MW00368436

PROMISED VALLEY

PROMISED VALLEY

THE NOVEL

LANCE WILLIAMS

TILLMAN S. BOXELL

Adapted from the Musical Play
Book and Lyrics by Arnold Sundgaard
Music by Crawford Gates

Connie,
Well, here it is, I hope you enjoy this work. It was a great experience to write. All the best,
Lance Williams
'95

Paramount Books
Box 379
Seaford, New York 11783

Landmark Press
48 West Broadway
Suite 1407N
Salt Lake City, Utah 84101

For information address Landmark Press, 48 West Broadway, Suite 1407N, Salt Lake City, Utah 84101.

Library of Congress Cataloging in-Publication Data
Catalog Card Number: 91-90530
Williams, Lance C.
Boxell, Tillman S.
Promised Valley.
1. Promised Valley—Fiction. I. Title.
2. Mormons—Historical—Fiction
ISBN 0-9630321-0-0

Printed in the United States of America
1 2 3 4 5 6 7 8 9 10

To Tad Danielewski, who believed in me enough to give me a chance and who has been a constant source of inspiration—himself never giving up the fight.

—Lance

To my father, the writer, who taught me that creative art, like creative life, is 1% inspiration and 99% perspiration.

—Tip

The novel *Promised Valley* was composed using computer equipment supplied by Burgoyne Computers Incorporated of Salt Lake City, Utah. This support is gratefully acknowledged. Without it, many trees would have suffered and we would be in traction with writer's cramp.

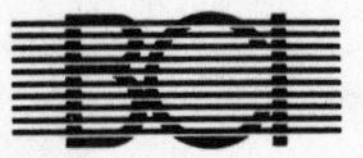

Acknowledgements

Very little is ever accomplished alone and this work is no exception. Many people unselfishly dedicated much time and effort on our behalf and we owe them a tremendous amount of thanks. We also wish to acknowledge their efforts and give them the credit they deserve.

We were most fortunate to have the support and boundless talents of our editor, Victoria Morgan Hyde, from the incubation stage of this book. Vicky's keen sense of direction continually kept us on course through the long voyage of development, writing, (many) revisions, and completion. She made us stretch when we didn't especially want to and would never let us write something "just to get by."

We received additional excellent editorial advice from our friend and former university newspaper editor, now attorney, Holly Armstrong. From editing the newspaper to technical journals and all manner of books, Holly was able to bring a different dimension to the project.

As always with the creation of a book, readers played a very important role and each of our readers contributed something of themselves which helped make the book what it is. We especially want to say thanks to one in particular, Duane Hiatt, for providing us with a much-needed reality check. Our other readers who played equally important roles include: Pat Coker Hall, Liz Christensen, Owen and Elizabeth Smoot, Brendan and Evelyn Gibney, L. Wendy Crowley-Williams, Flora C. Coker, Richard and Marion Williams, Tricia Ormsby, Michael Bennett, Richard Dewey, Janet Watkin, Ken and Pat Nix, and R. Shane Williams.

The talented eye of Ken Lindquist helped guide the technical aspects of our artistic direction. His unselfish input contributed to the visual success of the novel.

Without the tireless and cheerful efforts of our research associate and proofreader, Debbie Gibney, this book would not even be close to ready. Debbie always took up the slack when we would find ourselves buried under seemingly insurmountable piles of work. And, like Vicky, she was always positive in the face of adversity.

There are two people whose influence greatly affected this work although they were not directly involved. They are Diane Hixson and Kim Rennicker. Their subtle, but long term contributions are gratefully acknowledged.

A special thanks to Richard D. Poll for allowing us to use his original concept of the "Liahona" and the "iron rodder." Mr. Poll's words on the subject can be found in at least three separate works including his own book, titled, *History and Faith.*

The authors owe an immeasurable debt of gratitude to Arnold Sundgaard and Crawford Gates for their original inspired material and providing us such a wonderful framework upon which to create. As this is an adaptation of their musical play, we also thank them for their vision and understanding as we expanded the story into the novel it is today.

For all the other forms of help and support we received from all the other people in our lives, past and present, we thank you whole-heartedly. To the pioneer men and women who made the "trek west" and the "march south," we acknowledge your sacrifices and know that without you, this book could have never been written.

Introduction

By the Authors of the Musical Play "Promised Valley"

Myths are made of many fabrics and can be cut to many shapes and patterns. But the threads employed in creating those fabrics are invariably made from raw material culled from a mass of actual fact. The voyage of discovery, in which Keats, the poet, saw Cortez and all his men "silent upon a peak in Darien" staring at the broad Pacific, probably began in a grimy port in Spain when a tiny ship was loaded with very ordinary cargo. By the time Keats turned that voyage into the iambics of his immortal sonnet, the ordinary cargo had been alchemized into a poet's pure gold.

The arrival of the Mormon pioneers in the valley of the Great Salt Lake in 1847 was similarly a voyage of discovery. It had its parallel in the story of Moses leading his people to a Promised Land. Like the children of Israel, those early Mormons under Brigham Young had left their own embattled Egypt (a burning Nauvoo and a bloody Missouri) behind them. By the year 1947, a century later, much of that story had taken on the epic dimensions of a legend, yet all of it was drawn from a mass of actual fact.

This was the raw material providing the writers of the musical drama, *Promised Valley*, with the threads for their particular story. It was conceived and created on a commission from the State of Utah for the state's Centennial. Now, more than four decades later, it has provided the writers of this novel, based on that musical, with additional threads for creating a fresh new garment. It is hoped that it will appeal to and fit the needs of a later generation.

Yet little of the original cloth has been lost in the process, so skillfully have the new threads been woven into the older material. The story of the Mormon pioneers does not dim with the passage of time. Like Cortez and his men on that peak in Darien, Brigham Young and the Mormon pioneers stand eternally at the head of Emigration Canyon gazing at their own vast Pacific on an arid desert plain below. How they arrived there is the stuff of drama as well as history. It is the stuff of the novel as well.

This transmutation from musical play to novel will be followed at a later date by yet another sea of change: to that of epic film. In that version the elements of the musical drama and novel will be combined for a wider screen and even wider audience. It serves as key to the cinematic technique employed in the present narration.

The writers of this foreward recall with pleasure their collaboration on the original *Promised Valley*, that tremulous moment when the first word of dialogue and opening notes of music were written almost a half century ago. It was a happy time then. We hope it will be an equally happy time now.

Arnold Sundgaard
Crawford Gates

From the Authors

The year was 1947. Harry S. Truman was president of the United States, television was just catching on, and me, well, I hadn't even been born. In fact, I guess you could say I was once removed from this life since my parents were still busy living out their youth and were as yet unacquainted, much less married.

My grandparents call this period "the good old days." My generation associates the '40s with the post-World War II era. Those I talk to in the "younger generation" stare blankly at me when I ask them about what they think life was like in '47. "That's ancient history, dude," is something like the typical response I get. No matter where you were, if you were, or how you feel about the "age of swing," I think everyone would agree upon one thing: life was a lot less complicated then.

So why am I suddenly on a nostalgia kick? I'm not, really. This is more of a historical kick. It was the year 1947 when the musical *Promised Valley* actually began. The story has a long and fascinating history all its own. It is one we will probably share with you at some later date, but for now, it will suffice to give those of you unfamiliar with *Promised Valley* the condensed history version. A brief chronology of how and why this whole thing got started will help you understand the reason why the book was written. It also illustrates the impact and enduring effect *Promised Valley* has had on millions of people all over the world, myself being one of them.

There was a storm brewing in Salt Lake City — not a weather pattern, but a party being planned with a whirlwind fervor. Herbert Brown Maw, Governor of the state of Utah in '47, commissioned a committee to prepare for the Centennial celebration of the discovery and consequent settlement of the Salt Lake Valley. It was decided that one of the events would be a musical play. A big musical play full of singing and dancing to be staged like the hit Broadway musicals of the day. These were pretty lofty goals for a little state like Utah, but the commission did not stop there. They decided that the show would be written and composed by some of those very same Broadway playwrights and composers. Professional designers, technicians and performers from New York would also be hired to ensure the highest quality production possible. Even Ed Sullivan would have agreed this was to be "a really big shew."

The first question they faced was: "What should be the story of the play?" What about the establishing of a settlement in the Salt Lake Valley and how and why it came to pass? That seems obvious. So far, so good. OK, now, "who should write it?" This question took a bit more time and effort, but the committee finally settled on a very successful playwright by the name of Arnold Sundgaard who had two running hits playing on Broadway, called *Down in the Valley* and *The Great Campaign.* The logical choice for a composer was Kurt Weill, also a very successful Broadway talent. It was logical because Weill had worked with Sundgaard on many occasions, forming a loose partnership writing and composing. Fate, however, steered *Promised Valley's* musical destiny in a different direction. Kurt Weill wasn't available for the project due to another commitment, so the Centennial committee scrambled to locate another "Broadway music man." They found someone better—Crawford Gates. Crawford was a young, but accomplished musical whiz, orchestrating the dynamic music performed daily by KSL radio's in-house thirteen piece orchestra in Salt Lake City. Here was a local with the talent and vision to pull off such an awesome assignment. Contacts were made, Sundgaard met Gates, and the rest, as they say, is history. Well, not quite yet.

Remember, this is a greatly condensed version. A lot of very important and fascinating "stuff" happened along history's way, but I won't muddy this account with too many details.

With the script written and the music composed, Alfred Drake, probably best known for his portrayal of "Curly" in the original *Oklahoma!* on Broadway, was cast as Jed, the male lead. Celia, the female lead, went to Jet McDonald, who had played opposite Drake in the Broadway production of *Beggar's Holiday.* The supporting cast fleshed out in good form with actors and actresses from New York and Salt Lake City. There was a certain magic surrounding the production. Everyone was charged with energy and, as word of the play spread, the populace of Utah positively buzzed with anticipation.

As sometimes happens, those closest to the project were oblivious to the excitement being generated by Promised Valley. Gates and Sundgaard were buried under their deadline. Their commitment to excellence permitted nothing more than complete dedication of self in order to render what must be, so that the project would succeed given the scale on which it was conceived. Those on the state level who had commissioned the work were busy seeing to other details for Utah's Centennial, but the word was out and everybody was talking.

Finally opening night arrived. Everything was as ready as it could be, all last-minute changes incorporated, and a few firsts added. A local inventor by the name of Harvey Fletcher had effectively wired into the existing sound system a relatively new thing he called stereo. You can imagine what that did for the quality of the music. Even though Mr. Fletcher invented stereo sound in the twenties, it still wasn't widely used. Walt Disney's *Fantasia* was recorded in six channel stereo and one of the most successful uses of the medium at the time. For

Promised Valley, Harvey used a three channel system. Stereo sound would revolutionalize the sound and music industries and, in later years, Promised Valley would benefit further from this technological innovation. As for me, these advances helped shape my professional destiny along with the destinies of many others.

The stadium was filled to capacity but, when the lights went out, more than 8,000 audience members fell silent. There wasn't a sound until the first strains of the overture began. From that moment on, it truly was "a really big shew."

Promised Valley ran for three weeks in late July and into early August of 1947. When it closed, some 170,000 people had seen it. In some amazing way, all of them experienced the history of a people and the triumph of the human spirit. *Promised Valley* was now making history. A lot of this history would later draw me into the inner circle of the magic that is *Promised Valley.*

Although it was commissioned solely for the purpose of commemorating Utah's Centennial, *Promised Valley* didn't end with the celebration. For more than four years, a condensed version of *Promised Valley* was performed six days a week, for eight weeks of the summer. The performances were staged in an area of downtown Salt Lake City, with the LDS Temple as its backdrop. The site became known as the Temple View Theatre until it was razed in 1971.

It was in the Temple View Theatre that I first experienced *Promised Valley.* I couldn't have been more than ten or eleven years old, when, on a summer's evening, I went with my best friend and his family. Like just about everybody who saw the show, I was captivated by the story, the singing and the dancing. I immediately wanted to play the lead, but I was disappointed to learn that the only parts for little boys were those of Fennelly's sons. Still, the experience stayed with me and as I returned every year to see the spectacle, each year I wanted more to be involved than I had the year before.

Even without me, success for *Promised Valley* continued to grow and become a very positive tourist attraction. Families from all over the nation planned their vacations around a trip to Salt Lake City to see *Promised Valley*, the musical. Popularity increased until the play outgrew the outdoor theatre, so a late Victorian style theatre was purchased and extensively remodeled as the permanent new home for the attraction. The building was originally a "legitimate" theatre and later a movie house which I frequented often. When it was announced that *Promised Valley* would be moved there permanently, I was delighted. Since my performing career had advanced into full swing, I was sure that if performances continued as they had in the past, I would eventually play the lead role. The newly remodeled theatre was aptly named "Promised Valley Playhouse" and in this new home the summer tradition continued, but once again, sadly, without me. My career took a turn toward motion pictures and I was off to California.

Theatres in states other than Utah began staging the show. It performed in small venues, huge "bowls," university auditoriums, recreation halls, and in theatres all over America, including California. I was never far from a performance and continued to enjoy it from the audience. *Promised Valley* played such halls as the Greek Theatre in San Diego, the Pasadena Playhouse in Pasadena, the Hyart Theatre in Wyoming, the Scottish Rite Auditorium in Stockton, California and the Hunter College Playhouse in New York City. The musical became a truly world-class work when it was ultimately translated and performed in six foreign languages.

That should bring you up to speed, except perhaps for one thing. To date, it is estimated that well over five million people worldwide have seen *Promised Valley*, the musical. Now with the creation of the novel, it is my hope that not only will the three generations who grew up with *Promised Valley* rediscover it, but that many new generations will read of the struggles and triumphs of one group of people who were intricate threads in the woven tapestry of our fledgling nation's history.

Though it is true that this is a story about the "Mormon" people, *Promised Valley* is a story for all people. I know the original work was inspired. I hope this writing is inspired; I know I was while writing it. A legend this good deserves to be told and even though I never played the lead, I am extremely pleased that I could be involved in some small way.

After you've read the novel, share it with someone you know and then let us know your thoughts. Whether you are rediscovering it as an old friend, or just now meeting the people of the "Promised Valley," we would like to hear your story about our story. Who knows, perhaps when we write the concise history of *Promised Valley*, it will become part of the legend.

— *Lance*

In the summer of 1961, when I was fifteen, I got a chance to work on the New York production of *Promised Valley.* I felt like quite a man as I rode the train from my home in Connecticut to Grand Central Station and then uptown on the Lexington Avenue subway to Hunter College Playhouse on the campus of Columbia University. I did a little of everything you can do backstage — hung lights, assembled the set on stage, handled the pin rail and, thrilling for me, pulled the curtain on opening night.

There were plenty of young men who labored in the wings or dashed out on stage to sing and dance as Mormon pioneers or Indians or Mormon Battalion soldiers. We all fell in love with Melva Barbourka who, as Melva Niles from Salt Lake City, had won distinction with the New York Metropolitan Opera. She was our delightful Celia Faraday. I remember her black hair and sparkling eyes. I remember her girlish speaking voice which enchanted us and her soaring singing voice which awed us as she filled the theatre with her dynamic rendition of "The Wind is a Lion." I remember wanting to be like Art Lund, who was our tall, handsome Jed Cutler. Art was fresh from his London and Broadway triumphs as Joey in *The Most Happy Fella.* He taught us how to court a woman with his velvety crooning of "I'll Build You a Home in the Valley."

No one could fail to be stirred by our chorus and principals singing of the burning of Nauvoo while our "lobsterscope" created a horrible red sky with rippling flames and billowing smoke. Contrasted with that sublimeness, many audience members remembered the comic relief of the easily flummoxed Fennelly Parsons. Along with Emma Faraday, Celia's mother, and Bishop Quimby Leighton, we shook our heads over his antics with his eight sons and their color spectrum of hand-me-down shirts.

One night, a dashing young actor named Robert Peterson visited us backstage, taking a moment away from his great opportunity to replace Robert Goulet as "Lancelot" in *Camelot.* Little did any of us know that Bob would become one of the great Jeds in the long history of *Promised Valley.*

Later, I performed and worked at the Promised Valley Playhouse in Salt Lake City, but this was after the time when the LDS Church had used the Playhouse to showcase *Promised Valley* every summer. I met and worked with artists who had presented the play to generations of Salt Lakers and visitors from all over the nation, first at the outdoor Temple View Theatre and later at Promised Valley Playhouse. I myself, however, knew almost nothing of the proud forty-year history of *Promised Valley.*

I went on to schooling and career in theatre, film, television, and literature, never forgetting that very satisfying production and all that I had learned from it. I have since acted with Robert Peterson and enjoyed him from the audience, but I never saw Melva or Art or any of the others again except in my mind's eye as they lived the great story of the Mormon Exodus to the west and the trials of the Latter-day Saints fighting through the dangers of this world until they could find their Promised Valley.

Then one day in the Fall of 1989, my friend and partner, Lance Williams, asked me, "What do you know about the play *Promised Valley?*" I replied that it was a much-loved story of the Mormon pioneers put forth in musical theatre and a big attraction in Salt Lake City. I reminisced about the production I worked on. He said he had a strong impression that we should create a prose adaptation of *Promised Valley* that would delight all those who had seen the play and excite a whole new and much wider audience with the Mormon story. With my fond memories, I caught Lance's vision and I said, "Let's do it."

Lance set out to learn everything he could about the history of this work. He met with Arnold Sundgaard and Crawford Gates, the original creators. He delved into the history of his own family, which included a member of the Mormon Battalion and other early pioneers. We evolved a project wherein we would create a novel version adapted from *Promised Valley*, the musical. If this novel were to be successful on a large enough scale, then our next logical progression would be a big-screen musical film and, of course, in our day and age, a video.

The play had the mature man-woman love of Jed and Celia, persecution, and exodus. These elements were universal in appeal. To heighten that appeal today, we added an antagonist, a rival, a threat. We decided this character must not be an embodiment of the general threat of the hateful world — a melodrama villain. No, he must be a threat from within. He must have an honest point of view that dissents from the mainstream. Our worldly, sophisticated, yet idealistic and committed Mormon acts as rival to Jed and temptation to Celia. He puts into the piece a lot that is contemporary and of great interest to our modern audience as well as the audience that has loved *Promised Valley* since the beginning.

The new world-wide audience will also see that we have expanded greatly what Jed does and how he proves himself worthy of his position as protagonist. Modern women's issues and points of view also find expression as Celia grows and develops. This adaptation presents our history with a modern understanding. In *Promised Valley*, the novel, we see the origins of the people we are today and we recognize ourselves in our ancestors who built the promised valley we now enjoy.

We hope to express what we have put into our novel in all the latest cinematic possibilities with the panoramic scenes and physical action we have described. That would be a big screen musical that would really open this story to the world, but, for now, I am excited by the achievement our readers hold in their hands. May we all appreciate the people who come to life within its pages.

—*Tip*

PROMISED VALLEY

THE NOVEL

TABLE OF CONTENTS

1

The Hated City of Love

"Don't go into the woods . . . ."

A little voice echoed briefly, then was lost. The forest was dark and silent in every direction except for one small clearing. At the edge of the trees, eight-year-old Hattie called to her sister Clarissa, "Here's some clean snow! Bring the molasses!" Clarissa trudged up to Hattie with her arms wrapped around a big jar of black goo.

"My mama *and* your mama said don't go in the woods," lectured Clarissa, darting sharp glances into the dark treeline at the edge of their clearing. The difference between the clearing and the forest was literally night and day. As long as she stayed clear of the trees, Clarissa felt safe. She wasn't about to admit her fear to her sister, but Hattie already knew. She was afraid too.

The girls were the same age and played together all the time, but Hattie always had to take charge of Clarissa to get her to do anything. After all, Jean, Hattie's mother, was the first wife, and that made Hattie feel more like a big sister. That didn't stop the children from running to Clarissa's mama, Dorothy, for hugs and help just as often.

The pale sun reflected off the crust of icy snow, formed from the thawing, freezing cycle of the late fall season. Its effect brilliantly illuminated the clearing where the two girls lived and played. This was the only clearing for miles, and everybody knew it. Trails meandered into the little pocket, worn through the trees by the wagons and animals of the prairie people who fearfully brought their products down to the great river and the disturbing city beyond.

"Don't be such a scaredy-cat," sneered Hattie. "There are no mobbers around here." Reassured by her sister's words, Clarissa commenced creating candy by pouring black molasses on pure white snow. The place seemed quiet enough. Still, Hattie snuck a few glances into the dark forest all the same.

The forest around the clearing was low and quite open between the trees because it was made up of squat hardwoods like maple and hickory, as well as smallish soft evergreens like box elder and yellow pine. Nevertheless, even in fall, there were enough evergreen boughs and interwoven leafless branches to keep the light out of the forest. To look from the clearing into the surrounding trees was to look into darkness.

The two little girls had stopped just a few feet from where the forest reclaimed the land. Behind them, in the middle of the clearing stood a big, well-chinked log building. It was their home but had also served as an inn and supply store for many traveling through the wilderness. Those were better times.

"Now you hurry with them hogs," yelled Will Simpson to Henry, his fourteen-year-old son. Will studied his clearing, squinting hard through the blazing reflection off the diamond snow. His breath steamed in time with his strides as he crunched along from the house, past the barn to the clearing. It had been only days since the Legion had stopped by his farm to warn him of the possible danger of mob attacks. The leader of the Legion, Lieutenant Cutler, had nearly begged them to move into the city, but the family loved their home and wanted to stay.

Henry was feeding cornstalks and old squash to the hogs and Will knew his boy would spend all day playing with them if he could. Even though Henry, the oldest of the Simpson children, knew the hogs were livestock needed for food, he couldn't help but love them as his pets. Will looked at his son. *Was staying the right choice?* he wondered.

Hattie inspected the glob of molasses candy they had just formed. It was a fine looking creation, the best so far. "We will give this one to Father," Clarissa announced. "He will be so proud of us!"

Clarissa looked back toward her father and smiled—then she heard it. The sound of a horse snorting was no stranger to her and, whirling around in the direction of the noise, she stared into the forest. Clarissa sucked in her breath as her eyes fixed on a long line of horses, steam blowing from their enlarged nostrils. The beasts, shaggy with their winter coats, advanced slowly, pawing at the frozen earth with strong hooves. At first it looked like shadows, ghosts floating on a mist. Clarissa searched for the faces of the riders, but found only the faint outlines of headless men. A thought flashed through her mind. *Mobbers paint their faces black!*

"Run, Hattie! Mobbers!" screamed Clarissa as she dropped the molasses jar and ran. Hattie took one paralyzing look and bolted toward the house.

"Papa, Papa, Papa!" they both cried as they ran down toward the safety of their father. "Mobbers! Mobbers!" Will Simpson stood very still with only his eyes moving rapidly as he took in the situation. About thirty mounted men with muskets in their hands burst forth from the trees and thundered down on the desperately fleeing little girls, who had perhaps a hundred-yard start.

"Henry!" barked his father, but Henry was already inside the barn getting the loaded musket that was always kept there. Henry emerged and vaulted the pig fence. "Give me the gun and get in the house. Close up and load up . . . may God bless you and keep you, my son. You are the priesthood now." Will turned away from Henry's agonized face and sprinted with all his might toward his little girls. He was in his fifties, but strong and quick. "Get to the house," he yelled to his daughters as they ran past.

Two little girls trodden under the feet of a mounted mob, it would have been over in seconds, but as they advanced, the mobbers broke up into groups. Some were galloping for the barn, presumably to steal the livestock. Others were sweeping around the house to cut off the road to the river. Will only had to delay a half-dozen or so black-painted men to ensure that Hattie and Clarissa got to the house safely. Inside, there were enough muskets, pistols, and shotguns to arm the women and the older sons. They knew they would have to hold out long enough for the mobbers to move on to easier game or, better yet, to attract the Legion to the sound of the shooting.

Will had to forget about all that and think about shooting. As the six riders thundered down on him, yelling like demons, they aimed at him with their weapons. One fired, then another, each taking a turn, but all missed. Will smoothly thumbed back the hammer of his flintlock, knelt, aimed, and squeezed the trigger. The biggest of the six rolled off his horse, hitting the ground without another sound. There was only time for the one shot, then the others who had fired were on top of Will.

A silver glint of light flashed as one swung a sword, but Will was inside the swipe of the blade and grabbed the sword arm of the rider, pulling the man off his horse. With a crunch the man landed on his head and lay still. Another man made his horse rear in Will's face. Hooves flailing before him, Will stumbled back, raising his musket to his face for protection, but the gun was kicked from his grasp. The remaining four mobbers gathered around the farmer like a firing squad around a condemned man. Will heard only one giant discharge, but the balls of four muskets flew their deadly course, crushing the air from his lungs.

Will fell in a heap and rolled over on his back. He did not feel the coldness of the snow against him as he looked up at the sun. The sounds of the mob galloping down to his house filled his ears. He heard shots coming from inside the house and curses from the mobbers, but he could not move. "It'll be over soon . . .," mumbled Will, coughing blood from his throat. "Soon."

The fresh thunder of horses and rough shouts of many men filled his ears, but from a different direction. There was a rippling volley of musket fire exploding behind his head, much more than could come from the house. The mobbers were screaming and shouting, and what sounded like a whole herd of horses clattered away until the clearing was quiet again.

Will Simpson's vision was darkening around the edges as he waited to die. He visualized each member of his family in turn and prayed for them as they appeared in his mind. The face of a ruggedly handsome young man with thick, rusty blond hair and bright blue eyes suddenly came into Will's view. Will peered at him with an expression that began as anger and fear, then resolved into a kind of peaceful sadness. "Joseph?" Will whispered. "Brother Joseph?"

"No, Brother Will, it's just me, Lieutenant Cutler," intoned the face, gravely. Jedediah Cutler knelt over the fallen farmer. The Lieutenant was not only the leader of the Nauvoo Legion, he we also a respected leader in the city itself. Tall and strong, he was indeed of the stature of Joseph Smith. Still, Brother Simpson's confusion startled Jed.

"Oh. I thought for a minute I was already gone," gasped Will.

"No. You are still with us." Now Will could feel this man's arm under his shoulders.

"How is my family? Did they survive?"

"They are all fine. We are gathering them now . . . and as many of their things as may be taken." The voice was sounding farther and farther away, and Will could not see any longer.

"I should have taken them to the city. There we could have been safe," whispered Will. He could barely hear himself.

"Don't trouble yourself, Brother. The city is surrounded by our enemies as well. Our people leave daily for the West."

Suddenly Will Simpson smiled slightly. "A city that is set on a hill cannot be hid." They softly chuckled together. Then Will struggled to continue. "City of Joseph . . . white temple . . . golden temple . . . Jean . . . Dorothy . . . We must go there." There was twitching in his muscles as he struggled to move.

Jed took Will's hands to calm him. "You have been sealed to your family in the temple, Brother, and will be with them again. Our enemies may well hate our city, but there is still love within."

"Yes, the temple! Praise God that He provided a way for us to be married and sealed together for all time. Don't let them knock it down!" Will began to gurgle in his sudden agitation. "Save it. Preserve it. Find a place where . . . " The gray-haired man's breath ran out, and he was dead.

"He thought I was the prophet Joseph, come to take him to the other side," Jed recounted, looking up at a circle of men in blue-gray flannel uniforms. They were home-made soldiers, not regular in their appearance, all friends, fellow Elders of Israel. Some wore their own whipcord riding breeches. Some wore their own wool greatcoats or riding boots. Like the mobbers (who were supposedly state militia, not unlike this Mormon Nauvoo Legion), their weapons and ammunition were government issue—carbines, pistols, sabres, cartridge boxes.

"Perhaps Joseph will greet him on the other side," said a Scottish voice. Everyone looked at a ruddy, freckled man, with thinning red hair and pale blue eyes.

"Perhaps," agreed Jed, looking into Will's face.

"Should we say a prayer?" another brother-soldier asked.

"Is there time?" worried the Scotsman, looking around sharply.

"I think so," decided Jed. "Just for a moment. Jamie," he said, facing his Scottish friend, "Why don't you be the voice?" Jamie rose to his feet and took off his billed legion forage cap. The others reached for their assortment of legion caps and broad-brimmed felt hats.

At that moment the two wailing wives and numerous shrieking children came running up to the circle and burst through to throw themselves over the body of their husband and father. The Legion men stood aside stiffly. Some stared, mesmerized. Others looked away. Once more, they were seeing what they had sworn they would never again permit—bullet-riddled bodies, distraught wives, quivering children, merciless wilderness. Haun's Mill, Far West and Carthage Jail had presented the scene too many times. After a short interval, Jed said firmly, "We must go."

It was a sad parade. The large group of legionnaires accompanied the Simpson family through the thick forest paths to the river. Legion patrols were carried to the western banks of the Mississippi on giant ferry boats that serviced the two shores. Without them, the remaining Mormon families in Iowa would be cut off from the city.

The ferry boat that set out from Montrose, Iowa to Nauvoo, Illinois had to be poled by stout legion arms out of the shallows and into the main channel of the mighty Mississippi. Lieutenant Cutler grabbed the first pole and lined the men up along each side of the boat. He was big and lean, and he threw his weight on the end of his pole using big, hard, farmer's hands. "Let the littlest man steer with the huge oar over the stern," he called out to his men. Jed would get the boat moving and the others would fall into the rhythm he had established.

It was a big enough old scow that it could hold the Legion patrol, their horses, the Simpson family, and a mound of family belongings. The two wives sat on the end of the bench that ran down the middle of the boat with Will's body laid out between them. They could both lay a hand on his head or shoulder and hold him in place as the boat rocked on the waves piled up by the bitter wind. The children—except Henry, who still kept his musket slung across his back and helped the men work the ferry— sat on the deck around the feet of their mothers and looked at nothing. Every muscle in Henry's face was tight and twisted, and he made no sound.

The Scandinavian and English seamen among them raised a big, square lugsail on a low, thick mast and sailed the ungainly rectangular craft across the channel.

When they slipped into the shallows of the eastern shore, on the Illinois bank, they drove some horses over the side and men jumped on their backs. They rode off, paying out ropes tied to cleats on the ferry. They trotted, very briskly indeed, through the icy water and up onto a towpath along the river bank. One dashed ahead to alert the city they were coming.

It seemed they had voyaged forever out in the cold wind. The blue sky and the glinting, heatless sun would soon begin sinking toward the lumpy horizon on the Iowa side. The little children were whimpering now, and the whole family was packed together against the legs of their mothers and the lifeless head of their father.

As they rounded the bend to the northeast, the hill that rose above the river fell away like the drawn curtain of a theatre, revealing the great city of the Mormons. It was the city built by Joseph Smith, rising from the waterfront up the terraced Temple Hill to the magnificent white building on the crest, with its glorious golden dome.

All aboard turned to gaze at the elegant red brick buildings on the hillside with their white painted trim and well-glazed windows, their handsomely carved doors and sweeping lawns. The thin crust of frozen snow coated everything and the spidery branches of the trees zigzagged upward in a tangle of black lines, but the city was still beautiful for its order, its solidity, its proclamation of civilization.

Everyone on the boat studied it silently. Even the chilled and hungry children sat straighter and lifted their heads higher. A feeling of calm began replacing that of fear.

A city that is set on a hill cannot be hid. That was the joy and the sorrow of the City of Joseph, thought Jed. *The Kingdom of Heaven is invisible here on this earth, but in this haven built by the poor dead prophet, the kingdom was almost visible, almost real. Here it was practical to be good. Brother Joseph had called it Nauvoo. In the School of the Prophets, he taught that this meant "the beautiful" in the language of the Hebrews.*

"Is that the Mansion House?" asked Dorothy, pointing at a big, square, three-story, brick building.

"It is," answered Jed. "You will stay there tonight. Look, here are the women of the Relief Society to take care of you."

Hattie reached up and gently tugged Jed's sleeve. "What is a Relief Society?" she asked, puzzled.

"It is the wives and mothers in the Church who look after folks like us, Hattie," Jed responded warmly. "These women learn about all kinds of things that help with the work of the Church and assist members in need. It's an organized way for us to help ourselves. You can be part of the Relief Society one day when you are older." Jed wasn't sure she understood, but Hattie nodded her head and returned her gaze toward the Mansion House.

Jed leaned with all his strength on the big steering oar and the scow turned toward the shore. The horses were cast off and the boat glided in to the nearest dock. "That is Celia Faraday, one of the leaders of the Relief Society waiting for us," Jed announced to Hattie, with an anxious smile.

Standing on the dock was a beautiful woman. Jed fastened his eyes upon her, still working the steering oar astern. Her eyes sparkled on meeting his though her expression remained solemn. She was tall and straight, with shoulders back and chin up. Even with a long wool coat over her dress, with knit gloves, muffler, and bonnet, she seemed trim and lithe as she leaned forward to assess the situation in the boat. The late afternoon sun—full in her face—suffused her wonderfully modeled features with the glow and softness of the rose petal.

The old gray ferry boat bumped gently against the pilings, and the hairy rope fenders groaned as a few Legion men jumped to the dock and secured the craft. Jed leapt easily from the steering platform to the rail of the boat, then to the dock. His movements were quick and deliberate, and he pulled the woman to him. Tall as she was, she still fit nicely under the arm of the big man, with her head of thick wavy hair at the level of his muscled shoulder. She pressed herself against him as his arm tightened around her, and she laid a cheek on his broad, sturdy chest. They were far apart in coloration, she with honey brown hair and deep green eyes and he with rusty blond hair and blue eyes. The briefest glance at them drawn together would convince anyone that they were well matched. "My dear Celia," whispered Jed in her ear.

"I thank God you have returned to me safely once again," Celia sighed, her lips against Jed's neck.

"But poor Will Simpson wasn't so lucky, the old fool."

"Sssh. They'll hear."

"I'm sorry," sighed Jed. "He was a fine man, but he shouldn't have exposed his family to danger simply for material gain."

"Who attacked them?" asked Celia, looking into Jed's face.

"It was the Missouri Wildcats again."

"Was Colonel Price with them?"

"Not this time. I wish he had been there."

They broke apart as Jed turned to look at the line of carriages jingling to a stop at the head of the pier. One by one good sisters alighted from each and beckoned to the Simpson family to come ashore and get in. The first sister on the pier was as tall and straight as Celia, although much more ample. This woman's iron gray hair was smoothly tucked up under her large bonnet, and she swept forward with graceful, purposeful strides. Though her face had folds and wrinkles, it was clear that Celia was her daughter.

"Thank you for coming, Mother," said Celia.

"Yes, thank you, Sister Faraday," agreed Jed.

"I am happy to be able to help," replied Celia's mother with a serene smile. "Thank God you are safe, Jed, and you, too, Jamie Logan, not that they'll ever catch an ornery Scotsman such as yourself."

"Aye, Sister Faraday, that I am. Still, I'm glad for your confidence in me," grinned Jamie before they began helping children out of the boat.

Several of the Legion men helped Henry lift the body of his father and carry him to a small wagon. The two widows walked in stately manner on either side of their husband. A very tall, slender man with a crooked nose, kind eyes, and a gray lock of hair that fell across his forehead joined the women and directed the men where to take the body. Quimby Leighton, bishop and friend, was always there to help when trouble was present. As a bishop in the Mormon church, Quimby was not only a spiritual leader over a designated group called a ward, he was also responsible for the members' well being. Even though the Simpson family wasn't part of his ward, Bishop Leighton did what he could to lessen the suffering of those afflicted wherever he encountered them. Jed and Celia could hear Jean and Dorothy murmuring, "Thank you, Bishop. Thank you."

Celia waved to the wizened little man who drove the first carriage in line. "Hello, Father. Thank you for coming," she called out.

"Good afternoon, Caleb," added Jed.

The old man's eyes became slits as his face broke into a benign smile. "Glad to help, my dear. Good to see you safe and sound, Jedediah. We are all ready for tomorrow."

With the carriages loaded, Caleb waved his arm and led the column away toward the Mansion House. This centerpiece of the city had served as Church Headquarters, City Hall, and the home of the late Joseph Smith. Tonight it would serve as a refuge for the latest victims of a vicious mob.

Jed paused a moment as he reflected on Caleb's words: "We are all ready for tomorrow." They seemed out of context for the situation, yet strangely normal too. Jed perceived the sad reality that death and hardship had become almost commonplace in their lives, and the citizens of Nauvoo had become accustomed to it. *Perhaps the oddest thing,* Jed thought, *is that life must go on even in the midst of such adversity.* Celia recognized Jed's anxiety and kissed his cheek.

"Are *you* ready for tomorrow?" Jed asked, studying Celia's face.

She was preparing her answer when the last Legion soldier, leading several horses, shouted, "Lieutenant Cutler, do we ride again in the morning?"

"Tomorrow being my wedding day, I hope not; and as President Young is supposed to marry us, I expect not!" The two men smiled, but Celia didn't.

Late that night, Celia sat on a bench by the giant hearth in the front room of the Mansion House, staring at the blazing pine knots popping and sparking. The Simpson family had been bathed and fed and their prayers offered. Now even the wives were fast asleep in featherbeds on the upper floors. The lively widower Fennelly Parsons had just left after entertaining the children with funny and tender songs played on his mandolin.

Jed stepped out of the dark and sat beside Celia. After a moment of holding hands, he said, "Shall we be married tomorrow, despite . . . all this?"

Celia looked down at their intertwined hands. "Yes, please. Let nothing stop us. I want it to be so."

"Then get some sleep, my darling," he said, with worry in his voice. Jed kissed her as dearly as he could, touched her cheek, then disappeared back into the dark.

Celia lay stiffly in her bed, staring at the ceiling. Her bedroom door opened ever so slightly and Emma looked through the opening. A mother's suspicions confirmed, she entered the room and joined her daughter on her bed. Emma stroked Celia's hair. "How did you know I was lying here thinking?" Celia asked as she looked into her mother's smiling face.

"You never said you were certain about your choice of Jed over the *others* who professed love to you, especially one other in particular. I knew it would be on your mind."

"Of course you mean Peter. Mother, you're reaching into my past."

"Not long past, dear."

"If you knew that I would be feeling confused, why didn't you stop me from agreeing to the wedding tomorrow?" Celia asked with a bit of a frustrated whine.

"It is not for me to stop you. You are a grown woman now, and I know that you did not take the decision of marriage lightly."

"You have always taught me to be prudent, Mother. I have weighed the situation and looked at it from every point of view. When I made my decision, I took it to the Lord in prayer."

"And your answer was Jed?"

"Jed is the one who loved me faithfully. He is the one who stayed in the Mormon community, an honest farmer, to give me the life I wanted and needed. Mother, I'm not that little girl who wanted all the boys to chase her at the same time."

"Indeed you aren't," agreed Emma. "You have grown into a fine example of a Latter-day Saint woman."

"I tried to have your elegance and your strength, Mother. It's not that I don't love Peter. He'll always have a special place in my heart; but even though he visits Nauvoo often, Peter has gone out into the world to seek his fortune, to achieve his own goals. I was left behind, Mother, not to be a part of that. It is Jed who loves me. Jed is the better man for me."

"I have something I would like to give you, then," Emma said, rising from the bed. She smoothed her dress and walked from the room, soon to return with a large box. Emma resumed her place next to her daughter. "I realize that you have spent a good deal of time trying to make the wedding dress you have always dreamed of being married in. Heaven knows it hasn't been easy with all the turmoil around you. Have you finished it?"

"The dress is done, Mother, but I just haven't had time to add the lace. I was going to ask you to help me finish it tomorrow, but I felt bad after making such a fuss about doing myself."

Emma handed Celia the box and waited for her to lift the top from the carton. "Maybe this will help," Emma replied.

"Oh Mother!" Celia cried, eyes full of emotion as the top came away from the box. "Your wedding dress! But what have you done to it?"

"I had a feeling you were struggling to finish, dear, so I took the liberty of helping you. I've changed a little of this and that on the old dress in hopes it might suit you."

"Mother, it's simply perfect! It's exactly how I imagined it," Celia exclaimed, hugging Emma tightly. "Thank you, Mother. I love you so much!"

Celia stood in front of her mirror, holding the dress in place against her body. It was perfect—a bodice of lace, sweetheart neckline, and long tapered sleeves. The skirt was fine satin and the entire dress was accented with glistening pearl-like beads, hand-sewn by a loving mother in anticipation of her daughter's wedding.

"My baby," Emma whispered through her tears. Celia sensed more than heard her mother's heartfelt cry and rejoined Emma on the bed. In each other's arms, mother and daughter laughed and cried.

"I promised myself I wouldn't do this," Emma sighed, wiping the tears from her eyes. "Do you really like the dress?"

"Oh yes, Mother. I'm so happy! The dress is simply magnificent, and the best part is that you wore it at your wedding," Celia said with a sniffle.

"You will look like a princess, my dear, but only if you get some sleep."

"I feel much better now, Mother."

"You will sleep, then?" asked Emma, trying to act stern.

"Yes, Mother. I will sleep."

Up on the driver's seat of a small trap carriage sat the tall, calm, strong-faced widower, Bishop Quimby Leighton, who had helped the Simpson widows and who would preside at the funeral right after this wedding. Jedediah Cutler sat in his bishop's carriage with his arm tightly around his bride-to-be. Her dark maroon wool cloak and bonnet covered her splendid wedding dress, draped with lace. She held her wedding cap and veil inside the cloak. It was a cold, clear fall afternoon but with no chilling wind to blow away the frosty breath of the wedding party and the two horses. Celia Faraday held out her fingers, graceful in one knitted glove, to be squeezed by her soon-to-be groom's big leather-gloved hand. Her mother and father, Caleb and Emma Faraday, were the only other people in the carriage. The other wedding guests who would witness the sealing were Jamie and Jerusha Logan and the widower Fennelly Parsons, all friends of both Jed and Celia. They rode in Jamie's wagon behind the others. The wedding party rode along silently, looking at each other and gazing out over the city as they ascended Temple Hill.

Jed wished his parents were still alive to be with them on this special day, but they had both passed on not long ago, his mother only last year. He looked around at the now-abandoned buildings he knew so well, shuttered and cold, with smokeless chimneys. It was becoming a familiar scene, a melancholy scene, as many families left everything they owned, fleeing to safety.

They all huddled together and gazed quietly at those handsome brick homes as they passed slowly by. Ahead and behind, other carriages and carts carried small, sober wedding parties slowly up the hill to the temple where President Brigham Young was going to spend the afternoon and evening sealing as many couples together for time and all eternity as he possibly could. He had done so off and on for ten months now. Other apostles of the Church had also sealed many couples. Their temple was finished, but the city was doomed. There was no time to lose.

Brother Brigham had spent many months shuttling back and forth along the six hundred miles of caravans and camps by the wayside as 15,000 Mormons moved in stages out of their warm, delightful city homes toward a rough prairie rag tent camp called Sugar Creek, on the Iowa side of the river. This small camp served as the first way station for the continuing exodus of the Mormons from Nauvoo. Brigham returned to Nauvoo as often as possible to hurry the last few thousand Saints out before the final wave of mobs cut them off.

Jed thought about the beautiful city all around him. He felt a twinge of sadness settle over him as he realized he must soon leave Nauvoo as so many had already done. The sadness wasn't from having to leave Nauvoo particularly. The Mormons could make a home anywhere other people would let them. Problem was, no matter where they went, the hatred soon followed.

Jed had never been to New York, where it all began. His family had joined the Church in Ohio and helped to build the lovely little community of Kirtland, but they met with persecution in Ohio. So they moved to Missouri and built the exciting frontier settlement at Far West, but they met with persecution in Missouri. Finally they had come here to Illinois and built Nauvoo, a city bigger than Chicago. Nauvoo was a Mormon model for the world to follow, disturbing as that was, and the persecution wasn't about to go away.

Now they would go . . . where? Wherever they went, however, they would go married. Jed smiled and rubbed Celia's arm. She smiled back at him and kissed his cheek. They looked up and saw Caleb and Emma looking on them lovingly, both smiling at the future bride and groom. Their eyes were brimming, and not from the cold.

The carriage neared the top of the snow-covered hill. Nauvoo's houses and town buildings lay silent and white below them, shimmering in the afternoon sun. Whatever the season, Nauvoo was a sight worthy of an artist's canvas, and this white scene before them was no less so. Still, Celia's thoughts were of another time, when the city stood in the sun, dappled with the moving shade of the gently blowing tree boughs. She noticed the others lost in their own thoughts and wondered if they were also thinking of sunny days. *I remember our pride as we came home from work,* she thought. *I remember children running downstairs and the sight of the fields through the door. I remember peaceful evenings on the banks of the Mississippi, on the green western prairie.*

This was the clean, wealthy, happy city in the midst of a depressed, largely unorganized frontier region. Hate came as much from envy as from anything else. This was the city that had voted in a Mormon body against the corrupt governor and his "mobocrats," ruining the careers of many an elected sheriff and judge. So it was that, two years before, the Prophet Joseph Smith had ridden forth "like a lamb to the slaughter" to his murder in jail by soldiers poorly disguised as Indians.

Jed had helped lift the riddled corpses of Joseph and Hyrum out of the wagon that brought them back to Nauvoo after the mob had finished with them. That was 1844.

Jed's parents had taken him to listen to Joseph preach in their little Ohio town. That was fourteen years ago, in 1832. He was fourteen then. He had looked up at the smiling, well-muscled prophet. He enjoyed the clear, strong, humorous voice. He believed the honest words that came so easily and surely to the large visitor. This man was like the big brother young Jed never had.

Jed learned that Joseph had prayed for God to tell him what church to join when he was fourteen, the same age his excited listener was now. Jed believed it when somebody told him of the answer to that prayer.

His family joined the Church and moved to Kirtland, Ohio, where his father helped build the Kirtland Temple. His mother gave her mother's china to be ground into the stucco to finish the temple walls which made them sparkle in the Ohio sun. The Cutler family prayed to be sealed together in that temple, but before the Prophet Joseph could receive the entire ceremony from the Lord, their horrified neighbors drove the "blasphemous Mormons" out of Ohio and took over the beautiful temple and its School of the Prophets because it was such a curiosity. That move killed Jed's father.

In Missouri, the Cutlers built a new home in the Mormon settlements. They farmed, hunted, and met the first Indians Jed had ever seen—Lamanites, he reminded himself. They were descendants of the people he had read about in the *Book of Mormon.* Jed went to school with a big boy from Saint Louis named Peter Van Cleef. The two were meant to be friends. All the girls loved them, but Celia Faraday won their attention and was the one who got to be with them. She was the boldest, and wasn't afraid to talk to both boys, even at the same time. They studied the scriptures together in Sunday School. They wrestled with faith, repentance, baptism, the gift of the Holy Ghost, and with their developing triangle of affection.

Even as a child, Celia had been striking. She didn't have an easy time growing up in the frontier wilds traversed by her family. The living conditions were often less than desirable, but it was more than that. Celia realized and understood a personal struggle within herself very early in her life. Because of her beauty and fine features, she was treated gingerly by family, friends, and members of the Church. She enjoyed the attention and felt very feminine clothed in the beautiful dresses her mother made for her. That was all well and good in its place, but Celia wasn't content playing the part of a china doll. She often felt compelled to shed the ruffles and lace for dull cotton and flannel so she could go play in the trees or work in the fields with the boys.

As Celia got older, the considered opinion of her held by certain members of the Church began to change. To them, she was more a tomboy than the precious little girl they thought they knew. Emma knew Celia had a mind armed with an intelligent forthrightness that enabled her to deal equally with men. She took little notice of those who would try to mold her daughter into their own ideas of what she should be. Emma knew Celia's zest for living life was altogether healthy, and she encouraged it. She also realized that, as her daughter was growing up, Celia was struggling to understand herself and her place in their unstable world. Jed and Peter, in the midst of their own adolescent confusion, tried to help Celia find that place, as Celia tried to help them. It was a wonderful time in her life, and her childhood experience had made her strong, both in body and character. This strength, Emma knew, her daughter would often need to draw upon later.

Another move, another state. Celia had learned to cherish the tranquil times when they were to be had. But the raiding mobs came again. Terrified Mormon families who had farms out on the prairie wondered why. It didn't take much looking to find the answer. The inhabitants of Missouri observed the industriousness of their new neighbors. They also observed that these neighbors succeeded without the benefit of slaves. Worse yet, these Mormon converts from New York, New England, Ohio, Canada, and Britain were appalled by slavery and shunned it earnestly. Missouri, however, was a hard-bitten slave state and was not about to relinquish that way of life. The Missourians felt threatened and continued their raids, driving the Mormons away from their homes and grabbing up all their good property in Jackson County. Never mind that it was only good after the Mormons had irrigated it with their sweat and paid for it with their blood.

Celia watched her two admirers, Jed and Peter, become young soldiers in Zion's Camp. Being a soldier wasn't for Peter, however, and he left the ranks before he ever saw battle. He preferred handling things quietly, his own way. Jed, on the other hand, knew he had to defend his people, even if it meant real battles against those who would take away their rights. Joseph Smith moved back and forth from Kirtland to their settlement at Far West, Jackson County, Missouri, helping the Saints move their homes to new opportunities and riding as the leader of Zion's Camp whenever possible. Zion's Camp served as a militia and a kind of permanent posse, hearing rumors and reports of mob action against Mormons and rushing to the scene. Sometimes they arrived at the wrong place. Sometimes they arrived at the right place, but too late. Sadly, sometimes they met the enemy and battle ensued.

When Missouri became untenable, the Prophet took them to a little collection of hills connected by swamps on the Illinois shore of the Mississippi. There the men made habitable and the women made beautiful a place refused by the grubby frontier people. They drained swamps and made them rise into good building lots with tons of fill dirt. So—literally—rose the city, Nauvoo.

But for the Mormons, the nightmare continued. Colonel Price and his Wildcats successfully convinced the Carthage Grays, their counterparts in Illinois, to give up protecting Joseph and Hyrum in jail and help in their murder instead. The treachery worked, and the Prophet died. No matter what promises the next life held, life here was colder and darker than ever. There was no peace to be had.

Jed became a lieutenant in the Nauvoo Legion, the regularized Illinois militia unit organized and commanded by Joseph Smith. The highest ranking government official in the state of Illinois, Governor Ford, commissioned Smith lieutenant general over the Legion. Later, when the persecution of the Mormons escalated and there were rumors Smith would use "his army" to retaliate against non-Mormons, the commission was disavowed and the Legion ordered to disarm. By the time the order to disarm came, however, a mighty army had become seasoned in the ways of frontier battle, skills that would later serve them well.

Under Joseph Smith's command the Legion was uniformed, trained, and equipped. It was overpowering in its maneuvering and skirmishing with Price's mob militia, but Mormons were not safe outside the arc of the Legion patrols. In fact, it had become sickeningly clear that the people of Illinois who had once welcomed them had now joined with the people of Missouri in hatefully expelling them. During the fall of 1846, wagon trains of

Latter-day Saints streamed out of Nauvoo toward Sugar Creek, the temporary shelter in Iowa, even as the strongest Mormons, like Jed and Celia, finished their second great temple, white and gold, on the hill overlooking the city—and prepared to defend it.

The goal of marrying Celia was the soft place in Jed's life, a place of light and warmth. That was more possible now that Peter had left all the trouble behind to return to Saint Louis. If there could only be peace. Jed would accept anything life in the world could deal him, if only he could be sealed to Celia in the temple.

The wedding carriages pulled up beside the lofty edifice and the wedding parties stepped down one by one. They left the cold, blustery day and entered the side door of the massive building. In the serenely beautiful and intricately decorated chapel, the brides and grooms, suited, gowned, and veiled, waited quietly, talking in whispers, gazing up at the vaulted ceiling. They could proceed to the sealing room only when the authority who would marry them arrived. That was none other than Brigham Young, but President Young was late, nowhere to be found. With the troubles closing in around the city, it was easy to understand why.

Celia realized that her thoughts found old feelings, and she felt a shock of pain echo through her heart. She wasn't doubting her choice; she was just remembering. She must not think of her childhood with young Peter. *But where is he now?* she wondered.

2

Duty

Peter Van Cleef rode hard across the Missouri prairie, desperately trying to reach the city, Nauvoo, to warn the Saints. He was also desperate to talk to Celia before she married Jed. Peter respected his friend but did not believe Jed understood what a great-souled lady like Celia would require in a husband. He did not want to lose his chance at happiness without at least presenting himself and what he had to offer her. This he hoped to accomplish in the nick of time.

To look at him, it was obvious he was a young man with an eye for business and the determination to succeed. Peter Van Cleef was proud of his position in the business community. His dress, his manner, his speech—all proclaimed with a touching, almost poignant pride, the image Peter had for so long cultivated. Even now, as he rode, decked out in the finest trousers, foxed with rawhide, knee-high leather boots, and brushed suede jacket, he looked somewhat out of place on the frontier. His horse was completely adorned with the finest tack, including bedroll and supplies. The stallion was large and strong, however, and didn't notice the weight of its load. Every detail had been personally seen to and nothing left to chance. Peter, Jed, and Celia were all in their late twenties, but Peter knew he had the sophistication to seem older. Tall and handsome, his dark eyes and olive complexion hinted at his European heritage.

In some ways, Peter was out of place with the Mormon settlers in Nauvoo. He was not content with the simple farming lifestyle or the anonymity of the average citizenry. He rankled under the yoke of the consecrated Mormon life. Celia had been intrigued by that. Some women love a rebel. But Peter was a member of The Church of Jesus Christ of Latter-day Saints and a believer in his heart. As for activity, though, he would go to church and other functions when it suited his purposes. In fact, that was pretty much the case with his business and personal life as well. Everything, all his energy, was geared to successfully meet his ends. It was just that living in Nauvoo meant expending a lot more energy to meet a lot fewer ends.

Nauvoo was certainly a sharp contrast to Saint Louis, where Peter hailed from after emigrating from Great Britain as a young boy. His Flemish parents had come to England after the defeat of Napoleon at Waterloo. Mormon missionaries had converted the Van Cleefs in Birmingham shortly after Peter was born. They soon resolved to gather with the Saints in America. There was a certain something about the big city that Nauvoo lacked. This gateway to the West had a hustle-bustle attitude that meant progress. The city was old, yet new, always growing and changing. That usually meant confusion and disorganization, but to Peter, the more confused things were generally, the better he liked it. It seemed to give him an edge.

Business was the topic at hand in Saint Louis and the pungent scent of money was in the air. After finishing school with Jed and Celia in Kirtland, Ohio, Peter decided he must return to Saint Louis to begin his career. Yet when it came time and the call went forth for Mormons everywhere to band together and help finish the new city, Peter had decided to move with his people to join other members of the Church who had already spent years building what had become known as Nauvoo, the beautiful.

It was fine at first, a kind of new adventure. Nauvoo was beautiful, more beautiful than any city Peter had ever seen, or heard of for that matter. It was even more modern than Saint Louis. But something was missing, something Peter needed. It didn't take long for him to realize what it was. In Nauvoo, there wasn't the challenge of competition that there was between him and his "big city" business associates. Maybe the beautiful city required a little greed. Yes, greed! Peter could admit it to himself. Nauvoo was too calm, too "Good morning, Brother Van Cleef," or "Good morning, Sister Faraday." The excitement he felt in Saint Louis was lacking. Oh, there were other reasons for being in Nauvoo besides looking for new ways to make his fortune, one particular reason, in fact, but she had become a part of this new place. Peter needed that energy he had lost. He needed the heartbeat of the big city where he could feel challenged. Soon, ambition won out as he became bored and restless looking to uncover new opportunities. The young entrepreneur knew it was time to leave. His one big reason to stay, Celia, would get by without him . . . at least for now.

Peter had crossed over that invisible line from "The city that is set on a hill and cannot be hid," into "Babylon," "The World." "After all, every man has to have a job and every job should get you a little further ahead," Peter was fond of saying, and Babylon afforded him such liberty. Back in Saint Louis, however, his character and love were such that, when danger threatened the people he still considered his, he acted immediately. It was this passion that had nearly cost him his life just a few weeks before. Although Peter had escaped, the original target of the persecution, whom he had tried to save, was killed at the hands of those who hated the Mormons.

Until recently, the persecution in Saint Louis hadn't been as severe as it had in Illinois and other Mormon settlements. Peter concluded this was so because Saint Louis was, after all, a "civilized" city. What problems there were seemed to be occasional, isolated incidents with little consequence, often because he was able to thwart whatever rabble tried raising a hand to his brothers. He always accomplished it anonymously, always without detection and, to Peter's great satisfaction, always without violence. He used his cunning and intellect to outsmart his foe. Generally that wasn't difficult, given the mentality of those who got themselves riled to the point where they would become motivated to action. That wasn't to say those educated and in high standing were not involved. No, they simply allowed the ones who weren't as bright to do their dirty work for them. Still, Peter had been lucky. Luck, however, is a fickle thing subject to change.

And change it did. A new pattern began to develop. This one was much more destructive, but not in terms of injury or death to the Mormons in the area, not initially anyway. The death came in the opposite camp, among those who not only fought against, but indeed, those who would but merely speak out against the Mormons. It was bad enough that these oppressors were being killed, but to make matters even worse, their material wealth was also being plundered. Although there were never any witnesses, circumstances seemed to point a finger at the Mormons, and anti-Mormon sentiment was fanned into hatred everywhere. Rumors of a group calling themselves the "Danites," established to kill prominent people who spoke out against the Mormons, were rampant in the area. It was widely believed that the "outlaw" Porter Rockwell led these Danites. Saint Louis buzzed with talk of the "Mormon plague," and many who had persecuted members of that religion were afraid to speak out.

The threat of death didn't deter everyone, however, and there were those who continued to stir up the people against the Saints. They saw these events as new material for their stable of lies. One such person was Peter's close friend and associate, Morgan Cain, one of the more outspoken Mormon critics at the time, though not totally reckless. He hired a tough drifter named Charlie Bates to be his bodyguard against the "plague." Bates had only been in Saint Louis a few months before he had established a reputation as a capable fighter not afraid of anything. Under the circumstances, a bodyguard seemed to Morgan like a very good idea and the meaner, the better.

Anxiety poured over Peter and he puzzled, "Who is killing our persecutors?" Not that he minded them meeting their Maker particularly, but Peter knew that ultimately, the consequences would be devastating to his people. He knew it couldn't be Rockwell because he wasn't in the area. True, Orrin Porter Rockwell would not have hesitated dispensing with the likes of those who were causing his people such hardship, but as far as Peter knew, there wasn't anybody else about who championed the Saints the way Rockwell did. *One thing's for sure,* Peter thought, feeling he had made the right decision to keep his membership in the Church a secret, *no one can think I am the man!*

Peter kept his eyes and ears alert to the movements and activities of known "Mormon haters." This was easy, as he enjoyed a certain popularity within the inner circle of Saint Louis society where Mormon-bashing was high fashion. It wasn't some act of violence toward the Saints, however, that ushered Peter into the world of deceit and corruption, educating him to the reality of the situation. It was in fact, the inner circle itself.

On the eve of the annual Governor's Ball, the entire elite of Saint Louis were busy getting ready for what had become the "must attend" event of the year. There were always dances in Saint Louis, one every Saturday night, in fact; but this was the granddaddy of them all and by invitation only. The invitations were coveted by many, but received by few, and it only happened once a year. Everyone wanted to go, and Peter had been no different. This year would be extraordinary though, because this time Peter Van Cleef would be there. "Yes, it is true," mused Peter, feeling more than a little proud of himself. "I have worked hard for this and I'm going to enjoy it."

Peter admired his reflection in the mirror as he finished tying his fine black silk bow tie. In a lot of ways, it was a matter of acceptance, a sort of coming-out party for Peter, and he wanted to be prepared. It would mean being sociable with the very people who were most active in persecuting his people, but tonight he would put all that aside. Still, it seemed a bittersweet compromise.

There was only one thing left to do. With great reluctance, Peter had decided to accept the offer of one H. Percival Rawlins, a prominent Saint Louis banker whom Peter had the unavoidable displeasure of working with. This displeasure stemmed from Rawlins' outspoken sentiment toward Mormons. The old man himself was likeable enough, but his politics were black. Rawlins, on the other hand, had developed an interest in Peter and offered to introduce him to "all the right people." Another reason for Peter's reluctance stemmed from the fact that acceptance of Rawlins' offer meant Peter would not be escorting his usual dancing companion, Miss Mary Ellen Moore. It was a decision that had to be made, and since Peter and Mary Ellen spent a good deal of time together, he was certain she would understand. Peter was to meet Rawlins at his house precisely at eight o'clock in the evening, at which time the two men would go forth and present themselves at the ball.

Peter decided to arrive early at the Rawlins home in case H.P. (as he was known to his friends), wanted to critique Peter's appearance. Besides, it was quite a little carriage ride to Rawlins' house and the most direct way to get there was directly through town, which slowed a traveler down considerably. This was to be expected; Rawlins lived in the most exclusive part of town.

As Peter's carriage drew near the Rawlins mansion, Peter could see a frenzy of activity around the house. There was much confusion and noise as servants from the houses in the area were running about and clutching one another in consoling fashion. There was also a man at the door with a musket. It was Conor O'Malley, the big Irishman Rawlins had hired to be his bodyguard. Peter had spoken to him many times in between dealings with H.P. and considered him a friend.

Peter stopped the carriage and grabbed one of the male servants as he ran by. "What's the meaning of all this?" he demanded. The man responded that old man Rawlins had been murdered by the "Mormon plague" and they believed the house servants had the man who did it trapped inside. Instantly, Peter ran toward the front door, but was stopped by Rawlins' bodyguard.

"Whooooa, Peter, you can't go in there," O'Malley insisted, in his thick Irish persuasion.

"Let me go, Conor! I've got to help find Rawlins' murderer," Peter lied imploringly. He was really more concerned with finding out whether or not it was really a member of his church doing all the killing. Regardless of the reason, the big Irishman held him firm until it became obvious to Peter that he wasn't going anywhere.

"Now Peter, me boy, there's no sense in gettin' yerself all riled up. The deed has been done and there ain't a t'ing you can do about it."

"What are *you* doing about it, O'Malley?"

"Well now, I'm guardin' this here door, ain't I?"

"I can see that, Conor, but don't you think you should go in there and get the murderer?"

Without even thinking about Peter's question, O'Malley shook his head back and forth, letting the flustered young man know that he had no plans of trying to apprehend the murderer, inside or out. He told Peter that Rawlins had given him the night off and he had been in the guesthouse reading when he heard the commotion.

"Mr. Rawlins' house servants have the killer trapped in the attic; I'm guardin' the door; and the sheriff has been summoned. He should be arriving soon to handle the whole affair."

"You're telling me that all that stands between the murderer and his escape are a few servants?"

"Now there ya go again gettin' yerself all excited. Don't you worry yer head about it. They have a scatter gun."

He could just imagine the scene. Two or three scared black house servants holding a murderer at bay with a gun. It took some doing, but Peter finally managed to convince O'Malley that he should let Peter go in to at least help the servants. "Think of it, Conor. If we can get this killer before the sheriff gets here, you'll be a hero instead of it looking like you were sleeping on the job. Heck, you may even get a reward!"

"So what do you want me ta do then?" asked O'Malley sheepishly.

"You just stay here and guard the door, just in case he tries to make a break for it. I'm sure he'll run out the front door if he does." O'Malley was too busy thinking about a reward to register Peter's cutting remark.

"All right Van Cleef, butcha better be careful. I don't t'ink whoever is in there would hesitate killin' again."

Peter slowly opened the door of Rawlins' mansion and quietly slipped inside. He made his way up the beautiful staircase and down the hallway looking for those acting as guards, but he could find no one. He began opening doors, peering into mostly darkened rooms. As he inched along, he came to one door that was slightly ajar. Light was coming from the room, but not a sound. Peter paused and listened for a moment ... nothing. He carefully reached for the doorknob and pushed open the door. At once an arm reached out, pulling Peter into the room and onto the floor.

Peter looked up, stunned, a gun barrel at his throat. "If you move again, I kill you," came a voice from behind the gun. Peter made no attempt to move. He quickly looked around the room so as to understand his predicament.

"I'm Peter Van Cleef, a friend of Mr. Rawlins," Peter croaked. "I was supposed to go to the Governor's Ball with him tonight. I've come to help you catch the man who killed your master . . . O'Malley let me in!"

"I ain't no slave," came the reply, with an increasing amount of pressure from the gun barrel against Peter's throat. "I be a free man. I work fo Misser Rawlins."

That explains his confident actions. A slave would never threaten a white man with a gun, Peter thought. He lay still and waited for the man's next move. After a moment of thought, the man lifted his gun and let Peter stand. Now he could take in the whole scene, and he saw two others in the room with them. One was a woman, the other a young boy.

"Name's Samuel and dis is my wife and boy," the house servant said. Peter shook hands with the man and nodded. He noticed the woman had a pistol, old and rusty. Both she and the boy kept looking up at a small staircase leading to a closed door.

"Is the killer up there?"

"Yessir and as far as he know, they ain't no other way out neither."

Peter pointed to the pistol the woman clutched so tightly. "If you will allow me to take the pistol your wife has, Samuel, I aim to go up there after the killer." Both Samuel and his wife looked at Peter like he was a mad man, but after a moment, Samuel reached out for the weapon and handed it to Peter. Samuel stopped Peter with one big hand as he started for the door.

"Not that way, Misser Peter. He barred da do' behind hisself. Anyway, you go through that do' and he shoot you dead fo sure."

"Can you show me another way, Samuel?"

"You go across da hall to da liberry. Next to da fireplace in the ceiling is a small do'. Use da book ladder to reach it."

Peter went to the library and found the door Samuel had said was there. It was far enough away and behind the main entrance that he felt he could get in undetected. Still, he wanted the best chance he could get, so he planned a diversion. He instructed Samuel to count to ten and then start yelling and pounding on the main door into the attic for another count of ten. Peter decided to keep the library dark so no attention-attracting light would burst into the attic when he lifted the hatch. He heard Samuel counting as he made his way back to the library, climbed the ladder, and prepared to enter the attic.

". . . Nine, ten!" From the other room, the pounding began. Peter lifted the hatch slightly, looking through the space created. It worked! He could see the figure of a man moving toward the door Samuel was fiercely beating upon. He slipped silently through the opening into the dimly lit expanse cluttered with H. P. Rawlins' forgotten memories.

As the shadowy figure reached the door, he lifted a gun to shoot through it. Peter quickly leveled his gun on the man and shouted for him to drop his weapon or die. The choice given was not a difficult one, and the gun dropped to the floor. The man turned to face his captor. Peter could not at once make out the features of his prisoner. The same was true for the other man. Halfway between them, sitting alone on an old trunk, was an oil lamp that barely lit the room. Carefully making his way to the lamp, Peter turned up the burning wick. The unveiled twisted smile of Charlie Bates glowed in the brightness of the increased light.

"You!" exclaimed Peter. "You're the one doing all this killing." Somehow, the situation seemed strangely clear to Peter now. He had always felt uneasy around Bates, like a horse near a rattlesnake. Bates was a profiteer. That's why he had taken the job as Morgan's bodyguard; but killing wealthy people, it seemed, was just a little more profitable.

"Well, young Master Peter, all duded up fer yer fancy dress ball. Come to avenge yer 'friend's' murder?" Bates sneered. "Don't act so surprised, Van Cleef. Every man has to have a job, and every job should get you a little further ahead; don't you agree?"

Peter couldn't believe what he had just heard. *How does this prairie trash know my philosophy, and how dare he apply it to such a twisted accomplishment?* Peter thought. Bates could tell his comments hit Peter like a shot fired from a Colt pistol. He seemed to relax just slightly and took a step toward Peter. "Stand like a tree!"

Peter declared, raising the gun, bringing eye and sights in line.

"Spare me your silly masquerade, *Brother* Van Cleef," Bates hissed. Peter's eyes widened at this, and he realized his religion was no longer a secret. "Oh yeah, boy, I know all about you. In fact ya might say I owe my successful new business to you," Bates continued. "It's like this: I was a Mormon once, until ol' Joe Smith decided to go to Illinois and leave me behind to tend to my missus, sick from all our bein' chased around. She died, Van Cleef, while you and all your stinkin' Mormon 'brothers and sisters' were buildin' Nauvoo the beautiful. But ya ain't gettin away with it . . . none of ya! I went to Nauvoo after I buried my wife and was taken in for a time by the Faradays. Pretty little Celia spoke so highly of one Peter Van Cleef. Ya know, I think she fancies you." Bates sneered at Peter, grinding in the resentment, knowing the pain he was inflicting on his adversary. Peter locked his stare on Bates and his eyes again narrowed, peering through the sights of the gun. "I heard all about yer great success in Saint Louis and how much money there was to be made."

"If you touched even a hair on their heads . . . ."

"Relax hero, I ain't stupid. To them, I was a 'Saint' and they trusted me with everything. When I told them of my plans to journey to Saint Louis, they asked me to bring some mail for you and the discharge papers from your short but revealing service in the *Mormon* militia known as 'Zion's Camp.' Seems the brethren finally got around to making it official. Celia wanted you to have them and I graciously offered to deliver them."

Peter's heart sank. Back in Ohio, as the Saints were preparing to move to Missouri, he and his good friend Jedediah Cutler had joined a small, loosely organized group formed by the Prophet Joseph Smith. Its purpose was to discourage persecution, by force if necessary; but it wasn't to Peter's liking, and he didn't remain with the group long. Now it seemed, after all this time, that the Church decided to recognize those who had been involved. Their timing couldn't have been worse. Peter had been so careful to conceal his religious background and cloak all association with the Mormons since returning to Saint Louis. Now Bates had documents that not only proved he was Mormon, they also tied him directly to a force whose only function was to fight those who lifted their hands against that people.

" . . . So I came to Saint Louis lookin' for you and your money, but bumped into Morgan Cain instead. Besides, I knew you'd turn up sooner or later. Oh, and by the by, I can't claim total credit for my good fortune since being employed in Mr. Cain's service. It was his idea to kill off those who'd speak out agin' the Mormons so people would think it was Mormons doin' the killin'. It was a good plan, but Morgan is too weak to accomplish it. Little did he know I would use that plan myself. Takin' their money was my idea, but you understand that, don't ya, Peter? After all, business is business."

Peter's head was spinning with confusion. Fury burned inside him, yet he was ashamed that he might have had something, anything, to do with the terrible events of the past few months. He unlocked his stare on Bates and lowered his gun.

"What about me, Bates? Why didn't you tell Morgan I am a Mormon?" Bates smiled and again made a move toward Peter, who returned the gun to a threatening position, but slower and less assuredly this time.

"I was plannin' to blame you all along in the end, but ya done too good. Yer too powerful. Besides, why ruin a good thing? If I told them who you were, they might find out I'd bin a Mormon too and, who knows, somebody might believe you more than me. Your little play actin' has made me rich and got me revenge too. The way I got it figgered, yer trapped, and that's your hell!"

The faint sounds of horses and excited voices could be heard rising up from the front of the house. Bates moved slowly to the tiny porthole window in the attic dormer and looked out. Peter didn't have to see to know it was the sheriff arriving. "Looks like we're both about to experience justice, hero," Bates concluded, a little uneasy. "I wager that when they find out yer a Mormon and I tell 'em yer my accomplice, they'll hang you right along with me. That is, of course, unless I escape and nobody finds out."

Everything was happening too fast and Peter needed time to think, but time was running out. If the sheriff apprehended Bates, everyone would surely learn of Peter's secrets. He had to choose. "All right Bates, you win . . . for now. There is a small door, there, next to the chimney. It will take you to the library. Rawlins' servants are in the other room, behind the main attic door, but if you are quiet, they won't know you're there."

Bates picked up his gun and began easing toward the trap door. He paused when he reached Peter. "If you get any funny ideas about goin' to the sheriff about me, I'll just have to reveal that you're a Mormon and the leader of the plague. I've arranged to have your discharge papers published in the Saint Louis Gazette should anything happen to me." With that he struck Peter with the butt of his gun, knocking him, unconscious, to the floor. Without another sound, Bates was gone.

Peter was beginning to stir when Sheriff Beeker, O'Malley, and the house servants came through the attic door, guns in hand. O'Malley helped Peter to his feet and looked after the wound inflicted by Bates' gun. "I told ya not to do it, didn't I?" O'Malley said, shaking his head.

"I guess he got away," Peter offered, wiping the blood from where Bates hit him.

"Did you recognize him?" Beeker asked. "Can you describe him?"

Peter just shook his head. "It was dark, Sheriff. He hit me before I got a look at him."

The sheriff stormed out of the attic, and the others followed after a few moments of disbelief. On his way from the house, Peter saw the undertaker arrive and take away the shrouded body of H. Percival Rawlins. The sight made him stop dead in his tracks. He couldn't help but feel some remorse for the old gentleman, even if Rawlins had hated the Mormons. It figured that there was probably more ignorance and pride on H.P.'s part than genuine hatred toward Peter's church.

There was no point in going to the ball now. With Rawlins dead, it would put a damper on the festivities, and Peter knew anyone he might meet wouldn't be in the frame of mind to be impressed by him. Especially since everyone knew H.P. was to bring this bright new addition to the city with him to the party. For a moment he was glad his secret was safe and no one knew him from before or that he was a Mormon. Peter's heart raced and he began to sweat despite the cold that hung heavy all around him. The air was bitter cold, but he couldn't feel it.

Peter didn't move for the longest time, partly because he couldn't and partly because he didn't know what to do. Finally he found the strength to start for home. He returned to where he had left his carriage, only to find it gone. Charlie Bates had surely taken it for his own evil ends, so Peter had no other choice but to walk home in the cold autumn night.

He thought about his life as he walked. He thought about what had happened this night and what would surely happen tomorrow and the next day and the next. He felt as if a part of him had also died in that house back there, and the point was driven home as Peter's path took him right past the governor's mansion, where the ball attendees roared with astonished conversation about the murder and the "plague."

There was no other choice but to continue his masquerade a little longer. In fact, he would spend next Saturday night as he had for many a social season—dancing with Mary at the usual affair. His fate and that of his friends might just depend on it. The rumble from the mansion seized his unconsciousness, and Peter could feel the devil walking beside him.

In the days that followed, Peter was present for the opening and closing bells of the Saint Louis Stock Exchange. He managed to buy low and sell high even with his mind on the troubles of his people. He looked at property. He borrowed and lent. From his position of influence in Missouri and Illinois, moving among the rich and powerful, Peter knew all the politics. He knew that, across the river, Governor Ford of Illinois did not want the Mormons to vote in the '46 elections. Even with most of them already gone, there were enough to turn the tide against Ford, and the Mormons held him personally responsible for the death of Joseph Smith. Militia generals slipped in and out of high-powered offices and then made fiery speeches to their grinning "soldiers," but none of it appeared in the newspapers. As Peter left meetings about real estate, he heard tidbits of how to snap up abandoned Mormon property once the "poor fools" had left without being able to sell.

In the company of some of Saint Louis' most aggressive politicians and businessmen, one of whom was Morgan Cain, Peter became party to a conversation about "them damn Mormons." Obviously not knowing their associate was a member of the Mormon church, the conversation flowed freely, a situation Peter later reflected upon, feeling ashamed he had not been more active in his beliefs. Persecution of Mormons was a common and ongoing pastime now, but the occurrence of such persecutions had reached a state of near frenzy. It was a popular attitude; many were worried about these strange people who called themselves Latter-day Saints. This being the case, anyone active in political circles took it upon themselves to further the cause of stirring up the public against the Mormons. This evening, Peter just happened to be there to hear it.

How is it possible that this much hate could continue for so long? thought Peter. It had been little more than two years since the Prophet Joseph had been killed in Carthage. Most Mormons, Peter included, had believed the persecution would stop since the wolves had gotten what they were after in killing the Prophet. But it was not to be, and Peter felt his heart leap into his throat, beating so hard and loud he was sure everyone in the room could hear it. As he listened to the stories his "friends" were telling of their own efforts to thwart the Mormon plague, his palms became moist with sweat and he found it hard to breathe. Still he listened. Had he heard correctly?

A mob would descend on Nauvoo to drive out the last of his people by any means, including the killing of more innocent people. This was bad enough, but clearly not the end. It was Peter's close friend, Morgan Cain, who boasted a plan to burn the city of Nauvoo to the ground!

Everyone congratulated each other and laughed over their perceived victory. Everyone but Peter. A significant part of him had hardened and cracked when the Prophet Joseph was killed two years ago. He would be destroyed before he would allow his people to suffer any more death and destruction from the hands of these "gentiles." Peter felt sick inside and the rage welled up almost to the point where he could not control it, but he fought down his bile. As he excused himself, he felt the tears come. The emotion graciously waited a moment longer before completely overtaking him as he burst through the door into the cold Saint Louis night. Helpless and alone, Peter Van Cleef wept bitterly.

Instincts are good things, or so Peter had been taught in the hard school of business. After all, both beasts and merchants survive on instincts and, more importantly, fortunes are made by them. Peter's friends with political aspirations would have said it was those instincts of self-preservation and self-aggrandizement that guided him out of Saint Louis this night, but Peter knew better. It was something much stronger and infinitely more definitive that prompted him to leave. It was something he learned as an earnestly curious young man debating and discussing with the bright-eyed Celia and the grinning Jed. It was in fact, the gift he had been given without understanding its value until now. He knew he was prompted by the Holy Ghost.

There was no question in Peter's mind what he was to do. He had to travel to Nauvoo and warn the city of the impending mob attacks. As he cantered his big white stallion down the deserted road, he realized an urgency inside him like he had never known before. Yes, he must get there in time to warn the Church leadership, but there was also something else. Something even deeper that gnawed at his heart . . . Celia.

Peter shuddered at the thought of Celia at the mercy of people like Bates. She was in his past, but the feelings were still tender, as were the memories. It had been too long since he had seen her. Interwoven with soothing images of that time lay the dull pain that would never let him forget how he had left her to pursue capital gain in Saint Louis. It seemed never-ending as the pain became tangled with loneliness. He had lost Celia to another. What was worse, he lost her to his best friend, Jedediah Cutler. Worse, ha! Peter half laughed at the thought. Celia was much better off being married to a strong, stable farmer like Jed, not a worldly nomad like himself. He could feel the self-pity coming, but fought it off by thinking of happier times amongst the three friends.

Peter and Jed had been friends since their school days, an unlikely friendship at first glance. Peter was always self-assured, aggressive and cocky, while Jed was calm and steady with a deep spiritual conviction. It was a two-headed coin that worked. One supported the other like a fine team of chariot horses. Jed brought the Gospel to Peter, and they shared it as only true friends could. They learned together, went to church together, and met Celia together.

Even as a young girl, Celia was like a precious stone. She was beautiful to behold, strong in character, indeed truly remarkable in all her facets. She often found herself the subject of the two boys' rivalry, innocent as it was. Peter always had the edge over Jed, though. His charisma and charm captivated Celia, as did his dreams of what life would be like in New York, Saint Louis, or even the new adventures out West—California perhaps. Jed listened too, but his heart was with the land and he heard another call. He knew that, as capable with money as the members of his church were, they were farmers more than anything. He was a farmer and his father, and his father before him, were farmers. That was the way of things. Even though he secretly loved Celia, he could see she had bright lights, not seeds, in her eyes.

Fate is a cruel mistress and favors no one. She can, however, be guided somewhat by man's decisions. Peter knew this as well as any man. He had decided on the sparkle of gold, and fate obliged. The more success he attained, the greater became the distance between the life he left in Nauvoo and the life he had in Saint Louis. This was not so much in terms of miles, but in the empty expanse of his own heart.

Celia felt a much greater distance than Peter ever did. By the time he realized it, she was gone. At first it hurt her deep inside where no such emotion had yet penetrated. She had hurt similarly when the Prophet Joseph had been killed and because of the seemingly never-ending persecutions wrought upon her people, but this was different. This pain was searing.

Through Celia's letters, Peter knew she had spent many difficult hours alone contemplating what she should do in his absence and many more hours in prayer. Although she never actually said it, Peter knew Jed had tried to comfort Celia.

"Perfectly natural," Peter said aloud as he rode along. He had been so lost in thought, his vocalization surprised him, but did not stop the process. His mind raced on to find answers to questions too long ignored. Yes, it was perfectly natural. After all, Jed was Celia's friend too. Peter recalled how Celia wrote to him recounting how excited she was when Jed won the Nauvoo wrestling games and how she had felt so helpless when she and Jed delivered a beautiful calf after staying up all night, but how Jed was so wonderful and gentle. He especially remembered how Celia's letters seemed to glow when she would talk about helping Sister Cutler at home making bread or mending Jed's clothes.

The heart of a romantic woman goes out to a frightened hero, standing alone for what he believes in. Later she must think about the future, the children. Then the hero she seeks is her protector. So it was that Celia's interest turned from the dark-haired, dark-eyed man who wandered and sought adventure to the blond, blue-eyed man who stayed stubbornly at home to defend all he held dear.

All these things Peter remembered, and more. He hadn't realized at the time what they meant. He never suspected he had withdrawn from the contest to the point that Celia could forget "their memories" and make new ones with someone else. He stopped his horse and dismounted, frustrated at the anxiety he felt. *Why must I go through this realization now,* he thought, splashing icy water on his face from a nearby running brook. *My first duty is to reach Nauvoo and warn them before any harm comes to them, but I can't stop thinking about . . . .* He didn't dare say it; his lips froze with her name. Peter sighed as the realization swept over him that it was his arrogance and greed that kept him from Celia.

She, meanwhile, sat patiently but unhappily beside her beloved all afternoon in the chapel whose beauty was growing increasingly less interesting. The group was restless, and friends had gone out looking for Brother Brigham. He, however, was never where informed people said he was. He had always left just before the wedding searchers arrived. Caleb and Quimby urged Jed and Celia to be married by a member of the temple presidency, but they declined. Brigham had been good to them both and had relied on Jed in many difficulties. They knew he wanted to marry them, and they were willing to suffer a little now to treasure that experience forever.

The sun was low against the horizon and the crisp blues of the autumn sky gave way to the golds of twilight. It would be dark soon, and Peter knew he needed to make camp for the night. He had hoped to reached Nauvoo before nightfall but was too tired to continue. After all this time, he still remembered the Mormon farms on the Iowa side of the river well enough to know old Brother Simpson's place wasn't far. He would stop there for the night.

The farm was deserted, Peter found—no animals, no people. The yard was scattered with pieces of household goods left behind by looters. The scene stood in the sunset as mute testimony to the mobs scourging the Mormons away from all their outlying settlements and into the city. Peter looked on the scene with anger, finally coming face-to-face with the result of an advancing army of hate.

No matter; it would provide a shelter against the wet and cold. There was plenty of wood around with which to build a fire. That was the first order of business. The second was his thoughts.

Peter sat gazing into his fire, half-watching the crackling embers dance upward from the flames and disappear into the blackness of the massive stone hearth. He pictured Jed kneeling in front of his fireplace proposing marriage to Celia. He could see it just as she had described it to him in her letter. "Forgive me, Peter," she wrote. "Forgive me and wish me happiness." Peter had never answered that letter. He hadn't known how. At the time there weren't any words of congratulations, no happiness to be wished. Now it was different. He knew he ought to feel joy in their union and should tell them so. Their bond of friendship was still strong, and he knew he loved them both. The thought of this made Peter relax a little and warmed him inside with a happiness he hadn't known for a long time. He drifted off to sleep knowing tomorrow he would be with Jed and Celia once more.

The front door to the cabin flung open, crashing against the side of the wall. Peter jumped to his feet still in a sleepy daze, having only been asleep a few minutes. He looked toward the door and beheld the shadowy figure of a large man. The man had two pistols drawn and pointed in his direction. The wind blew hard into the cabin, whistling through the abandoned sticks of furniture. He couldn't see the face of the intruder except to know the man had long hair and a beard.

"Who are you?" Peter demanded.

"Name's Rockwell" replied the figure. "And just who might you be and what're you doin' in old man Simpson's house?" Peter laughed a sigh of relief.

"Port, it's me, Peter Van Cleef," exclaimed Peter, calling him by a nickname used only by Rockwell's closest friends.

He wanted to run to the frightening figure in the door who was his old friend. He wanted to embrace him, beard, bulk and all . . . . Rockwell didn't lower his guns.

It scared him to see Rockwell act this way. Orrin Porter hesitated only a moment before lowering his weapons after Peter identified himself, but it seemed like an eternity.

Orrin Porter Rockwell had been a good friend of the Prophet Joseph and was also a friend of Peter's. Rockwell had befriended the boy years ago in Kirtland, Ohio, after Peter's parents were killed emigrating to America from England. Peter learned the skills of the outdoors from Rockwell and gained his deep, abiding respect for nature and life through Porter's lessons. As Peter grew, Rockwell became more of a recluse and a traveler. He often acted as personal aid and bodyguard to Joseph Smith, duties which could keep him gone from the body of the Saints for months at a time. Even though it cost him his marriage, Porter had never flinched at what he considered his duty to Joseph and the Church. For Peter, Jedediah Cutler would take over as friend and companion, but Rockwell would always be like an older brother to him.

"What are you doin' here?" Porter asked, his voice ever so shaky. Peter went to him and told him of the mob coming to drive out the Saints.

"Why did you leave the safety of your gentile life to get mixed up in all this trouble?" Rockwell wanted to know.

Peter stammered, "I am still a Mormon, Porter, and . . . when I learned of the plot . . . I knew it was my duty to warn the people."

"Did you also know that Colonel Price and his Wildcats have crossed the river already and are joining with an Illinois mob?" Peter shook his head. He was surprised Rockwell knew more than he did, and the information was obviously more recent. Port smiled knowingly and asked, "Did you know that today was the wedding of Jed Cutler and Celia Faraday? Fact is, they're probably headin' for the temple right now."

Rockwell was known for his sense of humor, especially at the oddest of times. Peter jumped to gather up his gear and moved to saddle his horse, ignoring Rockwell's vain attempt at levity. He exclaimed excitedly that they must push on to warn the city. Porter just laughed and shook his head.

"Well, what did ya think we were going t'do, stand here and watch?"

As Peter and Rockwell eased their way through the woods, they observed columns of men, some mounted and some on foot, with all kinds of weapons. They were laughing, singing, and reeked of "white lightning," the harsh frontier whiskey. Unseen by the hurrying swarms of sinister black-painted men, Rockwell guided Peter along hidden trails that brought them to Cobb's Ferry ahead of the mob. They rowed themselves and their horses across the Mississippi on the raft-like ferry boat, held on course by a line of tethered buoys, and clattered into Nauvoo, whipping their exhausted horses up Temple Hill.

The wedding party was falling asleep in the chapel pews. Suddenly a door opened and Brigham Young strode in. Quietly but urgently, he spoke to the assembled company. "Forgive my tardiness, brothers and sisters. There is so much to do attending to the needs of the Saints in the camps north. I commend you for your patience. Of course, your sealings this evening are equally vital to the Lord's plan." President Young turned to lead the way further into the temple. "Let us begin. I . . . . " A great clamorous noise outside stopped him.

Peter and Rockwell galloped up to the temple grounds, reined in, and jumped to the pavement outside the side door. What to do? Peter had no recommend signed by a bishop. He could not enter. He stood back and looked up at the monumental walls towering over him. Everything he loved most dearly was inside, and he was not worthy to enter.

"Celia!" he cried out, and his cry was echoed back to him off the massive building. He strode up to the door, Rockwell watching it all with intense interest, and beat upon its polished timbers. After a moment, a temple worker opened the door, took one look, and closed the door. Peter was debating opening the door and entering when the wedding group came out to see him. Last out was Celia in her beautiful wedding dress.

Everyone (but especially Celia) was shocked to see Peter. Jed was hurt, angry, and suspicious. Rockwell and Peter spilled out their story, pointing excitedly to the icy river glowing in the waning, heatless sun and to the dark brush and forest beyond. Immediately Brigham ordered every man to his post, telling Jed to call out the few remaining members of the Nauvoo Legion; but Jed was rooted to the spot, studying Celia and Peter. It was Jed's friend Jamie Logan, a guest at the wedding who had come with his wife in his own cart, who departed to find the Legion soldiers. Brigham hurried away to gather the Quorum of the Twelve, the group of men who acted as the governing body of the Church. They would plan the response of the last Nauvoo Mormons to the final assault on their city. The Faradays got into their carriage and were ready to be driven off to their home by Quimby.

As the sunset gleamed on the massive temple and a winter night wind whipped up, Jed, Peter, and Celia stared at each other, tormented and confused. Celia was standing by the huge temple doors looking out over the city, trying to hold back the tears, as she listened to the two men fence with words heavy with stifled anger. "The Faradays must pack up their household goods, load their wagon, and, when instructed, head for either the thickest ice or the ferry," said Jed stubbornly.

Peter replied angrily, "In a few hours, there won't be a city left to leave. They had better gather food and coats, take horses and get out now!"

Celia then saw winking lights on the far shore, hundreds of torches. She saw long black columns, crowned with the dots of light, moving out onto the ice, converging on the city. She pointed and the men followed her finger. Rockwell began to examine his weapons and tighten his saddle girth. Peter and Jed stopped arguing. Jamie rode up at the head of an armed and mounted body of Mormon men, wordlessly requesting Jed to take his place at their head. It was now time to break away from their triangular problem and do their duty to the group.

With great anxiety, Jed asked Peter to help the Faradays get out. Celia turned to the two men. For just a moment Peter's eyes met Celia's. She was not expecting to be so impressed with him, and he wasn't prepared to leave her beauty so soon after regaining its healing presence. Jed was now too preoccupied to notice the exchange between Celia and Peter, but in his heart, Peter felt that somehow Jed knew. There wasn't time for words. Their eyes unlocked, and events took

control of their lives. Lieutenant Cutler waved his men on as he swung into his saddle. The remnant of the proud Legion cantered off into its last battle.

From the hilltop, Rockwell, Peter and Celia could hear gunfire, shouting and screaming from the Nauvoo riverfront. Then flames appeared among the buildings down below.

"If we're gonna do any good, we got ta get down there," said Rockwell roughly. "Looks like you'll have ta ride behind, Missy."

From the temple steps, Peter swung Celia up behind him on his big horse, wedding dress and all, veil flying, hopes abandoned. Rockwell leading, they galloped down the hill and deposited Celia at her parent's home, where she rushed inside to change.

Peter and Rockwell pressed on toward the skirmish line of Mormon men, whose attempt to hold back the mobbers' tide was marked in the night by the sparkle of muzzle flashes and the rattle of their musketry. They were very near now and could see the flames and feel the heat. Up ahead a small group of men were forming just outside the city, silhouetted in flames.

"They ain't here ta greet us," Rockwell yelled to Peter. Rockwell put his bridle reins in his mouth and drew both pistols. He took aim and fired again and again. Peter looked at him in amazement. He was a businessman, bred to be an aristocrat, not a gunfighter. His thoughts were abruptly stopped, however, as a burning pain screamed through his upper body. It took his breath away and made him dizzy. Peter could feel warm blood against his shoulder and he knew he'd been hit. He could hear Rockwell yelling at him, though it sounded miles away. "Get yourself together or you'll die where you stand." Peter could hear shouting and guns going off. Rockwell pulled an extra cap and ball revolver from his saddle holster and threw it to Peter, who took aim at the crowd of mobbers.

As the mob began to sustain losses from the combined firepower of Peter and Rockwell, they began to flee into the night, undoubtedly to regroup for another cowardly assault on less-prepared citizens of Nauvoo. Porter, unscathed, rode back to check on his young friend. "Ya done good, boy," Rockwell said. "How bad ya hit?" For the first time, Peter looked down at his shoulder.

"Not bad, Port. I'm all right," Peter replied.

"They're gettin' behind us, boy," Rockwell said as he twisted in his saddle to look around. "The whole city is afire." Peter turned his horse around to gape at the scene ignored in his concentration on the fight. The sky was on fire above the trees and, above that, the heavens were an inky black, thick with smoke. Wide-eyed and shaking, Peter whirled around to face Rockwell. The contrast between the two men was stark. Rockwell's expression was set; it was one of hatred. The squinting of his deep blue eyes only accentuated the emotion. Then Rockwell tossed Peter a grin, "You better get your girl out of there."

"Can you help me, Port?" gasped Peter, through clenched teeth.

Rockwell hesitated uncharacteristically, then spoke with the roughness of a painful decision. "No boy, I can't. I got ta find Brother Brigham. I wasn't there for Joseph. I can't let the vermin get Brigham. You'll have ta handle this on your own, Peter." With that, he whipped his horse and was gone.

Peter rode through clouds of blowing sparks and ash toward the Faraday home, spurring his terrified horse down flaming streets with Mormons and mobbers intermingled, all loaded with boxes, cases, and bags of every description—saving or looting the possessions of a lifetime. A panic suddenly gripped at Peter as his mind caught the impression of Celia. Would he be too late?

"No!" He beat the thought back and coaxed his horse even harder.

Peter had to dodge mob violence and burning buildings as he made his way to the river. The pain in his body from the gunshot wound nagged at him. He clutched the saddle horn tightly in agony at each rhythm of his horse's canter. Even more painful, though, were the sounds of death and destruction all around him. He could hear the cries of women and children, buildings collapsing as they burned, and the occasional crack of a gun. Still, he pushed onward with one purpose in mind.

As Peter rode parallel to the river, he caught sight of a scene that confirmed his fears. The Saints were fleeing Nauvoo. But where would they go, he wondered? Still, he rode on. It wasn't difficult to find the house where Celia lived. It was far enough away from the town that the mob hadn't reached it yet, but they were moving quickly. So was Peter.

He reined up in front of the Faraday home to see four men rushing toward the front door. One suddenly reared back with a pitchfork stuck in his throat and wiry little old Caleb Faraday hanging onto the haft of the pitchfork for dear life. The gentle little Saint was defending his home, with wife and daughter inside. Almost instantly, the other three were on Caleb, punching and kicking. Peter dismounted and lurched toward the pile of bodies. He slammed his pistol against the back of a mobber's head, and the man collapsed against his comrades. The three dark-clothed men struggled to their feet and ran away from the gaping muzzle of Peter's pistol. Peter examined Caleb while striving to maintain consciousness himself.

With a loud crash, a burning tree limb fell on the roof and in a moment the Faraday house was alight. Peter left Caleb, dashing inside to find Emma gathering food into a table cloth in the kitchen.

"Sister Faraday, see to Caleb out front," called Peter, as loudly as he could. Emma looked up in shock, and then ran past him to the door. He heard her screaming as she reached her husband.

Peter crawled upstairs calling for Celia, but was met by Jed coming out of the bedroom with his arms full of clothes. When it became painfully obvious that they were hopelessly outnumbered, Jed had disbanded the Legion and sent every man to attend to his family.

"Peter, what are you doing here? You're hurt, what's . . . ?"

"Listen, Jed," cried Peter, "the mob . . . the city . . . it's burning. We've got to escape." Smoke from the fire was getting thick, and Peter frantically shook his friend with his good hand. Jed and Peter went back into the bedroom to get Celia. Peter put a blanket around her and the two of them made their way to the door.

By this time, more members of the mob had gathered outside the house. When Peter opened the door he thought he saw someone, but kept moving anyway. A ball, fired from a mobber's gun, whistled past his head and splintered the door. Immediately he pulled Celia back inside the burning house. Peter took aim on the shadowy figure who had fired at him. One shot was all it took. The mobber fell and the rest fled.

The two tried again to escape the house, which by this time was engulfed in flames. They had made it outside when Celia realized Jed was still in the house. She screamed for Jed and tried unsuccessfully to re-enter the flames. Peter held on to her tightly, refusing to let her succeed in the attempt. He assured her he would do everything he could to save Jed, but before Peter could get back to the house, Jed called to him from the roof over the front porch. He had escaped through a window with the clothes, which he threw down to Peter. Jed, in turn, jumped from the roof.

Just then Quimby Leighton came rattling around the corner in his light wagon and team of two, pulling up in the yard. The men gathered up Celia, Emma, and Caleb, and lifted the whole Faraday family into Quimby's wagon. They fled to the river with Jed and Peter as a galloping rear guard, firing their last ammunition at any mobbers who threatened them.

At the river's edge, Quimby had a big Durham boat ready for them. Jed and Quimby hurled everything that had been saved from their homes into the boat. Mother and daughter helped poor bloody Caleb aboard. Jed was splashing out to climb in when he saw Peter let go of the horses and sink to his knees. Running back, he picked up Peter, who was as tall, but more slender than the muscular farmer. He laid his friend in the boat and rolled himself over the gunwale. Grabbing a pair of oars, he rowed in good coordination with Quimby, who had already taken position with another pair. The boat was in a fast-flowing eddy of the river that prevented a thick ice sheet from forming, so they gingerly picked their way among slowly moving ice floes, working across to the Iowa shore. Meanwhile, further upstream, Mormons were thundering over the river ice in fully loaded wagons.

For the first time in what seemed like a lifetime, it was quiet. The sounds of the burning city and the mob's rampage faded as the boat moved further out in the river. Neither Jed nor Celia said anything as Jed rowed mightily and Celia opened Peter's clothes to stuff a fine linen shirt over the wound. She hoped it would stop the bleeding, but it just became darkly sodden. Peter fought the pain in his chest. He wanted to maintain control of his breathing and his writhing limbs. The oars lapped at the water or bumped against the ice, which still innocently reflected the reds and yellows from the devil's own fire behind them. She wrapped Peter in the blanket he had wrapped her in and held him as his life flowed

from the wound inflicted by the hatred of an angry and ignorant people.

They could see other Saints making their way across the river to escape the mob. Their boat had floated downstream a little before Jed and Quimby managed to get it on course. This meant they would have to crunch along through ice-crusted snow, north along the Iowa shore, for at least a quarter of a mile, in order to rendezvous with the rest of the Saints who had crossed the river. In their condition, this was impossible for Peter and Caleb.

Their friends and neighbors already on the Iowa shore would wait for as many of the Saints as possible to cross in safety. They would, as they had done many times before, gather together before moving further inland where they would be safe from the mob. The destroyers would not follow the fleeing Saints across the river. They had accomplished their evil task and would not risk further danger to themselves. For the citizens of Nauvoo, the horror of the night was almost over. Soon they would have to assess their losses and begin to once again rebuild their lives.

The moon was rising as the boat grounded on the Iowa side of the river. The more the silver light shone down, the more obvious it was that the city that was set on a hill and could not be hidden was shining out with the light of its own destruction, and the most hideous beacon of all was the blazing temple on its hilltop. Everyone in the boat wept as they watched it collapse.

Then Jed looked down and saw that Peter's face was the color of the moon.

"We've got to get Peter to a doctor," he told Celia.

"But how? We've lost everything."

Peter looked like he was dying. Celia cried as she continued trying to stop the blood from his wound. She rocked Peter in her arms and whispered, "Don't die, Peter, please don't die."

"I ain't gonna let that happen, ma'am," came a voice from behind them. It was Porter Rockwell, and they knew he could take care of Peter if anyone could.

3

The Long Autumn Night

Rockwell had done all he could against the mob in Nauvoo. Brigham released him from service after Rockwell had opened the gates of hell to the black-painted cowards and ushered more than a few of them through. In addition, Rockwell had effectively secured the safety of the Prophet. As the night dragged on, he couldn't forget Peter's wound and began looking for the three friends, extending blows to the mob at every turn. Now that he had found them, Porter attended to the wounded young man with a skill Jed knew Rockwell had acquired from seeing to the afflictions of many of the Saints over the years. Rockwell had never been shot or wounded himself, but there were plenty of other Mormons who were.

Rockwell also helped Quimby and Emma work on Caleb, but under the wispy gray hair was obviously a fractured skull, and inside the cracked ribs, Rockwell was sure there were damaged organs. Here, Porter could not do much.

Bishop Leighton stepped forward and reached out his arms to Jed and Rockwell. "Then, if we have done all that we can do, we are right to ask for the Lord's help in prayer. Come, let us draw upon the power of the priesthood to bless our brethren." It was the Lord's healing blessing they would ask for through the power of the priesthood, which they all held. These men, like other worthy men in the Mormon church, were ordained to this office by another member of the Church with the authority to perform such an ordinance. It was with this power and through their faith that such blessings were accomplished.

Rockwell didn't hesitate a moment to step up and place his hands on Caleb's head. After a deep breath, Jed held out his hands to join with those of the Bishop and Rockwell. The three lightly touched Caleb's head, as far away from his injury as possible. When the Bishop had finished being the voice for a blessing of healing on Caleb, they all moved over to Peter, preparing to perform the ordinance again. Rockwell looked at Bishop Leighton anxiously. Quimby read his thoughts and asked Porter to be the voice for the blessing on their young friend. Wasting not a minute more, Rockwell lowered his head and pronounced a blessing on Peter.

Celia moved quickly to pack fast-reddening strips of a flannel nightgown against the hole in Peter's shoulder, but she knew Rockwell had the skill Peter needed. "The Lord will work through you, Porter," Celia said, smiling through her tears, looking up at the big, hairy face that loomed over her. Porter smiled with a meek gratitude very much at odds with his bulk and flashing features.

"Caleb is much more surely in the hands of the Lord," whispered Emma, cradling her husband. They all worked to build a stretcher after the fashion of the Indian medicine sled, which would allow Rockwell to get Peter to safety. At the same time they used a door from a nearby burned house to make a four-handled litter for Caleb.

"You two go on now," Rockwell said to Jed and Celia. "There ain't a thing you can do here." Celia kissed Peter and Jed shook hands with Rockwell. "Now get," Rockwell said, trying to give the couple a reassuring smile. "You'll see this boy again." They both thanked him and said goodbye. Rockwell then hurried to save his friend as Jed, Celia, Quimby, and Emma made their way toward the other survivors, each carrying a corner of Caleb's stretcher as they stumbled through the icy snow and gnarled, thorny bushes.

Rockwell didn't take Peter far from where Jed and Celia left them, just enough to be out of earshot. He knew he had to act quickly if he was going to save Peter's life, but just in case it was too late, he didn't want the others to know Peter had died. They had enough to worry about. Porter knew the first order of business was to get the mobber's demon lead out of Peter's body. He also knew Peter would probably scream from the pain of the knife, and if the others heard it they would come running, especially Celia.

At a point Rockwell deemed safe, he stopped his horse. Making a frontier fire was no challenge to Porter, and he soon had the flames licking the blade of his buck knife.

Peter lay on the makeshift stretcher, fading in and out of consciousness. Confusion and pain danced in front of his eyes whenever he was awake. During those moments, he wasn't sure of anything except that he couldn't move, then he would slip into a different world where the pain was gone and his mind was clear. *I remember fighting the mob in Nauvoo*—the thought filled the blackness of Peter's mind—*but it seems so long ago.* Then would come the pain. It all became something of a dream to Peter—a nightmare, really.

Rockwell was startled by Peter's weak voice, "Just let me sleep. I just want to sleep." He wheeled around from the fire, knife in hand, and shouted at Peter to try and hold on. Rockwell's voice was loud and tense, even though he was but inches from his dying friend. Porter kept talking as he cut away Peter's shirt. The knife was still hot from the fire when he began his operation.

Peter wrenched in pain from the burning blade as it cut deep into the muscles of his shoulder. The already-damaged flesh that was ripped open from the ball's wound seemed to melt away like butter when Rockwell's knife encountered it. The scent of burning flesh was strong and pungent, but it both looked and smelled worse than it really was. Rockwell understood the benefits of cauterizing the blood vessels in the area of the wound, and the hot knife accomplished the task. "Besides, the hot blade cuts easier," Rockwell yelled at Peter, as if to reassure him, but he wasn't even sure Peter could hear him. Still, it was worth a try.

There it was. *Tink*, the blade of the knife made contact with the metal ball lodged firmly against Peter's rib, just above his heart. Rockwell maneuvered the blade under the intruder and with a quick prying movement, expelled the bullet from his friend.

Again Peter wrenched in pain as the ball left his body. Rockwell watched as Peter drew a deep breath for the first time since they got him out of Nauvoo, but as he exhaled, Peter's body relaxed and he lay quiet and still. He did not breathe in again. Rockwell stopped dressing the wound for a moment and stared in disbelief at the pale, motionless figure.

"No, Peter! Don't die," Rockwell yelled. As if he could change anything, he scrambled madly to finish what he had begun only moments before.

"Yer tougher than this, boy," Rockwell yelled at Peter, as big drops of water welled in his eyes. "Yer tougher . . . . " Rockwell stopped mid-sentence. He stood and turned his back from the body of his friend. In pain and frustration, he kicked the frozen ground. For a moment, Orrin Porter Rockwell wept, something he didn't do often and not since the Prophet Joseph Smith had been murdered. Rockwell finally turned back to the silent form. He knelt down, lifted Peter off the cold ground and stood like a statue in the glow of the beautiful autumn moon in the white Iowa night.

"I'd trade places with ya if I could, boy. Yer young and had so much to live fer." Rockwell drew in deep breaths, but they weren't evenly spaced or smooth. Each breath was jerky and seemed to get caught up on a piece of Porter's broken heart as the air made its way to his lungs. A broken heart was no stranger to this rugged frontiersman. He had experienced it twice before, but it didn't make it any easier the third time.

When it first happened, it was slow in coming, perpetuated by the agony of losing his family. In the beginning, everything seemed to be normal in their lives. Porter Rockwell had married Luana Beebe in 1832, while living in Jackson County, Missouri. Soon, persecution of the Mormons made it necessary to move, and move, and move again. In the midst of all the troubles, Luana bore Porter four children, and they struggled to raise them under the harsh conditions of the wilderness. Because Rockwell was away a lot of the time on business for the Prophet, much of the weight of raising the children fell on Luana, and she soon grew weary of that sole responsibility and her present way of life. While Rockwell was in hiding with the Prophet Joseph Smith, after a particularly harsh attack by Mormon haters, Luana made the painful decision to leave her husband. The estranged Rockwell, deeply depressed and delirious with grief, had wandered throughout the region for the better part of a year, trying to deal with his pain. Two years later, his heart was only just beginning to heal when news of the death of the Prophet

Joseph Smith reached him. Porter's heart broke all over again.

Word of Joseph's death came swiftly and without warning, unlike the long, drawn out ordeal with his ex-wife, Luana. The loss shook Rockwell to his very soul. He recovered from his first heartbreak over Luana, but in some ways, he would never recover from the loss of his boyhood friend. Now he had lost Peter. *Will I ever feel happiness again?* Porter wondered.

With Peter still cradled in his arms, Rockwell stared in the direction of the Saints' encampment. *What am I going to tell them?* He didn't see Peter's eyes open. He didn't feel the young man's shallow breathing, but as surely as the moon illuminated their faces, the magic Rockwell had performed worked, and Peter would live.

Peter looked up at this giant of a man and felt the love and security he had known as a boy when Rockwell was his brother and teacher. "Big crybaby," Peter said weakly. It was as if the voice had come from inside his own head and not from Peter's mouth; still, Rockwell looked down at his friend. All at once the realization swept over him like a wave, and he grinned wide enough to light the night. Peter smiled back as best he could and said, "I'm cold, Port."

Rockwell built up the fire in no time and bundled warmly a part of his life he had given up for dead only moments ago, all the while dancing around and whooping like some drunken sailor away on shore leave. For just awhile in the midst of such an overwhelming tragedy, there was joy in life.

Unknown to either Peter or Rockwell, two others would also experience their own version of joy amidst pain. Jed and Celia had made it to the encampment of the displaced Saints. The sun was beginning to rise about the time they were finally able to stop and gather themselves together. A thought whispered to Jed, reminding him that today was to have been his first day of marriage. The thought caught him off guard, considering the events of the night before which had brought them to this point. He looked at Celia and felt very blessed to still have her with him and to be safe, even if their safety wasn't sure. Not all of them had been so lucky. Caleb, Celia's father, had been badly beaten and could die. Many of the other Saints had also suffered extreme hardship at the hands of the mob. As Jed watched Celia and Emma attend to Caleb, he noticed an overwhelming flood of emotion beginning to overtake him. Jed closed his eyes and concentrated, *Not now, please Lord, I mustn't cry now,* he thought. *Celia needs me and I must be strong.* Jed was strong and everyone knew it. He was also right. Not only Celia, but all the Saints looked to Jed for strength and would continue to do so as time went on. Right now, though, Jed needed the strength for another matter, a very personal one, and neither man nor devil would stop him this time.

A gentle reassuring hand on his shoulder broke Jed's concentration. He had been resting his head in his hands and now looked up to see Celia. She knew Jed was struggling. Although she also felt like crying, she would be strong for him. Celia's warm smile chased away Jed's anguish, and he felt renewed in his convictions. Jed jumped to his feet, firmly placing his strong hands on Celia's shoulders. His arms extended, he held her away from him so he could take in her beauty. Celia could tell Jed was serious and had something important to say. They locked eyes and gazed at each other lovingly until Jed spoke. "I won't see another sunset or travel another mile a single man, Celia Faraday!"

Her heart beat wildly. This was more than she had dared hope. When the temple in Nauvoo was destroyed, with it went Celia's hopes for marriage. Now the man she loved stood ready to take her as wife under any circumstances. "Who knows what tomorrow will bring, or the next day, or the next," Jed continued, "but whatever will be, we'll face it together and do it as man and wife!"

Celia broke Jed's arms-length hold and embraced him tightly. She didn't have to be strong any more and the tears came freely. After a moment, Celia looked up at his handsome face and said, "I'm ready, Jedediah."

Getting Brigham Young to slow down was never easy, and that proved even more the case as Jed tracked him from group to group within the encampment. President Young was busily working to reassure the Saints and organize them into functioning bodies. From a distance, Jed spotted Brigham surrounded by Fennelly Parsons and his eight children. He was instructing them to assist the women and older members of the camp. When they saw Jed coming, they all greeted him warmly. Usually such a meeting would be casual and leisurely, but Jed was determined to take Brigham back with him to perform the marriage that was interrupted by the mob. This left him with little time for pleasantries.

Brigham smiled as he extended his hand to Jed. "I'm so pleased to see you safe, Jedediah," Brigham said. Jed thanked President Young and returned a similar greeting, but Brigham could sense the anxiety in young Jed. His smile was replaced with a stern look when he let go of Jed's hand. "We'll get through this all right Jedediah, the Lord is with us. Don't you worry." Jed nodded and thanked his leader. Deep inside, Brigham knew that what Jed was feeling was even more personal and immediate than his own general well-being. Still, Brigham gave Jed the opportunity to speak his mind. "What is it, boy? Speak up!" Brigham coaxed, feeling a bit fatherly toward Jed. At last, Jed had his chance to ask a favor of the Prophet.

"President Young," Jed began, "I know it may seem strange what I'm about to ask you in light of what we've just been through, that is, but . . . . "

"But you want me to perform the wedding between you and your beautiful Celia, don't you?" asked Brigham.

Jed's reply was an emphatic, "Yes, Sir!"

"Good!" continued Brigham. "I was hoping you would feel that way. I think such an event would not only be good for the two of you, it would also rejuvenate the spirits of the Saints. Heaven knows we could all benefit from such a happy occasion." Jed could not contain his joy. He grabbed Brigham's hand and shook it mightily, thanking him all the while. "So, Jedediah, when shall we perform this happy ritual?"

Still shaking Brigham's hand, Jed replied, "Oh, right away, President, right away!"

By this time, all the Parsons boys were gathered around Brigham and Jed. President Young turned to them and asked, "Well, what are you waiting for, lads? Go gather the Saints!"

In a gesture of grandiose bravado, Brigham Young raised his arms to the crowd gathered around the cold clearing on the Iowa river bank. "Brothers and Sisters, even in hardship there is joy. I have asked you to congregate here to witness such joy in the union of two of our finest young people, Brother Jedediah Cutler and Sister Celia Faraday. It is true that the heathen mobs have destroyed our beautiful city of Nauvoo and forced us out of our homes, but the Lord Almighty has blessed these two young people and they know that wherever they are, as long as they are together, man and wife, there, too, is their home. Their faith is strong, and the Lord would have you be lifted up in that faith."
Brigham stopped for a moment to look over the gathered Saints. He was right. For the moment, they put away their own pain and suffering to share the spirit

and happiness due the occasion. He turned to Jed and Celia. "Brother Cutler, please take Sister Faraday by the right hand. Do you, Jedediah Cutler, take this daughter of our Father in Heaven . . . . "

So it was that they were married under the same new sun, bathed in the same beautiful morning light that befriended Peter and Rockwell. Jed and Celia would wait until they reached their new home and could build a temple so they could be sealed to each other forever. For now, in their complete joy, all thoughts of Peter Van Cleef escaped them . . . for now.

4

Babylon

Blurred lights and hollow sounds were all that greeted the reluctant young hero, who by all rights should probably be dead. Peter blinked wearily and tried to make sense of his situation. The more coherent he became, the more he realized he was in great pain. *Where am I? What happened?* Peter wondered.

Although beads of sweat were racing down his face, he shivered from the chills that encased his body. Then he remembered . . . . "Celia!" he cried with a feeble attempt to raise himself.

The word was painful, not just to Peter, but to the owner of the hands that gently stopped him from reopening his wounds and guided him carefully back down to the bed. "Ssssh Peter, I'm here," said the young woman. "Everything will be all right."

The sound of a female voice comforted Peter and he rested his head deep in the soft pillows, fading back into unconsciousness.

Mary Ellen Moore had not left Peter's side since the tall bearded stranger had arrived at her door. He carried in his arms the young man she had fallen in love with, what seemed like an eternity ago. She had met Peter after he had returned to Saint Louis from Nauvoo the first time. Peter had achieved success as a businessman of solid reputation and great promise. He was well-known not only throughout the business district, but in social circles as well. Even though Mary was not at all active socially, her step-brother, Morgan Cain, was.

Morgan and Peter had become fast friends in the fast world they both lived in. Morgan admired Peter's strength of character, something of which Morgan possessed little. His prominence was handed down to him from his family's position, and Morgan was apt to adopt whatever sentiment was popular or politically advantageous at the moment. Still, Peter found him exciting to be around because Morgan was always getting fired up about something. And Peter had to admit, in all fairness, Morgan was a good orator. Furthermore, when he wasn't doing business or on his soap box about something, Morgan was jovial, with a definite sharp wit that Peter particularly enjoyed.

It wasn't long before Mary and Peter were introduced, with a captivating effect over Mary. True to form, Peter was much too busy to let himself fall victim to the charms of this beautiful woman. He did, however, very much enjoy her company, and they spent as much time together as Peter would allow. Besides, there was always Celia.

As in better times, Peter was once again safe in Mary's house. He was going to survive, but it would take some time and Rockwell couldn't leave the Saints long enough to see Peter back to health. He realized he had no other choice but to bring his young friend back to Saint Louis. After Nauvoo, there was no place left to go. It was several years past that Peter had written to Rockwell of Mary and how she felt about him. With that in mind, Porter felt secure that she would more than look after his wounded friend. That left only one small problem. Peter was now in hostile territory. Indeed, he was back in the very lion's den from which at least part of the savage attack had been launched against his people. Did they know of Peter's attempt to warn the Saints? Would anyone recognize Peter from the fight? After all, many of the mob had been killed or wounded, and Peter had done his share of inflicting those blows. It was certain he would be mobbed himself if recognized.

Mary didn't hesitate for a moment to accept the responsibility of Peter's well-being from Rockwell. She didn't even question how he knew to bring Peter to her or, for that matter, what had happened. Rockwell was glad she knew the difference between what did and did not need to be said. A gun wasn't the only thing Rockwell was quick with. He immediately concocted a plan to keep Peter safe. "I'm a friend," Rockwell had told Mary, "and I'm much obliged ta you for lookin' after Peter in the past."

Mary blushed with the realization that her true feelings for Peter were known not only to him, but to this stranger as well. Rockwell saw the reaction, but chose to ignore it. He didn't know Mary and wasn't about to do anything that might make her any more uncomfortable with him than she already was. He softened a little and continued. "He needs ya now, ma'am, more than ever. He needs yer friendship . . . he needs yer lovin' care." She looked up at Rockwell and tried to smile.

"I need yer help too, ma'am, ta keep this boy safe. Ya see, there was some trouble over in Nauvoo—them Mormons again. This boy here got caught right in the middle of it on his way back from visitin' me in the mountains. Yes ma'am, just a poor innocent bystander run over by those rabble rousin' Mormons." Rockwell felt his story was progressing fine, so he continued. "While they was a-tryin' ta rob him, he beat up one of 'em pert' near senseless, so they shot him. I heard the shot and came a-runnin'. I'm afeared they may come lookin' for him, so we need to keep this quiet until he's better and can take care for hisself."

Rockwell could see Mary's eyes well up with tears that fell one by one down her soft white cheeks. She didn't say a word to Rockwell, just nodded. Porter was satisfied and excused himself to begin his trek back to the Saints. He felt awkward thinking his story made Mary cry. Little did he know her tears weren't for Rockwell's lies, well meaning as they were. As was usually the case for Mary, the truth was much more painful, and she knew its ugly entirety this time.

Discerning between truth and lies was nothing new to Mary Ellen Moore. Being the only child of a traveling revivalist minister who drank whiskey by the keg and frequently beat her, Mary grew up with half-truths and more than her share of black lies. In order to survive, she had made a game of figuring out where the truth stopped and the lies began. Consequently her mind was quite keen and perceptive. The game came to a sudden end when Mary's father was killed in the company of another minister's wife. It was, in fact, this woman's husband, the minister of a neighboring sect, who killed him. Religion for Mary became as lifeless as her slain father, but she always held on to her deep belief in God.

The Moores, mother and daughter, moved to Saint Louis to find work after Reverend Moore's death. They found Addison Cain instead. Perhaps it could be better said that Mr. Cain found them.

There are some men who use power to their own end. That wasn't the case with Addison Cain, although he was probably the most powerful man in Saint Louis, next to the governor. He had worked his way up through the ranks of the courts as a young lawyer, married well, and was very happy. The year Addison received his appointment to the bench, his wife died giving birth to their only child, Morgan. Addison clung to the memory of his wife and saw her likeness in their son, consequently spoiling the boy at every turn. Nevertheless, Addison was blindly proud of his son and planned to pass the reins of his law practice to Morgan. Unfortunately, his son didn't share his propensity for keeping power in check. Morgan reveled in it.

Mary's mother, Françoise, on the other hand, had suffered from the lack of power her entire life. She was a beautiful French woman who, in her youth, had danced with ballet companies all over Europe, but had wearied of the tyrannical demands on a prima ballerina. She fled to America and married the Reverend Moore, only to discover he was simply a different kind of oppressor.

From the first day the Widow Moore arrived in Saint Louis, waves of reaction rippled through the various social circles. Talk of "the beautiful French woman and her young daughter" who were looking for work reached the ears of Judge Addison Cain. He became intrigued and dispatched an aide to invite Mrs. Moore and her daughter to work for him and live at their estate. The Cains lived in the best part of town. Their mansion was on a beautiful bricked circle with those of the governor and H. Percival Rawlins, Saint Louis' chief banker.

The widow was much too dazzling to be a housekeeper, Cain had decided. She appeared, instead, more as a hostess. Employment turned to courtship, and marriage followed soon after. Overnight, young Mary attained a new stepbrother in the arrogant but charming playmate she had come to know at the house. The playmate, of course, was young Morgan.

What Rockwell didn't know was that Mary had loved Peter for a long time before Peter left to warn the Saints in Nauvoo. He didn't know Peter had confided in Mary that he was, in fact, a Mormon. Under the circumstances, Mary didn't feel the need to go into it with Rockwell. What difference did it make at this point anyway? The damage had already been done. Mary had tried to talk Peter out of going to Nauvoo. Now he lay wounded and in pain, but at least he was alive. At least he was back with her. Rockwell was gone, Peter was unconscious, and Mary allowed the tears to come freely. She cried for her love who lay so still, so pale. She cried for the emptiness of lost youth echoing the futility of adjusting to a grown-up world festering with greed, pride, and ignorance. Most of all, she cried because she knew Peter was no innocent bystander in all this and, as much as she didn't want to believe it, she knew Morgan was behind the attack on Nauvoo and, consequently, responsible for Peter's wounds.

Pieces of the puzzle were beginning to fall into place for Mary. Some things about Peter had never seemed quite right to her in the past. Not in a bad way, but Peter just didn't quite fit the image he worked so hard to perpetuate for himself. There was no doubting his abilities in business, but his spirit was outside the counting house. There was something creative in his eyes, in his character. His manner was much kinder and more considerate than the cut-throats he dealt with at the financial exchange. She had seen first-hand Peter's concern for the rights of individuals and often wondered if, secretly, Peter aspired to political power, like her stepbrother Morgan. The two men were friends, after all; but it wasn't political gain that motivated Peter, and Mary understood that now.

In the weeks that followed, Mary had a lot of time to reflect on all that had happened. She nursed Peter day in and day out, slowly bringing him back to health. No one in Saint Louis knew Peter was there, not even her family. Mary knew she would have had trouble keeping the secret from her mother, but Françoise had journeyed back to Paris to visit her parents. As for Addison and Morgan, they well knew of Mary's independent and stubborn streak. She was left pretty much to do as she pleased and, with that liberty, went to great lengths to keep Peter a secret.

Peter improved steadily and, as he did, Mary would spend long hours sitting with him, talking. She asked him about his people. She wanted to understand what on earth, or in heaven, could make a man risk everything for others. She had a sneaking suspicion Peter was the way he was because of his faith, and she wanted to know why. It was difficult for him, at first, to talk about being a Mormon. He was so used to being hated for it, it didn't come naturally; but he soon discovered he felt exhilarated as he unfolded for Mary the stories from the *Book of Mormon.* Mary listened intently to what Peter told her, drawn to his words as if by a magnet. He told her of the Prophet Joseph and his murder at Carthage. He told her of Brigham Young and how he must now lead his people to a new land, as Moses had done in the Old Testament. He told Mary of the fight in Nauvoo and the horrors he had experienced. They both cried in pain, but it was all a part of Peter that Mary wanted to understand.

The one thing Peter neglected to tell Mary about was Celia. Mary and Peter had grown ever closer since Rockwell placed him in her care, but Peter hadn't forgotten about the girl he left behind. Memory of Celia made his recovery easier, and he fought to get strong so he could rejoin the Saints and be with her.

During Peter's recovery, Mary had, herself, played sick in order to keep people away. She insisted she be left alone to recover so as not to cause anyone else the discomfort of her affliction. It was a good plan that worked—for a while.

"Mary Ellen, you open this door now," came a voice from the front porch of Mary's house. She went to the bedroom window and carefully pulled back the curtain to see who it was.

"It's Morgan!" gasped Mary, turning to Peter.

"Now, Mary, you open up. Nobody's seen you for weeks, and I've come to check up on you," came the voice below them. Peter sat up in bed and stared out the window.

"You'd better let him in, Mary. Just don't let him upstairs."

Morgan pounded on the door until Mary opened it, ushering him inside. "Now what's all this fuss about?" Mary asked her step-brother.

Morgan laughed at her good naturedly and said, "Well, somebody has to look after my spinster sister." His comment annoyed Mary, though she knew Morgan loved her and meant no malice by it. Mary fixed them some tea, and they sat together and talked. Peter could hear their muffled voices from the bedroom, where he himself was quietly busy trying to gather his things together. After a time, Morgan finished his tea and rose from the table. "Thanks for the refreshment, sister. I'm glad to see you're feeling better. That being the case, I must be off."

Mary saw her brother to the door and thanked him for coming. Morgan kissed her cheek and descended the porch steps. He paused at the bottom and turned back to Mary. "By the way, have you seen Peter Van Cleef of late? He hasn't been to the exchange in weeks and there have been some mighty strange stories bein' passed around." Mary swallowed the lump in her throat and clutched the door casing tightly.

"You know, Morgan," Mary replied, "I was just thinking about Peter today and wondering why he hasn't been 'round to comfort me." Morgan laughed and began walking to his carriage.

"Sister," he yelled back, "you wouldn't hardly see your own kin. You would have just turned him away, too. Peter hates bein' cast off, same as any man; but don't fret. I'm having his quarters and his office watched over for any clues to his whereabouts." With that, Morgan laughed and drove off.

With a sigh, Mary slowly closed the door and went directly to Peter's room. What she found startled her. "Peter Van Cleef, what in the name of heaven above do you think you're doing?" Peter was standing, fully dressed, by the window. He didn't reply, but continued to survey the front of the house outside the window. Mary could see what was happening, but she didn't believe it. "Peter!" she said, "You can't leave. You're not well enough!"

Peter turned from his gaze and went to comfort her. "I have to leave, Mary. You know that," Peter said. "People are becoming suspicious, and my being here has put you in an awkward predicament." Mary laid her head against Peter's good shoulder. She knew he was right, and even if he wasn't, nothing she could say would change his mind.

After a long pause, she looked up at him and said, "They'll kill you if they find out you tried to warn your people. I couldn't bear it, Peter." At that moment, he recognized the depth of Mary's compassion, and he knew he was starting to love the beautiful young woman who had sacrificed so much for him. But he also knew now was not the time, nor was this the place, to follow through with such emotional luxuries.

Peter smiled at Mary and said, "I don't aim to let that happen."

Gathering his belongings, Peter made his way to the door. He moved slowly because his shoulder still hurt from the wound. He had fashioned a sling for his arm to rest in, and it limited him as to what he could carry; but there wasn't much anyway. The two went downstairs and Peter went to the back door. "Don't worry about me, Mary. I'll be fine."

Mary went to him at the door. "Where will you go?" she asked. "Morgan's friends watch your townhouse. Your men of business haunt your office. You cannot even get money at your bank without the tellers spreading the word of your return. Besides, you're not well enough to travel."

"Don't worry, on many a night I have successfully reentered my home late without causing talk . . . as you well know," Peter teased her with a grin. She tried to return the smile, but his joke caused her pain as she thought of the wonderful hours they had spent in her house or in town, all without any commitment from Peter. In all truth, he kept her love at a distance. Her woman's wisdom knew that he cherished hopes for someone else with the same ardor that she lavished upon him.

He stepped out into the cold Saint Louis morning and made his way down the deserted street. Mary watched until he was gone.

To most, it was just another day when the door to the Exchange Social Club slowly opened. A progressive silence swept over the crowd like a dark cloud. No one said a word as Peter Van Cleef stepped back into a world he had hoped never to see again. Peter hadn't known what to expect when he once again saw his former associates and "friends," but it surely wasn't this. He walked into the large elegant room where he had so often sat amongst these very same people. Peter thought to himself, *It's as though they've seen a ghost.* It soon became apparent he was not far from the truth. Murmurs from the group filled his ears.

"He's alive."

"I thought they'd buried him."

"How'd he get away?"

Peter figured that, at any minute, the crowd would explode and it would all be over. Right again, but not exactly the way he thought. All at once, everyone in the great hall erupted with applause and cheers. Many rushed forward and patted Peter on the back; others shook his good hand. Peter was amazed and confused at the same time.

"Ya done great!" came one greeting.

"Ya gave 'em hell, Peter," came another, but it was the third that really caught his attention.

"Yer a hero, boy!" came the cheer. The statement caught Peter totally off guard.

"A hero?" he asked.

"Yes, a hero!" sounded a familiar voice from the crowd. It was Morgan Cain approaching Peter, hand extended. Morgan was wearing a grin from ear to ear as he shook hands with his friend.

"We all wondered if you were dead," Morgan said. "After getting jumped by that group of renegade Mormons, we figured you were done for."

Peter had to think fast. "It was a tough fight and a close call," he said, trying to show some enthusiasm.

Morgan put his hand on Peter's shoulder and said, "We didn't even know you were going to help us against the Mormon blight. Next time, tell somebody instead of trying to go it alone." This was Peter's chance to find out just what in the world was going on.

"I'm sorry I didn't tell you, Morgan. I didn't want to make a big to-do out of it. But how did you find out?"

"I told 'em, kid!"

Peter turned in the direction of the voice and locked eyes with Charlie Bates sitting at a table against the wall. The blood left his head and Peter felt dizzy, but he fought to maintain composure.

"Why, Charlie, good to see you again," Peter managed. *What is Bates doing here and why would he lie for me?* wondered Peter, his mind racing for answers.

"That's mighty nice of ya to say, Van Cleef," snorted Bates with his usual sneer.

The group broke up to their separate affairs. Peter and Morgan sat down at Bates' table. Peter told them he had to get home to rest, but he had wanted to come see everyone again first. After a few more congratulations from club members, Peter excused himself. Bates assured Morgan he would see Peter safely home, and the two men took their leave.

Once outside, Peter turned to his self-proclaimed enemy and asked, "Why, Bates? Why did you cover for me like that?"

"Don't flatter yerself, 'hero'," Bates said. "I thought they'd planted you back in good ol' Nauvoo. I had already spun the tale of yer death at the hands of 'renegade Mormons,' and I was just usin' the circumstances to my own benefit. With all the great financial minds in Saint Louis grievin' for their fallen comrade, it would be easy for me to stir up all the anti-Mormon feelin' I need . . . " Peter interrupted and completed Bates' thought, ". . . to rob more people and blame it on the Mormons."

Charlie laughed at Peter, mocking him. "Yer quick boy; very good." Though Bates was making light of Peter, there was still irritation in his laugh. "Now that you've miraculously returned from the dead, I can't very well tell everybody the truth, now can I? It would look poorly fer me and would be very deadly fer you," Bates continued. "Besides, since the mob didn't finish you in Nauvoo, I figure you owe me fer not turnin' yer lousy Mormon hide over to Cain."

Peter stopped dead in his tracks, his face flushed with anger. He turned to face Bates again. "I owe you nothing," Peter retorted, "and I'll be no part of your schemes."

Bates scratched his chin. "I guess I'm just gonna have to tell Cain that his friend is really a stinking Mormon traitor. I'm sure he'll know what to do with you."

Peter knew he was trapped. He hadn't recovered enough to flee Saint Louis, and if Bates turned him in . . . "What do you want from me?" Peter asked.

"Oh, not much," grinned Bates, "just a way into Addison Cain's home, that's all." Peter's eyes grew wide as Bates revealed his plan. "I figger it this way. Why settle fer one cherry, when you can have the whole pie? There's enough wealth in that house to keep me rich for the rest of my life, and you're gonna make it possible fer me to get to it without so much as creatin' a stir. Everybody's heard that ol' Addison has a secret way into his mansion, and since you and Morgan have been such good friends all this time, I figger you know yer way around the house pretty good."

Peter thought for a moment and asked, "What about me?"

"Oh, it don't make no nevermind to me," Bates replied. "Once we get done with our little business, you can do whatever you like. I'm headin' out to the Republic of California to enjoy life." Peter didn't say anything; neither did Bates. The two men stood in silence until Peter turned and began walking. Bates yelled after Peter, "You'll be hearin' from me . . . hero!" Peter just kept walking.

A week went by, then another. Nothing happened, nor was there any mention of Addison Cain—or anyone else for that matter. Peter kept to himself, except when Mary came by his townhouse to look after him. All he cared about now was healing himself so he could leave Saint Louis, and he was very near that goal.

As the weekend approached, Peter knew everyone would be getting ready for the usual dance on Saturday. It had always been such a wonderful occasion for mingling with new and often important people in the community with Mary, a beautiful example of Saint Louis' high society, on his arm. A smile found its way to Peter's face as he remembered. Those were good times. The smile quickly vanished as the rough and cold voice of Charlie Bates invaded his consciousness.

"Open the door, Van Cleef. We've got business to talk." Peter hesitated and fought back the desire, indeed the urge, to put an end to his torture by killing Bates. No doubt Bates had maintained his setup of having the discharge papers printed if anything happened to him, so Peter controlled his ire. Finally he opened the door. There was that mocking smile again, and Peter felt sickened. Bates was sitting in the carriage he had stolen from Peter the night of the murder of H. Percival Rawlins.

"I brung back yer buggy, hero," Bates said, stepping down from the carriage. He went inside and made himself at home. "You don't look happy to see me," Bates continued. "Well, no matter. We'll soon be rid of each other." Bates told Peter he would meet him Saturday night and the two men would go to the Cain's house an enter through the secret door after the Cains had gone to the dance. Once inside, Bates would be able to leisurely "select" the best treasure to steal. Before anyone knew what had happened, he would be gone. "No fuss, no trouble, and nobody gets hurt," laughed Bates.

"I'll help you on one condition," Peter declared. This brought Bates up short, not expecting any resistance from Peter.

"I guess you ain't figgered it out yet. You ain't got no choice. Remember, I still got your discharge papers!"

"That's my condition, Bates. You give me the papers and I'll show you where the secret door is, but no more. From there, you're on your own."

Bates' eyes narrowed and he cocked his head slightly to one side as he thought about Peter's demands. A smile slowly made its way across Bates' face. "Sure, hero. I'll give ya the papers. They won't do me any good in California anyway." Peter agreed to go along with Bates in order to retrieve those discharge papers that could expose his true beliefs.

"I see yer pert' near all healed up," Bates said as he left the house. "Just don't get any ideas about leavin', Van Cleef. If I tell Cain who you really are, he'll stop at nothin' to see you dead! Besides, I've taken out a little insurance policy." Peter said nothing. He didn't want Bates to think he was overly interested in anything the reprobate had to say, but this reference definitely caught Peter's attention. "It's like this, hero," Bates continued. "I know about yer little association with Mary Ellen 'Cain.' So to keep you from leavin' town and to prevent anythin' bad from happenin' to me, I've arranged to have Mary 'looked after' until we conclude our little business. It's from a distance now, and you can keep it that way by doin' what you're supposed to, but try anything and there ain't no tellin' what might happen to her." Bates slammed the door in Peter's face and laughed as he walked away.

Peter felt like a bad luck charm. Now Mary's safety was at risk. Bates had thought of everything and left Peter with little choice but to cooperate. It was one thing for him to be in harm's way, but he couldn't allow anything to happen to Mary. Peter knew he wouldn't sleep tonight.

The sun came up over Saint Louis as it always had. The air was crisp and clean like it always was . . . just another day to most people . . . but not to Peter. There was nothing he could do to escape from helping Bates steal from those who had been like family to him. He felt almost as if it would be better to die than to be a part of such treachery. It wasn't that Peter couldn't do anything to remedy his situation. He thought it out and realized there was one possible thing. He sent for Porter Rockwell.

After Bates informed Peter of his intentions, Peter had dispatched Simon Pratt to find Rockwell and bring him to Saint Louis to help. Simon was a fiery young boy in his own right, left orphaned when the mobs killed his parents in previous attacks on the Mormons living in Missouri. He frequently helped Peter, but was never needed more than now. He was bent on revenge, willing to do anything to get back at his afflictors. Only Peter was able to keep his energy harnessed and going in the proper direction. Peter felt sure Simon would find Rockwell if anyone could, but there had been no word and now it was too late. Had he been wrong to send a boy out across the wilderness to do a man's job? He wondered if he would ever know the answer.

Peter waited all week, hoping Rockwell would arrive and help him out of his dilemma. Problems like these were Rockwell's specialty, but where was he? Peter paced his room like a caged animal and tried to think of any possible way of getting out of his trap. He even considered going to the Cains and telling them who he really was and what was being planned against them. This idea, however, quickly departed after an unscheduled visit from Morgan and Mary in the late afternoon of the day.

"Van Cleef, ya old war horse," yelled Morgan from outside. Peter went to the door and looked out. Morgan was standing in his carriage. "Get yer tired bones out here and greet us proper." It was an entrance typical of Morgan, loud and arrogant, but Peter was nonetheless happy to see them and quickly moved to open his home to them.

"What are you two all about today?" Peter said warmly.

Mary stepped from the carriage and went to greet Peter on the front porch. She kissed his cheek and said, "You didn't think for one moment we were going to let you sit around by yourself today, did you?"

"Besides," interrupted Morgan, as he always did, "you haven't been out of this house in weeks; you need some adventure, some excitement!"

"So what's the big to-do, Morgan?" Peter asked. "There is a dance every Saturday night. You're acting like it's the Governor's Ball." Morgan joined them on the porch and Mary put her arms around him.

She said quizzically, "It's true, Morgan. You've been acting like the cat that got the canary all day, and you promised to tell me why."

"Well, boys and girls . . ." Morgan began, playfully dancing around the porch with Mary, ". . . it's better than the Governor's Ball. Tonight isn't simply just another dance. Tonight we celebrate our triumph of totally expelling the Mormon plague from what was so distastefully known as 'Nauvoo the beautiful,' and the acquisition—legally of course—of that very property!" Morgan beamed with self satisfaction. Peter felt anger swell up inside, but said nothing. Mary's cheerful countenance completely left her, and she looked at Peter, knowing the emotions he must be experiencing.

"Morgan, that's dreadful," Mary said, turning back to him.

"Now what's wrong with you two?" questioned Morgan with a bewildered look on his face. "Our Peter here is one of the local heroes! Mother will be back from Paris and Father will be giving a speech!" Although Peter wanted to lash out at Morgan, he knew it would only set him back and jeopardize his situation.

It was painfully obvious that he could expect no compassion from Morgan. Therefore, there was no reason to believe Morgan's father, Addison, would be any different.

"I'm not proud of what happened, Morgan," Peter said. "I did what I had to do for . . . my friends."

Peter felt uneasy with this double meaning. He couldn't even look at Mary. He felt ashamed because she knew the truth, but Mary sensed his anxiety and slipped her hand into his, giving it an understanding squeeze. For a moment, Morgan didn't know what to say. His perplexed look and speechless demeanor were so unusual that both Peter and Mary couldn't help but be amused, and they both laughed out loud. The tension having been broken, Morgan quickly recovered his good-natured feelings and said, "Fine! You two are like dark clouds on a sunny day. If that's the way you want to be, it's bully by me, but don't expect me to stick around and get rained on." He climbed back into the carriage and waited for a response. Peter told Mary that, under the circumstances, he would rather be alone for a while. It was wasted breath, though, because Mary already knew and she understood completely. She kissed him goodbye and left with Morgan.

Peter stood on his porch, watching as the carriage pulled away, Morgan snapping his horses to a brisk trot. He stood in silence until they were out of sight, then realized he was feeling the cold of the wind against his face. "Neither Mary nor Morgan really knows me at all," Peter thought, as he returned to the warmth and safety of his parlor. The thought left him a little empty, so he fixed his mind on it to contemplate a while longer. "It is true that Mary knows me better than Morgan, but even having shared as much as I have with her, she can't see my soul. Its roots are deep and planted in the rich soil of a world she knows little of." Peter drifted off to sleep, but his mind was still very active—working on the questions and concerns still fresh in his heart.

In and out of his semi-consciousness, Peter tried desperately to grasp the thoughts that swirled around his mind like winds through the naked trees of winter. He knew that, not unlike his friendship with Jed and Celia, he, Morgan and Mary were outwardly friends too, yet it was different. Their bond was as strong as ever, each one's own secrets safely tucked away, deep in a closet or buried in a hole, or locked up tight in some nether region of the mind. Two of the three friends were trying desperately to overcome the limitations and fears their segments of society molded around them. The other couldn't have cared less, but how much deeper the friendship would have truly been with prejudices gone. Sadly, however, this was not to be. Mary chose to follow the light and the light was in her heart. Morgan chose to walk darker paths, shunning the light, claiming the natural man; but the natural man is an enemy to God. For his part, Peter wasn't committed to a certain path and found himself wandering. Thoughts kept coming from nowhere and then vanishing back into nowhere.

As quickly as he had fallen into his deep sleep, Peter awoke with a start.

It was time. The sun had already set on the people of Saint Louis. The social set went to the party; Peter went to the Cains'. A full moon rose over the steeples and roof peaks of the city, illuminating the winter white below and painting gloomy images on everything it touched. There seemed to be only two colors present: the blackness of the shadows and the blue-white glow from the moon's light. Unlike the incident in the Exchange Social Club, Peter really felt like a ghost, pale and fluid as he made his way through the darkness. Another figure loomed from the shadows ahead. There was no question who it was.

"What kept ya, hero?" snapped Bates. "We ain't got all night!"

Bates was dressed in a dark prairie duster with his hat pulled down over his face. In one hand he held a rope, in the other, a few pieces of paper.

"Let's just get this over with," Peter replied coldly. "Did you bring the papers?"

"Of course," replied Bates, holding up the discharge papers. "A deal's a deal, right?" Bates handed the papers to Peter, then climbed into the carriage. They drove on in silence toward the Cains' house.

Peter had been a frequent guest at the Cains', either to visit Mary or Morgan when they still lived with their parents. He was well-known and well-liked. His familiarity was precisely what Bates was counting on to gain entry and unlimited access to the house with all its wealth, but there was more to his plan than Peter knew.

They rode past the mansion that belonged to H. Percival Rawlins. Peter wouldn't look at the house, but Bates acted as if it were a side show in the circus, gawking and pointing. He laughed mockingly. Peter began pulling the carriage over to the side of the road. "Don't stop here," Bates snapped. "Drive on to the house and stop the carriage in Cain's driveway."

"Don't you think that will be a little conspicuous? Someone is bound to recognize my carriage."

Bates pulled a gun from under his duster and thrust the barrel into Peter's ribs. "Just keep drivin', hero. After tonight, it ain't gonna matter 'cause yer gonna be dead, and I won't even have ta do it. Addison Cain will do it for me!" Peter had known he couldn't trust Bates and had almost resigned himself to the possibility that he would be killed. He began to say something, but decided there wasn't much point. The two men left the carriage by the front door of the Cain mansion. Bates motioned to Peter to lead on.

The "secret door" was hardly that. Addison had allowed the vines outside his library the liberty of growing uncut. Ultimately, the foliage covered the entire wall, including the door into the garden, making it virtually undetectable. Addison joked to his friends about his vine-covered door and, from his friendly exchanges, rumor spread of his secret entrance. It didn't matter to Bates. The vines would provide him cover to break in. If he could get inside without being seen, the rest would be easy.

Peter stopped in front of the wall of vines. "Why are we stopping?" demanded Bates.

"You wanted the door, this is it."

"Where? I don't see nothin'!"

"If you could see it, it wouldn't be a secret, would it?"

"You better not be playin' games, Van Cleef. I can kill you right here as good as anywhere!"

Peter went to the wall of vines and cleared away a section like pulling aside a curtain. The door was there, just as Peter had said. Bates was very pleased. It didn't take him long to get the door open, and he was deadly quiet about doing it. Bates motioned with his pistol for Peter to enter the house first. Once inside, Bates began looking around. He seemed determined to search the entire house. They walked past the study, down the great hall where Bates began to climb the massive circular staircase. Ascending the stairs, he momentarily disappeared from Peter's view as he reached the reverse of the staircase curve and the darkness of the second story. Remembering Peter below, Bates returned to the great hall, and the two men continued to the sitting room, lit only by the glow of the hearty fire dancing in the parlor's fireplace. The only sound was the ticking of the massive, hand-carved grandfather clock Addison Cain had had imported from Germany.

"I oughtta kill ya now, Van Cleef, but just in case something goes wrong, I want you around for cover," Bates snickered, beginning to uncoil his rope. He pushed Peter into one of the delicately beautiful, spoked, fan-backed chairs in the sitting room. Peter could tell Bates had once worked cattle by the way he roped and tied Peter's hands and feet. It was almost like being hog-tied. Bates tied Peter's hands together behind the chair, but didn't secure the ropes to the chair, leaving Peter some mobility.

"I thought you wanted me to help you locate valuables," Peter stated, searching for a clue to Bates' plan.

"Bet ya did, hero, but I don't need yer help. You just sit and relax, while ol' Bates here shows you how it's done. Who knows? You may just learn a thing or two and decide to go into business for yerself . . . if you survive." Bates left Peter and began his hunting and gathering routine, refined from years of practice. Peter immediately began trying to free himself.

Although Mary didn't play to the social set, there was something about the Saturday night dance that she always looked forward to. It really wasn't the people so much as it was the beautiful setting, the rainbow light dancing everywhere through the crystal, and the music, which always carried her to wonderful, far away places. At least she imagined it that way. Of course, it was always Peter who swept her off her feet. Mary wondered if tonight she would see this man who had so completely captured her heart. After the way Morgan had carried on at Peter's house earlier, she wouldn't blame him if he didn't come to the dance. *Anyway, Peter isn't yet completely healed and might need to rest,* she rationalized, but she knew she was only inventing excuses for him.

Everyone at the dance was having a splendid time—everyone except Mary. It wasn't that she didn't have the opportunity to dance without Peter being there. Plenty of the young men pressed her for a turn, but it just wasn't the same. After all, her heart wasn't in it, since Peter remained its sole possessor. Still, she would dance with them so as not to be impolite.

For years now, the Cains had shared one of their traditions with the young man they hoped would marry their daughter and become one of them. As the dance began, the Cains and Peter would gather at the massive fireplace and drink a toast to "life, liberty, and the pursuit of happiness!" This night, Peter was conspicuously absent.

"I heard your young man had returned," declared Addison Cain to his daughter with an inquiring tone.

"Yes Papa, so he has," answered Mary heavily. Addison eyed his daughter with the knowing eye of a father and saw Mary's regret that Peter wasn't by her side for the toast and the evening. Addison tried to lighten the mood, but only made it worse.

"Well, where is he then? He'll miss out on life, liberty, and all the happiness." Mary just sighed and lowered her eyes. Addison looked at Françoise with one of those "What did I say?" looks, but she was as puzzled as he was.

"Ah, don't mind her, Father," Morgan offered, already a little drunk from the fine spirits served at the dance. "Peter is just being a little too self-righteous tonight."

"Sometimes, Morgan, you are intolerable!" Mary quipped. She excused herself and stormed off, getting lost in the crowd.

Addison put his hand on Morgan's shoulder and resumed his role as father, a role which he relished. "Now, Morgan, you look after your sister tonight."

"Never fear, Father. I will see to it every eligible young man here dances with her."

"Mary came to the dance with us this evening, but you are going to have to take her home. Your mother and I will not be staying for the entire affair. She is feeling a bit tired after her trip . . . Then I can depend on you, Morgan?" asked Addison, noticeably agitated.

Morgan's attention was already wandering. "What? Oh, sure, Father, I'll see to it. Don't you worry," came the reply as Morgan wandered after a pretty young lady.

Judge Cain and his wife retired to the governor's private room, where they spent the rest of the evening. The governor and his wife were anxious to hear about Françoise's trip to Paris.

Mary tried not to feel hurt over Peter's absence. She even worked on feeling cheery, dancing with some of the men at the party, but with very little effect. After a particularly undesirable dance, Mary decided to leave altogether and go find Peter, which was where she really wanted to be anyway. She attempted to locate her parents to inform them of her decision so they would not waste time looking for her when the dance was over, but try as she might, she could not find them. She did find Morgan, however. That was easy.

Morgan was making an especially big fool of himself this evening, so Mary always knew right where he was. At the moment, he was in the middle of the ballroom floor dancing the gavotte with a woman at least a hand taller than himself. Morgan was never known for his stature. Mary boldly presented herself in front of her now fully inebriated stepbrother and asked him the whereabouts of their parents. Without missing a step, such as they were, Morgan informed her that they had gone home and left her in his capable care. With that, Morgan danced into the crowd again, leaving Mary standing on the dance floor alone.

Ha! Capable hands indeed, but I can't just go, Mary thought. *Morgan's too drunk to even get himself home, and mother and father worry so. I'll visit them before going to Peter's house and let them know not to worry.* She gathered her coat and left the dance. Moments later, Addison and his wife emerged from the governor's room and began saying good-night to their friends.

Bates was usually high-strung and nervous, but as the evening wore on, Peter sensed something else was wrong, causing him to feel even more pressure than he normally would. Bates was acting like a frightened animal as he scurried around the house. From time to time, he would stop and listen, as if he had heard something, first from the study, then from the kitchen. At one point, he froze dead still in the great hall. "What was that?" Bates said out loud. Peter had heard the noise too, but he acted as if he hadn't. The possibility of someone else in the house wasn't something he wanted to think about.

Bates quietly looked from room to room to see if anyone else was in the house, but he could find no one. After a few moments of silence, Bates resumed his thieving. The things he took from the house, he loaded into Peter's carriage. Back and forth Bates went, filling every space he could with the Cains' possessions.

Peter had managed to free his feet, but couldn't stand because of the way Bates had tied his arms around the back of the chair. The chair back fanned out very wide at the top, so there was no way of simply pulling his arms up and over. He worked feverishly to undo the knots that were keeping his hands prisoner.

Some time had passed before Peter heard the sound of another carriage coming up the drive. He looked at the clock in the great hall. It was only 9:30. The dance was far from over. Peter's body tensed, and he focused his attention in the direction of the door. Bates ran into the sitting room. He looked at Peter, and Peter could see the fear in his face. *That's why Bates has been so nervous,* Peter realized. *He must have felt jinxed on his biggest and last robbery.* Now his worst fears were coming true in the home of one of the most powerful men in Saint Louis.

"What are they doin' home so early?" gasped Bates, voice strained.

"It's over," Peter replied. "You lose, Bates."

Bates was panicking and it scared Peter. "Not a chance, Van Cleef," he said, pulling the pistol from his belt. "The Cains will just be the latest victims of the Mormon plague." Bates rushed out of the hall and disappeared through the back door. Peter got to his feet, lifting the chair on his back. He managed to shuffle over to the window and look out.

Outside, Addison Cain was walking around the treasure-laden carriage. "This is Peter's carriage, isn't it, dear?" asked Addison of his wife. Françoise nodded.

"But why would it be loaded with our things?" she asked, puzzled.

"Well, we'll just find out about this," Addison huffed.

Peter saw Bates sneaking up on the Cains as they made their way toward the front door. He knew Bates wouldn't harm the Cains outside at the risk of being seen. Peter didn't have to guess at what Bates would do once they were all inside the house. He needed time to get free and come up with a plan. There wasn't any time left.

With all his weight, Peter fell back on the chair, sending it crashing to the floor. He knew it would be painful, but he had to risk it. The force of the fall broke the spokes and the frame surrounding them. Even though he was still tied, he was no longer a prisoner of the chair. Peter rolled his arms behind him, under his legs, where he could easily access the knots that still held the rope tight around his hands. It took only seconds to loosen the rope and he was free. Now he could do something, but what? Peter thought for a moment. "The study!" he said out loud, but before he had time to move, his mind caught the image of his discharge papers. Without hesitation, he removed them from his coat and threw them into the nearby flames, then made his way down the great hall to a room he knew well."

Addison had often shown Peter and Morgan his gun collection, and it was known to them that Cain kept several loaded guns in his house. Peter knew of two in particular, his favorites—a loaded brace of the new-fangled Colt cap and ball revolvers in the top drawer of Addison's desk. Peter yanked open the desk drawer, pulling it completely out. The contents, including one of the guns, spilled all over the room. Peter grabbed the gun and looked around hurriedly for its mate, but it was not to be found. He abandoned the search when he heard the front door of the mansion open and made his way back down the hall coming face to face with Addison Cain and his wife.

"What is the meaning of this?" thundered Addison, but before he could say another word, Peter raised the gun, eyes focused behind the Cains.

"Stop, Bates!" Peter yelled, aiming his pistol. The Cains turned to see what Peter was seeing. Françoise screamed and a shot rang out. Behind them, as he toppled to the floor, Charlie Bates dropped the pistol he had leveled at the Cains. Peter looked around to see where the shot had come from. He hadn't fired his weapon, but there wasn't anyone else in the room except the Cains and the crumpled body of Charlie Bates behind them. Addison turned back to confront Peter. Everything happened so fast, Peter didn't have much time to react.

The moment Peter took his eyes off the Cains, Addison reached into his coat and drew a small Derringer pistol from his vest pocket. Without hesitation, he trained the weapon on Peter and told him to drop his gun. Peter was stunned by the events, yet he still had enough sense to do what Addison said.

The beautiful pistol Peter held fell to the floor. Addison tried to comfort his crying wife as he moved her away from Bates' body. He instructed Peter to kick the gun to him and keep his hands up high, which he did.

Addison picked up the gun, still not knowing it had not been discharged and turned it on the young man.

"What have you done, Van Cleef?" Cain demanded.

"I did not kill that man, Mr. Cain!"

"Do you take me for a fool? You'll pay dearly for this," Addison said in his most authoritative voice. "How could you steal from your friends?"

"Mr. Cain, no, it's not what you think," Peter exclaimed. "Let me explain!"

"Tell it to the sheriff, Peter. I'm of no mind to listen to a murderer." Peter was shocked. His head was spinning.

"Mr. Cain," pleaded Peter, "I just saved your lives!"

"Saved us? Ha!" Addison said, still trying to comfort Françoise. "Seems to me you just killed the man who tried to save us. Mr. Bates was my son's bodyguard and very loyal."

By this time Ol' Jim, the Cains' head houseman, and the other house servants were all gathered, having heard the noise and the gunshot. Jim stood over Bates' body shaking his head.

"My guness, Massa Cain, whatever coulda' happened here?" he asked. At once, they were shocked to see the matching pistol of the brace, dangling from Jim's wrinkled, skinny hand.

"Great Scott, Jim!" Cain yelled at the hapless slave, who jumped with fright. "What are you doing with my pistol? Did you shoot this man?"

"No, Massa," yelped Jim, practically tossing the revolver to Addison. "I stubbed my toe on it as I come a runnin' ta see what all da noise was about. Dat dere pistol was lyin' next ta da servant's do'. I figgered you be wantin' it, so I brung it."

Cain put away the Derringer and now pointed both Colt pistols at Peter. "Good work, Jim. Now, go fetch the sheriff and get our belongings back into this house!" All the house servants scrambled to accomplish Cain's orders.

5

The Wind is a Lion

The wind blew across the frozen grass. It blew all day and all night with a harping, keening wail. As it danced over the rolling prairie, down the clay bluffs from the western unknown, it happened over a dirty encampment known as Winter Quarters. Although it felt like another trial sent just to afflict the already downtrodden Saints, the wind knew no master and kept on blowing right past them to the east over the Missouri river . . . east from whence they came. When the Mormons contemplated moving west, they thought about what it would be like trudging into that wind. They knew the wind would dry and slow them. What they had not considered to be a problem turned out to be the most difficult challenge of all, as the blowing force coated everything and everybody with dirt.

Soon they would leave this artificial town at Council Bluffs that had begun as a rough camp on the westward trailhead. They had begun by building temporary shelters of canvas and lodgepoles. As a year passed, they absorbed the flow of Mormons north out of Nauvoo; a

Mormon community, with its typical intense orderliness and snug practicality, developed. They farmed and built up herds of livestock over and above camp consumption. As the seasons passed, they had to keep telling themselves that soon all would head west to a promised land that would never be taken from them.

They had to keep expanding a cemetery with its shallow, gravelly graves. Celia, Jed and Emma had stood singing hymns with other members of the camp, while Bishop Leighton dedicated graves with prayer. They had seen the faces of beautiful Nauvoo friends shoveled out of sight and tried to think of the celestial world to come, a new life without fear or sorrow. Even with six hundred husbands, wives, sons, and daughters dead at Winter Quarters, the living had to keep living, hunched against the wind and dirt, never really warm, never clean, never safe, and never would that wind be still.

Winter Quarters at Council Bluffs—the name suggested to Jed endurance of defeat and a burning desire to try again, to move on, like Valley Forge or the first winter for the Plymouth Pilgrims. If he had not been able to come back each evening to Celia and his little cabin, he would have ridden off alone and crazy or been shoveled under with the others. Now it was spring in the year of the promise.

The wind is a lion from March until May, thought Celia as she looked hopefully at the sun. The robins had come back to the plains and Celia sang along with them. There was no doubt about it. The sun conveyed some heat now. There was much more daylight. Each day was less raw and bitter. Spring would come no matter what they did.

It helped for her to take care of somebody else. Celia and Emma tended the crippled Caleb. They tried to sit him in the sun whenever there was enough of it to warrant the risk, bundling him to the nose in blankets. The sun seemed to cheer him, even if it could not touch his skin. His eyes watered in the wind, but he smiled and was grateful. Wife and daughter knew without voicing it that he had recovered from his beating as much as he was going to.

Celia reminded herself every day that she would go mad without the antics of their widower neighbor, Fennelly Parsons. He was helpless without his wife, yet he had to take care of eight sons who had nothing to rely on but their father's childish bravado. Fennelly couldn't make himself do what he didn't want to do. It was hard, however, to call him lazy, because he worked so frantically to avoid working. Despite his incompetence, he was carried along by his brothers and sisters, who understood his difficulty since losing his wife. Raising eight sons was tough under the best conditions. For a man who didn't know hearth from home, it was nearly impossible, and his fellow Saints were always ready to lend a hand. It wasn't that Fennelly was any more deserving than other members. The Mormon people, as a rule, were simply loving, concerned folks, who looked after each other. Their long-suffering support under Fennelly's floundering arms was a testimony to everything right and wrong with the Mormon collective spirit.

Celia watched the eight sons of Fennelly Parsons, from age three to fourteen, line up by height to work at their laundry. In front of each was a wash tub. The tubs rose in size according to the heights of the boys. At the end of their line was the littlest tub with no littlest boy stationed at it. At the head of the line was the ninth and largest tub, obviously belonging to Fennelly, who had not come to his washing yet.

At length Fennelly arrived with his usual loose-jointed good humor. He counted the boys and tubs, looked for the missing boy, found him in the largest tub, and marched the little lad to his own tiny station. Fennelly had on a dark maroon shirt. Each of the sons had on a slightly less red shirt, faded according to his size. The smallest boy had on a pink shirt. *This is a very artistically satisfying hand-me-down,* thought Celia.

The boys washed silently. Finally Leonard, the oldest of the eight boys at a ripe old age of fourteen, and therefore spokesman for the lot, looked up from his work and queried, "Papa?"

"Yes, Leonard," said Fennelly, quickly dropping the newspaper fragment he was reading and grabbing a soapy shirt.

"What if we don't leave today? Won't all this washing and packing be a waste of time?" Leonard asked wearily.

"When was any kind of preparation a waste of time, my son?" replied Fennelly, scrubbing industriously.

"But we've had no word when we'll be going. And we've done this every morning for weeks now," complained Leonard.

"Just the same, when the time comes, my son, we must be ready," Fennelly pronounced.

"Yes, Papa," sighed Leonard.

The eight sons resumed their washing, and Fennelly resumed reading his newspaper fragment, thinking the children would not notice. From her vantage point, Celia stifled a chuckle.

"Papa?" asked Leonard.

"Yes, Leonard," replied Fennelly.

"We're tired," said Leonard.

"Tired? Where would I be today if I permitted myself the luxury of getting tired? No, my boy, remember a good Mormon never gets tired," beamed Fennelly, smelling something wonderful cooking in the Faraday cabin and following his nose toward it.

"Yes, Papa," sighed Leonard again, this time more deeply.

"We all have a job to do here," lectured Fennelly, tiptoeing toward the Faraday's cabin. "I have a job. You

have a job. Everyone has a job. Jobs create order in the human family. Without order we lose our meaning. We lose . . . ."

"Papa," called Leonard, causing Fennelly to whirl around just as he was about to put his nose in the Faraday's door.

"Yes, Leonard," groaned Fennelly.

"Why don't you do your job?" asked Leonard pointedly.

Fennelly leapt back to his tub and scrubbed furiously. They all labored quietly until the last piece of laundry hung on the line. Leonard mustered the courage to confront his father one last time. "May we go now, Papa?" requested Leonard.

"Yes," Fennelly said, returning to his lighthearted tone. "On one condition: that you all take a long walk. When we start on that two-thousand mile hike I told you about, I want all of you in the pink of condition—the very pink," said Fennelly, in a weakly disguised attempt at being stern.

"Why don't you come with us, Papa?" queried Amos, the precocious seven-year-old, who never needed to gather his courage to speak.

"Me? Oh, I've got much too much work to do," retorted Fennelly, taken aback.

"Don't you like to walk, Papa?" Leonard questioned.

"My dear boy, there's nothing I like better. But I've got to carve up that buffalo and roast the meat for eating on the way," Fennelly replied, groping for an excuse.

"All right, Papa," said Leonard, gathering the rest of the boys together. "You fix the buffalo."

In the manner of a military drill, Fennelly prepared the boys for their walk. "Remember now, take deep breaths, long strides and a steady pace," he said. "Line up. Mark time. One, two, one, two. Forward march!"

The eight sons marched off singing in improvised march tempo. Celia, all the while watching, tried desperately to stifle her laughter by burying her face in her apron and retreating into her cabin.

Fennelly, meanwhile, mopped his brow in relief and returned to his own cabin. "Now where did I put that buffalo?" he wondered aloud. Fennelly went to the side of the cabin and gingerly picked up a dead squirrel. He was trying to figure out what to do with it when Emma came out of her cabin.

"Good morning, Brother Parsons," said Emma, cheerfully.

"Good morning, Sister Faraday," replied Fennelly, smiling and encouraged by her cheerfulness.

Emma reached in her door and brought out a reclining chair made out of straight pine boughs. Then she pulled out a brightly colored rag quilt. "You look puzzled, Brother Parsons," observed Emma.

"Just figuring out a way to make this squirrel taste like a buffalo," Fennelly offered, almost to himself.

"Is that all?" Emma joked lightly.

"That's all," resigned Fennelly, inspecting the squirrel from all sides.

Emma put the chair in an angle of the cabin open to the sun, but blocked from the wind. She arranged the quilt over it—preparing for the daily airing and sunning of her invalid husband.

"Do you mind if Caleb sits out here for awhile?" asked Emma.

"No," Fennelly exclaimed, with over-stated sincerity. "Go right ahead, Sister Faraday." Everyone felt badly about what had happened to Caleb in Nauvoo, and Fennelly always did his best to make the Faradays feel comfortable around him.

"Nice day. I want him to get some sun. He always feels much better after being out for awhile," said Emma.

"Yes, plenty of sunshine. It's one thing we Mormons have been given plenty of," Fennelly said in his usual attempt at levity.

Emma called to the cabin, "Celia! You can bring your father out now."

"Sister Faraday," Fennelly asked, as he approached Emma. "Would you happen to know a good place where I might borrow a wee pinch of flour?" He had been waiting for the optimum moment to present his question, and this seemed like the time.

"Have you been to the Church storehouse?" returned Emma, patiently waiting for Celia and Caleb.

"They said I'd been a bit too lazy last week to get my full allotment. Came late for wagon mending three days in a row."

Emma smoothed the folds of her dress and thought for a moment. "Then it wouldn't be right for me to give you any either, would it?" she said.

"No, it wouldn't," agreed Fennelly. "It would be very bad."

"However, you won't be late again, will you?" quizzed Emma.

"No, Ma'am. You can depend on me for that," Fennelly stated with definite resolve.

Emma smiled and softened her pretense of sternness. "Then you can depend on me for a little flour."

Celia brought out her father and wrapped him in the quilt Emma was holding. Mother and daughter had to help Caleb do everything. Such was the nature of his afflictions. Fennelly watched as the two women carefully lowered Caleb into the chair. It never dawned on him to offer his assistance, as he was still preoccupied with dinner.

"Easy now, father," said Celia. The time since Nauvoo hadn't been easy for Celia. They had always been close, father and daughter. She grew up admiring her father's strength of character. Caleb was always a deep resource when she was afraid or confused. To see him now, in such a frail and broken condition, wrenched at her heart.

"Over this way, Caleb—in the sun," Emma coaxed. If it was fair to say that seeing Caleb in his present condition was hard for Celia, then it would have to be said that it was nearly unbearable for Emma. The many years of persecution may have rolled off her, but the lingering suffering and steady destruction of the man she had loved and with whom she had built her family caused her endless torment. Her prayers were full of desires to be worthy of the Celestial Kingdom where she and all her kindred would live together in the brilliant perfection denied to the dark world.

"I feel guilty being pampered like this. Don't you think they pamper me too much, Brother Parsons?" whispered Caleb.

"Now you take it easy, Brother Faraday; there are plenty of us here to help," said Fennelly, hovering around the two women who struggled with Caleb's arms and legs, finally getting him comfortable in the chair.

"I'll get the flour," Emma said, slightly out of breath.

"You sure you don't think less of me for having asked?" queried Fennelly.

"Not in the least," replied Emma, making her way into the cabin.

Fennelly, head bowed and chin resting on his hand, seemed to be in deep thought for just a moment. "Oh, one other thing," he said, holding up his finger, as if he had just intercepted a great idea.

"Yes." Both Emma and Celia gazed calmly at Fennelly.

He stood up straight and asked, "It seems I'm out of salt, too."

The two women looked at each other, half expectingly. Emma shook her head. "Brother Parsons, you need a wife."

"I know, but I need salt, too," Fennelly responded, apologetically.

"I'll give you a little," said Emma.

"What about sugar?" Fennelly said, taking advantage of this quick response.

"I might find some," came Emma's answer.

Fennelly took off the floppy-brimmed hat he often wore and held it in both hands in front of him. "You don't think I'm terrible for asking?"

"Not yet. Anything else?" Emma asked, knowing full well what was next.

Fennelly shuffled his feet and wrung the hat in his hands. Celia again found it difficult to hold back her giggles. He always provided them with such amusement. "What about a fire? Is there a fire in your stove?", he finally ventured.

"Y-ees," said Emma, pretending to think about it for a moment.

"I'd only be using the oven, of course," offered Fennelly, most anxiously.

Emma walked over to Fennelly and took him by the arm. "Brother Parsons, wouldn't it be simpler just to use the whole kitchen?"

Jumping at the chance, Fennelly replied with glee, "You sure you don't mind?"

"Not at all, Brother Parsons. Go get your 'buffalo' and I'll help you," Emma said with a smile.

Fennelly snatched up his squirrel and hurried into the Faraday cabin where he knew the squirrel would be prepared with the greatest of care. Celia could only smile and shake her head.

Times were not idle at Winter Quarters. There was truly movement and excitement. Jed came back from meetings of the Captains of Hundreds grinning and drawing maps in the dirt. He told Celia of the plan to trek west. It would be a Mormon exodus for the children of Israel in the new world, led by the new "Moses" of the last dispensation. There was wagon mending, which Fennelly was almost always too busy to attend, and harness repair instructed by Jamie, the perfectionist Scot. Horses, mules, oxen, and cows were brought up to their greatest strength and training by men who listened to Jed as a master of husbandry.

Every day was full; every minute had purpose. But even with as much as he had to do, Jed often found himself pausing to reflect on his true love, Celia. *Without her, I would be like the dirt that is blown to and fro by this prairie wind,* he thought, smiling broadly. *As surely as each day passes, my love for her grows and I am amazed, since I don't know how I can love her more than completely. And that I already do.*

Celia too, often found herself disproportionately happy, given the circumstances of her life. Yet, each day found her more in love and happier because of a man she knew also loved her. The happiness felt by Jed and Celia was delightfully infectious and brought joy and hope to many of the Saints camped at Winter Quarters. There were so many in camp who had suffered much hardship and loss from the persecutions wrought upon them, and the Cutlers' happiness, indeed, any happiness, was seized upon and held most dear. In addition, the population of the encampment continued to grow. Some came because of hate; some came from love.

As May arrived, Celia decided she was sure that she now carried Jed's child. As if she were in harmony with nature, the winds died down, and the prairie erupted with blooming flowers, signaling its approval. Celia would sit with her hands placed where she envisioned the new life to be growing inside her. She could picture the baby in her mind and envision what it would be like to have a child, a family. An enveloping sense of warmth swept over her as she dreamed of her child and experienced the love she felt for it.

"Thinking about the baby?" Emma asked, bringing Celia back to the moment.

"Yes, Mother," replied Celia.

"It is truly wonderful, Darling. But now that you are sure you are pregnant, don't you think you should tell the father-to-be?"

"I've been waiting for Jed to come home all day, Mother. I will tell him then."

As the moment approached, Celia joyously prepared her announcement to Jed as he came in from the corrals, but Jamie intercepted him and dragged him away to yet another important meeting. She sighed and accepted the wait.

Within a few days, the wind finally died away to a gentle, caressing breeze that took the sting out of the sun. Emma and Caleb dozed together in their chairs against their cabin wall, holding hands.

Celia looked at them through the window as she washed dishes. Suddenly Caleb stiffened and gurgled in his sleep. His spasmodic clutch woke Emma. Celia was outside in two long strides.

"Is he all right?" gasped Celia.

"Yes, if I relax him here," crooned Emma, massaging Caleb's twisted limbs.

"He must get strong again so we won't be left behind," said Celia as she helped Emma rearrange Caleb's position. "How long do you think it will take for us to cross the plains and find this new home they keep talking about?"

"Your husband is in charge of this part of camp. He'd know better than I," Emma said. "Why don't you ask him?"

Celia sat down next to her mother and laid her head on Emma's shoulder. "I don't want to worry Jed. He has so many things to care for," she replied softly.

"Why should that worry him?" Emma asked, stroking Celia's hair. "Haven't you told Jed that he may be the first new father in the new land?"

"He's always so busy," said Celia.

Surprised at her daughter's reponse, Emma looked at Celia very intently. "No man is too busy for that."

Celia could tell her mother was serious, but Celia had her own reasons for not telling Jed. "I don't want to say a word if it might delay us. Jed is so eager to go. I don't want anything to stand in his way."

A terrific crash from their kitchen disturbed the gentle conversation. Fennelly stuck his head out of their door.

"Quick, Sister Faraday. Something's wrong with your stove," stammered Fennelly. Emma rose wearily and strolled into the kitchen.

Celia continued to sit quietly, stroking her father's head. Suddenly she smiled as Jedediah, followed by two Mormon Scouts, Milo and Lorenzo, strode into view.

"Celia!" cried Jed as he hurried to her. "I'm sorry, dear, I know I kept you waiting again." Jed turned to his companions and said, "Here, Milo. You and Lorenzo take these dispatches to the sixth, seventh, and eighth hundreds."

"Yes, Captain Cutler," said Milo, and they respectfully withdrew.

"What did you find out?" inquired Celia.

"We're pulling stakes by the end of this week, Celia. There's no question now that the ground is firm enough to support the wagons," Jed excitedly declared.

Celia's heart raced. *Could this really be the time?* she wondered. Maybe, then, this was also the time to tell Jed her little secret. Even in her excitement, Celia worked to remain calm. "Sit down a moment, Jed. You look tired," she managed.

"We've got to get packed," Jed replied, not letting up for a moment, even though he let Celia seat him on the bench in their front yard.

"We are packed, Jed," Celia said, taking his hands. "I've been ready for weeks."

"But what about the others?" asked Jed with a concerned look at the Faraday cabin.

"They're ready too," Celia assured him.

Looking into her calm beauty, Jed felt her strength and the moment of concern drifted away with the light breeze. "Well, I guess this is it, then," he said.

"I hope so," Celia added. "We've moved so much. We've tried to settle down so many times. And always it ended the same for us . . . blood, death, and heartache." Celia's eyes filled with tears as she took Jed's face in her hands. Jed took her hands in his and kissed her palms.

"Celia, no one can trouble us out there. It doesn't even belong to the United States," Jed reminded her, indicating the prairie ahead.

"Maybe we'll never have to move again. Then we can really settle down." Celia spoke tremulously, preparing to tell Jed about the baby.

"That's right, darling; it's got to be. This time it has to be," Jed proclaimed, getting up nervously. "Well, at least I know this part of the camp is ready. My hundred is in order."

"You're quite a leader, Jedediah Cutler," Celia said, standing up with him. "You'll always be looked up to, and people will always follow you." Her dark eyes flashed with the overflowing love she felt for her Captain Cutler.

"Oh, I don't care about that," chuckled Jed, shaking his head. "All the hard things I have learned leave me with a simple dream. I dream of a home in the valley we seek. I know it will be a hard place, but I will make it green. You will make it lovely. I just want to put you in a lovely place of your own and enjoy it with you. I try to do my duty, but it isn't a duty when I work to build something good for us. I am so glad to be going. The sooner we leave, the sooner we find our home."

"Are we really going to find a home where we will be safe, Jed? Is there such a place for us?" questioned Celia. "After Nauvoo, I don't know if I can believe enough to work that hard again."

"Course there is, darling. We'll find a place of peace and contentment," said Jed. "We'll keep Nauvoo in our minds and transplant it to this valley we've been promised. Now, tell me again what you want when we arrive," he asked her with a grin.

"Well," she giggled, playing their little game. "I think the house is white; the barn is red. I know that's the same as back home, but I've never seen a prettier arrangement for a farm. Maybe I'll have more imagination when I get there."

"I love your imagination," encouraged Jed. "And we'll find you a place with the spring running cool, and down the road a mile or two a little schoolhouse for our . . . ." Celia could see it coming. Jed was leading her right into the very subject she so desperately wanted to talk to him about. It seemed like the perfect opportunity and she was so excited, she cut Jed off.

"Jed, before we go I'd like to tell you something," declared Celia.

"Yes?" said Jed, so openly and calmly that it strengthened her.

"Now I don't want it to worry you or anything like that," warned Celia, moving closer to him. She began feeling warm and tender inside. It was a welcome feeling, and she knew what she had to say would make Jed feel the same.

"Why? What is it?" asked Jed, now knitting his brows with concern.

"Don't get excited, Dear," Celia replied, herself getting excited. Jed wasn't feeling the warm tenderness yet. In fact, he was getting knots in his stomach, and the protector in him was clearly beginning to show.

"What's wrong? What's happened?" demanded Jed, grasping her by the shoulders.

"It's nothing to be upset about. I know that much," Celia managed, unnaturally. She was taken up short by Jed's seemingly insensitive manner. Celia imagined a much different situation for the announcement of their first child.

"Who's upset?" questioned Jed, not understanding this sudden change in attitude. After all, to him, he was responding exactly the way he thought he should, presented with the possibility that something was wrong.

"Well you certainly aren't calm," cried Celia, mouth trembling.
She sat up very straight and pulled away from Jed slightly.

"I am calm . . . . I'm very calm," Jed offered quietly. He could tell he would have to turn the situation around if he was ever going to discover what it was Celia was trying to tell him. He put his arm around her and sat quietly, taking long deep breaths until Celia felt content.

"All right, then . . . let's see . . . . How shall I start? Well . . . it's like this . . . I . . . Do you love me?" asked Celia earnestly, twitching her hands around Jed's neckerchief. Jed beamed.

"Oh . . . Celia, that's no secret. I love you. I love you very, very much," declared Jed, stroking her hair.

"Good," Celia continued. "In that event, I think it's only proper to . . . ." Just as she had cut Jed off moments before, so too did she get interrupted at the moment of revealing her secret. It seemed that fate had a way of rearranging even her best plans. Jamie Logan came stamping up and hollering like there was no tomorrow.

"Jed! Jed!" Jamie called out.

"Just a minute, Jamie," snapped Jed, now fixed intently on what Celia was telling him.

"No! No! This is important, Laddie. I have to speak with you alone, as the poet said," replied Jamie with ill-concealed excitement. Jed ignored Jamie and encouraged Celia to continue, but she knew the moment had been lost—again.

"Go ahead and tell me, Celia," coaxed Jed, fiercely, turning back to her. He also felt the moment slip away, but wasn't willing to let it go without a fight.

"It's nothing I want to tell your friends, Darling. You talk to Jamie," sniffed Celia. "I can always see my husband later."

"No, Celia, tell me now," pressed Jed, Jamie in the background still calling to him. Celia was at an end and tried very hard to maintain her composure. It wouldn't be proper to cry in front of Jed's friends. She gave it a good effort, but couldn't hold back.

"It's nothing that can't wait. And I'm sure Jamie has something to tell you that's far more important," Celia cried, crumpling into tears as she turned away, rose from the bench, and almost ran back to their cabin.

"Celia!" Jed called after her, leaping to his feet with such vigor that the bench toppled over. Jamie closed the distance between him and Jed and rested his hand on Jed's shoulder, almost leaning on him. He peered after Celia, watching her as she slammed the door to the cabin.

"What does the lass want to say, do you think?" asked Jamie, raising an eyebrow, genuinely curious and genuinely oblivious to the trouble he had caused.

"I might have found out if you hadn't butted in," snorted Jed. The two men stood in the yard, awkward and discomfitted.

"Well, she could have told you with me here. I can keep a secret as well as the next man," Jamie exclaimed, still without a clue that he might have had anything to do with the situation.

"I think she was only teasing," Jed rationalized. "I've been away so much." Jed didn't believe his own words, but what could he do about it now? Celia would tell him later, in her own good time. Besides, Jamie had something important to tell him and there was still much to be done before the trek west. Jed decided it was best to put this experience behind him and get on to business. Jamie, however, hadn't quite reached the same conclusion.

"Now isn't that just like a woman. Teasin' and tauntin' a man's troubled mind," clucked Jamie. His seemingly never-ending good-natured spirit was infectious, and it was breaking down Jed's sour mood.

"Well, what is it, Jamie?" asked Jed, tring to remain serious. It was as if Jamie hadn't heard a word Jed said. His eyes were fixed on the cabin and he scratched his chin as he appeared to be in deep thought.

"My Jerusha's like that," ruminated Jamie, still ignoring Jed's question. "Of course, I thought it would be different once we were married."

"Marriage doesn't always cure a woman of her tantalizing ways," Jed sighed, shaking his head.

"No?" asked Jamie, now interested in what Jed was saying.

"Uh-uh!" said Jed.

"I had hopes it might suppress a few," Jamie acknowledged, somewhat resigned, but still with a smile. Suddenly, almost as if their previous conversation had never taken place, Jamie returned to his original excited state and asked Jed, "You know that big meeting at headquarters we must attend at noon?"

"Yes," replied Jed, not understanding Jamie's newly revived excitement.

"Well, it's not about planning the move west. There is an honored guest, an army officer." Jed's eyes narrowed, and the hair on the back of his neck began to tingle.

"An army officer. What does he want? If they have some more high-handed threats for us, why we'll . . . ."

"Easy, Laddie," Jamie cautioned. "As I say, he's an honored guest and President Young wants us to listen to him. It'll be starting now, so we'd better hurry."

This did look like an important meeting. Men like Jed, strong and unfazed, were hurrying from all parts of the camp toward the central pavilion where Brigham Young made his headquarters. These striding men were the captains of ten, and of fifty, and of a hundred. Jed could see bishops and other called spiritual leaders of the camp, including Quimby Leighton, who was covering ground as rapidly as any with unhurried strides of his long legs. There were even the old Legion officers. This was the leadership, all the men on whom Brother Brigham relied to keep the camp united, motivated, and disciplined. This meeting to which all the men were called was clearly to announce the fate of the Saints. Soon Jed would know where he and Celia would spend the rest of their lives.

Jed entered the pavilion of canvas and thatch. It was filling fast with murmuring groups of men, all known to Jed, but the first person he noticed was a U.S. Army officer. This man stood vivid in blue uniform with red sash, twinkling brass buttons, and shiny black dragoon boots. His hands resting comfortably on sword hilt and pistol holster, he chatted with the much smaller President Young beside him. The shoulder straps on his uniform displayed gold embroidered leaves on a sky blue field—an infantry major. Every eye was on the smiling major, which was odd, because Jed was used to the leaders of the Saints having their attention riveted on the dynamic expression of Brigham Young.

The major was not slender and not stocky. He was well set up, but fleshy. A close look showed him to be not particularly young, but with a pink smoothness and eager, ingratiating expression—*a big child,* thought Jed . . . *Or is it just that we have lost all our youth too soon?*

"His name is Major John Broderick of the United States Army. He's the recruitin' officer," whispered Jamie.

"I hope he doesn't expect any of us to join his army," Jed replied sourly without any attempt to muffle his voice. This unfolding situation was not something Jed cared to be a part of, and he made no bones about it.

"That's exactly what he does expect," declared Jamie. Jed looked at his friend in amazement. He couldn't believe what he had just heard. What about the trek west? They were finally going to pull up stakes and begin what would be the last move before settling down once and for all. Jed knew he wasn't ready to give up that dream of going west with his beloved. Too many Saints had died for it, and the ones remaining would need him on the journey.

"Well, he has a long wait coming before any of us does that," Jed announced after a short pause. Jamie knew what Jed was feeling, but he wondered if Jed understood the importance of the visit and request soon to be levied upon them.

"Do you have red blood in you, Laddie?" asked Jamie. He was firm with his question, but compassionate with its delivery.

"Sometimes I wonder," Jed retorted. "So much has been bled from us." Jed felt a feeling that he hadn't for some time. It was sadly familiar and it didn't take long for him to recognize it for what it was. The hardness of heart that had become a means of personal survival for Jed in the early days of the Mormon persecutions was still with him. He thought it had left him since his marriage to Celia. It wasn't a part of himself that he was proud of, but there was no denying what he was feeling.

"You'll have to buck up a little then," Jamie continued. "Are you able-bodied, Laddie?" Jed resisted his friend's question. He knew Jamie was right, but he couldn't at once admit it. Still, Jamie persisted. "Well, are ya?"

"Oh, I suppose so," Jed finally relented.

"He expects every red-blooded man to volunteer for the Mexican campaign," continued Jamie.

"Well he's too late for us, Jamie," proclaimed Jed, still trying to fight the inevitable. "We're leaving the country!" Jamie shook his head slowly. He looked at Jed with pale blue eyes, narrowed in Scottish cleverness.

"That's a tragedy then. Because he expects every able-bodied man to volunteer along with his red blood," Jamie said, slyly.

"Haven't we gone through enough getting this far? Won't they ever leave us alone?" asked Jed angrily.

"It's my belief—ignorant man that I am—that the army can recruit if and where it pleases. I believe this Major Broderick is looking for you now," said Jamie.

Some of the Mormon leaders could be seen pointing Jed out to the major as he approached Jed eagerly. Jed felt his mouth go dry as his throat tightened. For just an instant, he felt like leaving the meeting and simply not dealing with this army intruder, but his character was such that he could not do it. He would stay and face the problem.

"Good morning, Mr. Cutler, I believe. I've been told you're the captain of the finest hundred in this camp," said Broderick, with a certain air of confidence about him.

"These men are all of the finest quality, Major," Jed returned with a quick riposte, uneasy at this tacky flattery.

"Of course. When you were described to me, I didn't expect anybody so young. I'm Major John Broderick, U.S. Army," he said, offering his hand to Jed.

"I'm Jedediah Cutler. This is Jamie Logan," Jed responded, as they shook hands. Whether or not Broderick sensed Jed's sullenness, he continued with his warm smile and friendly voice.

"I'm here on a rather arduous military mission. I thought I'd take advantage of the opportunity to sound out sentiment in your part of camp, as it were," said Broderick.

"I don't think you'll find us very sentimental," Jed replied coldly. He wasn't about to give in to this smiling uniform until he knew precisely what Major Broderick had on his mind.

"That's exactly what I wanted to find out," Broderick continued. "I've already spoken to your president and council. They've decided that I must speak to the assembled captains."

"I'm afraid their answer won't be very favorable . . . Sir," said Jed confidently, not giving an inch.

"You say that and don't even know what you'll be used for," Broderick said reproachfully.

"A soldier's a soldier," declared Jed, stubbornly. Jamie had been watching the two men intently through their verbal exchange without interfering. Remembering what Jed had said to him just moments ago, he felt it was time he entered the conversation.

"We're all set to leave the country, Sir," said Jamie.

"Yes, I know that," Broderick responded, now addressing Jamie. "But we need men for a march to California,"

"Well, perhaps we'll be going to California ourselves," Jamie rebutted.

"This is a military mission. The pay is good, provisions adequate, honorable discharge on arrival," Broderick pressed.

A few men had drifted in close during this exchange. They stood curiously by, wondering which side to take. One of them stepped shyly forward and asked, "I beg pardon, Major, but if a man joined what would happen if he took along his wife?"

"That might be all right—if he paid her expense," answered Broderick.

"In that case, Sir, you can count on me to come if you're payin' what you say and the Church says it's all right," said the solemn young fellow.

"But Brother Zarabel," interposed Jamie. "You've got two wives." Zarabel hooked his thumbs in his vest, proudly defying Jamie's inference.

"Well, what of it? Do you think the Major will deny me the chance to serve my country simply because God has been kind to me?" queried Zarabel. Major Broderick ignored this exchange between Jamie and Zarabel and turned to make a general address to the assembled group.

"Our route is over the desert, by way of Santa Fe. Your pioneers will go over the mountains. We'll be out of touch completely." A murmur swept over the crowd and the men looked at each other. Jed recognized the hesitancy in the group and was quick to seize the moment.

"We can't afford to give up the men," announced Jed with finality.

"And if I asked out of loyalty?" Broderick responded.

"My feelings are mixed on that subject," acknowledged Jed.

"I hardly think you mean that," said Broderick, struggling to regain the crowd.

Jed didn't appreciate the Major's intrusion into the personal world of what he did or didn't believe and he told Broderick so in no uncertain terms. "I mean it from the bottom of my persecuted Mormon heart! I've never seen anybody try to protect us but ourselves. Where were you, Major, when we were driven out of Missouri?

What help did you offer when we were burned and beaten in Illinois?" Pointing toward Caleb, Jed said, "Do you see that man over there—my father-in-law? Once he was strong and powerful. Could plow a field like ten men. Now what is he? Ill with fevers and sick from the beatings of mobs who claimed to be our fellow citizens."

"I admit I know little about that. Perhaps it's the neglect suffered all too often by minorities. But I have a job to do; I'm in the service of my country, our country," Broderick replied.

Jed pressed on. "Do you think we like the idea of leaving our country? Do you think we willingly give up so much that we loved? Where do we come from? Ohio, New York, Vermont. We belong to this country. But we've been forced out of it. In order to exist at all, we've no other choice."

Their voices must have been rising in pitch and volume because Bishop Leighton was moving very fast to reach the Major and Jed in short time. Arriving at the back of the now very large crowd, Quimby stood firm, looming over them.

"Brother Cutler, Major Broderick—the President and Council would like to begin," Leighton announced.

"Thank you," Broderick said as he withdrew.

Brother Brigham was uncharacteristically quiet as he introduced Major John Broderick, U.S. Army, to the group.

"Brethren, Major Broderick has an interesting proposition to make to which we should all give our utmost attention," announced Brigham, meekly and politely. To the astonishment of the assembled captains who knew him so well, Brigham stepped carefully away from the center of the standing assemblage and sat down behind the crowd. This left Major Broderick alone in the center, with every eye on him and every mouth set with hostility.

The Major set forth his proposition with considerable hemming and hawing. He kept looking around, appealing for support and getting none. What he proposed was so outrageous that it struck the Mormons dumb. They just seethed quietly.

"We . . . uh . . . that is . . . the government, President Polk himself, desires the best Mormon men to join the army to fight in the war against Mexico. As you know, our forces under General Scott have landed at Vera Cruz and are marching on Mexico City after their great victory at the Battle of Buena Vista. But the gallant citizens of California have risen against their Mexican overlords, under the leadership of our own General Fremont, and are striving to establish an independent republic. We must send forces to help them secure California for our own, just as we admired the Texas revolution against Mexico which brought that great land into our . . . . "

"Will California be a slave state like Texas?" interrupted a voice in the back.

"I won't help the spread of slavery," added another voice. This provoked a rumbling which Brigham quelled, standing with his hands raised.

"Brethren, let us hear the major out on this matter."

Recovering his aplomb, Broderick went on, trying to respond to the objections he felt radiating out to him. "I know you men are 'free soilers' and don't want the Southerners to get all the good western land for their slave plantations. I know you want a place to put all your immigrants and build your new society. I'm a Northerner and I want that, too. America must push west and settle new land. Both North and South agree that it is the manifest destiny of the nation to expand west until it reaches the Pacific Ocean."

His explanations were met with stony silence, so the major left great issues and moved on to money. "All of you who join up will receive excellent pay, eleven dollars a month, in addition to your own issue of food and clothing, of course. That money would be a godsend to your families preparing to pioneer westward, would it not?" suggested the major.

"The unit you form will be sent to California where you will help conquer and settle a bright new land. Maybe California could be the new home of the Mormons." Jamie and others lit up at this.

"Also," the major continued, "America is watching the Mormons. Your countrymen wonder if the Mormons really consider themselves to be fellow citizens, or are they an alien cult, disloyal and conspiratorial? Here is a chance to prove your patriotism."

Jed could stand no more. These were not children having to be coaxed into fulfilling a weary parent's expectations, and he would not be treated as one. He stepped from the crowd and moved to the center of the platform next to the major. Jed interrupted the major in a voice firm but aroused.

"First of all," retorted Jed, "it is not the Latter-day Saints who need to prove their patriotism, but the government and the army. The Mormons have always walked up to every covenant they have ever made. They have obeyed all laws and availed themselves of all rights, protecting the same on behalf of their neighbors wherever they went. The Prophet Joseph Smith published a revelation from the Lord commanding the Saints everywhere to honor, obey and sustain their governments. He further prophesied that the Constitution of the United States was divinely inspired and would hang by a thread in the latter days only to saved in the nick of time by the Latter-day Saints."

The crowd shuffled and the men murmured in resonance with what Jed was saying. President Young did not attempt to quell this response.

"Joseph Smith would be alive today," thundered Jed, "if he had been willing to disobey the law and refuse to surrender himself for trial on an improperly drawn charge that had not been attested to in any court! But no, he went to Carthage Jail like a lamb to the slaughter.

"There he was murdered, he and his brother," continued Jed quietly, "this man who had done more for the salvation of the world, save Jesus Christ only, and by whom? Who shot him to death as he had one last chance to escape the mobbers who had already killed his brother and wounded his friends? Who? Soldiers! The Carthage Grays, urged on by their inspiration from across the river, the great Colonel Price, whose Missouri Wildcats are even now making headlines in this glorious war, that's who!

"And who is this government we should serve?" sneered Jed in the Major's face. "Is it the government of the sovereign state of Missouri whose voice was Governor Boggs saying, 'Exterminate all Mormons who will not leave'?

"Is it the great national government in Washington whose President told the Church, 'Your cause is just, but I can do nothing for you,' as he withdrew the regular army soldiers from the protection of Nauvoo? We protected ourselves with the Nauvoo Legion, the largest and best unit in the Illinois Militia and the only force for law and order in the south half of the state, until this great and glorious government ordered us to disband as a threat, a *threat*, to peace and safety!

"With the army—our brave defenders—pulled out, our own Legion disbanded, in came the mobbers, led by Colonel Price, whose lust for Mormon blood knows no bounds. They proceeded to destroy Illinois' largest city.

"And as for this war with Mexico, we attacked them—oh, no, don't protest, Major. Nobody believes the Mexicans crossed the border first. We all laughed at the President when Congressman Lincoln wanted to know the exact spot where we were invaded by the Mexican hordes and nobody could tell him. We take their land, we beseige their capital, and you want us to show our patriotism by allying with this wickedness? And for what benefit to us? For money? So that our fellow Americans will stop trying to kill us?"

"Yes," said Brigham Young, quietly. Everybody turned to look at him. "Yes, that is right." The president of the Church seemed to be looking at something only he could see and hearing something only he could hear, and everybody in the pavilion except Broderick knew what was happening. Brigham went on with labored difficulty as though he were receiving dictation, which, of course, he was.

"Everything Brother Cutler has said is true, but it is vengeful. 'Vengeance is mine,' saith the Lord. 'I will repay.' We cannot change the past. I have been as wrathful as any. I have said we must get clean out of this country and make our own, but it *is* the destiny of our country to rule from sea to sea. We will be a part of it. We must participate in its affairs if we are to claim its protection. Some of our brethren must leave their families. Those wives and children will make the westward journey without the support of husbands and fathers. Only in that way can they earn the money that must be paid to outfit us for the journey.

"But have faith, brethren. Know that we who pioneer will care for your little ones while you soldier. Know that your new life will be waiting for you in some promised land that we shall find in the tops of the mountains.

"And know this, brethren: If you will perform your duties as soldiers of your country with all the character that is in you, if you will willingly and loyally obey your commanders while always obeying the commandments of God, living the Gospel of Jesus Christ even to the steadfast keeping of *temple covenants*, then you will not be soiled by your participation in this war. You will be counted among its heroes *without harming anyone.* This I know. Amen."

The group mumbled "amen," including the confused Major Broderick.

Jed stood silent, head bowed. The men in attendance looked back and forth at each other and at Jed. "How many recruits do you want, Major?" asked Jed quietly, lifting his head to meet the calm gaze of their prophet.

"Five hundred," replied the awed major. "We shall form a battalion."

"The Mormon Battalion!" cried out Jamie and everyone gave a cheer. As the noise died down, Jamie became somber. He looked at Jed, who was clearly puzzled by his own about face. "I'd better go and tell Jerusha," said Jamie. "I'm sorry, Laddie. I didn't expect to be a soldier so soon." He left them all quiet with this new realization.

The decision had been made. Everyone knew what they had to do. Each man in turn left the pavilion and returned to his camp to tell his loved ones the news. Jed was the last to leave, uncertain of what he would say to his beloved.

Celia was standing in the doorway of their cabin as Jed approached. "Are you going, Jed?" asked Celia, quietly. Jed stopped dead and looked at Celia with wide eyes. "Bad news travels quickly, especially among women," she continued, with tears in her eyes.

"I'm afraid so," Jed finally managed.

Celia put her hand on her stomach. It was growing, but not yet expanded. "Where will you join us?" stammered Celia, fighting back her emotions.

"No one knows," Jed replied, taking the last few steps to Celia. "California, we hope."

"Oh, Jed!" Celia exclaimed, breaking down. Jed caught her as she began sliding down the wall of the cabin. He sat down with Celia, holding her tightly and doing everything he could to comfort her.

"It won't be long," promised Jed. "We won't let it be!" He cradled her in his arms, rocking her slowly, until she stopped crying.

"No. Of course not . . . . Only . . . only, I'll worry so. When do you start?" questioned Celia.

"Right away . . . . I'll have to go pack my things," Jed replied. "Come and help me, Darling." Jed could feel a dull ache in his heart, and he wondered what Celia must be feeling. "Celia, what was it you wanted to tell me before?" asked Jed.

Whatever Celia had been feeling before, Jed's question made the pain burn all the stronger, but Celia would not make Jed's inevitable departure so much more difficult by revealing her secret. "Oh, nothing," came her response. " . . . Just a dream. I wanted to tell you about a silly little dream."

"I'm afraid both our dreams will have to wait a time."

"Yes, Jed. I know."

6

The March South

The dawn was raw red rather than pink. It was an army dawn, a reveille dawn. It drove men who did not want to move into a functioning mass of bodies. After assembling on the double, they sat quietly at a little berm of earth that ran parallel to the edge of Winter Quarters. These young men wore the most serviceable work clothes they had, with bedrolls under their arms or across their backs. Major Broderick, in his blue uniform with brass buttons winking in the sun, sat on his fine gray stallion. His dragoon saddle blanket was stamped with a gold "U.S." and his gleaming sabre hung down behind his left leg.

The recruits for the Mormon Battalion looked across at their families, who had gathered solemnly to watch them go. Husbands and wives, fathers and children looked at each other across this gulf of one hundred yards that would soon be one thousand miles. The little brass ensemble that had survived as a remnant of the magnificent Nauvoo Legion Marching Band huddled around their conductor and oom-pahed out "Columbia the Gem of the Ocean." They were musically correct without having to think about it, but there was no passion as their chords and parts sounded dully over the prairie. The wives put their arms around their children, and the children waved to their fathers, who waved back, smiling bravely.

Everybody was exhausted before they began, but still the men and women smiled secret smiles at each other and waved tenderly. The evening before, the Nauvoo orchestra had set up in the bowery and begun to play. Undoubtedly Brother Brigham had arranged it. Hearing the dance music, everybody took the hint and turned out for the going-away dance. Mormons were thought to be dour fanatics, and there had certainly been room for gloom in Winter Quarters that night. But there they had gathered, dancing on the hard-packed dirt under the dried out bowery.

As word spread, the bishops and the captains announced to their people they would "dance to the canto of debonair violins, the cheer of horns, the jingle of sleigh bells, and the jovial snoring of the tambourine. French Fours (*Le Quadrille* to the knowledgeable), Copenhagen Jigs, Virginia Reels, and the like will all be executed with spirit." There were to be no polkas, however. President Heber C. Kimball, First Counselor to the Prophet Brigham Young, insisted that the polka required entirely too much of a man's hand on a woman's torso and, therefore, brought the Devil in to spoil the fun.

It was a dance with a mood of poignancy and exaltation that the book readers said was like the great ball in Brussels before the Battle of Waterloo. The gentlemen of the company bowed to their partners and the ladies curtsied low, with grins all around as the lines formed for the next reel. Jed thanked the Lord again that he had learned how to dance. Many a night before a roaring fire on the stone hearth of their cabin in Ohio, Jed had danced with his sister while his brother played the "squeezebox." All the children had imitated Mother and Father, clog stepping and skipping through the figures of the reels.

Celia was an excellent dancer and had taught dancing in Nauvoo. She loved to dance with her light hand on Jed's strong arm and his sensitive fingertips gliding over her waist or shoulder. They had tantalized each other often at the elegant balls staged at the Mansion House in Nauvoo. Brother Joseph, straight, tall, and beaming, had led out with his beautiful wife, Emma, and all the young couples had followed them around the floor.

Now, on the dirt floor of the bowery, Jed watched Brigham clap his hands and tap his foot as he smiled over the whole group from his vantage point next to the orchestra. Celia skipped lightly behind the line of swaying ladies, and Jed kept pace with her behind the line of men, looking at her all the while. As they arrived together at the head of the reel, Jed remembered Peter at those Nauvoo dances. The tall, dark Peter with his flashing smile was so casually confident in all the fanciest steps. Jed could keep up with Celia, but Peter used to lead Celia through the most intricate dances in a way that awed her and provoked murmurs from dancers nearby. Now Jed and Celia joined hands to twirl down the lane of the reel, but in the moment their eyes met at the beginning of the movement, Celia saw Jed's awkward, fearful expression. Her eyes went wide in alarm for just an instant, but they both recovered and grinned at the other dancers as they flew past them.

With a crashing finale, the dance ended and the laughing couples straightened up from their final bows and curtseys.

"Oooh," gasped Celia as Jed walked her to the edge of the bowery. "I cannot keep up with these youngsters as I once did."

A night breeze blew across them and Jed pulled his wife under his arm. "You do look pale, my dear. Tell me truly, how do you feel? Is it the matter you wanted to tell me about before? We can walk out on the prairie and talk, if you like."

They walked out from under the pine boughs beneath the vast sky full of stars. She twisted her fingers in her shawl. "Please tell me what you wanted to say before." He looked deep into her eyes, and suddenly she felt a surge of something very unloving.

No, I can't tell you, she thought. I*t would keep you from what you have been told is your duty to others; but why must it come before your duty to me?* Trying to be strong and unselfish, she reeled back from that second of hatefulness. *Unworthy . . . unworthy,* she thought. *He is tormented by this task as much as I am. Be grateful that you have an honorable man.* "I wanted to tell you," she began slowly but levelly, "that I knew what you would be called to do, and I have a testimony that it is right."

Jed was silent a moment, studying her. Once again, he banished his envy of Peter, which seemed so ridiculous at times like this. "Thank you, my love," he whispered. "You knew more than I did, but I have faith in your spirit." With smooth strength Jed enfolded Celia in his arms and kissed her softly.

"Tch, tch, tch," clucked Brother Kimball from just inside the bowery. The squinty-eyed, bespectacled, bald-as-an-egg First Counselor muttered, "Bad example for the young! Bad example for the young!" He was about to descend on the couple gazing up at the stars when suddenly Brother Brigham clapped him on the back cheerfully.

"Just the opposite I'd say, Heber," and he winked at the orchestra which struck up a lively polka. Brother Kimball stared at President Young, mouth wide open.

"Just this once, Heber. They're going away for a long time."

A freckle-faced lad commenced to sing, and all joined in as they whirled around the floor.

> Sitting in a corner on a Sunday eve,
> With a tapered finger,
> Finger resting on your sleeve;
> Starlight eyes are casting,
> Casting on your face their light.
> Oh bless me! This is pleasant,
> Sparking on a Sunday night.

Jed and Celia were drawn back into the crowd by the singing and the whirling dancers. They joined in and clapped their hands with the music, although something told Jed that Celia wasn't up to the frenetic movement of the polka. He had received the message of her spirit that if she whirled dizzily, she would surely be ill. That would reveal her condition immediately—to the women at least, but both Jed and the crowd were painlessly oblivious to Celia's dilemma as everyone sang and danced on.

> One arm with gentle pressure lingers round
> her waist.
> You squeeze her dimpled hand,
> Her hand, her pouting lips you taste.
> She freely slaps your face,
> Your face, but more in love than spite.
> Thunder ain't it pleasant,
> Sparking on a Sunday night.

Jed and Celia had kept up with the liveliest of the youths for a good long time, but, before the polka and long before the others gave it up, Celia was heavy-legged and drawn looking. They finished up with a gentle waltz, dancing close together if only so that Jed could hold Celia up. Together, they sat on one of the rough benches lining the sides of the bowery, Jed's arm around Celia. They swayed together gently in time with the music and sang the last song with the assembled company while only the strongest danced to their singing.

Oh, come and join the Saints here.
Come join the merry throng.
Help drive the aching from your heart.
This parting won't last long.

No parting tear must ever fall.
No sadness ever dim the eye.
The Mormon folk are singing.
Their songs will reach the sky.

The Upper California,
Oh, that's the land for me.
It lies between the mountains
And the great Pacific sea.

For we can be supported there
And taste the fruits of liberty.

The morning sun began to rise up full and strong over the plains. Jed felt added pain as he saw his wife look at him out of a peaked face that seemed positively ill. She looked like she would turn away sick at any moment. It seemed to Jed that morning was an odd time for nausea. He had never seen Celia this way, and she had stayed up all night plenty of times for reasons much less pleasant. But it would now be up to Emma to look after Celia; it was time for him to go.

Major Broderick spoke out firmly but quietly, "Battalion will form column of companies." Jed and the other elected captains in command of the five companies got to their feet and stepped out into the trail south.

"A Company, fall in!" barked Jed with the command voice he had learned in the Legion. After the Battalion column had faced to its right, Jed looked over at Celia as he slowly moved past her. She smiled and waved until the wagon top blocked him from her sight. *We do have a dream that leads us on,* thought Jed, trying to send his thoughts to Celia. *Keep hope in your soul, my darling. Keep sight of the goal. Keep sight of the goal.*

They weren't even enlisted yet, but they felt as if they had been on the march forever. Five hundred weary men trudged along in a thick, shambling column. When they weren't raising dust, they were slogging through mud as the unsettled spring alternately baked them with sun or soaked them with showers.

Major Broderick rode his horse at the head of the column, resplendent in his regalia. Let him have his pomp, the Mormon men agreed. After all, they were hiking right back across Missouri, scene of so many hateful persecutions. They needed the government to protect them now, and it took only one government officer to keep back the hostile farmers and townspeople who came to the road's edge to glare at them.

The illustrious major also had the money to buy them food. They knew they could drive a harder bargain than he could, but they were under his command now and would have to mind their place. They hoped the money (and, therefore, the food) would hold out until they got to Fort Leavenworth in Kansas. But the hard-muscled farmers and workers were spirited enough to sing hymns as they marched along, at least when no Missourians could hear them. Jamie would think of what to sing and lead the long, moving choir, walking

backwards and waving his arms. More often than not, however, the men were too tired to pay much attention to his conducting.

One night after they had camped, eaten, and settled in, the major walked among them, very thoughtful. "Evening, men," said Broderick quietly.

"Evening, Sir," replied Jed.

"Not going to sleep?" questioned Broderick.

"No matter how bloody tired we get, Major, we're all just so restless when it comes to the night," Jamie answered.

"Maybe so, but this'll be the longest infantry march in military history and you'd better get as much sleep as you can," suggested Broderick, taking a seat next to some of the men. "Well, if you aren't going to sleep directly, may I sit awhile?"

"Sure," Jed replied, sensing there was something more. "What's on your mind, Major?"

"I must admit I expected a little trouble. Until I came to your camp at Winter Quarters, I knew very little about your people—except for rumors."

"And what did the rumors say?" came a voice amongst the men.

"Well, I've never been one to listen to rumors, but I was given to believe the Mormons were a cult and not Christians. Since our association, however, both have proven to be utterly false. Yet, I understand why outsiders could be stirred up to violence against your people. You Mormons have some interesting beliefs and, as soldiers, I never knew any who wanted to come less and yet who came more willingly."

"The quicker we get this over with, Sir, the quicker we can join our people," Jed stated bluntly.

"You may think me a trifle thick, Jed, but why are your people so intent on living alone?" wondered Broderick. "You've crossed half the continent—just to be alone."

"We like it alone, Sir," Jed replied. "Those outsiders you mentioned seem to want it that way too."

"Do you think your people's troubles are always the fault of others?" queried Broderick. "Like I said, perhaps outsiders don't understand what you and your religion are all about. I surely didn't. Now that I'm beginning to understand the Mormons some, I see they aren't a threat to anybody. But a lot of people don't believe that. Maybe you need to try harder to let outsiders know what you Mormons are like. Besides, do you really think you can ever escape other people, closing the door of the world like you were going down to some private storm shelter?"

"We've done all that, Major," Jed insisted. "Do you really believe that they will ever leave us alone as long as we live in the United States? Alone we do just fine. We've our strength, our belief."

"If you can really do it, God bless you. Only I think it may be a tough job," Broderick said unassumingly.

"It'll be easier when we've left this country," concluded Jed.

"I doubt if you'll ever be able to do that," said Broderick, not unkindly. "Keep in mind that part of this campaign is to secure this entire region for the United States. It's rather ironic that you who sought escape should be part of that campaign."

The men were silent, having been reminded of the reality of their situation. For a moment, no words were said. The only sound came from the crackling campfire. "Then you think we'll never get away?" asked Jed.

"You can try, my friend, but I doubt it. You see Jed, no journey which moves away from man ever ends," Broderick expounded.

"But Major, we *have* to get away, just in order to *survive!*"

"Jed," questioned Broderick. "You believe in the Bible, am I correct?" Jed nodded affirmatively. "'. . . And the lamb shall lie down with the lion'—we must all learn to accept each other, see the good in each other and live together in peace."

They were good words that came from the heart of a good man, but it didn't comfort those who heard them. They knew they were on their way, not to live in peace, but to risk their lives in war.

They marched out of Missouri and into Kansas, from a hard-bitten slave state which had been the western frontier only twenty years ago, into a contested area. This land was being fought over by those who wanted Kansas to be slave and those who wanted it free. These were tough issues that tore at men's souls and caused much bloodshed. It wasn't the only issue either. There was still the matter of the hostile Kiowa and Southern Cheyenne Indians, who were not ready to relinquish the Cimarron country of western Kansas to the white man. Many more good men would die in this conflict before Kansas would be secure.

Under a huge crystal-blue sky, the column trudged over rolling plains of tall prairie grass. There were no fences here, and few settlements. The white man's plow had not broken this land. The men peered watchfully about them, surveying the far horizon. They were fearful of Indians and bandits, especially since they bore no arms with which to fight off any attack by hostiles. The sad truth was, they were protected only by their oblivious major who rode in front of the men, presenting himself as a splendid target.

At length, they arrived at Fort Leavenworth, tired but unscathed. To the amazement of everyone, Leavenworth was not really a fort at all. It was a collection of ramshackle, whitewashed, low-slung buildings. These post facilities were scattered about a sun-baked dirt parade ground. This so-called fort sat in the middle of a featureless prairie that stretched to all horizons. The men walked into the enclosure of dead grass with their last energy, stimulated by the excitement of seeing real soldiers marching around in blue uniforms and black leather equipment. Some of the units were almost marching in step, and some even had muskets on their shoulders.

Major Broderick led them to an open field away from the other units. The space they were to occupy was devoid of man or beast, except for a long line of canvas bundles evenly spaced down the center of the field. Jed had seen such bundles before, as had most of the men who served in the Nauvoo Legion. The "green" recruits didn't know they were army tents that would soon serve as their new homes. Major Broderick put Jed in charge and rode off to headquarters to report their arrival. Jed had the men laying out company streets and pitching tents before the major was out of sight. He organized groups and put the old Legion men in charge of them. Soon the long rows of taut tents filled the open field.

When Major Broderick returned, he rode into camp with another mounted officer. This new man was a sour looking, skinny little fellow whose mouth was hidden behind a huge, light brown walrus mustache. His long, curly, cinnamon-colored hair flowed out from under a campaign hat (complete with plume), at an outrageous angle. A wispy goatee came to the rescue of a chin weakened into non-existence by the overpowering mustache. His beady, china-blue eyes stared out of an incredibly freckled and squint-lined face. Those eyes burned into everyone he looked at, but as he would not deign to bend his stiff military neck, he always seemed to be looking sidelong into their faces. His intense military bearing (as tall as possible in the saddle) made him seem contemptuous of everything and everybody.

The uniform of this officer was correct in every detail, and tightly tailored to his thin, but straight, torso. It was also bleached and streaked by sun and rain. The polished boots he wore were wrinkled with much wear, undoubtedly from the same campaigns that scratched and dented the scabbard of the sabre he wore at his side. Sheathed inside, however, was a blade sharp and spotless. His leather gauntlets were soft and shaped to his hands.

It was a surprise to Jed to see that the new officer was only a first lieutenant, although clearly of the regular army. He was cavalry, with silver bars on the yellow field of his shoulder straps. The low rank made Jed look again and see that the man was actually rather young, in his late twenties, about Jed's age. This man was all soldier. It appeared to Jed that he had come straight from West Point to the frontier and had stayed there for about ten years of Indian fighting and keeping the Kansas peace.

Jed felt the men were instantly afraid of this wizened little lieutenant, and the lieutenant knew it and liked it. *Now he has a real war and he can achieve the glory that will take him to the top, even if his troops are only Mormons,* thought Jed.

"Are you people organized yet?" barked the little lieutenant in a nasal, irritatingly high-pitched, extreme southern accent.

Oh, no, thought Jed. *South Carolina.*

Major Broderick, thoroughly cowed by the lieutenant's harsh command presence (he was, after all, only a "brevet" major, a junior officer given a higher rank for the duration of the war), mumbled that the men hadn't even been enlisted yet.

Jamie dared to speak up. "We have our captains of ten and of a hundred."

The lieutenant snorted a humorless chuckle and spat. "I would be obliged, Sir," said the lieutenant to the major with an elaborate but fish-eyed courtesy, "if you would take these people to the post sergeant major, for enlistment. If you permit me, I will say a few words." He saluted sparely and the major returned the salute timidly. The lieutenant faced the mass of men and looked down on them from his horse.

"I am First Lieutenant A. J. Smith, late of the 4th Dragoons. I shall be adjutant to the commander of this Battalion, although the commander has not yet been chosen," he said rapidly in his thin but penetrating voice. He smiled sarcastically; his teeth could barely be seen under the mustache. "I will be responsible for your training." He turned to the open-mouthed and blinking Major Broderick, saluted crisply but hastily, "Good morning, Sir," and rode off at an easy canter, lithe in the saddle and unconsciously at one with his horse.

For a moment, nobody moved or made a sound. Then the major stirred and said quietly, "Come along, men." On his horse, he led the way to Post Headquarters, followed by the shambling column of five hundred homesick men.

"Company, tench-HUT," shouted Captain Jed Cutler, late of the Nauvoo Legion, Illinois Militia, now commanding "A" Company, Mormon Battalion, U.S. Volunteers. With his first lieutenant, Jamie Logan, and second lieutenant, Zarabel Cobb, setting the example, the hundred men of the company did a creditable job of popping to attention, as did the other companies. All of them had been hastily instructed by the old Legion men. Smith could not hide the fact that he was impressed, which, of course, instantly made him furious.

"I see you have organized," he barked viciously. "You think you know the drill book? Form column of companies to the right. If you cannot do it, you shall double quick the one mile to Post Supply."

Without looking back, Smith trotted his horse out of the Battalion area. That way, he betrayed no respect when he heard the correct commands being given. He was both agitated and impressed when he heard the command to face companies to the right. Following execution of the order came the command for leaders to take column position, which enabled the companies to step off in sequence.

When the Battalion marched up to the long, low, whitewashed warehouse with its board porch and simply-lettered sign that said, "Post Supply," they saw with a start that soldiers in blue-gray uniforms were lounging all about the area. Their uniforms were willfully dirty. Their beards, hair, and mustaches were scraggly. Some whittled with Bowie knives. Many were spitting tobacco juice. They were hard, lean, and hateful. They were the Missouri Wildcats, about equal in number to the Mormons.

Whoever at headquarters sent us both to supply at the same time is ignorant of recent history, thought Jed.

As the companies each halted under their captains' commands, the Mormons saw their own A. J. Smith leaning on the Dutch-door countertop of the Supply Issue Room. He was talking to a white-haired old supply sergeant who was sucking on a huge corn-cob pipe.

The Mormons stood at ease and glared at the Missourians, who lounged and grinned at the Mormons.

"How come they allow abolitionist nigger-lovers in this man's army?" came an anonymous taunt. Others joined in.

"Damn Mormons should be white slaves . . . low trash."

"Like to take over our land, huh? Whup you 'til you holler—or die!"

And then from the Mormon ranks:

"You killed the prophet."

". . . and Hyrum."

". . . and my child."

Then a Missourian:

"Nits make lice. We'll git you all. You cain't hide out west."

Smith and the supply sergeant jumped when they heard the roar of a thousand voices and the rush of two thousand feet as battle was joined behind them.

Jed had spotted a man he thought he remembered from that night in burning Nauvoo and went straight for him, although it didn't really matter. The Missourian had a long drooping mustache and gave a banshee yell as he swung at Jed's head. Jed ducked and began thudding his big fists against the man's tough but slender midsection. The man expelled a loud groan and went down. Next he turned to find the man who had said "nits make lice," but a brother who had lost his son at Haun's Mill was sitting on the man, smashing at his face, which the Missourian tried to protect with both hands. Jed saw Jamie struck down from behind by a piece of whittling wood. The assailant turned on Jed, but he ducked under the flailing log, lifting the man off his feet, and threw him to the ground. He kicked at the writhing torso but the man rolled away.

In just moments, the huge mass of swinging arms and legs had kicked up a dense dust cloud, and all eyes and mouths were full of it. No one could see more than a few vague, nearby shapes. The dust cloud glowed yellow with the sun beating down on it. The noise was tremendous. These men filled their arena with the pent-up hatred of twenty years of persecution and struggle.

Out of the corner of his eye, Jed saw a flash in the cloud. He turned to face it and leapt away from the thrust of a big, wicked Bowie knife. The knife slashed again and Jed had to fall flat on his back to avoid it. A coffee-colored face with incongruous gray eyes hurtled down toward him and the double-edged tip of that thick blade was arrowing for his throat.

Suddenly, there was a loud clang as a heavy sabre blade entered Jed's vision and the Bowie knife twirled out of sight. The dark-faced Missourian was kneeling, holding his hand and wrist, uncut but throbbing with pain. Jed looked up to see Lieutenant Smith standing over him, sabre *en garde*. Strange how Smith could make that piping voice so powerful.

"Get back on your own sides, all of you!" shrieked the little man with the big sword, eyes bulging, mustache quivering. "On your feet and into ranks or you'll wish your mothers never met your fathers, you . . . you . . . volunteers."

The Mormons and the Missourians warily got to their feet and separated back into their own groups, although everybody looked the same under their coating of dust. Sullenly, both units formed up in their own lines of companies. Jed noticed that nobody was seriously hurt. The old supply sergeant gazed out on the scene, smiling and puffing on his pipe.

From out of the dust rode a darkly handsome colonel in a very resplendent version of the Missourians' blue-gray uniform. He trotted his big bay horse between the two formations.

"What is going on here?" he barked, his plume trembling in agitation. Spotting Smith, he rode up to the lieutenant until the horse was breathing directly into his face, but the little man remained motionless. Still holding his drawn sabre in his right hand, he abruptly swung it upward in the sword salute. This brought the blade flashing right past the eyes of the colonel's mount and the horse squealed, reared slightly, and backed off. The colonel was discommoded and the Mormons chuckled, causing some Missourians to edge forward, growling.

"Good morning, Sir," said Smith "I am Lieutenant A. J. Smith of the *regular* army, late of the Fourth Dragoons, and now adjutant of the Mormon Battalion. And whom do I have the honor of addressing?"

"That's Colonel Price, leader of the mob that drove us out," came a voice from the Mormon ranks.

"Silence!" screeched Smith "Captain Cutler, you saw that man as well as I. He shall walk punishment all night tonight. Do you understand?"

After a moment of silence, Jed replied slowly. "Yes . . . Lieutenant."

Price jabbed a finger at Smith. "Your Mormonist trash have attacked my men."

"There has been an altercation, Sir," said Smith evenly, through gritted teeth. "It would appear that there is bad blood between our two units. I suggest they be kept apart during all future training at this post."

"Hah! My men don't need training. We leave for the war as soon as we draw fresh equipment. As for your . . . men, they should be sent to prison . . . or hell! Stand aside!" With that, the furious Price rode up to the supply shed and his men followed.

A. J. sheathed his sabre and marched down to the Mormons. He stood in front of Jed. Suddenly he relaxed for the first time since the Mormons had laid eyes on him and spoke quietly. "Captain Cutler, I shall want you to explain a few things. Apparently my knowledge of your people is deficient."

"With pleasure, sir," responded Jed, grinning.

The Mormon Battalion waited patiently in the hot sun, nursing cuts and bruises, while the Missourians received their issue. It seemed like forever before they marched off (singing filthy, blasphemous marching songs with much leering in the Mormons' direction), ready for battle. Without further altercation, the Mormons lined up to file into the shed, past long tables behind which stood the old sergeant's supply soldiers. On the tables were stacked folded uniforms of all sizes, army shoes, cartridge boxes and bayonets on thick black leather cross belts, canteens, haversacks and blankets. Lastly, each man balanced on top of the personal pile he carried, a brand new flintlock army musket. The officers were also issued a beautiful army sabre as part of their uniform complement.

That evening, the elected officers of each company sewed on their shoulder straps of rank insignia, and the non-commissioned officers did the same with their sky blue stripes. The sound of hymns and lilting folk songs floated up from their camp, and they went to bed early and contented.

It was just as well that the Mormon Battalion went to bed early. The next morning Lieutenant Smith had them fall in for inspection of their proudly worn uniforms and equipment. He stormed up and down the ranks, complaining, insulting, threatening. "You're an embarrassment to this man's army." He ordered the men to present arms—which they did with some reservation. As before, the little lieutenant berated the quality of their preparation. "These muskets are disgraceful. I can't wait to see the sabres of your so-called officers!" He pulled a sabre from the scabbard of a nearby captain and wailed. "Don't you children know anything about army regulations? These sabres are part of the uniform of an officer, whose name must accompany the weapon! When I come back, this Battalion had better be in order or you will all walk punishment. And officers, get your names on those sabres. I don't care if you have to scratch them on with your bayonets!" Smith stormed out of the barracks, leaving the "so-called officers" embarrassed, but the overwhelming emotion among all the men was anger and resentment for their lieutenant.

A. J. Smith simply couldn't have cared less.

After much effort on the part of the men, adjusting, sewing, and cleaning, Lieutenant Smith returned and inspected his batallion. When he once again drew a sabre from the sheath of an officer, he was surprised to see the name, "Captain Jedediah Cutler, U.S. Volunteers, Mormon Battalion," beautifully engraved in the blade, just below the hilt of the fine sword. Smith hadn't realized that within the ranks of these volunteers were craftsmen from all walks of life, including engravers. Every sabre he inspected was equally adorned. The little Carolina gamecock finally "humphed" his approval. The Mormons thought it was time for lunch and Smith agreed, but it would be five miles distant after a conditioning march. Upon completion of lunch, he explained with much pleasure, the Battalion would spend the rest of the day and the next two days and two nights in the field learning to bivouac, forced march, picket their area, deploy from column to line of battle and back again, and on, and on, and on.

"He must have thought one sentence of civility was making him soft," laughed Jed to Jamie as they trudged to their tents to pack up.

In the month that followed, no one had time or breath for civility, not to mention singing, but there was correctness, thoroughness, and fairness. Everything made sense, as Smith taught five hundred farmers, tradesmen, and artisans the school of the soldier, the art of war. Nobody liked him. Everybody feared him. They didn't know yet that they respected him.

With training complete, the Battalion paraded in front of Post Headquarters, commands being given by the adjutant, A. J. Smith. The general commanding Fort Leavenworth sat on his dappled stallion, facing the troops, his staff behind him.

Beside the general sat a beaming old colonel on a very passive roan gelding, his mane limp and head down in the heat. The colonel, however, was obviously very happy to be there. The gray whiskers that went all around his face positively vibrated with his smiling at the proceedings as the troops marched in and dressed their line. His soft, brown eyes took in everything with great satisfaction.

Toy soldiers, thought Jed. *We are his new toy soldiers.*

Sure enough, the post commander announced that the venerable gentleman, Colonel P. Saint George Cooke, U.S. Army, had been named commanding officer of the Mormon Battalion.

Colonel Cooke made a resounding acceptance speech about Roman legions reaching out to the edge of the known world, and the guests from the fort's population applauded politely. There was a wiry mountain man among the crowd who stood out from everyone else. It wasn't so much his appearance that caught the eye. He was runty in height, moonfaced with a scraggly mustache, slit eyes, and a slash mouth, but he was jumping up and down making all manner of noise. Accompanying his raucous approval of the speech was an odd gesture of his arm with his fist thrust upward. The beadwork and fringes on his filthy tattered buckskins flailed around as he threw himself off balance with his enthusiasm. Abruptly, he fell with a thud, making his grey-streaked black hair leap up and flop down. The soldiers in ranks struggled to keep mouths set and eyes front, but many could be seen to shake a little with suppressed laughter.

He's part Indian, thought Jed as the assemblage ignored the old cuss, *and he's drunk. The lieutenant will kick him into silence with his big boots for destroying the glorious moment.* Smith, however, ignored the reprobate along with everybody else.

Without even a shadow of movement, eyes locked to the front, the five hundred soldiers studied Colonel Cooke to learn his worth as a commander, and they studied Lieutenant Smith for his reaction to the appointment. All present knew why they were studying, but they could learn nothing more than what they already knew. Cooke was old and kindly. Smith was young and hard. They instantly liked Cooke. They grudgingly respected Smith. Perhaps Smith's training and Cooke's leadership could get the Battalion through to California. Only the march across the continent would tell them. And, after all, these soldiers had a revelation from the Lord to fall back upon.

At sunrise the following day, the Mormon Battalion marched out of Fort Leavenworth, into the unknown. Lieutenant A. J. Smith, adjutant, instructor, and a better friend than they understood, watched as the column filed past the undefined boundaries of the fort.

Jamie stepped up to Jed as they marched from the parade ground. "Why is it our adjutant is staying behind? We need him."

"Look at him," Jed responded. "He wants to come, but he can't. His orders are to stay behind and train more volunteers for the campain."

"So they give us a Brevet Major and a broken down old Colonel to lead us?"

"Perhaps it will be up to us now, Jamie."

Only now did the men learn why everyone ignored the antics of the half-breed trapper. He was their scout. If any man knew about the uncharted wilderness ahead of them, it was Jean-Baptiste Charbonneau. It turned out that this Charbonneau was the son of Sacajawea, "Bird Woman," the Shoshone girl who, back in 1803, had guided Lewis and Clark. She had led those famous explorers up the Missouri River, across to the Columbia River Basin, and down to the Pacific Ocean.

Her story was known to every American who lived in the Louisiana Purchase. Having been kidnapped from her family by raiding Crow Indians in a place the trappers called Cache Valley, she had been sold as a slave from tribe to tribe on down the Missouri to Saint Louis. There she was bought by a particularly nasty French woods-runner named Toussaint Charbonneau. He "married" her and fathered a son—Jean-Baptiste. Sacajawea agreed to go with Lewis and Clark to get

away from the old drunkard's beatings, even though it meant carrying her papoose on her back all the way to the Pacific.

The story of Bird Woman always laid stress on Jean-Baptiste, who, unfortunately, had grown up like his father even though raised by his mother. The soldiers didn't care. The main thing was, could Charbonneau guide them across the desert to California?

The Mormon Battalion stepped out in route column, no marching, just hiking along, singing songs, every man chatting with his neighbor. All their provisions would be carried by them—what provisions they could wrench from the army. The only horses were those of Cooke and the batallion's scout. Because horses were in short supply, even Major Broderick had to walk with the men, his beautiful stallion having been assigned to the ridiculous but indispensable Charbonneau. It was another perfect example of the poor treatment the Mormon Battalion had received from the army since being inducted to service. Sometimes they were deprived of food, other times, sleep, but this was the first time a non-Mormon associated with the Battalion had been affected. Major Broderick was none too happy about it either.

The liveliest discussions had to do with how far it was to California and when they would get there. Jed Cutler, walking along at the head of his company, did not enjoy that debate. He was thinking of Celia. She was his comfort in the midst of this hardship, even though he knew she was experiencing hardships of her own. His thoughts drifted back to the brawl with the Wildcats which, in turn, took him back to Nauvoo. Now his mind caught another image, that of Peter Van Cleef.

Although thoughts of Peter came and went throughout the months since that terrible day in Nauvoo, Jed had chosen not to dwell on them. With everything happening in his own life, that was easy. It wasn't that

Peter's well-being didn't concern him, but it was out of his control, and now Jed had his own survival to worry about. Still, as he trudged along, he wondered if Peter was still alive. Jed also found himself wondering if the destruction of the last Mormons in Nauvoo was the only thing Peter had wanted to forestall.

They marched into Santa Fe in good order, even though they had sand in their shoes from walking across Kansas and Colorado. The Battalion camped for a short time in Pueblo, Colorado, with a weary band of Latter-day Saints, from Mississippi of all places. It was a comfort to see Mormon families again and to learn that these people were full of hope. When the order to march was once again given, the Battalion headed west and the Mississippi Saints headed north. The Mormon soldiers looked long and hard at their people heading for the new gathering place in a high valley that had been promised to the faithful.

The wagon train carried the soldiers' letters to their families, who would be in the new settlement before the Battalion returned from the war. Before the pioneers left, Jed wrote to Celia. While deep in concentration, Jed's usually straightforward letter began to take on a more romantic air. Thoughts turned to daydreams of his beautiful wife, her dark hair glistening in the sun. Jed could see her in his mind's eye and he longed to look into her eyes, touch her soft white skin, and hold her close to him. He found himself penning verse as he wrote:

> "My love for you is like a growing tree. It grows and never asks the reason why, for as long as it is nourished. My love is always nourished by your smile. The earth which feeds my soul is you, my beloved wife."

Jed sent his letter along with the many others written by the men of the Battalion, but he knew it would take months to reach Celia. Still, the writing helped him pour out his spirit. It was this spirit he sent by an express much more sure—on the wings of a mighty prayer, to his wife far to the north, soon to begin her parallel journey. At another fire in another place far away, Celia straightened up from tending her father and felt the warm reassurance that her husband loved her and wanted to help her. She almost laughed. She almost cried.

The Mormon Battalion knew, as they marched into Santa Fe, they were getting close to the war. As they came to a halt in the Plaza of the Governors, they were studied by haggard soldiers resting in the colonnades. These were men who had stormed the fortified town and the Mormons remembered the fresh cemetery outside the walls, including mass graves for the Mexicans.

The Battalion was billeted in some burned-out houses. Colonel Cooke went to headquarters to report and Broderick went to find food. The men began to eat what they had carried in from the plains and instantly Mexican children materialized from piles of burned beams, chunks of adobe, and shattered tiles that seemed to serve as their shelter.

Jed shared his hardtack biscuit and beef jerky with some silent children clad only in long filthy shirts. Their black hair was filthy, too, and covered with dust. Snatching the food solemnly, they ran away. He couldn't help but think about these poor children and what it would be like to be a father one day.

When I have children, Jed thought, *I pray they never feel pains of hunger and destruction as these children have.*

It didn't take long for Jed and "A" Company to give away or eat all that they had. While his men dozed, he rose, painfully, and worked his leg muscles as he walked toward the town's now greatly enlarged cemetery. At the head of each grave, there was a board pounded into the ground. On it was carved or burned the name, rank, unit, and state of origin of the dead soldier beneath. They were from all over America, when the regulars were considered. Sure enough, there was a disproportionate amount of southerners. From the northern militia and the regulars there were a lot of Irish and Germans.

Jed abruptly stopped his tour of the cemetery. He was standing in an area surrounded by the graves of some Missouri Wildcats. More than a few of Price's men had received the "ultimate" surprise. Without being ready, they had crossed over to the other side. *Do they think differently of the Mormons now?*

Jed had fought. He had heard bullets crack past his ear, from the weapons of these very men, but he had fired his weapon at the faces of men like these in order to save his wife. Were they thinking exalted thoughts of glory or honor or the cause of the country when they dashed through these burning streets? Or were they still haughty bully boys enjoying the fear they caused, until they met a Mexican who was unafraid enough to squeeze his trigger?

They were beyond Jed's vengeance now. He had wanted to kill them—and they had been killed. The trouble was, after a man is dead, his poor, puny, harmless body must be buried. Jed felt sorry for them. He forgave them. He prayed that *he* might be forgiven.

Jed did notice that Price was not among the dead, and he learned that the Wildcats had marched on, looking for more war.

As for the Mormon Battalion, they cleaned up after the Wildcats' battle over Santa Fe. Colonel Cooke was long in his expressions of distress at having missed the battle. Broderick had to be tougher with the men than at any time since they had started as he drove the companies through fatigue duty and provost guard duty. The men could say, however, when it was done, that they had helped the citizens rebuild Santa Fe and organized the town so that the people could live. They had seen all but a small garrison force march away, further south and west, fanning out in a broad invasion of the Mexican territory.

One quiet evening as the sun burnt red against the horizon, a lookout spotted a caravan of pack mules, led by a scandalous mixture of Mexicans, Indians, and mountain men. They made no attempt to enter Santa Fe, but camped nearby.

Charbonneau called them "Comancheros" and ran off to greet them ecstatically in a preposterous blend of French, English, and Spanish. When he came back he told everyone they were making their way to old Mexico to escape the rule of the advancing United States government. "Deyz outlaws," emphasized Charbonneau.

"Shouldn't we arrest them or something?" wondered the major.

"We have no grounds, Major. They have done nothing to us or to anyone else that we could prove," replied Colonel Cooke.

Everyone could see the items being unloaded from the Comanchero mules were personal effects of many different kinds of people. There were dresses and men's trousers and coats, Indian blankets and jewelry, shoes and boots, saddles and tools. This bounty undoubtedly came from victims of Comanchero raids, but the Mormons knew nothing of the outlaws. They did not ask Charbonneau about the goods, nor did he volunteer any information. Colonel Cooke could see horses and pack mules in abundance within the outlaws camp. "What are the chances of making a deal with the Comancheros?" he asked Charbonneau.

"What do you have in mind, Sir?" queried Major Broderick.

"Major, you of all people, I'm sure, will agree that we need another horse, not only for you to ride, but just in case something happens to one of our other mounts. Perhaps we can bargain with these Comancheros and secure one."

"*Oui, oui,* Colonel. Dat's good idea. I will talk to dem."

"We will form a detachment," announced the Colonel. "Major, assemble 'A' company. Charbonneau, you will accompany us." The small force made their way to the camp of the Comancheros and were received by them. Under normal circumstances, Comancheros did business their way, usually taking from others. When they traded, it was always for money or gold. Charbonneau asked the leader of the Comancheros what would be their price for a horse. He laughed when he heard the answer, amused by the boldness of the outlaw.

"He say he will not sell dis horse for gold or silver, dey got plenty," Charbonneau told Colonel Cooke, trying to contain himself. Not willing to let his chance at a horse go easily, Major Broderick stepped up to Charbonneau.

"What does he want then?" asked Broderick. Charbonneau laughed again, pointing at Colonel Cooke.

"He wants dat nice army sword."

Jed watched from his position in front of his men. He was close to the colonel, so he heard everything that transpired. It was a curious situation and all the men wondered what was happening.

"My sabre? Why, that's preposterous," snapped Colonel Cooke.

"Dem's good horses, Colonel. Dey cost you plenty if you pay with gold."

"Perhaps they would accept my sabre," offered Major Broderick, looking hopefully toward his superior.

"Absolutely not, Major! Next to myself, you are the highest ranking officer in this Battalion and I expect you to maintain your complete uniform accordingly. If you were a volunteer, that would be an entirely different story, but you are not, so we will simply have to give them something else."

"No sword, no horse, Colonel. Dey not change dere mind."

"Begging the Colonel's pardon," Jed said stepping up to the officers. "I believe the Colonel's decision to obtain an additional horse is a prudent one, and if I may be so bold, Sir, I request the Colonel's permission to volunteer my sabre for the acquisition."

"That's very noble of you, Captain, but your duty does not require such a sacrifice."

"Sir, it is my belief that an additional horse will better serve our cause than my sabre. Even without it, I have sufficient arms with my musket and bayonet. Another horse would give us greater flexibility for sending scouting parties as well as relieve some of the burden of packing supplies. I do not therefore consider being relieved of my sabre a sacrifice."

"Well spoken, Captain." Colonel Cooke thought for a moment then continued. "Very well, Captain Cutler. If the Comancheros will accept your sabre in trade, we will make the exchange."

Charbonneau translated the offer to the leader of the Comancheros who heartily agreed. After the exchange was complete, the motley band of outlaws took their leave of the Battalion, heading south for the Mexican border. Jed felt pleased he could contribute to the success of his mission. Mostly, however, he felt relieved of five pounds of steel he no longer had to carry. The detachment returned to the shelter of Santa Fe and waited for new orders.

Finally, it was their turn. The old colonel positively cantered his horse into Battalion headquarters shouting the orders to the assembled officers. They would march for Tucson, in the Mexican province of Arizona.

"Tucson must fall to the Mormon Battalion! Then we shall have the honor of securing the southern entrance to California," gabbled the colonel. He received for a reaction only Broderick's worried glance and the unhappy silence of the company officers. They were trying to be correct but were thinking how narrowly they had missed the battle and how sorely tested the prophecy of Brother Brigham would be.

Still, the order went out, the men once again piled their lives on their backs, and their column wound out of the town onto the road west. The last thing they saw of Santa Fe, looking back into the rising sun, was a pole flying the U.S. flag the Missouri Wildcats had raised. Now, like Columbus, they disappeared over the edge of the map. They walked west into a desert, guided only by Charbonneau . . . and a prophecy.

7

The Trek West

That same prophet said it was time for the pioneer company of Saints to leave Winter Quarters and do their part by going west. Celia went to where Caleb sat resting. "Come on, Father," she said, helping him from his chair into the cabin.

"Are we moving again, Celia?" asked Caleb.

"Yes, Father. We're moving again."

The wagon train stood in line, mules and oxen hitched to every kind of freighter, Conestoga, and light wagon that was ever built. Cows were tied to many wagons, and there was a small herd held together by teenaged boys next to the train. The young men who would act as scouts ahead of, and outriders around, the train stood in a group near the front of it, holding their horses' bridles while the spirited animals shook their heads and stepped about here and there. President Young and his first counselor, Heber Kimball, rode slowly along the train in their light wagon, inspecting every rig.

Bishop Leighton called his ward together for a prayer of blessing upon the journey. Celia, in the bowed group, put one arm around her mother and one around her father. The men took off their hats. The bishop, towering over them by a full head, prayed.

"Heavenly Father," he said, in his calm, clear voice, "we leave this place thankful to Thee for pointing the way to our fresh travels. Some of us have been asked to serve our country, and we depart with deep conviction that soon we will meet again. Watch over us and guide our way, we ask thee, in the name of Jesus Christ. Amen."

The cry came down from the head of the train to get moving and the huddle broke up. Everybody helped each other into the wagons and, one vehicle at a time, the train lurched into motion along the trail west. South had gone the would-be soldiers in a long caterpillar of striding legs. Now, west went the pioneer wagons with a giant creaking of heavy-laden wheels and whips cracking over straining withers and thrusting hooves. Brigham had said they should try for twenty miles a day. He said if they could keep up that pace, they would get there (wherever "there" was) in ninety days. Jed had already been on the road longer and traveled farther than that. Celia decided that what Jed could do, she could do.

Each morning Celia had trained herself to sit up the moment she regained consciousness. That way, she was not startled by the wretched bugle braying out its crackling version of "reveille." It would be five o'clock in the morning, with the stars as bright as at bedtime. There were coughs and low voices each morning, accompanied by the rustle of clothes in every wagon. Emma always made good beds with thick straw pallaises laid over flat-topped chests. The dear old mother tucked everyone in with plenty of blankets and rag-filled comforters. They even had a few down-filled pillows from home. That made for sound sleep when they flopped into bed at nine in the evening after family prayer and an unsatisfying rendition of some insipid lullaby on that ridiculous bugle. The young man who played it was so proud of his important function that nobody cared to tell him how irritating his music was.

Warm, soft beds made it hard, however, to swing bare feet onto the floor of the wagon and rush to get dressed with everybody's breath steaming in the small space. The dew-soaked canvas top sent a stabbing chill through anyone who brushed against it. Caleb, of course, stayed in bed, bundled against the searching cold, until the bright sun would make a warm May day. Emma was always the first woman in sight when she appeared at the back of her wagon and jumped down to the ground, but she never beat Quimby, who would stand up from making a fire and chuckle at her.

"Who can tell the price of a virtuous woman? She ariseth early, before any that are in the house." Emma lowered her eyes and smiled.

The fires flared up as usual around the wagon circle, and the women cooked Johnnycakes, beans and the last of the ripening bacon. This morning, however, there was excitement in the air, instead of the usual bracing for all-out effort. Brother Brigham had said they would not travel today but would get fresh meat.

They were in the heart of Nebraska now, at a place on the North Platte River called Grand Island, and the men would try their hand at buffalo hunting.

All across Iowa and Nebraska they had seen nothing but waving grass, rolling clouds, and begging Indians. The bishops and the captains had kept the women out of sight whenever the little groups of braves had ridden up to the train on their colorful ponies. Celia and Emma listened through the canvas as they muttered "How-how" and pealed out their chanting, sing-song language with Porter Rockwell, Howard Egan, and Brother

Brigham trying to make sense out of the few words they knew and could catch. Pawnee . . . they were Pawnee, Celia learned. She glimpsed the hedge of hair down the crown of an otherwise shaved skull and their beads, fringes, and feathers. Always Rockwell and Egan would shout some explosive nonsense syllables and back the aggressive Indians away. Always the Indians would shout back in a threatening tone. Brigham would order bacon and some flour, maybe molasses to be given to the deputation, then mutter instructions to keep the stock inside the circle tonight.

It was discussed around the fires that there were no buffalo any more in Iowa or eastern Nebraska. The outriders had shot an occasional delicate little antelope—nothing more. Too many wagon trains had passed through. Too many wagon trains had stopped and begun settlements at all the water points. So it was grudgingly agreed that the Pawnee had a point in demanding food as a toll to be paid by the travelers who ground down the prairie.

But now, at Grand Island, they met a different kind of Indian, taller, straighter, with better clothes and equipment, and thick heads of flowing black hair. "Lakota" they would say, tapping their chests with great dignity, never breaking eye contact with the man to whom they spoke. "Sioux" is what Porter and Howard called them. These Indians brought goods to *exchange* for food. They brought buffalo robes and other hides, well-dressed, suitable for constructing moccassins, leggings, or gloves. They brought bird bone whistles, grass lariats, and other items useful or interesting. Brigham smiled and gave them a whole live cow with not a whisper of disagreement from Rockwell and Egan for the Lakota were many and had wiped out every previous ancient enemy.

The sun was full up now and breakfast was finished. The wagons were all packed and the oxen and mules hitched up, but the train did not move out. Everyone fidgeted and chatted. The men who would try their hand at being mighty hunters were gathered in little groups making plans. Always one question provoked discourse: How exactly do you hunt buffalo?

The Lord provided the way to learn when whooping Sioux Indians galloped by yelling, "Tatonka, Tatonka!" They gestured to the Mormons to come with them and swatted the flanks of their horses with their hunting bows of hardwood backed with bone and took off for the river. Buffalo! Buffalo! Many! Enough for all, enough and to spare. The young pioneer men jumped on their horses, grabbed their muskets, and galloped after the Indians. Later the word came down for the wagons to follow the hunters. Emma and Celia worked together to drive their yoke of oxen as fast as the others, with Caleb bouncing around in the back, making not a sound.

They came over a rise and saw a huge vale spread out before them. It trended gently down from the rounded ridgeline on which they stood to a meandering stream bed at the bottom, and then gently up to the far horizon. Emma and Celia saw a huge, moving, brown cloud shadow on the far slope, constantly changing shape as it moved over the tawny grass. With a jerk of their heads and a gasp, they both looked up at the same time. The brilliant blue sky was cloudless and the combined sight was breathtaking. Their eyes came back down to the brown mass. Buffalo. They noticed a fringe of dust bordering the edges of the mass. There had been no dust cloud to inform them of what they saw because the mass undulated slowly over the slope which was, after all, covered with grass. Next they saw little lines of dust materializing along the flanks of the enormous herd with a little bug-like movement at the head of each line. Although they couldn't make them out, they knew these were the mounted hunters, galloping along with the herd.

As they took in the expansive scene, the women dropped their eyes to the near slope and saw dark brown humps rising from the tall grass, scattered here and there all over the slope. From some of them rose the slender shafts of arrows with brightly colored feathers at the top.

Then as if with one mind, the wagons on the ridge crest headed down the slope among the fallen buffalo. The oxen pulling the Faradays went along with the others.

"We must look for the ones with bullet holes instead of arrows," pronounced Emma. "They will be our share." Jumping down, she ran forward to grab the oxen's nose rings, pulling them to a stop. Celia got down carefully, and together they walked over to a huge bull on his side, dead eyes staring into infinity.

"My goodness," chirped Celia, trying to grin as her stomach heaved within her. "The men will have quite a time dressing out this beast.

"No," replied Emma, pointing with a huge butcher knife. "Apparently, this is women's work." Celia followed with her gaze the point of Emma's knife and saw Indian women and children running to the various animals they claimed and falling to with their long knives. Celia noticed that flies were already beginning to gather with their annoying buzzing.

Unexpectedly, an Indian girl ran up to their buffalo and excitedly stuck her knife in the buffalo's mouth. There was a juicy sawing sound and she withdrew from the mouth a soft, slippery, blood-dripping but clearly recognizable giant tongue. With great joy, she offered it to Celia, whose world began to whirl around her and grow dark. The last sound she heard was her body hitting the ground.

Later, when their buffalo had been transformed from a dead creature into food, Celia rejoiced with everyone else. Delicately sliced and lightly braised, the tongue was delicious, and they made buffalo stew with their dried peas and corn. Also into the pot went the tuberous roots of the Kamas bush, called "prairie apples," to serve in the place of potatoes.

Angry with her weakness, Celia pitched in and made buffalo jerky, racks and racks of the drying strips, glistening with salt under the midday sun. Every wagon would have bags of the chewy, savory pieces so they would not have to devote another day to hunting for the rest of the journey.

Refreshed and resupplied, the wagon train continued on.

The journey wasn't all drudgery. There were things to smile at too, like "the mile machine," "The Professor," and "The Official Chief Grumbler."

The irrepressible William Clayton was, indeed, the bright young man of the Mormons. As his people clustered in the snow drifts on the west bank of the Mississippi, that dreadful Winter when they left Nauvoo, he had written their hymn of exodus—"Come, Come Ye Saints." Not only was he a musical artist with at least one flash of inspiration, but he was the Mormon Morse or Colt or Fulton: the boy genius inventor.

When the day drew near for the pioneer train to leave Winter Quarters, he had begun to sketch on a rare piece of paper in camp. He measured the exact diameter of his front left wagon wheel with a ragged old seamstress' tape measure. Muttering and whistling to himself, he began to furiously whittle wooden gears of many sizes and assemble them in a wooden casing he carefully fabricated. All the gears were on their own little whittled axles.

At length, he had taken his left front wheel off and sweated a stoutly fire-hardened wooden ring gear onto the inside of the wheel hub. With the wagon wheel back in place, he bolted his crude looking gear box to the side of the wagon in such a position that a gear protruding from the end of the box meshed with the gear on the wagon wheel. He had painted numbers around the circumference of the gear at the other end of the box. Accordingly, the wagon wheel turned; the gears turned; the numbers presented themselves one after another. At the end of a day of travel, Brother Clayton could read off how many miles his wagon had traveled. He called his contraption an "odometer." Everybody else called it the "mile machine."

Meanwhile, there was even more science to assist the travelers. Back home in Nauvoo, the Prophet Joseph Smith had founded the University of Nauvoo, which met for classes in the Mansion House. Joseph delegated the administration of the university to Doctor Orson Pratt, a devout and enthusiastic believer in the Church and the Prophet. Doctor Pratt was a man of classic intellectual appearance. He was a small pale fellow, not given to spending a great deal of time out of doors under normal circumstances. His high-domed forehead accentuated his penetrating stare, which always seemed to focus far off into some distant plane. The usual darkness of his dress only added to his conservative, intellectual appearance, but it was a look that suited him nonetheless. Dr. Pratt was widely known among the Saints as the Professor. It was a title he accepted most proudly.

The Professor had read all the accounts of the explorers of the American West and had advised both Joseph and Brigham about the possibilities of western settlement for the Saints. He had studied the sketch maps of Captain Stansbury's 1832 expedition and Captain Fremont's 1842 expedition. Now he brought along on the pioneer trek his battered old sextant, shiny with much handling and carefully protected in its felt-lined case. Whenever there was a prairie horizon almost as straight as a horizon at sea, which was every few days, the learned man would step away from the train in mid morning and just before bedtime. He then would raise his sextant to his eyes and "shoot the sun" or "shoot the stars," calling off their angles above the horizon to Brother Clayton or some other bright young scribe who recorded the data in a notebook. All that remained was for him to close his eyes and rub his forehead and, marvelous to say, he would pronounce the exact latitude and longitude of the wagon train at that very moment. This invariably brought forth gasps of wonder and awe from those who had gathered around him for the twice daily performance.

Once, acting as spokesman for the assembled Parsons boys, young Leonard Parsons asked the Professor what he did when he closed his eyes and rubbed his forehead. The Professor fixed him with a stare and said in an irritated voice, "spherical trigonometry!" The Parsons boys scattered in all directions and carried the news throughout the camp, "It's spherical trigonometry! Spherical trigonometry!"

The good doctor used his sightings and other surveying to constantly update the one map brought along by the pioneers. This map was circulated among the bishops and the captains so that, each evening, one portion of the company could see where they began, where they were, and where they might end up. He also gave lectures on famous landmarks along the route, flora and fauna, and the remarkable customs of the indigenous inhabitants (subtitled "Injun ways" by Rockwell and Egan, who were consistent attenders and assistant instructors).

The position of "Chief Grumbler" came about because the Saints were normal (even though "the natural man is an enemy to God"). After about one month of twenty miles per day across a featureless plain under a hammering sun, grumbling had become excessive. *Why did Brother Brigham want to camp here instead of there? Why do we always have to pass up good water just because the sun is still high enough to make some more miles? Why do I have to ride guard around the herd all night again this week? Will somebody please break that damn mile machine?* And so on. And so on.

The most imaginative grumbler was known as Colonel Wright. He had a militia commission from somewhere and used his title to establish himself as someone who knew what to do as surely as did Brigham Young. People were listening to the Colonel, and his phrases were getting to be parroted around camp.

One evening the Colonel announced that thirty days of buffalo jerky was enough. They had to vary it with a little fresh meat. The jerky had too much salt for health. Enough was enough. Brigham Young assembled the Saints and made a short kindly speech, smiling broadly.

"Brothers and Sisters, our Colonel Wright is providing an invaluable service by noticing every deficiency in our daily routines. Therefore, it is my belief that all of you should rest from your critical labors and allow Colonel Wright to represent us all as the watchdog of wisdom. To that end, I hereby appoint the Colonel to be Chief Grumbler."

Everybody laughed and shook the Colonel's hand, slapping him on the shoulder with loud congratulations. The Colonel wilted under the sarcasm and was never heard complaining again.

Always on their left hand lay the seemingly motionless Platte River, a sequence of smooth-surfaced pools among sand bars with vertical banks cut through the sod and clay. Though it took straining and boiling, at least they camped by water every night.

One evening Quimby and Celia carried a tub of water between them into the Faraday camp just as Emma backed out of the wagon with some of Caleb's soiled clothes.

"How is he?" asked Bishop Leighton.

"He can't sleep," Emma sighed. "Celia, dear, would you please look after your father?"

"Yes, Mother," Celia replied, already making her way to the wagon.

Quimby put his hand on her shoulder. "Why don't you get some rest?"

"I'm not tired," Emma replied wearily. Then, almost tearfully, she added, "Thank you for the water." While she scooped water into a bucket dipped in the tub, Bishop Leighton got out the small parchment map which he examined in the light of the fire. Emma looked on. "If only Caleb could get some sleep," she whispered softly.

"We came a long way today," Quimby noted, trying to turn Emma's attention from her sorrow. "The mile machine said twenty two."

"I didn't notice the miles," said Emma, drooping with fatigue.

"I never knew it was such a big country. Even on this map it doesn't give you any idea of the distances," Quimby observed.

"It feels cool tonight," reflected Emma at the edge of the darkness.

"Have you eaten?" asked Quimby with concern.

"We finished the rabbit."

"I'll try to bring in something else tomorrow," Quimby encouraged.

"Thank you, Bishop Leighton."

Out of the darkness popped the ever-jovial Fennelly. He carried a shallow basket under one arm and greeted them warmly.

"Evenin', folks," he chirped.

"Evenin', Brother Parsons," Emma returned.

"Is Celia about?" asked Fennelly.

"She's trying to get her father to rest," said Emma.

"My young 'uns have made this basket for her. Ever since I told them she was going to have a baby, they've been workin' on it. I'm real proud of 'em," beamed Fennelly, putting down the basket.

"Thank you, Brother Parsons. Celia'll be proud of them, too," Emma assured him.

"They were goin' to bring it themselves but they were just tuckered out and fell asleep. Sleepin' like logs over there . . . eight little logs," said Fennelly.

"It will be a nice basket for the baby to sleep in," Quimby observed, inspecting the strength and design of the weave. Bishop Leighton looked up at Fennelly and smiled. He recognized the hand of a true artist in the creation of this little treasure, much more than eight little boys could muster.

Fennelly returned the smile and then quickly changed the subject. "Have we got much to go, Bishop Leighton?"

"I'm afraid it's a long way yet. A long way."

They were all good friends and had all gone through much together. Together, even in the middle of the wilderness, they found strength in each other. Fennelly sat down with Quimby and Emma. "Powerful dry out this way. Don't seem to rain much."

"Yes, it's dry," agreed Quimby. "It's not going to be an easy life out here."

"I've wandered around since I was ten, never had a chance to settle down. I'm lookin' forward to this no matter what it's like. I'm goin' to like it! I'm sure of that," Fennelly said bravely.

Emma looked anxiously toward the wagon and the others followed her gaze. They could see the expectant mother's silhouette against the light inside. She sang softly to her ill father. Without turning her gaze, Emma once again asked Quimby the question so often asked. "How much farther is it really? Is it too far?"

Her forlorn words struck Quimby deep inside and he felt helpless. He knew there really wasn't anything he could say.

After a few moments, Celia emerged from the wagon and joined her mother and the group around the fire. “Father’s asleep now,” she announced quietly. Emma showed Celia the basket that Fennelly brought her and Celia thanked him appropriately.

“Oh, the kids made it,” Fennelly said, blushing.

“Thank them for me, would you?” asked Celia, hugging the basket to her body. Fennelly smiled and nodded. She gazed thoughtfully at the basket while running her hand absently over her protruding middle. “Bishop Leighton, does that map of yours tell where Santa Fe is, although they must be far beyond that now?”

Quimby pulled the map from his vest pocket and opened it up so all could see it. “Yes my dear, it does show the location of Santa Fe, but I believe you’re correct about them being long away. I’m sure they are somewhere in the vast western desert.”

Celia took the map from him and laid it on the cold ground, but close enough to the fire for her to see by its flickering light. The others knew Celia’s mind was on Jed, so far away.

“Celia, I’m worried about your father,” Emma said absently. Celia put down the map and went to her mother with a comforting hug. She, too, was worried but had tried not to show it.

“How much longer can we go, Mother?” wondered Celia.

“The promised land. It’ll seem like an awfully lonely land if Caleb isn’t there,” Emma said reflectively. Celia didn’t register her mother’s mournful observation because she was deep in her own thoughts of loss.

“I don’t want it if Jed isn’t there,” thought Celia out loud.

“All right! That’s enough!” said Quimby hastily, rising to his great height. “We are working ourselves into a terrible state over things we cannot control. Shall I summon the Chief Grumbler or would you prefer to sing? We've just enough time for one song before the bugle blows. What shall it be?" Everybody smiled sheepishly.

Fennelly jumped forward with his hand raised. "I've got a song that I . . . thought of . . . as we were bouncing over that rocky stretch."

"Let's hear it then!" demanded Quimby. "Teach it to us."

"We'll need Brother Gledhill with his squeezebox," warned Fennelly.

"Right here!" called out a smiling face as the man stepped into the firelight, accordion in hand. Little did the group know Fennelly had been hoping for a chance to share his new song and had Brother Gledhill standing by for such an occasion.

Fennelly dashed about teaching all the parts and verses to the circle of people about the fire. The little circle grew deeper as more and more people came over to join in.

> Oh, the cushioned seat is the sin of man.
> It's bound to bring him grief.
> Comforts like that are not part of the plan.
> It's outrageous beyond belief.
>
> The proper way to treat your bones
> Is to keep them all upright.
> And though your body aches and groans,
> You'll sleep like a log tonight.

They sang, clapped, and danced so happily and so well that Brother Heber had to wait for a soft moment before speaking up sharply. "Ahem! Brothers and sisters, the bugle blew some time back. It's time for prayers and bed." Everyone laughed and embraced when the song was over. With cheerful and relaxed voices, they bid each other good night then dissapeared into the darkness. Emma wondered if the ruckus had awakened Caleb, but when she looked into the wagon she saw that he was sleeping peacefully with a smile on his face.

Morning seemed to arrive much quicker the next day. All too soon it was time to move on. Twenty more miles—that was the goal.

The rolling grassland changed to endless sage with huge plates of rock turned on end and sticking up through the crests of long, narrow ridges. It was true summer now, and the pioneers watched the flowers die a little more each day until they were gone. The rutted trail they followed, which had carried many earlier wagons to Oregon and California, now left the Platte River. Rockwell and Egan had to ride ahead and look for water every day. Brigham no longer had the option of saying they would push on for a few more miles past a water point.

Day by day, it became more obvious that Caleb would not see the promised valley. Both mother and daughter knew this without raising the point to each other. They watched him cease to struggle against pain. He became less and less fearful and fretful, until he was quite at peace, striving to appreciate each moment that remained to him. Indeed, he became more, rather than less, lucid as he sank. The women could see that Caleb was determined to do his duty as patriarch of the family and bless his posterity.

One morning, while Celia sat on the seat up front, keeping the oxen moving with an occasional tap on the rump with an old ax handle, Emma sat by Caleb's bed as they both gently swayed and jostled with the wagon's passage over the trail. She held his hand in hers, against her heart, and smiled into his face. He beamed back at her and chuckled. "I am weak now," he explained, "but I remember when I carried you over our first threshold."

"That was a considerable feat," Emma chuckled in her turn.

"Of course I practiced long hours loading hundred-pound bags of flour in your father's mill," he went on with a twinkle.

She tapped his cheek in a playful, mock slap and then smoothed the few strands of white hair on his head. "I remember that you built that first house," she crooned. "I remember that you always took care of us and . . . gave your life to protect us."

"And would again, my darling," he proclaimed as strongly as he could. Her eyes filled with tears. "I will always be close by. I will always watch over you and I know that you will be taken care of." She stared, shocked, into his smiling face. She thought the sensitive man had been lost long ago, to be replaced by the child-like invalid, but he had been aware all along. He knew. Emma began to sob. She laid her head on his chest and he stroked her hair. Up front, Celia listened painfully while she prodded the oxen and gazed at the far horizon.

Caleb exhausted himself with that benediction and soon lapsed into near coma for two days. Celia prayed that her father would not leave without also giving her his blessing. By the grace of God, as they all knew, he awoke the third morning just as calm and bright as if he were going to throw off his covers and jump up to enjoy the new day. Emma quickly took over the driving and Celia took the seat on the old cedar chest next to Caleb's bed in the wagon.

She fed her father some warm mush and brought him up to date on their passage over the sage land. Then he asked her about Jed and the baby. She replied that all was well with both of them as near as she could tell. After a pause to stroke her hands, he said quietly, "And what do you think about Peter Van Cleef these days?"

Celia recovered from her shock enough to move her mouth. "I . . . I certainly don't think of him much at all," she managed. "From time to time I wonder if he is all right, but all I care about is Jed returning safely from the war and joining us in the new land."

"Bless you for an honest woman, my dear," said Caleb kindly with an innocent smile. "I think of Peter quite a lot. He was a fine young man, and he saved my life in Nauvoo. I hope he has not come to a martyr's end in Saint Louis."

"Peter Van Cleef is no martyr," mumbled Celia.

"Perhaps not," soothed Caleb, "But he can always be counted on to serve the Lord and love his friends, wouldn't you say?"

"Yes, certainly," agreed Celia with all due solemnity. She wondered where this patriarchal father's farewell blessing was going.

"You are so fine. You have always been loved by everybody," Caleb continued, as he stroked her cheek.

"Then why do I feel so lonely, so abandoned?" she sighed.

"Why indeed?" asked Caleb, falling in with her frustrated tone.

"Everyone has other tasks and duties they must do rather than stay with me."

"Yes, even your father will be called away soon." Caleb said it reflectively, with no self pity, but Celia gasped in horror at her selfish thought and threw her arms around his neck. "No! No, I didn't mean . . ."

"There, there, baby. There, there." He patted her back with all the strength left in his arms and hands while she lay weeping across him. "I will never leave you. You will feel my presence nearby . . . if you have faith. Also, your husband is with you, seeking to reach out to you from wherever he is called. It is as the Lord said to his disciples, 'Lo, I am with you always.' You see, happiness and peace come first from loving, only then from being loved. Get your joy from giving joy, Celia."

"That seems like a recipe for abuse," she said against his shoulder with a coldness that surprised her.

"I know. Indeed, don't I know. All Saints know that. But it is from loving that you gain your power. It is from giving that you gain your security."

She sat up straight and looked at him carefully. "You have taught me this principle all my life, Father, but only just now have I realized what a hard doctrine it is."

"Yes, yes. But you will see," he urged. "Everything good that you send out will come back to you. You have always had faith."

"I have always had you and Jed."

"You still do, my dearest child. You still do."

Caleb lay back weakly. He had spent his last reservoir of energy trying to transfer his testimony to his only child. As he closed his eyes, she smoothed his covers and stroked his forehead. Celia realized her father knew she was not the perfect example of beautiful saintly womanhood she had always been told she was. She wanted things she could not have. She resented duty. It was a troubling blessing. Caleb drifted off into a deep sleep, leaving Celia to contemplate the words he had spoken to her.

The Professor indicated to President Young that they would soon see Independence Rock, the famous square butte made of gray and yellow sandstone. This landmark was so named because it marked total separation from the old world of the United States, the world of towns, cities, law, and order. After Independence Rock, they would be in a land the Indians called "Wyoming" which meant "end of the plains." From now on, the prairie would trend constantly upward and become a grand series of rolling hills, finally ending at the entrance into the mountain west. This entrance, said the Professor's map, was called South Pass.

Standing in front of the rock, Dr. Pratt told its history to everyone who had gathered to look at the landmark. "The rock was named for the independence from the past it conferred on all the emigrants who passed it and their hope for freedom in the future," he announced. Celia studied the dark rock silhouetted against the western sunset as the wagon train pulled into camp. She was filled not with excitement, but with foreboding.

It happened that the next day was the Sabbath, so the pioneer train lay over for a rest day, as it always did on Sunday. Other wagon trains, Oregon and California bound, always took a layover day at Independence Rock just because they needed it. Presumably, Brigham would have driven the Mormons on the very next dawn if it had not been Sunday. Another reason all emigrants stayed awhile at Independence Rock was the good water there, clear water not seen for days and not to be seen again before they entered the mountains. These Mormon pioneers would take advantage of the opportunity to wash everything, including themselves. Tomorrow they would have an exuberant Sacrament Meeting with fine singing, mighty prayers, and stirring talks. Spirits were high throughout camp.

After church, the Professor took all who cared to go and showed them the writing on the side of the rock. There were inscriptions by all the famous passersby, painted or chiseled, names, messages, and dates. Brother Orson lectured on the name of Marcus Whitman, the missionary to the Indians of Oregon, who opened that territory to settlement, and Jim Bridger, the greatest mountain man, whom they would all meet at Fort Bridger—the last way-station before the mountains. He showed them a particularly fulsome message from John C. Fremont, the glorious California pathfinder, who was even now establishing the "Bear Republic" in San Francisco and looking for the arrival of U.S.

troops to support him. Wouldn't he be surprised when he was rescued by Mormons? Celia hung at the rear of the crowd and thought her complex thoughts. Emma had, of course, stayed with Caleb. After the lecture, the energetic William Clayton climbed to the top of the rock and waved his hat to the cheering crowd below.

Celia walked pensively back to the circled wagons and was instantly apprehensive when she didn't see her mother tending the fire or doing anything outside. In a rush, Quimby ran by her. Obviously the spirit of discernment had told the bishop to get down there right away. Celia ran after him. As they both plunged into the Faraday wagon, they heard Emma crying out, "Caleb! Caleb!" The poor old man was gagging and convulsing on the bed. Emma had him by the shoulders, but was beside herself not knowing what to do.

"It's a stroke," Quimby said, joining her.

Celia began sobbing as she realized what was happening. "Father, please don't die!" she cried. Emma threw her arms around Caleb as he took his last breath, looking at her all the while.

They buried Caleb at dusk. The ward gathered for a funeral, but it was brief and fidgety, because the light was fading and the howling of coyotes disturbed the stock. They would have to be calmed and cared for before bed. Everyone regained their spiritual perspective, though, when Brother Clayton, sober but still clear eyed, with chin up, led them in his exalting song.

Come, come ye Saints; no toil or labor fear,
But with joy wend your way.
Though hard to you this journey may appear,
Grace shall be as your day.

Even though the last verse was supposed to be joyous, its words were sharp and painful to Celia and Emma.

And should we die before our journey's through,
Happy day, all is well.
We then are free from toil and sorrow too.
With the just we shall dwell.
But if our lives are spared again
To see the Saints their rest obtain,
Oh, how we'll make this chorus swell.
All is well. All is well.

When everything was done and all that remained of the summer sunset was red streaks over the hilltops, Celia trudged back up to the Rock. There, leaning against the giant slab that was covered with names and messages of hope and promise, she gazed out over the huge land. *My heart is lost and lonely in this place,* thought Celia. *I wonder if I will see him again—Jed I mean, but also Father. What am I imagining? What is real? Strange envies ask me "Did you love me then?" Will you return to me? Should I have faith?*

Returning to the wagon, she found her mother rigidly lying on the bed that Caleb had lain in for all of the journey, staring at the canvas overhead, mumbling prayers. She lay down with her mother and they wept together until they fell asleep. For the Faradays, there was no comfort, and tomorrow there would be no rest.

Celia and Emma were rocked back and forth with considerable violence on their seat as their wagon lurched over the crest of another long, wandering rise. When the oxen and wagon started down the other side, Emma applied some pressure to the brake lever, but it was not particularly steep. Together, they both gaped at the jagged, blue-gray crest of a mountain range that peeked over the next rolling rise. The dull, textureless smear of slate color contrasted with the bright blue sky above it. These mountains were enormous and still quite far away. "The Rocky Mountains," said Emma in an awed voice. "But where is the South Pass? I see no break in them."

She was not left to wonder long. As the wagon in front of them cleared out of the way of their vision, they saw a picturesque little log fort. It sat at the bottom of the vale standing next to a typical western river, typical in that it meandered along a seemingly level surface with vertical banks cut through the sod. The water oozed along in rivulents between the sand and gravel of its streambed. In spring, it probably roared with water, but now provided just enough for the fort. The structure looked like the old prints of the French and Indian War with a log palisade and corner blockhouses. The insides of the walls were lined with cabins. "Fort Bridger," announced Celia with renewed excitement. "It must be Fort Bridger."

That evening, Celia walked slowly across the wagon circle, drying her hands on her apron. Wending her way toward a big crowd of pioneers, she came to the rear of the group. She heard a whoop and a cackle, then a raucous voice call out, "No, sirree, Brig. You don't have to worry about nobody stakin' it out ahead of ya. Why, Father Escalante didn't even bother to bless the place when he come up here explorin' fer Spain in, I guess it was 1776, our year of independence."

Celia slipped far enough forward to see a roly-poly old man with a jolly red face, seated on a log and just finishing a big plate of food. He was bald on top with huge freckles on his scalp. The hair that grew on the side of his head hung down in iron gray ringlets that mingled with his curly gray beard. He had a warm friendly smile and grinned while he told his stories to the crowd. His teeth were yellow but at least they were in place. This was Jim Bridger, leader of mountain men, teacher of explorers, and master of ceremonies for the opening of the West. "Why, good gadfrey, brethren, even the Injuns go round that valley. If'n a bird wanted to fly across it, he'd have to carry his provisions in a bag around his neck."

President Young sat next to Bridger with his hands primly folded in his lap, looking mortified and darting glances at the Mormon faces around him. *He wishes Bridger would shut up and confer with him privately,* thought Celia, *but the old man has an audience.*

"Tell us about the Great Salt Lake, Mr. Bridger," Brigham went on, sounding uncharacteristically perky.

"Discovered by my old friend Jedediah Smith. One beaver season he come down out of the mountains and saw this marsh land with reeds twenty feet high. Well, Jedediah was always curious so he plunged in and marched through them reeds for nigh onto a day. Then he discovers he's wadin' in salt water. So he made him a boat outta them reeds and he paddled with his rifle butt. Finally he breaks out of the reeds and there is the Pacific Ocean. Leastways that's what he thought it was, a deep bay or arm of the ocean. Some weeks later he come yellin' and screamin' into our rendezvous sayin' 'I have found the Northwest Passage! Ships can go from New York to China now!' But o' course it was a great big salten lake. Captain Stansbury went all around it. It don't do ya no good, though, less'n ya need a pinch o' salt." Bridger cackled again and slapped his thigh.

"Is there no fresh water in the valley?" asked a man in the group of listeners.

"Well, yessir," replied Bridger. "Streams come down out of the mountains and drizzle their way across the valley and into the dead lake. But if you ain't livin' next to a stream you can dig a well pert'near down to Hell and you won't get nothin' fer yer trouble."

"We did well with dry farming back in Winter Quarters," said another man, trying to be helpful.

"Maybe, but that weren't alkali soil," reminded Bridger.

"We will wash the soil, if we have to," declared Brigham, standing abruptly. "We'll get water where we need it. This place is a natural fort in the tops of the mountains. It will keep us separate and safe." There was a hearty muttering of satisfied agreement with that thought. "Thank you, Jim, for your advice and hospitality," said Brigham, shaking Bridger's hastily wiped off hand. Turning away from the old man, he called out to his own people, "Tomorrow we head for South Pass. Once through that, we make our own road through the canyons into the valley. The end draws nigh, Brethren. Persevere here at the last and, I promise you in the name of the Lord, all will be well."

The sun wasn't even fully awake when Fennelly Parsons found himself crawling on his hands and knees into a thicket of dried, brambly bushes. His palms and knees sank soundlessly into a layer of soft, talcum-like dust. It was his day to be scout and, up until now, he had liked it. He could hear the road gang behind him by a quarter mile, shouting orders and encouragement to each other and to their animals. He could also hear the rush and rasp of logs being dragged through the forest and the sounds of hacking and chopping as men cleared away underbrush.

South Pass had been as easy as promised. Once through it, however, they turned southwest, quartering across the grain of the mountains, looking for canyons that led into the valley. Egan and Rockwell conferred with Brigham and the Professor every morning and then rode off in search of the best way to travel. They would return in the afternoon with good information. Brigham could always direct the road gang with firm guidance. The pioneers chopped a road for the wagons along the bottoms of canyons and zigzagged it up and over broad ridges. The road in its last stage was being made out of logs packed together and held in place by rocks and dirt. Army engineers had long since proven this manner of construction, calling it a corduroy road.

Behind the intrepid scouts on horses, courageously looking for a basic route and threats from Indians, animals, or whatever, came Fennelly, the lowly road gang scout. Feeling his way along, figuring out exactly where the road would go, he marked boulders that must be dug up, and decided what dirt and logs it would take to support the wagons. There would be no bloody blisters from swinging an ax or a hoe all day, no dragging trees with ropes like a human donkey. Nonetheless it was nerve-wracking, horrendously responsible work, scrambling along the route, marking things, dashing back to the gang foreman to tell him what must be done.

Still on hands and knees, he just knew there was something important on the other side of this thicket. He would crawl through and see what it was, then go back and report. Without warning, he heard a whirring rattle sound and instantly saw the black beads of a rattlesnake's eyes about six feet in front of him. The snake retreated into its coil and Fennelly retreated backward. Though it felt strange to him, he was determined not to give up. Crawling around the uphill side of the snake's lair, thrashing his way through the thicket, he fell out the other side and saw that he was at the head of yet another canyon. This one was a very steep-sided notch in the mountains. Like a target in a gunsight, however, at the end of this down-sloping canyon, was a glimpse of the floor of a desert valley.

"Oh my goodness gracious," blurted Fennelly aloud. "It is as was promised. The Lord has provided." He jumped to his feet and began whooping and waving his hat in the air. His excitment was so vigorous, he lost his balance and tumbled a short distance down the mountain. Laughing all the way, he picked himself up, dusted off and said, "Now what do ya know about that?"

Bishop Leighton walked slowly down the most recently completed portion of corduroy road. His flock descended from their stopped wagons and gathered around him. He had spent the morning on the road gang, and he was filthy, dirt clinging grittily to his sweat. The smile on his face was exalted, however, and his carriage was very noble. "What's the trouble, Bishop?" asked Emma, scarcely able to breathe.

"There is no trouble, Sister, no more trouble. We have reached the end of the trail. We camp tonight in the valley of our new home."

8

Prison

Peter's wrists were still sore from the shackles when he awoke in the Saint Louis jail on the morning after his arrest. Sheriff Beeker was in the front office making coffee, and the smell filtered back to Peter's cell. From hero to prisoner . . . . All Peter knew was that he was tired, tired of the charade, tired of the fight. Sitting in jail, he had had time to really examine his beliefs. He began to realize that worldly success, alone, meant nothing. Without true friends and family, he had little. Peter also realized his church meant more to him than he ever knew. The conflicting realities of the two worlds Peter bestrode led him to understand the joy and fulfillment of life in the circle of the Saints as compared to the dark uncertain struggle for survival outside that kingdom of light. The principles he had learned in Sunday School with Jed and Celia were never more important than now. The sacrifices his people had made for the truth, the mistakes he himself had made, his love for Celia—all crowded in upon him.

The emotions overtook him and he fought to hold back the tears.

"Cryin' ain't gonna do you no good, Van Cleef." It was Sheriff Beeker. He had a plate of something resembling food, and he shoved it at Peter. The appearance was bad enough, but the smell told the tale and Peter knew he did not want it. He shook his head no. "Suit yerself," yawned the sheriff. He dumped the contents of the plate on the floor of the cell and returned to the front of the jail.

It was late in the afternoon before Beeker returned. "Ya got visitors," barked the sheriff through the small window bars in the door between the front office and the cell block. "It's agin' my better judgement, but considerin' who they are, I'm gonna allow it." Peter got to his feet. He tried to make himself as presentable as possible. Using the blanket from the cell cot, he had already cleaned the slop from where Beeker had dumped it. When the sheriff opened the door, Peter threw the blanket to him. It caught Beeker totally off guard and right square in the face.

"Thanks for breakfast, Sheriff," Peter said, knowing Beeker couldn't retaliate since others were present. Beeker mumbled something obscene and returned to the front office leaving Morgan and Mary alone with Peter.

"I didn't do it," Peter said before the other two had a chance to say anything.

Mary went forward and embraced Peter. "I know, Peter. I know you're innocent," she declared. The words had barely left her lips when she felt herself being jerked away from Peter's arms.

"I don't," growled Morgan. He pushed himself between the other two, keeping Mary as far away from Peter as possible. "You're nothing but a money grubbin' fraud," Morgan continued. "You've been usin' me all along, and I fell for it. I could overlook that Van Cleef, but robbin' our folks; that's despicable!" Mary tried to push past Morgan, but he kept her at bay.

"He said he didn't do it, Morgan," Mary exclaimed.

"You stay out of this, Mary," snapped Morgan, pushing her away again, more violently this time. Peter grabbed Morgan by the lapels of his jacket and brought him up short. The two men were face to face, both charged with opposing energy.

"You idiot! I'm the one who was being used!" Peter said, holding Morgan firmly in front of him. "Your henchman, Charlie Bates, planned to kill your parents as well as rob them. He also killed Rawlins and the others. There is no 'Mormon plague.' It was just Bates' way of getting rich and shifting the blame away from himself!"

Morgan struggled to free himself, yet couldn't get free. His ego wouldn't allow him to call out for the sheriff. But Peter could tell he was getting nowhere, so he released his grip. Morgan brushed himself off and paced the jail cell.

"And just how do you know all this, Van Cleef, if you weren't a part of it?" Morgan questioned. "Could it be that it was really *your* plan and Bates just tripped you up?" Morgan wanted proof; there wasn't any to give him. "The evidence stacks against you, Peter," continued Morgan. "The property was in your carriage, *you* were the one with the gun. There wasn't anybody else there."

"What about the gun, Morgan? Did you check it like I asked you to?" Peter quizzed Morgan, pressing his point.

"Now why should we have had need to check the gun, Peter?"

"Because the gun I held wasn't fired, Morgan. That's why!"

"Nice try, Van Cleef, but which gun? As you well know, there were two. The sheriff took the bullets from

both guns and sho'nuf, there was one spent chamber. Now we all know it came from your gun, don't we? You'll have to do better than that, Peter, or you're going to find yourself at the end of a rope."

The tears Mary shed had turned to anger, and she said what Peter could not. She tried to make her step-brother see what a fool he was making of himself.

"Peter is our friend, Morgan. He could have stolen from us any time if that had been his plan. Besides, you know as well as I that any of us would have given him the shirt off our back had he need of it." Morgan did know it, but just knowing she was right infuriated him all the more. Morgan couldn't deal with the fact that his sister would not support him and, in fact, aligned her loyalty to someone Morgan now considered the enemy. His face turned red and he couldn't utter a word. Peter expected him to blow up with rage; instead, Morgan stomped out of the cell block.

Mary and Peter relaxed somewhat, and both sighed together. Their unified response made them laugh a little. It felt good. Mary put her arms around Peter and hugged him tightly.

"Don't worry, Peter," she said, not letting go. "I'll do everything I can for you." For a moment there was quiet. They found calm in each other's arms.

The calm, however, was broken by Morgan's angry voice summoning Mary. "Sister, we are leaving! Come along!"

"I'll be back later," she said, not wanting to leave. "There is something I must tell you when we are truly alone."

"Can't you tell me now?" asked Peter with some puzzlement. "What if your father won't let you come back again?"

"He can't stop me! I'll tell them I must bring you food and supplies, if they ask."

"One thing before you go, Mary. Until this trouble blows over, please, for me, be very careful. I don't want any harm coming to you."

"You needn't worry about that, Peter. After the robbery, Father hired a bodyguard for me, as well as a new one for Morgan."

"Very well. You'd better go now," Peter said, resigned.

Sheriff Beeker returned to the cell area and locked the heavy iron door that kept Peter a prisoner. He gave Peter a dirty look, but said nothing. Mary paused at the cell block entrance to give Peter a final reassuring smile. She couldn't help thinking that maybe she was trying to reassure herself. She could feel tears coming, so she didn't linger. Peter needed to see her be strong now. There would be time for tears later.

Many days passed before Peter saw Mary again, but she came as soon as she could. Her family had made it most difficult for her because she insisted on supporting Peter. Morgan had been especially adamant about preventing her visits to the jail, but Mary would not be controlled.

When she was finally able to return to the jail alone, she had more to tell Peter than just the secret she mentioned to him the last time they were together. Beeker was always an ugly sight, constantly plaguing Peter's day. As he opened the cell block door, Peter could only imagine what harassment he was in for this time. Much to his surprise, however, Beeker didn't say a word. Instead, he simply admitted Mary.

They both waited until the sheriff had left them alone before speaking. As soon as the cell block door closed, Peter embraced Mary. "Oh, it's so good to see you. It's been weeks."

"I know, Peter, I'm sorry. Everyone tried to keep me from seeing you. I think you've already been tried and found guilty in most people's minds."

"No matter, you're here now." Peter led Mary to the bunk against the far wall of the cell and they both sat. "Now, what is this big secret you couldn't tell me before?" he asked anxiously. "I've been wondering about it since you mentioned it."

Mary carefully looked around, making sure they were alone.

"First let me tell you what happened to me, Peter. One night, just after Bates was killed, a man was boasting that Bates paid him a lot of money to kill both you and me. He had been drinking and was getting out of hand, so the tavern keeper sent for the sheriff. When Beeker tried to apprehend him, the man drew a gun, but the sheriff shot him dead first."

Peter stood up and walked to the front of the cell. He grasped the bars and looked toward the cell block door in amazement. "Beeker didn't say a word to me about it."

"Of course not, Peter. Morgan has paid dearly to keep it quiet. He still believes you killed Bates, trying to rob our parents."

"Well, I guess I'm the only one who knows I'm innocent."

"Nonsense, Peter, I know you're innocent!" Mary said, joining him at his side.

"Of course you do, Mary, but you're in love with me. It won't stand up as evidence in court."

"I'm being serious, Peter, I know you didn't shoot Bates," Mary lowered her voice, ". . . because I did."

Peter didn't say anything. He just looked at Mary trying to understand what she was saying to him. *Surely she can't be serious,* he thought.

"I know it's hard to believe," she continued, "but Charlie Bates was going to kill my parents!" With that,

Mary broke down and sobbed. Peter laid her head on his shoulder, still dazed at what she was telling him.

"How did you know we were there?"

"I thought mother and father had gone home from the dance, and I was on my way to tell them I was going to visit you and not to worry," Mary said between sobs. "When I arrived at their house, I saw a man loading their belongings into your carriage. I knew you couldn't be a part of such a thing, but I had to find out what was happening, so I came in through the servants' door and listened."

Peter remembered the sound he had heard that night. It was Mary, and she had been there almost the entire time. Peter stroked her hair and tried to comfort her as she continued.

"I heard Bates threaten you, ranting about telling the newspaper of your Mormon past, so I knew you weren't involved. Then I heard my parents' carriage. I didn't know what to do, but I couldn't let you or my parents be hurt. I went to my father's study and took one of his guns, then climbed the servants' stairs at the back of the house." Peter's eyes widened when he remembered the missing gun. "Peter, I was above you in the dark on the back side of the stairs. I shot Charlie Bates!"

"Why, Mary, why didn't you just come forward? Your father is the most powerful judge in Saint Louis. Besides, you shot in defense of your parents."

"I panicked, Peter; I didn't know what to do. I was afraid that if I came forward the secrets Bates held over you would come out . . . . I don't know, perhaps I just wasn't thinking."

"It sounds like pretty good thinking to me," mused Peter as he tightened his arms around her. Mary dried her eyes and sat up, looking at his astounded expression. "Don't worry, Peter, I have decided to tell the truth. I can't let you be blamed for this."

It took Peter only a moment to realize what Mary was saying. "No, Mary, you can't say a word. Promise me you won't say anything! I'll think of some way to get out of this mess—I always do—but I don't want you involved."

Mary couldn't see what possibilities Peter might have, but he insisted, and she promised not to say anything, at least for a while. They held each other and talked of better times until Mary had to leave.

From that point on, Mary visited Peter daily. She brought him food and kept him informed of the news from the outside. It was lucky for Peter that the few judges Saint Louis had were all overwhelmed with their current case loads. The circuit judge had, therefore, been assigned the case on a priority basis, but was, at present, out of town. They knew it was only a matter of time, however, before the circuit judge would complete his rounds of outlying settlements and return to preside over Peter's case. The fact that Addison was the presiding judge for Saint Louis and couldn't rule on his own case was buying them time.

Peter sat in his cell waiting for the only good thing in his day—his visit from Mary. *She usually comes before now,* Peter thought to himself. He tried to read a little to pass the time while he waited. Still she didn't come. As the darkness began to creep into the cell block, Peter knew she wouldn't be coming, and he figured something was wrong. The sound of the jailer's keys clanking together, opening the cell block door, lifted his spirits in anticipation of perhaps seeing Mary after all. He went to the door of his cell and waited. Peter wasn't prepared for what happened next.

The door to the cell block opened, but Mary didn't enter. Neither, for that matter, did the jailer. The door stood open for a moment, Peter's eyes fixed on the sight.

Nothing moved, no sound was heard. Peter began to feel fear growing inside him, and well it should, as Morgan Cain entered the room.

At first Morgan didn't say a word. He simply walked into the cell area and stopped. Peter almost didn't recognize him. Morgan's face was contorted with rage, yet he controlled it. His eyes were ablaze with hate, yet it didn't consume him. His hand clutched a book so tightly, it buckled under the force.

Neither man moved. Morgan made no attempt to enter the cell as he had the last time he had come to visit. Peter felt compelled to back away from the bars, but just couldn't find it in him to do so. There was no mistaking it this time. Whatever it was that brought Morgan to the jail, the once-strong friendship between the two was gone. Hate now filled that void for Morgan.

Peter couldn't bear the silence any longer. The tension was beginning to take its toll on him. "I wasn't expecting you, Morgan," Peter managed. "It's good to see you."

"Good to see me?" Morgan said through his teeth in a tone subdued, but powerful. "You . . . lying . . . thieving . . . murdering . . . hypocrite!" hissed Morgan. "It was you all along. There is a Mormon Plague and you are both the Mormon and the plague!" Morgan raised his arm and hurled the book he had been holding at Peter. Instinctively, Peter ducked as the book crashed against the bars and fell to the ground. It came to rest binding side up and Peter looked down to see what it was. A helpless, sinking feeling came over him as he read the words *The Book of Mormon* on the cover and recognized it as his own personal copy.

"Where did you get that book?" Peter asked.

"What difference does it make, Van Cleef? We know it's yours and now the truth is out. We don't need any more evidence to convict you."

Peter moved from the bars and sat on his bunk resting his head in his hands. "Did you really stoop so low that you, my friend, would go to my house and search my personal belongings?"

Morgan walked over to the book lying on the floor and kicked it into the cell. It slid across the floor and stopped at Peter's feet. "You'll want this back, I'm sure. No casting pearls before swine, right, Peter?" jeered Morgan. "For your information, I was looking for something to help you. I wanted to believe you didn't do it. Mary was so sure you were innocent. You had us all wondering there for awhile, but not anymore. The word is out. Everybody knows."

Now it was Morgan's turn at the cell door, face against the bars. He never once raised his voice, and that scared Peter. There was a certain tone of finality in his voice, and he was in control.

"There has even been talk of mob violence against you, Peter, but I want you to know that as your 'friend,' I will do my best to keep you safe so you can hang lawfully." With that, Morgan turned and walked briskly from the cell, slamming the iron door. It echoed loudly, then all was silent. When Morgan closed the cell block door behind him, Peter was alone. It was night, and the room was in total darkness. As before, it would be days before Peter would have another visitor.

One morning just before dawn, Peter was awakened by the sound of a commotion coming from the front of the jail. He scrambled to his feet and made it to the front of the cell about the time the cell block door was opening. Peter could hear a male voice, noticeably agitated; but it wasn't Sheriff Beeker. Mary and a deputy entered the cell block, both trying to get through the door at the same time. Mary pushed the deputy out of her way and continued into the cell area. She was trying hard to keep her composure, though obviously upset about something.

"Glad to see yer up, Van Cleef," the deputy growled. "Yer girlfriend here dragged me out of my bunk fer this. It better be good!" Peter could only imagine what was wrong now, but he knew from the way Mary was acting that it must be serious. She was very impatient as the deputy opened the cell door, allowing her admittance. The deputy lingered, waiting to see what this was all about. Mary, however, wasn't going to put up with this behavior. She wheeled around and ordered the deputy out of the cell area. In Saint Louis in 1847, if a Cain said, "Jump," you jumped! The law was no exception. Mary's colorful behavior surprised Peter, her usual demeanor being somewhat soft-spoken. His curiosity was greater than his fear at this point, but Mary said nothing until they were alone.

"Peter, the combined mobs of Missouri and Illinois have begun massing to follow your people across the wilderness and finish them for good!"

"How do you know this?"

"It's common knowledge. The paper is calling for volunteers. That's why Sheriff Beeker isn't here." Peter sat down on the hard wooden bunk, a feeling of helplessness overtaking him. Mary sat next to him and took his hands in hers. "That's not the worst of it, Peter. The mobs are clamoring for your death first!"

"It may be too late for me, but there is still a chance for my people if I could just warn them," Peter said, shaking his head.

"I'll warn them," Mary offered.

"It's not your fight," said Peter, half wishing it were.

"Well, it is mine!" growled a voice behind them.

In startled surprise, both Peter and Mary looked up to see Porter Rockwell at the jail window.

"Porter, am I glad to see you!" Peter exclaimed, jumping to his feet.

"It's a mixed blessing, boy. I've got some bad news of my own. But first we're gonna get you out of here."

Simon's head popped up into view next to Rockwell. "I found him Peter, I brought him back like I said I would."

Peter smiled at the youth. "You did good Simon, real good!"

"Ma'am," Rockwell said to Mary.

"Hello, Mr. Rockwell," Mary returned warmly. "It's truly a pleasure to see you again."

"Yes'm. Thank you for lookin' after Peter here. He looks like he's mostly patched and back to gettin' hisself in tight spots again." Mary smiled at Rockwell's ability to be light-hearted even in such tough situations. She didn't know it was a trait Rockwell had respected and learned from the Prophet Joseph Smith. What she did know was that now, somehow, everything was going to be all right.

"We better git before we're noticed," Rockwell said, "but we'll be back to spring ya tonight."

As they took their leave, Peter called after Rockwell. "Porter, wait. How are you going to get me out of here?"

"We'll take advantage of all the confusion being caused by this Mormon witch hunt; you'll know what to do." Rockwell and Simon withdrew from the jail. "Just be sharp," Rockwell instructed as they left.

Mary hugged Peter with a feeling of relief. "You must go far away, Peter. Find your people," she said. "I'll miss you, but I know it's for the best." Peter turned and looked out the barred window on a city gone crazy with hate of a people. Mary, standing behind the man she loved, rested her head on his back. "How will Mr. Rockwell get you out of here?" she asked softly.

"He'll think of something," Peter said as a broad smile overtook his face. "He'll think of something!"

Darkness fell slowly over Saint Louis, more slowly than it ever had before. Peter tried to sleep for a while, but couldn't. Every time he closed his eyes, he thought he heard something. Time passed, and the night seemed endless. But the later it became, the easier it was to ignore any noise, and Peter found he was now fighting off sleep.

In the front of the jail, the deputy sat dealing cards to himself to pass the time away. He paused, looking up, thinking he heard voices. Everyone in Saint Louis knew Peter was in jail, and the situation warranted caution on the part of the sheriff and his deputies. They knew they had to keep Peter safe, at least until he went to trial. The deputy sat very still and listened. "Must have been a mouse," he assured himself when all seemed quiet again. He went back to dealing his cards, but was immediately interrupted again by the sound. "Here we go again," he muttered to himself.

This time the deputy put down his deck and went to the window of the jail. The sight before him made his heart skip a beat, and he reached instinctively for his sidearm. The deputy's face glowed from the reflection of the fire of torches being held by a large mob that was assembling outside the jail.

"We want Van Cleef," came a voice in the crowd and the others followed with similar demands.

"Don't be a fool, deputy," came another. "We know Beeker isn't there, and if you don't give us the Mormon filth, we'll burn down the jail!"

The deputy stepped back from the window and locked the front door to the jail. "You know I can't turn the prisoner over to you," he yelled out. "I don't care how the maggot dies, but I do care what Beeker would do to me if I let him go."

"You best be worried about what we're gonna do to you! Hangin's too good for that Mormon dog, but if you won't give him to us, we'll settle for a baptism by fire."

In the back of the jail, Peter heard nothing and his head bobbed as he once again drifted off to sleep. The crack of gunfire and loud voices brought him quickly back to full alertness. He scrambled to his feet and started for the window, only to jump back as a flaming torch screamed through the bars, landing on the bunk. Immediately the bedclothes erupted into a wall of flames, and the wooden frame quickly followed. As the cell filled with smoke and flames, Peter grabbed his water cup and began rapping it against the bars of the cell to attract the attention of the guard.

"This is the plan?" Peter said aloud, dragging the cup faster over the bars. The other prisoners now in the jail were the town drunk and other assorted riff-raff. They were yelling for the guard in between coughing and choking. Peter yelled at his cell mate to go to the window of the jail and breathe through the bars.

"Great plan, Porter. They're not going to have to hang me!"

In what seemed like forever, the cell block door finally flew open, and the deputy quickly made his way from cell to cell, unlocking the doors.

"It's a mob, Van Cleef," shouted the deputy. "They want yer Mormon hide, and seems they ain't takin' 'no' fer an answer. The entire building is on fire!" A new fear gripped Peter. He hadn't expected a mob. He expected Rockwell and Simon. He had seen what anti-Mormon mobs did to their victims, and it wasn't pretty. This, after all, was the way the Prophet Joseph had died. Peter knew that even if he did survive the mob attack, which wasn't likely, there wouldn't be a lot left to stand trial, or for Porter to rescue, for that matter.

The town drunk ran out of his cell past the guard, but when Peter tried to make his exit, he could see the deputy with his gun in hand and leveled at him.

"Just don't try to escape," the guard warned. "Yer still my prisoner. You could fry for all I care, but that might really anger the mob. They got hangin' on their minds." Both men left the burning cell block choking and coughing. They didn't have time to get outside before the front door of the jail, ablaze from the mob's handiwork, exploded into a million glowing embers as one of the mob rode his horse through it and into the jail.

Through the smoke, all Peter could see were moving images. Confusion was everywhere, and he caught himself remembering Nauvoo and the night they were driven out. There was shouting and the roar of the fire all around them; more gunshots and more fire. The rider made every effort to overtake Peter and the jailer, who began heading in the opposite direction. Their efforts were futile however, since the rider was more or less on top of them already, and there really wasn't anywhere to run. The deputy turned his pistol on the mounted intruder with full intent to use its deadly force, but before he even had it raised, the rider shot the revolver from the deputy's hand. Peter was amazed at the accuracy of the shooter. He knew only one person who could shoot like that.

"Could it be . . .?" In the burnt orange light of the jailhouse flames, Peter strained to see the man on the huge horse. Even with the painted face, there was no mistaking the hair and beard, and Peter recognized the face of his friend and deliverer. Moments later, Rockwell hit Peter with the butt of his gun and everything went black.

It was quiet when Peter regained consciousness. It was also very bright. The last thing he remembered was Rockwell, the jail, and the fire.

That was last night, Peter thought. *At least it was night. Just when, I couldn't be sure.* In fact, Peter wasn't sure of a few other things, like, was it really Rockwell he

had seen on that horse and, if so, why did his friend club him? One thing he did know—he wasn't dead, although the pain in his head made him wish he were. Peter lay still and tried to assess his situation. In the distance he heard a terrible noise, something like an animal makes when it's in pain. He listened to the noise and could tell it was getting louder, heading in his direction. Peter's confusion vanished in an instant as he realized the dreadful noise was, in actuality, Rockwell singing "Oh Susannah." He was amused by Rockwell's attempts at singing and the lightness in his soul. He laughed out loud as Porter approached.

". . . My hun's so cute, her name is Beth. Susannah don't you cry," sang Rockwell loudly with spirit.

"That's, 'The sun's so hot I froze to death, Susannah, don't you cry'," Peter said, shaking his head with a smile.

"Hun, sun, what's the difference?" Rockwell said, obviously pleased to see his young friend on his feet. "Besides, it's just an old song." Peter and Rockwell greeted each other with a bear hug embrace, Rockwell lifting Peter off the ground.

"If you don't put me down, I'll recommend you to sing in the ward choir," Peter groaned. Rockwell laughed and lowered Peter back to earth.

"Glad to see that little bump on your head hasn't affected your sense of humor." Peter rubbed the area of his head that had been introduced, uninvited, to Rockwell's gun.

"What kind of a plan was that anyway, Porter? First you burn the jail down. That could have killed me. Then you pistol whip me. That nearly did kill me!" Porter Rockwell was not an educated man when it came to book smarts, but it didn't take a genius to tell that Peter was a little sore, both literally and figuratively.

"It worked, didn't it?" Rockwell said, not letting Peter's ingratitude ruin his jovial mood. "Yer free ain't ya?" Peter tried to be angry with Rockwell, but couldn't. "Besides," Rockwell continued, "we had to convince that deputy we were the real thing and that a hangin' would be the next order of business. This way, they won't come lookin' fer us or you 'cause they'll think yer already dead." Rockwell again lifted Peter into the air, but this time dropped him over his shoulder like a sack of potatoes. "All this rescuin' has made me hungry, and since yer so fragile, I'll take ya to the food," Rockwell said, walking toward Simon, who was busy making breakfast for the trio. "My hun's so cute, her name is Beth. Susannah, don't you cry."

"The sun's so hot." Peter said, hanging over Rockwell's shoulder. "And yes, I am free. Thank you, Porter!"

After breakfast, the three men broke camp and cleared away any trace of their ever having been there in the first place. They mounted their horses and prepared to leave.

"What's our next move?" Peter asked Rockwell. He knew Porter had things well-figured out in advance, and all they needed to do was listen to him and they would be all right. Rockwell rode his horse up next to Simon's and put his large hand on the boy's shoulder.

"Simon, before you go back to yer kin, I need to ask one more favor of you, boy," Porter said. Simon didn't respond. There was no need. He would do anything for Rockwell. "I want you to go to Mary Ellen Moore and tell her Peter is all right and not to worry. She is a fine lady," he continued, looking at Peter, "and we owe her that peace of mind."

Simon nodded his head and said, "Consider it done, Mr. Rockwell." After they exchanged goodbyes, Simon galloped off to carry out his instructions, leaving Peter and Rockwell to themselves.

"Now I've got some bad news for you, Peter," Rockwell said. Peter had forgotten that Rockwell had mentioned bad news at the jail the night before the breakout. So much had happened since, it was easy for him to let it slip from his memory. Rockwell gently kicked his horse, starting the massive beast walking. Peter followed. He waited for Rockwell to tell him this bad news, but the words weren't coming easy. The lightness in Rockwell's countenance was gone.

"We've come through a lot, you and me," Rockwell began. "We've seen good times and bad together. We've laughed some even. Lately it seems like all we've done is run from those who want to see the Mormons dead or fight the ones we cain't run from."

Peter listened intently. There was something in Rockwell's voice, something about the delivery of his words that Peter had never heard before. It was chilling, and he dared not make a sound. As Rockwell continued, Peter knew what he would hear would not be pleasant.

"The trek across the wilderness took its toll on our people. We dern near lost Brigham to the fever before we got to our promised land, the Salt Lake Valley. Lots of folks died on the way. The stronger men fared a bit better, but we still lost 'em. The ones that made it to the valley are doin' pretty good now. What you prob'ly don't know, Peter, is that before we even left our winter encampment to go west, a large body of men numbering some five hundred left to go south and fight fer their country agin' the Mexicans."

Rockwell was right. Peter hadn't heard anything about Mormons fighting in the Mexican war, but he wasn't getting the message Rockwell was building up to. Still, he could feel the anxiety in his friend and he knew the worst was yet to come.

"On my way back to Saint Louis, me and Simon stopped at Fort Bridger fer supplies. There we met an army courier on his way East with news of the war effort in the West. He told us the Mormon Battalion had marched from Pueblo, Colorado into the desert. They ain't been heard from agin, and the army considers them lost to the desert. That means they died out there, boy . . . all of 'em."

Rockwell stopped his horse and turned to Peter. He paused a moment, surveying his young friend and the impact the news was having on him. Porter also found it difficult recounting the events and needed a moment to gather his strength.

"Five hundred of our men? When will it ever be over?" Peter half whispered. He seemed to be in a daze, numb from the unrelenting pain his life was filled with. "I can't take it any more, Porter!" he said, slumping forward in his saddle.

"Look at me, boy!" Rockwell said softly, but firmly. "Yer gonna have ta be strong fer a little while longer . . ." Peter brought himself upright and faced Rockwell, not wanting to hear anything else the big man might have to say, but he trusted Rockwell completely, and if his friend thought Peter needed to hear more, then he would listen.

". . . Yer gonna have ta be strong, Peter, 'cause Jedediah was with the Mormon Battalion and therefore among the men who died in the desert." Rockwell pulled something from his rifle scabbard and tossed it to Peter. It was a U.S. Army sabre, well-worn and dirty. "They told me that sword belonged to one Captain Jedediah Cutler, Mormon Battalion. His name is on the blade. It was retrieved after a army patrol fought it out with a bunch of cut-throat Comancheros that had been raidin' settlements. The army thinks the Comancheros had somethin' ta do with the demise of the Battalion. It's all that's left. I figgered you'd want to give it to Miss Celia."

For a moment, Rockwell's words burned in Peter's head, spreading throughout his body. Then he seemed to feel empty, the words echoing in a vast hollowness, a place where such things belonged. Peter could tell he was feeling two entirely different emotions. The first was the remorse of losing someone so close to his life, someone he truly loved as a brother. The other was an emotion he shouldn't have felt, but it was there nonetheless, and it was for Celia, the girl he loved. If Jed had really died in the desert, then Peter wouldn't have to compete for Celia. Moreover, the pressing question was, now that Jed wasn't in the Salt Lake Valley with the rest of the Saints, who was looking after Celia?

Rockwell let Peter work out his feelings in silence. He knew if Peter had anything to say, he would do so in his own time. Peter's thoughts kept jumping back and forth from Celia to Jed. He remembered their youth and the good times they shared. Finally he lifted his head and spoke. "Are you sure?"

Rockwell studied Peter before he answered. "Yeah, I'm sure. Least ways, sure as anybody can be—gettin' his news secondhand. I tried to cross that desert. Couldn't make it. Besides, the sword is Jed's. His name is on it. I believe the news."

"Is it possible that the Battalion became lost or perhaps got captured by the Mexican soldiers? Maybe they never made it to the desert."

"I suppose anything is possible, Peter, but the evidence stacks again' that bein' the case. It's never easy when somebody close to you dies, but it ain't gonna do ya no good to pretend it didn't happen."

Peter rolled over the sabre in his hands, studying it carefully. He thought about everything Rockwell had told him and he knew Porter must be right. *Jed would never be so irresponsible as to loose his sabre. Something or someone must have taken it.* His mind's eye once again caught the image of Celia. It was clear what he must do.

As if Rockwell could read Peter's mind, he nudged his horse in next that of his young friend's. Rockwell put his big hand on Peter's shoulder. "Miss Celia is gonna need yer help fer awhile. Jedediah would have done the same fer you if he were in yer place."

"Very well then," Peter said drawing in a large breath. "We're needed in the promised valley."

Rockwell felt the energy returning to Peter and knew he would be all right. They both positioned themselves squarely in their saddles and with firm kicks to their mounts, loped off at a lively gait toward a future neither one could imagine.

9

On To Tucson!

One day's march from Santa Fe, the Mormon Battalion found itself in a featureless desert of baked clay and rocks too hot to touch. By day, the only thing beautiful here was the sapphire sky, but no one could bear to look up at it because of the blazing sun. The long evenings were beautiful with their unending succession of perfect sunsets. Actually, it was more that the evenings felt beautiful due to the coolness accompanying them. That feeling of relief had to be cherished though, since it quickly gave way to apprehension of the cold night under the awesome display of moon and stars.

Back home in Nauvoo, the world and the sky over it were closed in by trees and hills. They seemed smaller, more manageable, as though they could be managed like a part of a home—like furniture or wallpaper. But out here, the land and sky were huge, endless, and overwhelmingly powerful. Indeed, here, a man controlled nothing except himself. These men knew that, without the even greater power of God on their side, they could accomplish nothing. That was the benefit of trying to live in this land, looked down on by this sky. It taught them to be united with God.

Jed lay in his blankets and looked up at the stars. *Celia is under this,* he thought. *She is pioneering the land, not even knowing the perils that move across her path, like an ant trying to cross a road.* He breathed in the cold, clear air. *We have to be together again. We have to have children and make a new home. When we do that, we will be as powerful as this sky.*

As he had once before, Jed pictured Celia in his mind and sent his spirit, his thoughts, and his desires across the vastness on the wings of mighty prayer. It was almost as if he could feel her presence, smell her hair. Sitting at a campfire on the Wyoming plains, Celia kissed her hand and blew the kiss to the wind. "Find my love," she instructed. Jed, touching his cheek, imagined her kissing him tenderly and, for just a moment, the miles between them vanished.

Every man fussed and labored to create the best possible sleeping spot, racing each other for the choice level areas and sandy textures. If a man could not sleep, he could not rise at first light. If he could not rise and work his legs, he could not march. If he could not march (and march twenty miles under the twin enemies of sun and pack before the next delightful sunset), he would die.

For these good Mormon men, it was no longer a matter of earning cash for their families to move west or of showing patriotism. Now it was surviving an alkali mouth and deep purple grooves in the shoulders from pack straps and pain that shrieked with every movement. It was cramps in the calves and hot sand in ragged shoes.

Jed did not think of Colonel Price or the Mexican War or even the Church and the gospel. He would relax and stride out with a lanky pace that ate up the miles and let his mind take him to a fantasy of Celia, reliving every moment they had spent together, from childhood on. He edited Peter Van Cleef out of his fantasies, but other than that, his thoughts of Celia were with him every moment . . . every sight, sound, touch, smell, and taste. Drawn back to reality, Jed heard heavy breathing and realized it was the men behind him trying to keep up. He had translated his joy of Celia into longer and faster strides, all the while smiling at the ground in front of him.

Jed was not a good officer during this time. He was just trying to get there like everybody else. He did not notice the longing looks many of his men gave to a caravan of pack mules, led by a group of fur trappers and traders that crossed the battalion's path, camping nearby. That evening, the trappers paid a visit to the battalion. After sharing food and tall tales with the soldiers, talk shifted to the journeys being undertaken by each group. "We are taking trade goods north to a new settlement we heard would be in the valley of the Great Salt Lake," announced a rugged soul, clad entirely in buckskins. Those battalion men within earshot held their breath at the news. "This new place is due north of us, up the trail with the Old Spanish Steps cut into the mountainside by the exploring priests, Escalante and Dominguez."

"Why go there?" asked Broderick. "I would think California would be the place to trade your goods."

"It's not nearly as far to the valley of the Salt Lake as it is to California," answered another man. He was a black man, obviously a free man, but he still bore the scars of slavery from shackles he once wore. "Some crazy white men were planning to build a town there in a marshy dead valley discovered by Jedediah Smith and the way we got it figgered, they are going to need everything we can carry."

Exhausted or not, many men lingered, talking to the trappers in depth about their plans. Jed tried to appear interested in the conversation, but his mind was elsewhere. He was also fighting sleep. He awoke fully alert when he heard Jamie asking the visitors when they would leave and how long it would take them to arrive in the Great Salt Lake Valley.

Late that night, as the moon hung high and the knifing cold was at its worst, Jed sat wrapped in a blanket by the coals of a dying fire. He saw the shape of a man slipping silently past him, loaded with pack and musket.

"Where are you going, Jamie?" asked Jed. The dark figure shuffled over to his captain.

"I couldn't sleep. I thought I'd take a walk." Jamie said quietly, unable to meet Jed's eye.

"Afraid someone would steal your pack and musket while you were gone?"

"A man can get a breath of air if he likes, can't he? That's not desertin'!" Jamie announced, betraying his own thoughts. At once, the responsibility of leadership returned to "Captain Cutler," and he also felt a friend's compassion for Jamie. He knew what his lieutenant was feeling because he felt the same way.

"There's no place to desert to, is there?" noted Jed.

The Scotsman slumped against the rocks next to Jed. There was no use in pretending any longer and Jamie confessed his dark thoughts to his one true friend, not his commanding officer.

"I can't stand this marchin' any longer, Jed. I never knew it'd be like this. We don't eat. Water's bad. And the sun—I never seen so much of it with no shadow at all," moaned Jamie. He covered his face with his hands and rocked his head back and forth.

"We'll be in California soon. Then you can see your Jerusha all you want."

"I'll go crazy before that," came the muffled response from Jamie's covered mouth. It was as if he was trying to hide with no intention of coming out from behind the camouflage provided by his hands.

"You'll have plenty of company when you do, Jamie," Jed joked, putting his big arm around Jamie's shoulder.

"What difference would it make if I left?" Jamie questioned, lowering his hand from his face.

The question was strangely familiar. Maybe all the men had it pass through their minds at one time or another. Jed had taken it a step further. "Where would you go?"

"Well, I'd try to find our people," Jamie began, imagining it in his mind. "I'll bet they have need of us." So far, he was right on course in his thought process, but Jed wondered if he had really thought it through.

"What would you say when you reached them?" Jed queried. "'I broke my word; I left my brothers in the desert?' Do you think they'd be proud of you for that? Would that be helping anybody?"

Jamie stopped shaking his head. Jed could tell he had struck a resonant chord.

Jamie thought about Jed's question for a moment before speaking. "I'm sorry, Jed, I get lost. I get lonely."

"Jamie, I get lost too. I get lonely," Jed acknowledged, not looking for apologies, "but . . . nothing should shake us. Nothing. Ever!" Jamie began to understand what Jed already knew. They were Latter-day Saints and indeed, the whole world was watching. It wouldn't be just another desertion if he, or any of them, left. It would be something else the world could use against the Mormons.

Besides, Jamie thought, *because we are Latter-day Saints, we can draw upon that strength to see us through.* Exhausted but content, the two friends slept better that night than they had in months.

Their lives were now in the hands of Charbonneau. Jamie was positively cheerful toward Jed as they tramped along and would often meet his eye, smiling, even though the men drank the last of their water and ate cactus pulp. Charbonneau not only scouted ahead but zigzagged back and forth to the flanks for miles on his bedraggled horse. The by-now-unsympathetic and unsentimental Broderick had told Charbonneau to find water or not come back to the column.

There came a day when it was drink or die. Poor old Colonel Cooke was the only one on a horse. He barely kept his seat, lying forward over his saddle bow, with Broderick on one side and Jed on the other, leading Cooke's horse and holding his swaying body onto his mount. The third horse, drawn and exhausted, was being led without rider to prolong his usefullness.

For ninety days they had boldly marched forth with every dawn, making their average of twenty miles per day like the Roman legion the colonel wanted them to be. On this day, they began with empty canteens. It was the end of August, and the sun was unrelenting. They had entered a table-level valley bottom, heat waves shimmering over the glistening white clay. For the first time, some of the men had to be helped to keep them from falling out of ranks. Broderick then forbade any rest stops, knowing the battalion would never restart once the men sat down. He had to let the pace slow, however; men were weaving, gasping, and moaning.

The horses lifted their heads, stared and sniffed. Charbonneau seemed to come out of a trance. He stared ahead with his eyes narrowed down to the merest cracks, mouth set, nostrils flaring. At this moment, he was all Indian.

Suddenly, Charbonneau jumped on his horse and brutally goaded it into a gallop out ahead. The column stopped to watch, amazed. The colonel sat up and Broderick mounted. When Charbonneau was a tiny figure, seen as a wavy blob through the heat, he abruptly stopped. He whirled around and headed back toward them. The men squinted in puzzlement.

Almost instantly, there was a rumbling and a thundering as hundreds of shaggy black buffalo erupted into sight, seemingly right out of the solid valley floor. They scattered in all directions with Charbonneau fleeing from the ever-expanding edge of their circumference. When Charbonneau and the buffalo reached the battalion, he reined in and faced the crazed animals, calling out in wild Indian cries. The buffalo parted and went around both sides of the column of mesmerized soldiers, who were perfectly agreeable to let them pass.

"Sink hole!" yelled Charbonneau and headed his horse back out to the front. Colonel Cooke and Major Broderick cantered forward and the men began to run. They could not run far, but they stumbled and shambled as fast as they could until a giant crater, perhaps three hundred yards across, became visible in front of them. They drew up at the edge and saw a pond of muddy water at the bottom. The smell of buffalo dung was intense.

Five hundred men were silent and motionless for a full minute until Charbonneau slid down the side and plopped into the water. Every eye was on him as he took off his stocking cap and opened his canteen. He scooped up a capful of water and strained it into his canteen. He poured from canteen into cap and strained it again, and again. Finally, he looked into his canteen, laughed a maniacal laugh and shouted at the top of his lungs, "Vive la Battalion Mormon!" and drank the water. Then he looked up at the men lining the edge of the sink hole and laughed again, but the men gave no response. He belched outrageously and still got no reaction.

Broderick cried out in a tortured hoarse croak, "Get down there and do like Charbonneau!" Nobody stirred.

The colonel's eyes and mouth kept opening and closing but he made no sound or motion. Broderick was shoving men over the edge and shrieking, "Get down there! Do it!" but the men he pushed just slid down and stopped at the water's edge.

Nobody noticed Jed raise his head from a silent prayer, but everybody watched him slide very deliberately down into the water. Cap in one hand, canteen in the other, he swept his gaze over the group, closed his eyes, and spoke. "Having been commissioned of Jesus Christ and by the power of the priesthood which I hold, I bless this water . . ." Jed hesitated, thinking, then continued. " . . . to the souls of all those who partake of it, that they might live to serve Thee and get home safe to their families. Amen."

"Amen," said Jamie and started down.

"Amen," mumbled everyone else, including John Broderick, and stepped down gingerly, trying not to add more dirt to the water.

One after another, the men repeated the procedure shown to them by Charbonneau, until all had drunk the filthy water that saved their lives.

The mixed blessing of hindsight manifested itself to every man in the battalion. It became painfully evident to the soldiers sitting around the sink hole that even though their bellies were full of water, they were barren of food. "We should have shot some of those buffalo," they castigated each other. "Next time, if we live to see a next time, we shall have our wits about us."

Colonel Cooke and Major Broderick were not concerned, however, because Charbonneau told them that Tucson was beyond the ridgeline, now visible on the horizon. After a sharp fight, they would replenish both food and water in the town, proclaimed the officers, not noticing the horrified looks underneath the dirt caked on their faces of their men.

The battalion spent that night hidden in the arroyos on their side of the rounded ridge line that separated them from Tucson. Colonel Cooke ordered Major Broderick to take Charbonneau and one other man he trusted most and reconnoitre. He gave the major charge of the three horses for use on the mission. Broderick went straight to Jed and asked him to come on the patrol. Jed agreed instantly.

Charbonneau helped them disguise their uniforms with hide vests and other items he had gotten from the Comancheros. They had to wear their uniforms, though, or be shot as spies if caught.

Under the midnight blaze of stars, they led their horses up a steep-sided wash that took them near the town, a whitewashed adobe village that gleamed in the silver light. Jed, Broderick, and Charbonneau left the horses tied and munching on a little sparse grass in the stream bed and belly crawled up to the adobe wall surrounding the town. They slunk along the wall, staying in its moon shadow, disturbing not a pebble or a twig with their gently searching feet.

The wall was the height of a standing man and it connected the perimeter buildings. There were heavy beam gates at each of the cardinal directions, closed and barred at night. Dominating the low tile roofs was the bell tower of the mission church situated in the center of the town. There was also a bare flag pole near the church, rising from what was probably the barracks of the garrison, on the other end of a central plaza.

When the men realized they had returned to their starting point on the wall, they looked at each other, puzzled. Broderick whispered, "No sentries." Jed nodded. Charbonneau shrugged.

Jed motioned with his chin as if to say, "We have to go over the wall and get inside." Broderick gulped and nodded. Vaulting the wall with a single leaping foothold was easy enough. They landed silently inside, instantly hunkering down to listen. Nothing moved. As they trotted from shadow to shadow, wall to wall, a dog barked, other dogs soon taking up the call. The men froze and waited patiently. The dogs settled down without anyone moving inside the houses or showing a light.

Advancing slowly, they came to the central plaza. They discovered that the church bordered one side of the plaza and a long, low, colonnaded barracks lined the other with the flagstaff rising before a heavily-linteled double door. But there were no sentries and no lights anywhere in the barracks to indicate a guardhouse. Where was the garrison?

The two Americans and their guide returned to their horses in the wash. When they settled down and the warmth of their exercise left them, they began to shiver with the aching cold of the desert night.

"What do you think?" whispered the major.

"I think we have to stay here until dawn and see if we can find out what happened to the garrison," answered Jed, trying not to cough. Broderick nodded reluctantly. Charbonneau was already taking the saddle off his horse. The two men watched as he removed the sweat-stiff saddle blanket and bent it around himself.

"Remember in the Bible when Caleb and Joshua spied out the land of Canaan? Did they depend on steaming horse apples to keep them from freezing?" wondered Major Broderick as he followed Charbonneau's lead. Jed likewise did as his comrades, and they all picked out a place to sleep, near, but not under, their horses.

"Whatever they did, we can do," yawned Jed as he sunk down and closed his eyes. He was smelling Celia's lilac perfume, not horse sweat.

Jed leapt up with a start when he realized the sun was bright on his eyelids. He looked over at his companion and gently shook him. Major Broderick similarly jumped up with a start. Charbonneau was gone from the camp. The two men climbed up to the edge of the wash and peeked over. Charbonneau lay flat, eyes fixed on the distant town. "Dat's good you come see, Major!" he said, with a chuckle.

Smoke came from chimneys in the town and they could hear the sounds of people and animals. As they watched, the gates of the town were opened by Mexican men in white cotton clothes and straw sombreros. When the gates moved, the church bells began to ring, and the two American soldiers heard the result of what Charbonneau had been watching so intently. The sounds of a babbling crowd grew louder as they gathered in the plaza, hidden inside the walls.

Jed pulled at Broderick's arm and pointed to a dust cloud emerging from between two barren, yellow hills. Now visible on the valley floor, crawling toward the town, was a dark line with many moving legs, already wavering in the heat haze that began as soon as the sun had cleared the horizon.

Jed and the major shaded and strained their eyes as they watched this column approach the town. It resolved itself into a double file of Mexican soldiers, dark faces with black mustaches or beards, shaded by black shakos with red plumes. They wore blue coatees with white crossbelts, dirty white trousers, and broken shoes—now gray, once black—with the dye rubbed out by the desert sand. Each soldier shouldered a flintlock musket with fixed bayonet.

In between the two files of soldiers stumbled a single file of nearly-naked Indians. Their hands were tied behind their backs, and they were roped together with nooses around their necks. They looked blankly at the ground in front of them.

At the end of this procession were some tiny donkeys, burros as the Mexicans called them. Three carried dead Mexican soldiers over their backs. Three more dragged travois made of tree limbs and covered with canvas. On each travois lay a soldier with lolling head and hands clenched in pain, bombarded by the sun.

Leading them all, on the only horse in the column, was the Mexican commander. He sat on his horse with back straight and head up. He gazed straight ahead from under his cocked hat. The right leg, which Jed and Broderick could see, had the trouser leg cut off and the thigh was wrapped in a blood-caked, dirt-covered bandage. The brass epaulets on the squared shoulders proclaimed him a captain. The only sign of his pain was the white teeth under the trim mustache, biting into the lower lip as the horse walked slowly, with stately gait.

After the column passed not a hundred paces from the two men pressing flat against the wall of the arroyo, Broderick whispered to Jed, "How many do you make it?"

"Fifty able bodied," Jed whispered back.

"And we know that's all because they took everybody from the barracks," mused Broderick.

"That's right," agreed Jed, watching the column enter a gate and receive a tumultuous cheer from the unseen folk inside.

"Listen!" hissed Broderick as they strained to make out shouts of individual voices.

They heard, *"Viva Mexico!"* and *"Viva Excellencia!"—"Viva El Capitan . . . Capitan Comaduran!"*

"Did I hear his name to be Captain Comaduran?" asked Broderick.

"Yes. I believe so," replied Jed. "I wonder what kind of Indians those are," he continued, louder now that the cheering had taken over.

"Navajo," said Charbonneau with conviction. "Dis Navajo land. Dey fight Mezzicans plenty."

"I believe we've completed our mission here," announced Broderick, quietly. "We will return to camp and report our findings to Colonel Cooke."

Each man in turn inched his way back over the edge of the wash. After retrieving their horses, they hurried back to where they had started their patrol. They rode into the center of the battalion line of soldiers who had lain under moon and sun since the trio had left them for their reconnaissance. Their return was greeted anxiously by the men. Jed and Major Broderick sat with Charbonneau and Colonel Cooke on the reverse slope of the hill between them and Tucson. The colonel listened with great interest as Major Broderick described the Mexican garrison.

"No more than fifty of the enemy you say?" chortled the old colonel, his pop eyes opened wide. "Then we are assured a success!" He looked up at the waning sun. "We will not attack tonight. We might shoot each other as well as civilians if we attacked in the dark and became confused in the town. No. We will form line of battle at dawn and attack down the hill with the sun behind us."

Jed noticed that Jamie had sat nearby and listened intently to every word of the conference, his wide eyes fixed on Jed. Refocusing his glance beyond Jamie, Jed realized that the will of the colonel was being passed down the line of soldiers, and they were all casting agonized looks at the party of officers in the center.

"Would the colonel entertain a suggestion?" Jed began slowly, raising his head to look frankly into the old man's face. Broderick studied Jed sharply as Jamie silently urged him on.

"Of course, Captain," rumbled the old gentleman, completely unaware of the tense byplay surrounding him.

"I am remembering the carnage at Santa Fe, Sir, the suffering of noncombatants and the considerable losses among our men. It's hard to forget the annihilation of the defenders."

"Yes, the place was stoutly held, and our brave boys overcame the defense to secure a vital objective."

"Exactly, Sir. Our orders are to secure Tucson for the United States, to create a protected route across the desert into California. With odds of ten to one in our favor, and a helpless civilian population in the way, would it not be more . . . honorable . . . even more glorious to bring about a Mexican surrender without a fight?"

"Captain Cutler," said Major Broderick, breaking in solemnly, "the Mexican commander we observed, proudly leading his triumphal procession with a terrible wound to torment him, did not appear to be the surrendering kind."

"That may be, Major," replied Jed, not to be outdone in solemnity, "but in the name of humanity, should we not try?

"With a parley, we will lose the element of surprise," said the colonel, rubbing his chin.

"Given the weight of numbers we enjoy, what matters surprise?" urged Jed.

Everyone sat still while the colonel mulled this thought over in his mind. The old man blew a deep sigh through his white whiskers. "After coming all this way, I had hoped for distinction in action. I have never . . . I mean, I had hoped to just once . . . ."

Jed did not know what to say. He dared not bring up the prophecy. Broderick saved everything when he said, "My ardor is aroused, too, Colonel. I wanted, just once, to strike a blow for my country in this war. But then I think of my responsibility to these men, and to those people down there who will now become part of our country. Duty, in this situation, seems to require a different course."

Nodding sadly, Colonel Cooke said, "You're right, of course." Then he turned his suddenly lugubrious eyes on Jed and said, "I suppose you wish to conduct negotiations with this Captain Comaduran."

"Yes, Sir," said Jed, smiling brightly.

"You will take Charbonneau, of course. I'm sure his Spanish is as barbarous as his English, but he is the only translator we have. But, remember, Captain, they must surrender by, say, seven in the morning—when the sun has fully cleared this hill—or we will attack."

"Yes, Sir," replied Jed, rising to his feet, saluting, and turning to go.

As a white flag of truce, they carried a tent pole on which was tied a big bandage from the medical kit. Charbonneau and Jed rode horses slowly over the plain leading to the east gate of Tucson, squinting into the western sun behind the town which sent long shadows out to greet them. When they neared the open gate, they saw civilians darting back and forth across the opening. They heard a quavering, squawking Mexican bugle and the menacing roll of drums. They saw the garrison turn out and man the wall facing them, plumed shakos and glittering bayonets visible over the parapet. The red, white, and green tricolor of the Republic of Mexico, with its centered golden eagle, fluttered occasionally from its staff in the plaza. The late afternoon air moved only slightly with the lightest of breezes.

Excited voices called back and forth, and fingers pointed. Jed turned in his saddle and looked back up the hill from whence he had come. Despite his determination to avoid a fight, he experienced a rush of hot blood and a prickling of hair on his neck as he saw the Mormon Battalion in battle line along the crest of the hill. In the center of the line stood the color guard, with the Stars and Stripes and the old Nauvoo Legion flag side by side, rippling very slowly with their bright colors lit by the horizontal rays of the languishing sun.

Jed looked forward again and rode with all the dignity he could muster through the gate and into the plaza.

With a sidelong glance, he saw that Charbonneau was actually relaxed. The man was truly an adventurer, and the part of him that was Indian made him love ceremonial occasions. Finding buffalo sinkhole water in the desert, trading with cutthroat Comancheros, entering an enemy position determined to fight to the last breath—everything was fun for Charbonneau, Jed decided.

There before them, in a gentlemanly pose, standing at the top of the steps leading up to the portico of the barracks, was Captain Comaduran. For all his courtly ease, he was as erect as a commander should be. He wore a fine uniform with fresh trousers and tall black boots. Under his ornate sword belt was a crimson sash. From under his gold looped cocked hat, he smiled up at Jed as the two horses halted before him.

With his wound, he dare not come down the stairs. *He would topple at our feet,* thought Jed, as he saluted. Captain Comaduran moved his good left leg to bring himself to a position of attention, heels together, never moving the damaged right leg. He then returned Jed's salute and gestured to the big, blond army officer and the outrageous half-breed mountain man, indicating they should dismount and follow him inside the barracks. Two Mexican soldiers came forward to take their horses.

At the proper time, he spoke. His voice was clear and cultivated, a baritone, not deep, not high. He spoke slowly and clearly, eyeing Charbonneau carefully.

He is an aristocrat, and my translator is a ruffian, thought Jed ruefully. But then Charbonneau revealed yet another facet and translated with aplomb, although Jed was sure that Comaduran was choosing simple words and grammar. Charbonneau had learned a lot from old Charbonneau, his French father, and from the Bird Woman, his Shoshone mother. The vast lands and peoples of the American West had also taught him much.

"Please, come with me into my office, gentlemen," requested the captain, through Charbonneau. The Mexican captain then turned and attempted to walk as naturally as possible, not waiting for his guests. He knew he must reach the shadow of the doorway before they dismounted.

"Si, mi Capitan. Muchas gracias," called Charbonneau after Comaduran's receding back. He winked at the gaping Jed as they got down from their horses.

When Jed and Charbonneau entered the captain's high-ceilinged office with deeply casemented windows, they found him seated behind a battered but ornately carved desk, gazing at them with total self-possession. "Please be seated," he said gravely. Charbonneau translated for Jed. As they found lacquered wicker chairs and perched gingerly, he snapped his fingers and a small Mexican sergeant appeared with a big silver tray loaded with decanter, glasses, coffee pot, and cups. "Wine or chocolate, gentlemen?"

"Wine," said Charbonneau.

"Chocolate," said Jed, glaring at his companion.

"Chocolate," amended Charbonneau, sorrowfully.

The captain joined them in sipping hot, thick chocolate. "So, the Mormon Battalion has arrived," mused the captain.

"You know of us?" Jed's response was one of surprise.

"The Indians tell us much . . . also refugees from Santa Fe."

Jed thought of a riposte. "Then you have interrogated your Navajo prisoners from yesterday?"

Now it was Comaduran's turn to be surprised and he darted glances back and forth at both of them. "Save your breath, Señor," interrupted the captain in perfect English as Charbonneau began to translate. "I speak your language." Charbonneau, unruffled, returned to slurping at his chocolate. Jed, however, was noticeably surprised. The captain considered Jed's question a moment and spoke. "Yes, I have, Señor. So, you have performed reconnaissance?"

"Yes, we have," said Jed flatly. "We know about your wound, and we know how many men you have." Some of the spirit went out of the Mexican captain, and he slumped just a bit. "You have seen our force and you know our mission," Jed went on remorselessly.

Comaduran lifted his chin and his black eyes flashed into Jed's blue ones. "My orders are that I shall not haul down the flag of my country. I shall hold this town for Mexico until relieved of my responsibility. This is the last obstacle in your path to California."

"But you know, Captain, that behind your defense most of California has already fallen. Most of its citizens, Anglos and Latins alike, prefer the Independent Republic just proclaimed. Also, if Santa Fe, with a much larger garrison, could not hold, what can you do here except die, with all of your men, in a wrecked town that will not shelter the women and children who survive."

"This was the message of our President Santa Ana to your Texas defenders of the Alamo, yet they chose to die, and you count them noble for their choice, no?"

"Yes, that is true; but they bought time for a cause that was rising. Here your sacrifice will buy nothing. Time is against your cause and history has passed you by. The Mexican territories north of the Baja are lost to you not only by force of arms but also because the new wave of settlers there, the people who will build up the land, are our people, not yours. I say this to you, Sir, not to boast over you but to mourn with you. My people, the Mormons, seek a place of peace, a place of freedom from fear and want. We thought to flee far from the United States, even though we love our country, to build a home in a portion of your territory you have no use for. Now our country has caught up with us. We can both see, can we not, that right or wrong, conquest or liberation, it is truly the destiny of my country to take unto itself all the western lands. I say this to you, ashamed of my government. I want nothing to do with their greed. But this is how it is . . . for both of us. If you fight a brief, miserable little battle here, and consign your men to a miserable death, who will praise you? Not your superiors. They will soon seek the armistice you spurn. Not the people of Tucson. In a town flattened by warfare and with no garrison to protect them, they will be destroyed by the desert and the Indians."

Jed ceased. Charbonneau looked discreetly at his lap, sitting primly on the edge of his chair. Comaduran looked out the window, at his flag, at his men still manning the wall. Then he turned his head to bore into Jed with his liquid black eyes. "I cannot surrender without a fight. I cannot pull down my flag and become a prisoner because it is expedient. I am not a member of the government to negotiate and be clever. I am a soldier. I serve where I am placed. I have my orders. There is a Latin word the Spanish are fond of. Your man cannot translate it. You must be Spanish to understand it. It is *misericordia* . . . an honorable and necessary suffering of the heart in doing that which is hopeless and required. Tomorrow we will all experience it. Thank you, Captain. You have done your duty well. You have a strange spirit that I like. You may go."

As he finished speaking, the captain blanched and nearly fainted. His chin sank to his chest. Jed realized that the man's resistance to his pain was nearly at an end. He thought of saying more, to exploit that pain, but felt prompted to leave the wound alone. The two visitors rose and left the room.

When Jed and Charbonneau stepped outside, the plaza at sunset was full of people with faces upturned to look at them. Even the soldiers on the wall turned to study them. The people began to speak to them in Spanish. Charbonneau once again translated for Jed, this time out the side of his mouth.

"Please, Sir, tell us what will happen."

"Will the Americans attack?"

"Will they kill everybody?"

"Will the captain surrender?"

"What is happening in the war?"

"Please, Sir, my little boys and little girls . . . ."

"Por favor, Señor . . . ."

"Por favor, Señor . . . ."

The people, distressed men and women with staring black eyes, broad brown faces and white teeth, closed in on Jed and Charbonneau as they mounted. Two soldiers came running to hold the people back and assist the men in turning the horses toward the gate. Picking their way through the outstretched hands, they went around the corner of a house, headed for the gate.

As the crowd disappeared from sight, their sound fading away, strong hands unexpectedly grabbed their bridles, pulling the horses into the deep shadow of a two-story adobe hacienda. With their eyes not yet adjusted to the gloom of the shadow after the level setting sun, Jed and Charbonneau couldn't see who had detoured them. They were pulled quickly but politely from their saddles by two men. Independently, yet simultaneously, both Jed and Charbonneau decided that this was an opportunity, not a threat. They both relaxed and went with the unfolding events.

"Dismount, Sirs, *por favor*."

"Come inside. Come this way."

They were hurried through an adobe arch with its wrought iron gate into a courtyard lined with flowering bushes. They continued through a heavy door, which shut behind them with an echoing thud. They were gently pushed into a tall room with western windows, high up, that admitted the last rays of the summer sunlight. A bald, stocky but not fat, vigorous but not graceful, man stepped forward and bowed. His heavy black mustache and side whiskers showed signs of gray. He wore the short jacket with decorative brocade and the flaring trousers of a land-owning gentleman. Looking keenly at the two, he spoke past them to his men behind Jed and Charbonneau.

"You may go, boys." The two strong, gnarled *vaqueros* in rawhide vests and chaparreras turned and left without a sound. Concentrating on Jed, this townsman said, *"Habla usted Español?"* Charbonneau explained himself and the man pulled them into massive wooden chairs. He leaned toward Jed and, face to face, spoke hoarsely. "I am Emiliano Guerrero-Martinez, Alcalde of Tucson, and you are from the American army on the hill, no?"

"I am Captain Jedediah Cutler, United States Volunteers, sent here by my commander to talk to Captain Comaduran."

"Who has refused to surrender, I believe."

"That is true."

The Alcalde hissed in a breath through his clenched teeth and absently thumped the arm of his chair with his hard, round fist. He seemed to be plunging into a decision that was frightening but carefully considered when he said, "The captain has only fifty soldiers, and I have that many town workers and *vaqueros* who will obey me. There are many others in the town who will help us. We can promise you an open town if you can promise good treatment."

"Certainly, but our wish is to prevent bloodshed."

"We will arrest the captain then barricade the soldiers in their barracks. There will be no bloodshed."

"How will you do this?"

"No time to explain. You must be seen leaving the gate before anyone thinks you stopped along the way.

Just watch for the flag to come down. Then meet me at the gate, and your troops can march in. Now go, and forgive my rudeness in not offering you my food and drink."

They all jumped up from their chairs and hurried out the way they came. Their horses were in the courtyard and they mounted and headed out the gate, but when they turned into the darkened street, they faced Captain Comaduran on his horse with a squad of soldiers in a line, muskets aimed at the three conspirators. The captain looked thoughtfully at Jed and the Alcalde and then spoke sadly. "It is a law of war that in a besieged town, there is always a traitor who will open the gates if the enemy will promise to treat him well."

"Don't be a fool, Captain," rasped the Alcalde. "You will get us all killed. My men will not allow . . . ."

"Your men will do nothing if you are my prisoner, just as my men would not know what to do if I were your prisoner. Leaderless, these people are nothing." The captain smiled at Jed. "This is not your democracy."

"It could be. Why not let the people decide this matter?"

"They are weak. They will betray the will of the whole people, of the Republic. You are not really much of a soldier, are you, Captain?"

Jed looked hard at the proud but frightened Alcalde. The soulful Captain Cutler spoke with the solemnity that had grown on him more and more as he had assumed greater responsibility for the fate of his friends. "You will not understand, my friend, but I am trying to save a promise here. We can work a miracle, you and I. We can win the war of life against death. There is an English word; my companion cannot translate it. It is *charity*. It is the greatest word."

The captain digested this and then slowly answered. "You are not a soldier at all, Señor. You are a missionary. But I have a different calling, and I will do what I promised to do. And now, because you have violated the truce with your misbehavior, I make you my prisoners. As for you, Don Martinez, you are a traitor and a dead man. No matter how the battle goes tomorrow, you will not see another sunset." He turned to his sergeant. "Take them to the guard room."

Charbonneau and Jed sat on the beam floor of a jail cell and rested their backs against the adobe wall, watching Martinez argue furiously through the bars of the door with a guard that he should accept a promise of a bribe to let them go. The soldier on guard harrumphed indignantly that they would all be dead tomorrow. What good was the Alcalde's money?

Charbonneau had put his head on his knees to sleep but Jed woke him to translate.

"Soldier," called Jed. "Why will you fight tomorrow? If all the soldiers turned against the captain and let the Americans in, no harm would come to anyone."

"Is that so, *gringo?*" The old soldier with wrinkled skin like a wind-carved desert tree leaned easily on his musket and spit. "And what of the harm to my country? We have pride, too, you know. We know about Santa Fe, and the gringo revolt in California, and the invasion of our homeland at Vera Cruz. Besides, the captain has saved this town many times from the Navajos and the Apaches. Maybe he can do it again. Maybe, with this little cockroach in jail, there will be some men in this town who will fight with us."

The Alcalde let out an exasperated grunt at the old soldier's comment. With a flurrying gesture, he took his leave from the front of the cell and sat in the shadows against the back wall.

Jed thought of his next words carefully. "I will guess that you have no wife . . . no children. Are there no young soldiers? No husbands or fathers?"

This hurt the soldier, and his trouble showed so readily that he backed away from the door to hide his face. "Yes, there are young soldiers, but you will not get to talk to them now." With that he stormed off, leaving them in their dark cell.

"Well, Captain," whispered Charbonneau, pulling a knife out of each boot and giving one to Jed, "We got to stay alive until our boys break in here tomorrow." He put the knife he kept for himself up his sleeve and then went most definitely to sleep.

Jed sat still in the dark with Charbonneau snoring beside him. He remembered that the Prophet Joseph had spent many a night like this, with no rescuers nearby mobilized to save him. Sometimes he was chained to a log. And his guards were not respectable old veterans, but Price's horrible blackguards who teased Joseph with stories of murder and rape among their Mormon victims. The story was told that Joseph would pray for the Spirit to comfort and strengthen him, and when it came to him he would rise and command his tormentors to be still or go straight to hell. They would feel his power and leave him alone.

Now Jed prayed for the Spirit to help him find a way to guide Comaduran to do what was right for his honor, for the people, and for the prophecy. Abruptly, Jed's cheek recoiled from Charbonneau's shoulder. Realizing he had slept for some time, he lay down and curled up on his side. His earlier thoughts returned. What would Celia say? This needed a woman's idea. He drifted off back to sleep, dreams of Celia filling his head.

The drums rumbled and the bugle blew, and the boots of the soldiers clattered on the barracks floor. Jed, Charbonneau, and Martinez all lurched up into sitting positions, like three corpses resurrecting. The morning light streamed in through the small barred windows at the top of the cell wall. Jed struggled to remember the dream of Celia, because it held the answer. Holding both his hands in hers, she smiled into his face saying . . . saying . . . . He had been trying to kiss her instead of listening to her. She had said, "Ask him again exactly what it is he must do."

Jed leapt to the door, dragging Charbonneau by his collar. Jed put his mouth between two of the bars. "Soldier! You! Compadre!" he cried out in English. The old veteran stayed on his side of the guardroom and handled his musket. Jed pulled his head back and pushed Charbonneau against the bars. The mountain man squawked out his translation as Martinez hurried over. "Take me to the captain!"

"I cannot."

"I have an idea, man. Let me tell it to the captain. Don't you want to live?"

Outside in the plaza, women and children were running into the church as the bells clanged wildly. Jed stopped short to watch a group of soldiers kneel in unison on the steps of the church, with a skinny, bent, old priest standing in front of them. They all took off their shakos and began chanting together. Jed could make out *"Mea culpa, mea culpa, mea maxima culpa."*

"Dey are being shriven," commented Charbonneau. "You know, confession . . . before you die?"

Jed looked around and saw Captain Comaduran standing on the eastern wall, using his drawn sword as a cane in his right hand, shading his eyes with his left against the brilliant sun that had just cleared the hill to the east. The sun illuminated a long, lateral, dust cloud moving down the hill toward the town. As Jed climbed the wall beside the captain and hauled Charbonneau up with him, against the dark hillside he saw the darker uniforms of the Mormon Battalion. Their five hundred muskets and bayonets flashed as the soldiers came from the carry to the charge. Their flags rippled. Old Colonel Cooke rode just to the rear of the center of the moving line. There was Broderick, double timing back and forth behind the line, barking at company commanders,

and Jamie, in the forefront of his company, where Jed would be as captain.

"Captain," said Jed, quietly and steadily.

"Yes, Captain," replied Comaduran without taking his eyes off the Mormon Battalion. The soldiers Jed had observed a moment before were finished with the priest and ran to their positions. The Mexican soldiers were under cover, aiming their weapons over the wall at their steadily approaching targets. The civilian men were in their homes. The women and children were in the church.

"What is it exactly you must do?"

The captain turned to look at Jed. "I beg your pardon?"

"I ask you to tell me your exact orders. What is it exactly you must do for honor's sake?"

The handsome captain wrinkled his brow as he studied Jed. "I must never surrender. I must never haul down our flag. I must keep this town under Mexican rule until I receive more orders from my president."

"Very well, then I have an idea that will preserve your honor from the stain of defeat as well as that of innocent blood."

The battalion had just prepared to fire volleys by ranks, preparatory to charging the wall. The front rank had knelt and every man was checking his flintlock priming when Jed and Charbonneau came galloping toward them from the gates of Tucson. The two haggard emissaries reined in before Colonel Cooke.

In great agitation, Jed saluted and asked, "Colonel, would you consider your duty done if we marched in triumph through Tucson and continued on without loss to California, leaving the town to be transferred to American control upon the conclusion of a general peace?"

The old colonel gobbled like a turkey as every eye turned to rest upon him. Major Broderick ran up to hear the answer. "Why . . . why . . . yes, yes I suppose I would." Jed turned and waved his arm at the wall. Captain Comaduran rose up into view and waved back. Then his fifty men also rose and pulled back from the wall. It was obvious from their firing positions that their first volley was meant for the old colonel on horseback. This caused the old gentleman to gobble again and a titter to run up and down the ranks.

And so it was that the Mormon Battalion marched into the east gate of Tucson with cracked drums beating time for the exhausted soldiers as the Mexican garrison marched smartly out the south gate led by their tinny bugle. The Battalion marched across the plaza without touching the Mexican flag which flew proudly from its staff. The people gathered quietly along both sides of the street filled with the dusty blue marching column, eager to see if the gringos would keep their promise to take not a grain of wheat nor kernel of corn, not a chicken or an egg or even a drop of water. And would they harm not a soul as the Alcalde had said?

When it became clear that they would not stop or even look to the right or the left despite their cracked lips and growling, collapsed bellies, the people cheered and the children danced about the soldiers.

Jed smiled at Alcalde Martinez as he marched past at the head of his company. He called out to the grinning little man over the shouts of the crowd. "Will the captain really leave you alone?"

"*Si, Señor* Captain, of course," replied the Alcalde jauntily. "He gave his word of honor. I wish my paper money was worth as much."

The Mormon Battalion passed out of the west gate of Tucson and continued on its way. Colonel Cooke would be able to report that he had penetrated the enemy's defenses and overcome all obstacles at Tucson without a single casualty. He had outmaneuvered an enemy force, now left to wither on the vine in a rear area.

The fulfillment of Brigham's prophecy had a cost, however. The whole point of taking Tucson, besides breaking through into California, had been to resupply the battalion with food and drink. For now they staggered on, over the last of the desert, with thoughts of the Santa Rosa Mountains still before them. There was no question—they were truly starving.

It was another baking hot day under a burnished sky. This was the ugliest stretch of the journey. At least the prairies, salt flats, and scrub-covered hills were beautiful to behold while the men toiled across them in pain, fear, and boredom. But this land was dirty yellow undulations that could not even be called hills. It was made of gravel and sand covered by a talcum-fine dust. Their ragged shoes had lost all their black dye and were a whitish yellow, and uniforms that had once been bright blue were so permeated with dust and faded by sun that they were now light gray.

Two of the three horses had quietly and apologetically sunk down under Major Broderick and Charbonneau, sighing out their last breath. Charbonneau instantly cut their throats, and everybody drank a little blood. Every morsel of horseflesh was removed, cooked, and eaten that night, while the sole surviving horse looked on impassively. Charbonneau had shown the men how to suck on cactus pulp for a little moisture.

But that was all days ago. In this part of the desert, there were no plants except for the most miserable weeds, and no moisture of any kind. Charbonneau said there was a ridge of rocks up ahead, with a spring. He called it "Needles." Now, however, they were down to one mile per hour, with many men being pulled along by two friends. Nobody talked, but everyone believed they would not make it.

At first, the men were too deep inside themselves to hear the slight rumbling up ahead. Jed's company happened to be at the head of the column, and he looked up from the ground in front of him when he heard a snort. He thought it came from the colonel's bedraggled horse and was hoping it would collapse like the others. But the noise was coming from out in front, just over the next little curve of the land. The men around him brought their heads up and pointed out the dust rising ahead with the drumming of hooves on the ground growing louder and louder.

The tips of horns flashed in the sun as the animals came over the rise, and everyone began croaking like a flock of birds. It was a herd of reddish cattle with huge wildly twisted horns spreading out laterally from the sides of their heads. Thundering hooves and bellowing snouts combined to create a hellish sound which transfixed the column of soldiers. Stunned or not, the herd was stampeding directly toward the battalion.

Jed looked over at the colonel and saw that he was frozen. Charbonneau was dancing around looking for even a rock to climb but there was nothing. "Dey crazy for water! Dey gonna kill us!" he shouted. Jed hobbled over to the colonel as fast as he could. He grabbed the colonel's thigh and shook it, forcing him to look down at Jed from his saddle.

"Colonel, would you like to fight a battle . . . win a great victory?" shouted Jed, smiling as best he could with his poor cracked face.

"Let us see the battalion's tactics," added Broderick who had just arrived on the other side of the colonel's horse. "Shall we use the drill we would have used at Tucson, Sir?"

The colonel now saw the cattle for the first time. They were thundering toward the mesmerized column on a front of perhaps three hundred yards, and they were three hundred yards away, closing fast. The colonel cleared his throat. Jed and Broderick waited with gritted teeth. The din of the hooves was overpowering now. "No, this is different from the action at Tucson. In this case, Battalion will form the hollow square and volley by ranks. See to it if you please, gentlemen."

"Yes, Sir!" shot back Jed and Broderick with one voice as they ran away from the colonel. Orders went back to each company and the aroused men obeyed with renewed spirit. At the double quick, they formed a hollow square one hundred paces on each side with three ranks forming the wall of men on each side, just like at the Battle of Waterloo. They were on time by a second, as the cattle surrounded them and lowered their heads to charge. Never did two opposing forces lust for each other's blood more fiercely or more literally.

"Front rank, fire!"

"Second rank, fire!"

"Third rank, fire!"

Oh, how the Mormon Battalion reloaded and fired, volley after crashing volley, and how the enemy went down in heaps. Finally the remainder of the beaten herd was turned and moved on as the companies charged with bayonets fixed and stout battle cries. They mercilessly dispatched the wounded. "We have met the enemy, and the enemy is our dinner," exulted Jamie.

In no time at all the men cleaned and dressed the animals whose death had saved them. After Charbonneau assessed their location, he noted with some irony that not far ahead lay the very pool of water the crazed herd had been searching for. No man complained when the order came down through the ranks for every soldier to pack on their backs as much meat as they could carry. When the order "resume march" was given, not a single animal lay wasted.

There was singing that night in the camp by the spring at the Needles as the men ate sizzling, red running meat, washed down with all the water they could hold. They stayed there for three days, making jerky, washing everything, and resting. Charbonneau called the place "Needles," but the men of the Mormon Battalion called it heaven.

10

The City Rises

They started with a wagon box fort in the dirt. It was a puny little camp in the middle of a large flat bench that filled the area within the near-right angle of two sets of foothills. They gave the stream running next to it the pretentiously hopeful name of City Creek. This was in the northeastern corner of the valley. The canyon they had traversed to enter the area opened out onto this smooth but slightly sloped surface. From here, the pioneers could look up at the mountains towering over the eastern side of the valley. Brother Brigham said the Utah Indians called them the Wasatch.

Some eager souls unhitched teams from wagons and hooked up plows to try the soil on this bench. They ruined a precious plow—bending the share and peeling it right off the frame—before they hastily ceased. The sod and the clay under it were baked almost to the consistency of brick. This was high desert all right, just as Bridger had said. Instinctively, the ever-clever Brother Clayton grabbed a hoe and ran up the green little canyon from which appeared City Creek. "I have an idea that might help 'soften' our troubles," he snickered on his way to the creek.

"Follow Brother Clayton," yelled one of the men who had tried to plow the clay ground.

"Where's he goin'?" asked another, scratching his head.

"Who cares? Brother Clayton can figger out this problem if anybody can."

Clayton began hacking out a ditch that would bring a flow of water to the place where they had attempted plowing. Other men jumped to the task and, in no time, the ditch arrived at the plot, spreading water over it in a miniature delta.

"Now what?" asked a stout fellow with a hoe in each hand.

Clayton looked at him in complete amazement and simply replied, "We wait."

After a couple of hours of soaking, the plow was tried again and, this time, it furrowed easily through the soggy dirt. With a counselor at either elbow, the still feverish Brigham Young said, "Irrigation. Yes, irrigation."

"Let's hear it for Brother Clayton!" came the cry, and the cheering pioneers hoisted Clayton on the shoulders of two brothers, to be paraded around in triumph.

Twenty miles across the valley floor rose the valley's western rampart, called the Oquirrh Mountains in the language of the desert dwelling Goshiute Indians. From their commanding bench, the entire settlement could see a line of cottonwood trees and Russian olive bushes running right down the middle of the valley. This gave away the presence of a deep, still river moving from left to right, or south to north. Before Porter Rockwell was summoned to Peter's aid, he had ridden along that river and around a sandy spine jutting out from the Wasatch.

He called it "Point of the Mountain," and the name stuck.

In the next valley to the south, Rockwell had observed that the river came from a huge, but shallow, fresh-water lake. Since the French explorer, Etienne Provo, called this area Utah Valley, Rockwell had decided it was only fitting to call the lake Utah Lake. Meanwhile, back at the northern end of the Oquirrh Mountains, that placid river ran into the shimmering surface of Jedediah Smith's Great Salt Lake, just as Jim Bridger had described it.

The word came down to the captains that, like Joshua in the Old Testament, their own Brigham Young had led the latter-day children of Israel into a promised land. Brigham himself carried that comparison further, noting that the Utah Lake was positioned like the Sea of Galilee. The river flowed into the undrainable and therefore salten lake that was in similitude of the Dead Sea. So Brigham decided the connecting stream could have only one possible name—the Jordan River.

The sun set right at the juncture of mountains and river and lake, daily performing a soothing spectacle that made everybody sigh with contentment as they ceased their labors and trudged . . . home.

"We will transport Nauvoo the Beautiful to this valley, body and soul," Brigham decreed. "Furthermore, we will make this desert blossom as the rose!" he continued, paraphrasing the scriptures. There was room on this bench to build a city ten times the size of Nauvoo, and Brother Brigham said they would need it all and more. "Villages and towns will arise on the valley floor and expand until they touch each other, covering the valley with farms, ranches, and homes." It took great faith to believe that one day their people would fill this vast panorama.

They called the road they built from the east, Emigration Road as it emerged from Emigration

Canyon, leading into the center of the settlement. Turning west, it went out to the lake and the Indian settlement the Goshiutes called Tooele. As the road continued out of town, it was called Tooele Road. Many a pioneer woman looked down that road each dawn and dusk, knowing it connected with the trail the mountain men used to get to California. *Would the Mormon Battalion return to them one day, marching down that road?* they wondered.

The pioneers watched the First Presidency of the Church: stubby Brigham Young; tall, bald Heber Kimball—Brigham's lifelong friend; and Willard Richards, as they puttered and muttered all over that bench with much pointing of Brigham's cane. "Here . . . here will rise the temple, the House of the Lord," declared Brigham, stabbing the dirt with his cane. It was to be built on a plot in the northern portion of the city. A lofty temple here would look out over the city and the valley beyond, with nothing to obstruct the view. Next to the city square that would contain the temple, Brigham lined out the area that would provide his home and the headquarters of the Church.

Brother Orson, the Professor, was directed to survey a huge grid of streets that would replicate, but greatly expand, the plan of Nauvoo. As in Nauvoo and, indeed, all over America, there would be wards which would serve as both neighborhoods and ecclesiastical units, like the congregations of New England or the parishes of Louisiana. Bishop Quimby Leighton would preside over a ward nine city blocks long and nine blocks wide. Each block was forty rods (640 feet) on a side and enclosed ten acres. There were no "Ward Heelers," however, because there were no elections, no politicians of any kind. Someday, there might be a municipal charter such as Nauvoo had enjoyed, but who would grant it?

The Mormon settlers were outside the territory governed by the Constitution of the United States. This was

Israel in the latter days, governed by the Priesthood of God, and to the pioneers, any other form of government was inferior.

Huge streets were surveyed and marked. Grading and surfacing of the new streets commenced. These were streets never imagined in America, longer, wider, and straighter than in the city of Washington designed by L'Enfant, streets to shame the Parisian Champs-Elysees or London's Pall Mall. *What grand structures will be built along them?* wondered the Saints as they looked out over the impressive sight. Whatever would be built, they would be well proportioned with the streets and sidewalks.

The undeviating streets were all eight rods (132 feet) wide with twenty-five foot wide sidewalks. A mandate was immediately adopted to ensure setback for buildings of another twenty feet. Freighters rejoiced that they could turn their huge wagons around within the street, even if they had eight span of oxen or mules. Brigham hinted at other vehicles that would fill these remarkable streets in the latter days.

A great north-south thoroughfare stretched from Church headquarters on the northern hill, through the center of town, all the way toward "Point of the Mountain" twenty miles to the south. This spine of the city was actually part of a long Indian trail that enabled the Shoshoni of the north to trade with the Navajo of the south.

The entire length of this road was under the gaze of the Prophet as he stood on his own lot at the foot of the hill. It was a grand sight, and it would extend further on to serve the entire region. The fledgling settlement would grow into a prosperous, free territory. Or would it? The counselors who knew Brigham's mind saw his determination that a state of the United States would be necessary if they wished to preserve and protect what was being built. Oh, he would keep the gentiles off balance with loud talk about an independent nation filling the entire Great Basin from the Rockies to California, but they still believed that the Constitution was God's work and that their destiny lay in the United States.

From the day he first laid eyes on the place, the tough little man with the jutting jaw and the clever eyes had never hesitated to proclaim that the Saints would make a "State of Deseret" in their new land. It would be a theocratic republic named for the industrious honey bee in the *Book of Mormon* and, as such, it would apply for admission to the Union. Washington might jeer at that notion with numerous citations of the Constitution and the Northwest Ordinance, but it was a gambit worth trying, thought the Brethren.

This first small company of pioneers used every bit of daylight preparing the city for the arrival of the body of Saints. This massive migration was continuing, even as they toiled all that summer. Tens of thousands of hopeful, yet frightened, people were arranged back along the trail and at Winter Quarters. Many others waited along the rivers, roads, and canals of heartland America and at the ports of Boston, New York, and New Orleans. At the same time, Saints were gathering at ports in London, Portsmouth, Southhampton, Bremen, Antwerp, Le Havre, and more. They organized their emigrant ships and over they came, gathering, always gathering.

Celia did her best to help, but it was daily more obvious that her main task was to incubate little Jed, Junior (if that was the gender and, judging from the kicking and wriggling going on inside her, this was a fair bet). Every time she heaved her ripening shape off the only Faraday chair and tried to at least wash clothes or cook, her mother would sit her back down.

"Young lady," Emma scolded only half playfully, "you stay in that chair and rest. I have enough to do without babysitting you."

"That's the point, Mother," Celia whined. "Everybody has so much to do and I want to contribute my fair share."

"Staying healthy for that new baby is your job. Besides, there isn't a thing here that I can't do myself. If something comes up that I might need help with, I can always ask Bishop Leighton to assist me."

"He really is a nice man, Mother," Celia said with a knowing smile.

"Now don't you start up with me about Bishop Leighton again," replied Emma, still only half joking.

"I think he likes you, Mother."

"Bishop Leighton likes everyone," sighed Emma, a little self-consciously. "But yes, dear, you're right. He is a nice man."

Bishop Leighton, though a beanpole, was a tower of strength. The city was laid out properly now, and the people were spreading out into their wards. They took up their deep, but narrow, lots with a home near the street. Each lot had a huge garden and small pasture behind. Quimby presided over the Fourteenth Ward, right in the central city area. Like all bishops, he was the "father" of the ward . . . the manager, the engineer, the judge, the land agent and a dozen other trades and professions. Nothing had prepared him for these responsibilities except his belief that this calling came from God through the Prophet.

When it was light enough to see, everyone in the ward could observe the bishop striding slowly out of his wagon box on his lot next to the Faradays. He moved deliberately, covering ground rapidly with his long legs. The older children nicknamed him "The Giraffe"—a humorous title not meant to be unkind. As the sun rose over the Wasatch, traversed across the valley, and sank behind the Oquirrhs, Bishop Leighton continued his daily walk. Without ever seeming to stop, he criss-crossed the ward, talking to everybody every day—or so it seemed. Under his calm, wise smile, the heads of households staked their lots, formed work gangs to clear them, graded the Eighth South Street which ran down the center of the ward, and chopped out the irrigation ditches along both edges of every street.

As more manpower arrived each month, they built canals and earthen aqueducts to bring the water into the network of ditches that watered each lot. City Creek filled the north-south ditches. A stream from Red Butte Canyon, out of the Wasatch, filled the east-west ones. The ditches were lined with gravel to purify the water as it tumbled over it. This system insured that every family could walk outside with a bucket and return with all the clear, cool, mountain water they needed. The baked clay surrendered to the water, and the oxen who pulled the plows fertilized it. Top soil was carted down from the life-sustaining canyons, and seeds went in. Even though the sun blazed day after day with never more than a few high, thin clouds, the irrigation made the fields and garden plots push up tender plants.

Houses went up, daily . . . log cabins and adobe. Lodgepole pine was dragged down from the canyons. Adobe pits and straw provided bricks just like those made by the Hebrew slaves in Egypt's Goshen. Roofs were thatch or rough, splintery shingles, sometimes made of sweet smelling cedar. Blue-gray adobe walls and dun colored shingles on low-lying, flattish roofs made for a colorless city, but it was solid and functional.

There was more city every day, too, not only as people moved out of their wagons, but more Saints were arriving as the gathering continued. The majority were British. The city had a Welsh choir now and sometimes at sunset mournful bagpipes would keen out "Amazing Grace." As the months wore on, the newest lot of arrivals were Scandinavian, mostly from Denmark. They looked up at the harsh mountains and out over the desert valley as though they were on another planet. They conversed with each other in their sing-song, consonantal language, which convinced others settlers that the Danes were from another planet.

No matter where the new settlers hailed from, America, Europe, or Africa, everyone worked side by side to build a new life in a new and promising land. The customs and languages blended into the very threads of the growing society, making it colorful and exciting for all. A steady stream of these pioneers were insured by the efforts of missionaries sent out by the church leaders to labor in lands far and near. Like the early Mormons before them, new converts left their homelands in search of a better life—one where they could worship as they saw fit. It was every bit the American dream for which so many non-Mormons and Mormons alike had given their lives.

Now, smoke went up chimneys every morning. The people reinvented the routine of home. All through the kiln-like day, the widower Quimby Leighton calmly pointed out the solutions to ever-changing problems. His only comfort came each evening when he sat down to supper with the widow Emma Faraday.

Fennelly Parsons drove his sons hither and thither creating a great show of farming and home-raising, depending more than anybody else on the help of the ward members. He was still funny and charming, but there was an edge of fear and shame to his antics now. This was a man who needed to be needed. He yearned to do something at which he excelled, and farming was not that thing. He and his sons did manage to raise a ramshackle house, but even Brother Brigham could see that something would have to be found for Fennelly that made use of the talents within him.

But what to do with the hands and mind of an artistic non-farmer was just one of the challenges of the new frontier. Such subtle challenges of the arriving souls, and indeed those of the very land they came to settle, were being tamed by the Mormon pioneers. It was this new and growing settlement they called "Great Salt Lake City!"

11

Dead or Alive?

Six weeks and four spent horses apiece is what it took for Peter and Rockwell to cross the plains, maneuver through the rugged Rocky Mountains, and finally reach the Salt Lake Valley. They had stopped at Fort Bridger for supplies and to try to learn more details concerning the Mormon Battalion. Of course, the army courier Porter had talked with on his way to Saint Louis had long since gone from the place. In fact, all the military personnel had departed the fort. The war was over.

As they broke through the mountain pass into what had come to be known as Emigration Canyon, Peter stopped his horse in awe of the spectacular valley that lay below him. Rockwell reined up his horse next to Peter and looked out at the expanse.

"It was here in this canyon where we broke through the mountains and first saw the Great Salt Lake Valley," Porter recalled. "Brother Brigham was sick with fever, but had a few of the brethren help him out of the wagon he was riding in. He just stood there, not more than twenty feet from where you are now. As soon as his eyes rested upon the valley below, he said, 'This is the place; for the Lord has shown it to me in a vision.' I knew right then that everything we had gone through was worth it. We were home!"

Peter was clearly in awe—overwhelmed may have been a better description. The expanse of the valley that stretched before him was great. Its rugged beauty seemed fitting for the new home of the Saints. *Ah yes . . . Saints,* Peter thought. He savored the word. It had been a long time since he had really considered himself a "Saint," but now, poised on the mountains overlooking the promised valley, he truly felt that he, too, might be home at last. The two men were silent for a moment as they looked out over the valley. Rockwell sensed Peter's pride, having already experienced it himself, and he was in no hurry to interrupt the event. Besides, the sight was still new enough to Rockwell that he didn't mind surveying it again.

As if he were summoned, Peter began the descent to the valley floor and the Mormon settlement. Rockwell followed. Still, they didn't speak. Thoughts of Celia and Jed flooded Peter's mind, but seemed to fight each other as he attempted to come to grips with what he would say once reunited with the Faradays. He half hoped the news would somehow have already reached Salt Lake, though deep inside, he knew it would be better if he told Celia himself.

Rockwell let out a loud whoop when they reached the valley floor. Both men nudged their mounts to a full gallop and headed for . . . . "Where are we going, exactly?" yelled Peter, trying to keep up with his friend.

"Brother Brigham will want to see us," Porter called back. "'Sides, we've gotta tell him about the Mormon Battalion."

By the time they reached Brigham Young's quarters, Peter was choking on the dust. "This Salt Lake City isn't much like Nauvoo, is it?" he said to Porter under his breath.

"It's rough yet, but give it time, boy," Rockwell replied. "Brigham says we'll make the desert blossom like a rose."

President Young was waiting for them outside his house, having been notified that riders were approaching. The dust cloud from the hasty approach of the horses remained behind them as dust clouds do in such situations. This held true, however, only as long as the riders advanced. When they stopped, the cloud overtook them, covering everything, including Brigham, with prairie dust. It didn't seem to bother President Young in the least. In fact, he didn't even break stride as he walked forward to greet his friends. A couple of coughs, and Brigham was shaking Rockwell's hand.

"Porter, welcome back. We've missed you while you were away, as always. And Brother Van Cleef," he continued, turning to Peter. "You have been away from us much too long. You are welcome here."

It was an amusing sight, to say the least. All three men were dusted from head to foot, but it was a heartwarming reunion just the same. Still, Brigham could sense there was something else, something wrong. "What is it, Porter? Is something the matter?"

"Yes, President, I'm sorry to say there is," Rockwell answered.

"Well, tell then. Let's hear the news."

"It's the Mormon Battalion, President. We have learned from the army that they are probably all dead." Porter related to Brigham what the army courier had told him when he had passed through Fort Bridger on his way to Saint Louis. "I fear the worst, President. I've been in that desert. A rattlesnake couldn't live there."

Peter looked at Brigham anxiously. "I've got to tell Celia," he said. "Jedediah Cutler was with the Battalion. Can you tell me where to find her?"

"Now just hold on here a fine minute," Brigham said, raising his hands. "It may be that this terrible thing has indeed occurred, but I feel moved to say that indeed it has not!"

Peter and Rockwell looked at each other. They were surprised at Brigham's statement and the power and conviction that accompanied it. "It is my counsel to you both to act with prudence until we can gather more definitive information on this matter."

After a bit more conversation, Brigham invited his two friends to take their leave and rest after their long journey. "But please come see me later, Porter. There is a matter of some importance I wish to discuss with you."

The two men said goodbye to Brigham and remounted their horses. When they were far enough away from Brigham's quarters, Peter turned to Rockwell. "Did you hear what he said, Porter? Can you believe what he just said?"

"Now simmer down, boy," Rockwell said, keeping his gaze straight ahead. "That is God's own prophet you're referrin' to."

"But you said yourself how nobody could survive that desert!"

"Never mind what I said. I ain't no prophet."

Peter thought about what Brigham had said to them, "Act with prudence . . . ." He thought about Celia. He had almost become used to the idea that Jed was gone and he would now take care of her. The thought of Jed's being alive hadn't even crossed his mind. He had accepted what Rockwell told him. But now, what if Jed really wasn't dead? *No!* Peter thought. *If Porter thinks no one could survive, then no one could! And Celia has the right to know.* Peter turned to Rockwell and said, "Where is she?"

Porter finally looked at his young friend. "Now, I know what you're thinkin', but I'm advisin' you to keep still about this Mormon Battalion story fer now."

"I know what I'm doing, Porter! Where do I find Celia?"

"You never learn, boy. Yer as stubborn as ever, and it's gonna come back at ya!" Peter just looked at Rockwell and didn't say a word. His mind was already made up. "All right, Peter," Rockwell groaned. "You go ta her; you tell her that her husband is dead!"

Peter's face was one of shock. First of all, Rockwell only called him "Peter" when he was irritated at him. Secondly, Rockwell hadn't said anything about Jed and Celia being married! "Oh, did I forget to mention they got hitched?" Peter didn't say anything. He was stunned by this news. "I didn't tell ya because I didn't want ta hurt ya." Still Peter was silent. "Well, what'd ya expect?" Rockwell continued. "Last time ya saw 'em, you interrupted their weddin', remember?"

"I had hoped I interrupted it for good!" Peter finally said softly.

"Why you selfish little beggar!" snapped Rockwell. "Don't you ever think about anybody else 'cept yerself?" Porter knew the young man did, but he was angry and felt he needed to make a point. "Do you not recall that the last time they saw ya, they thought you were dead, or at least dyin'? They needed each other!"

"Now Jedediah is dead." Peter said, almost smugly.

Porter felt his arm stiffen as he was about to pole-ax Peter right out of his saddle, but he took a deep breath and said slowly, "You don't know that."

"You said . . . ."

"I ain't no prophet!"

Rockwell stopped his horse. Peter followed suit. He could tell Rockwell was angry with him, but Peter knew Rockwell wouldn't stand in his way if he really believed in what he had to do. Rockwell was a firm believer in letting one make his own mistakes. "Why did we stop?" Peter asked. "I want you to take me to Celia!"

"Yer here, boy," Rockwell said dryly. He kicked his horse and began a slow walk away from Peter.

"Aren't you coming in with me?" Peter questioned with much anticipation.

"You do what ya gotta do. My cabin's the last one out of town goin' east." With that Rockwell rode off and Peter was left alone to face his past.

Peter rode up to the little cabin to which Rockwell had led him. He dismounted and tied his horse to the wheel of the Faraday's wagon. He stood outside the cabin for a few moments, trying to think of a way to tell Celia the news. Peter couldn't imagine any way to break it to her that wouldn't hurt. He made several attempts at knocking, but paused each time. He would have gone on that way the rest of the day, but Celia heard the noise outside and opened the door to see what was going on.

Peter was once again trying to get up the nerve to knock, hand poised ready, eyes tightly closed, when the door opened. "Peter?" Celia gasped. "Peter, is it really you?" She grabbed him, dust flying everywhere, and held him tightly. Peter did the same.

"I'm quite dirty from the trip," he told her, not really caring.

"Don't be silly. We've never let dirt get between us," Celia laughed through tears of joy. What did get between them was Celia's very large stomach. She was now in her eighth month and counting the days. Peter held her away from him so he could look at her.

"What's this, then?" Peter said softly, trying to conceal the impact of this unforseen reality. He stood dead still in a kind of trance and tried to wipe the tears away from Celia's face, but only succeeded in making mud.

Celia looked down, patted her stomach, and said, "We think it's Jed, Junior. So much has happened since we parted on the riverbank. We'll have time to catch up on all of that, but now I'm just so happy to see you, Peter. We didn't know how you were getting along, and Porter couldn't seem to tell us much of anything."

"Well, I'm here now and everything will be all right."

Celia invited Peter to come in and talk to her. She became very excited and charged with energy. Peter inquired as to the whereabouts of her mother. He knew he had to tell Celia the news, and perhaps it would be better if Emma was there too.

"Oh, she's just taking some supplies to Brother Parsons. You know how much he needs the help of the others," Celia smiled. Peter smiled too. He hadn't thought about old Fenelly Parsons and all his boys in ages. The memory made him warm inside. "She should be back any moment. You will stay until she returns, won't you? She'll be so disappointed if you don't."

"I'll stay."

"Oh, Peter," Celia exclaimed, suddenly patting her hair. "I must look awful. If only I could have known you were coming, I would have made myself presentable." And it was true, Celia looked a little rumpled; but it was nothing more or less than how any pregnant farm girl doing housework and chores would look. Her hair was tousled, her clothes were extremely loose and baggy. On top of everything else, she had mud streaks on her face, thanks to Peter. But Peter saw none of this. She appeared as beautiful to him as she did every Sunday morning in Nauvoo before the sacrament meeting.

"You look beautiful, Celia," Peter said, eyes lovingly fixed on her. "I have longed to see you these many months. It was the memory of you that helped me mend."

Celia blushed. She studied him uneasily. *It was always Peter who spoke to me with vivid intimacy. It was always Jed who believed his deeds made flowery words unnecessary,* she thought, remembering feelings and memories long put away. Celia suddenly felt awkward and she turned her out-of-proportion figure away from Peter. She was nervous and when she was nervous, she talked fast. "You must have so much to tell us. Whatever happened after Nauvoo?"

"Celia?"

"What have you been doing all this time . . .?"

"Celia, I . . ."

"Why haven't you come before now?"

"Celia, please!" She realized what she was doing and put her hand over her mouth. Peter could tell she was smiling.

"I'm sorry, Peter," she said after a minute. "You know how I am."

"Yes, Celia, I know. That's why I need to talk to you and for you to listen to me." She lowered her hands and folded them together on her distended lap.

"I just wish Jed was back so we could all talk together. I'm sure he has stories to tell also."

Peter felt his heart jump in his throat and tears well in his eyes. "Celia, it's Jed. I . . . ."

He wasn't able to finish his sentence. Not because of the lump in his throat or the tears in his eyes. He was simply interrupted. Emma had returned.

"Celia, who belongs to this filthy creature?" bellowed Emma from outside. Celia jumped off the stool she had perched on and ran to the door.

"Mama, you won't believe who's here!"

"Now calm down, dear," her mother said. "You don't want to get all worked up in your state of . . . who is here, Celia?" With that she was already through the door and saw Peter. "Praise be to our almighty God! Peter Van Cleef, you are back! Are you all right? What became of you after Nauvoo?"

"Mother . . ."

"Are you staying for dinner?"

"Mother!" Celia exclaimed, smiling, reaching for her arm. It was easy to see from whom Celia had picked up the habit. Peter smiled too.

"Dear me, I do go on so," Emma said, repeating the same hand to mouth movement Celia had made moments ago. "Caleb used to joke about it when he was alive, God rest his soul." Peter's heart again raced and vaulted into his throat.

"Caleb is dead?" Peter asked, trying to be strong in the midst of such emotion.

"Yes, dear," Emma replied. "He died on the trek west. After Nauvoo, he was never the same. Oh, but don't you fret about that. He is with our Father in Heaven now and much better off than he was before."

"Mother," Celia said. "Peter was just about to tell me of Jed when you returned." Emma looked surprised.

"Jed? Have you heard from him? Did you cross paths in your journeys?" Peter turned from them and walked to the small window cut into the logs of their cabin. The tears came now. He hadn't cried for Jed until now. Before, it was anger, disbelief. Now, faced with the chore of telling Celia and Emma about Jed, he realized that, no matter how strong were his desires for Celia, he felt Jed's loss deeply.

"Peter, what is it?" asked Celia, going to him at the window.

She put her arms around him, but it only made the pain more searing, and Peter couldn't help himself. He sobbed even harder, resting his head on Celia's shoulder. Emma joined them and she also tried to comfort Peter.

Jed's death was at the center of Peter's torment but, pouring forth from the same gaping emotional wound, came the poison from the past months since Nauvoo was burned ... the mobs, the violence, Saint Louis, Charlie Bates, and Mary Ellen Moore . . . yes, and Mary

Ellen Moore . . . but also, also, his aching need for Celia.

Images rushed past his mind's eye and suddenly stopped with a clear picture of the three friends, Jed, Celia, and Peter, greeting each other with laughter as they met to walk to school together. Peter's breathing settled down as he gained the courage to be comforted by these people he must hurt.

Celia and Emma worked their soothing magic until Peter regained himself. They were patient; Celia was content to have Peter back in her life, whatever was bothering him. She hadn't yet made the connection. Emma, on the other hand, grew increasingly worried. *Why would Peter react so strongly about news of Jed? Unless . . . .* She wouldn't allow herself to finish the thought. She would simply wait until Peter told them whatever it was he had to say. After all, there was no sense jumping to conclusions.

Peter dried his eyes and sat down on the milking stool. Mother and daughter likewise sat on their puncheon bench, saying nothing. Emma was somber and Celia realized that, indeed, something was very wrong. They all sat together for a moment before Peter spoke.

"I wish it wasn't I who had to tell you what you must be told," he began. "I would rather die than hurt you, you know that." Celia looked at Emma, beginning to feel the weight of Peter's words. Emma took her daughter's hand and held it tightly. "We learned from a courier in the U.S. Army," Peter continued, "that the Mormon Battalion marched into the Arizona desert and vanished. They were never heard from again."

Emma turned her head away and cried softly. Celia cried too, but it was more shock than tears. She sat next to Emma, breathing heavily. Her eyes were lost and hollow, not fixing on anything. The very air in the room seemed to be weighted with despair, and Peter was afraid to continue. He had no choice, since he started the whole mess. It might be more damaging to leave things unsaid.

"The courier told Porter that the official Army report would list the Mormon Battalion missing in the line of duty . . . all presumed dead."

Upon hearing the words, Celia could take it no more. She put her hands on her stomach and sobbed for her lost husband and their unborn child. Emma did her best to comfort her daughter, but there wasn't any comfort to be had. Peter wanted to do something to comfort Celia; he just didn't know what to do. He felt helpless and hung his head because he realized their pain was due, at least in part, to his selfishness. Maybe President Young was right. Maybe he should have waited until there was more word on the fate of the Mormon Battalion. Now it was too late. He had told Emma and Celia, and they would all have to live with it.

Celia buried her head in her mother's chest and clung to her as if she were life itself. Emma stroked Celia's head with one hand and held her with the other. Celia's tormented sobs were muffled in the folds of Emma's dress. It became apparent to Peter that Celia needed to cry, Emma needed to console, and that they needed to be alone.

"I think I should go," Peter offered. Emma nodded, not looking at him, but that was all right with Peter. Their hurt expressions were hard enough to take without looking into their eyes. "Please believe me when I say how sorry I am," Peter continued. "I loved him too." And with that, he was gone.

The bright sun outside was in stark contrast to what Peter just left. He rode out of town half looking for Rockwell's cabin and half wandering. He'd come so far, overcome so much, and for what? To feel continual pain? *Maybe I should just keep on riding,* Peter thought. But he knew he couldn't. Celia needed him now, more than ever, and he wouldn't let her down.

Rockwell's cabin was not only the last cabin to the east, it was the only cabin to the east, as far as you could ride and still be near the settlement. Porter had built it way out of town, but he always was a bit of a loner. Peter wasn't too surprised, though, because he knew how Rockwell thought.

It felt good to be able to rest. Peter looked forward to getting clean and with his discovery of a small stream not far from the cabin, his task would be relatively easy to accomplish. The thing that struck him as unusual was the absence of Rockwell. Peter fully expected to find Porter waiting for him when he arrived, maybe with some food. But it was not to be, and he was alone to fend for himself.

The sky was dark when Rockwell returned to the cabin. Peter was sleeping on the bunk, exhausted from everything he had experienced in the course of the day spent. Porter put his foot on the frame of the bunk and gave it a push, toppling both it and its contents. Peter crashed to the floor and emerged wide awake.

"What, who is it?" Peter blurted out, trying to gain control of his situation. He looked in Rockwell's direction and found his intense expression.

"Ya had ta do it, didn't ya?" Rockwell asked. Peter knew exactly what Porter was talking about, but still felt badly and didn't know what to say. "Whole town has heard the news now and if tears could be drunk, we'd never need rain again." Peter sat down and rested his head in his hand. Rockwell continued to explain the scene in town and was considerably animated about it. He looked like an old story teller in the reflected light from the fire in the hearth. He waved his arms in vast sweeping motions as he revealed to Peter the trouble he had caused.

"Everybody's mourning somebody. Brigham is right in the middle of the whole mess with people pullin' at 'im from all sides, askin' all sorts of questions. The men are bad enough, grievin' for lost sons, but the women folk are really carryin' on."

Peter didn't look up. He just shook his head, not believing the trouble he caused in such a short time. Porter lowered the tone of his voice a little and said, "Brigham told me I should educate you about the way things are done around here. He said that if you're gonna live here, and yer certainly welcome to, you need ta conform ta their way of doin' things or you won't fit in." At that, Peter looked up at Rockwell in disbelief. Porter had anticipated the reaction and was ready for it. "Now don't get yerself riled at me," Rockwell said. "I ain't sayin' it, Brigham is. Lord knows neither one of us has ever been much for conformin'. I suppose when it comes ta you, you can blame me fer that, but at least try ta be yerself in a way that don't hurt nobody else!"

"Are you sore at me?" Peter asked Rockwell.

"No, I ain't sore at ya. I just want everybody ta get along."

It was important for Peter to know that Rockwell had not withdrawn his support from him. After all, Peter's life wasn't all roses either. This land was just as strange to him as it was to anybody else, and Rockwell was right; Peter was an individual who never saw any need to conform just because everybody said to. But Peter knew he would work hard to preserve his identity while remaining a part of the covenant people.

"Thanks Port, I'm glad you understand," Peter said. "By the way, what did President Young want to talk to you about?"

Rockwell tipped the bunk frame upright and sat down by the fire. He watched the embers glow red and yellow, occasionally dancing up the chimney. "Looks like I won't be around to keep ya out of trouble fer awhile," he said. "Brigham wants me ta ride ta the California territory and bring back some mules. If we don't get some fresh stock soon, we won't be able to get the crops in next spring."

Peter went weak in the knees at the thought of another long journey, but that wasn't his reason for staying. "I can't go with you, Porter," he said.

"Go with me? I'll have enough ta do without havin' ta keep you out of trouble!" They both smiled at each other. Rockwell knew why Peter couldn't go. He wasn't about to ask him to. Besides, Porter needed some time on his own now. There were things in his own life that needed sorting out.

"How long will you be here before you leave?" Peter asked.

"I leave at first light, I hate ta say," Rockwell replied. "You can stay here in the cabin and look after things fer me 'til I get back, but tonight you sleep on the floor."

The two friends laughed together, and the sounds blended perfectly with the prairie symphony in the summer night. Peter tried to bury the feelings of pain and frustration he felt because of the sorrow caused by the news he had so thoughtlessly unleashed on the settlement. He finally decided that, tomorrow, they would all be back to the troubles at hand, but now, tonight, those troubles would be free to dance up the chimney with the sparkling embers.

12

California—The Land of Plenty

Captain Jedediah Cutler stood at the summit of the Cajon pass and gaped with astonishment. He looked back the way they had come. The desert below abutted the foot of the glittering granite Santa Rosa mountains, up which they had just toiled. Then he looked west at California. "It's the bloody Garden of Eden," marveled Lieutenant Jamie Logan, who had just clambered up the trail to stand beside his commander.

"It is beautiful," Jed agreed. "Look at that green." He took in a great breath of the clean California air, then exhaled a heavy sigh. Without taking his eyes from the scene, he fervently asked Jamie, "Can you get me down there right now?"

"Aye, Captain, but I can't alter the laws of physics," Jamie replied smiling. "We'll have ta walk."

Marching down the slope and on to the sea, they went through many villages and passed by missions and presidios. Everywhere the flag of Mexico was down and the flag of John C. Fremont's Bear Republic was up. They saw Anglo faces among the Mexicans who turned out to watch them tramp by. Even though Fremont had been warning the American backers of his "Bear Republic" about the wicked influence of the Mormons polluting fair California, the Anglos cheered the blue uniforms and the U.S. flag all the same. The Mexicans did not. Acceptance was in the air, however. There was no mourning for the *caudillos* and *hidalgos* of old Mexico, nor for the misfortune of El Presidente Santa Ana. The war was over, and the prophecy that had sustained the Mormon soldiers had been fulfilled.

In the beautiful little town of San Diego, the American occupation force made its headquarters at the tile and adobe barracks of the Presidio. Palm trees, such as these gringos had never seen, lined all sides of the quadrangle and kept the roofs in shade.

On the grassy expanse inside the quad, the Mormon Battalion was in formation for a mustering-out parade. The uniforms had been washed and brushed, patched and darned. Obviously their coats would never be the rich, dark Prussian blue that had been issued them at Leavenworth, and their trousers would never again match the color of the clear sky. Their brass buttons, however, sparkled in the bright sun. The black leather was soaped, oiled, and polished, reflecting the light from all its wrinkles and creases. The fading and fraying of their clothes were the only badges of honor they would ever receive, and the Mormon Battalion wore them proudly. All muskets and bayonets were cleaned, oiled, and wiped down. They looked like the "burnished arms" officers liked to talk about when they compared themselves to the Roman legions, the Greek warriors, and Napoleon.

The men were at "order arms" and the officers at "carry sword." Jed stood at attention in front of his company. *I remember back home when we paraded as the old Nauvoo Legion on the Fourth of July. Lieutenant General Joseph Smith addressed us with his sword held high,* thought Jed, as Major Broderick marched out to take his place as Parade Adjutant before the assembled ranks.

Colonel Cooke and civilians from Fremont's government walked their horses slowly out in front of the formation. Major Broderick brought his sword up and down in the graceful arc of the sword salute. "Sir, the parade is formed," he announced.

"Thank you, Major," replied the colonel in a soft voice, slowly and carefully returning the salute with his own sword. "Take your post." The major marched around beside the colonel and the guests.

Sheathing his sword, the colonel looked at the battalion sadly and for a long time. Jed noticed Charbonneau silently taking up a cross-legged position in between two pillars of the portico on the side of the quadrangle behind the colonel.

He is only a silly, pop-eyed, old walrus of a man with a young fool's ideas of glory and reputation. He rode while we walked! But, by rights, he should have died out there somewhere, and he held on, clinging to that horse and to life. He got us things we had to have, and he listened to reason at Tucson. The army could have sent us a lot worse. So ran Jed's thoughts as he waited for the colonel to begin his farewell speech. Meanwhile, Charbonneau continued to sit like a statue in the portico. Broderick stood at attention, looking up at the colonel.

"Men of the Mormon Battalion," began the colonel slowly and softly. "I congratulate you on our safe arrival to the Pacific shore—the conclusion of a march of over two thousand miles." Now the colonel straightened up in his saddle and gained in strength and emotion with each sentence. "History may be searched in vain for an

equal march of infantry. We marched through wilderness where wild beasts both threatened and saved us—desert where, for want of water, there is no living creature. The garrison of Tucson gave us no pause. We drove them out, but our intercourse with the citizens was unmarked by a single act of injustice. Continuing to march, half-naked and half-fed, we have discovered and made a road of great value to our country.

"Arriving in California, we cheerfully entered into a campaign to meet, as we supposed, the advance of an enemy, only to learn that California had been secured for the United States by the efforts of its citizens who are our countrymen. Thus, you volunteers have shown the high and essential qualities of veterans. Now you will leave the service and return to your families. You will then build up your own home, wherever that might be, under a government you helped to make into a protector of your lives and your fortunes."

After a brief pause, the colonel tried to continue. His voice cracked, and he looked around at the scene with his round eyes brimming with rheumy tears. "I thank you, comrades, for giving me a chance to . . . a chance to . . . ."

"Hooray for da colonel!" yelled Charbonneau so suddenly and powerfully that the horses shied, and every head in the battalion turned to look at him as though they had been ordered to do an "eyes right."

"Hip hip, hooray," yelled Broderick and the Battalion gave three cheers, with Jed laughing and shaking his head.

Jed luxuriated in his new, store-bought, civilian clothes. All the men had signed an order authorizing the army to send their pay directly to the Church, but now their mustering out pay had come to the men in cash, enabling them to get home. So, with the money he had earned, Jed bought a horse and tack and still had enough to outfit himself for the journey back to Celia. He was infantry no longer.

From the vantage point of his own horse, his own clothes, and his own money, Jed looked around at California. One night, a few days after mustering out, groups of battalion men sat around charcoal braziers in the barracks of the San Diego Presidio, where they were allowed to live until they pushed off for wherever they would go. There was a lot of talk about California.

"Good old Captain Sutter, he bought himself a mill up by that big bay . . . . "

"San Francisco Bay."

"Right. San Francisco Bay, and some of us from "C" Company are going to work for him. There's a town up there where Fremont and the Anglos kind of run things and . . . . "

"Fremont hates us. There'll be persecution up there."

"Oh, we don't think so. There's plenty of us, and the local people like how we handled ourselves in the army."

"Did you hear about Captain Hunt? He's going back to San Bernardino—that first town we saw when we came down from the mountains."

"How about you, Captain Cutler?" The smooth, freckled face of one of the Battalion's youngest soldiers looked up at him in the flickering firelight.

"We married men have to go back to our families, of course." Jed shifted uneasily as he leaned against a stucco pillar.

"But will you stay there in the valley of the Great Salt Lake?" wondered the earnest young man.

"We hear it is too poor for our new gathering place."

Jed tried to speak with strong assurance to these men. He was still a leader to them. "President Young, and even Joseph Smith before him, thought it was the right place, where we would be safe in the mountains."

"There are plenty of mountains here, more grass, more timber, water, more everything."

"It is a grand place," agreed Jed with a sigh.

The next morning, Jed came out of Headquarters with his discharge papers all signed and sealed. He saw a man in brand new civilian clothes from his broad brimmed hat down to his . . . army boots. Jed looked again and saw it was Broderick. "Good morning, Major," gulped Jed, recovering his voice.

"Not Major Broderick anymore, just Mr. Broderick now. I decided to leave the service, too," grinned Broderick with an infectious smile. "I may even get married."

"And stay here? But you invested a lot of years in the service," said Jed with great curiosity.

"Yes, but I don't want to invest any more. I served my country and helped it gain all this land and wealth. Now I want to help myself, while I'm still young enough to start a life of my own." Broderick inhaled a huge breath and blew it out with a big smile and a joyous look around. "The air is so clean and fresh in California."

"Well," said Jedediah, after a dumbfounded pause. "Do you have a woman in mind?"

"No. No, it is just a goal I have set for myself. There are plenty of opportunities around here in that area, as in all others, though I don't suppose I will find a beauty such as your Celia. You must be yearning to see her."

"The men with families in Salt Lake Valley leave tomorrow, and if they cannot keep up with this fine Spanish horse I bought, then I will pioneer ahead and beat them all to the valley. Their wives will wonder why they have dawdled along the way."

The two men laughed together and found themselves walking along side by side. "I bought a horse, too," said Broderick after a hesitation. "If it's all right with you, I would like to ride along with you for a few miles and show you something."

Jed looked intently at Broderick, "Certainly, Major. That would be a pleasure."

"Call me John, please," said the fresh-faced, smiling man. This was the same man who had drunk buffalo sinkhole water, reconnoitered Tucson, and now proposed to marry and live in a newly conquered province, not to mention his plan to show off a surprise on the following day.

"Right . . . John. Tomorrow we ride east, then," said the amazed Jed.

"Good." John Broderick stopped and faced Jed, and they shook hands. "I always relied on you as the natural leader of our band. Everybody did, I think. We counted on you to do the right thing and show the way. I think you and the other family men will like what I show you tomorrow."

"Thank you, John," replied Jed uneasily.

After they parted, Jed walked around San Diego deep in thought, taking in all the sights, sounds, and smells of the market, the plaza, and the homes.

Early next morning, when the sun was not yet above the Vallecito Mountains that looked down on San Diego by the sea, a column of horsemen, riding frisky horses new to their masters, set out from the Presidio. They headed east into the grassy and pine-forested uplands. John, Jed, and Jamie were in the lead. When they had ridden half the day, John led them off the main Camino Road and turned onto a forest trail, which led up and over a ridge.

On the crest of the ridge, John paused and motioned for the group to draw up around him. His companions did so and looked out over a splendid valley, carpeted with green. Treelines of poplar, pine, and cottonwood showed where streams crisscrossed the valley floor. Forested mountains surrounded the valley, but not so near or so lowering as to suggest a pocket that would be frigid in winter. Here and there were tiny dots of black or reddish brown which, if watched closely, could be seen to have white faced heads down next to the ground—cattle, hundreds of them.

"That grass is up to a horse's belly," said one wondering brother.

"And them cattle can eat all they want without moving," added another, pulling at his beard.

"Anybody live out this way?" asked a third man, directing his question to John Broderick.

"We do, if you like," announced John melodramatically as he turned in his saddle to sweep his concentrated gaze over each man in the group. "This is the Valley del Capitan. You are looking at Rancho de la Barona, which I bought with my mustering out pay."

"Majors must make a good wage," mumbled one of the men, looking down into his kerchief.

"I got a good price from an *hidalgo* who decided to leave California and take his family back to old Mexico," said John, grinning that new grin of his, "but it is too much for me alone. I will sell shares to any of you who want to throw in with me. Those five hundred head of cattle go with the place, and they are excellent breeding stock. We are riding the breeders of a fortune in horses. You can build any kind of home you want, stone, log, even frame if we have a sawmill. We are close enough to town to trade for anything. By thunder, we can build our own town if that is what we want! What do you say?"

"I'll build you a home in the valley," mumbled Jed, a little choked up.

"Truly, this is a promising valley," laughed the bearded man as he took off his hat and took in the whole scene.

"I must ask my wives, of course," said another.

"Of course," John agreed, solemnly.

"I don't even have one wife, but I imagine I could support half a dozen here," piped up the very young

freckle-faced fellow with a gap-toothed chuckle. "I believe I will throw in with you, Major, if you will let me work for my share."

"That is fine," assured John, shaking hands with the young chap. Then he turned to face Jed, who could not meet his eye. "How about you, Jed?" He waited for an answer.

Jamie cleared his throat and began officiously, "President Young has said that the Salt Lake Valley is the gathering place of the Saints. He is counting on us to come back and help build up the kingdom."

Still everyone waited for Jed to reply. Slowly Jed whispered, "I don't know."

"Eh, Laddie?" pressed Jamie.

Louder and with some anger, Jed rounded on the group, "I said I don't know! I have to see this Salt Lake Valley. I have to talk to Celia. I have to talk to Brother Brigham."

"That is right," came a voice in the back.

"John, this is a beautiful place, and you have done well to purchase it," Jed continued, earnestly, "but, as one elder of Israel, so called because of the responsibility of leadership, I was chosen to be a captain of a hundred families before I was a captain of 'A' Company. I am husband to a great lady who has suffered much to pioneer that valley called Salt Lake . . . yet I have a great love and respect for this land called California. I have to study carefully, and think who and what I sustain. If ever there was a matter for prayer, this is one such. Then I will act."

"Well said, Jedediah Cutler! I am beginning to think that Mormons are the best Americans I know!" proclaimed John Broderick, clapping Jed on the shoulder amid smiles and laughter from all. "You do what you have to do—all of you. But I want you all to know that there will always be a place in my *hacienda* and in my heart for each of you."

13

A New Life, A New Chance

Everything a society needed was taking shape in Salt Lake City. And, of course, there were babies born in the new homes. For Celia, it started in the middle of the night. Actually, it had started that same morning when she looked her first Indian in the eye.

He had ridden up the old Indian trail that the pioneers were beginning to call State Road. He was mounted on a strange breed of horse that was solid brown except for white spots on its rump. She watched him warily as she beat a rag rug, grateful for the heavy club in her hands. The brave scowled at her with intense curiosity as his long-striding horse glided past. His body moved unconsciously in perfect rhythm with the muscles working underneath him. His beads and ribbons were as colorful and as dilapidated as Celia's rug. Slowing his mount as he approached, he looked at the pregnant pioneer. He had no weapons, but he still looked fierce and dangerous. Peter walked to the edge of the street with a heavy hoe in his hands to watch the visitor ride up to Brigham Young's house.

That night, Celia flinched violently when the Indian leapt upon her with a horrible cry, matched instantly by her own shriek. She tried to protect the baby inside by turning on her side but the Indian had her pinned as his hands reached for her throat. "Jed!" she cried out. "Jed, please help me!" But Jed did not come. She remembered with an endless fall to despair that her husband was dead. She tried to push the Indian away, but he was too strong. Suddenly strong hands tore the Indian off her and Peter was holding her in his arms as she wracked herself with huge sobs.

Dazed, she heard her mother's voice crooning, "There, there, dear. It was only a dream. Lie back down now." She looked over Peter's shoulder and saw that there was no Indian and that her mother was kneeling beside her bed. Peter was real, having stopped by to check on the two women. He was, in fact, holding her and now eased her back down onto her pillow. He looked at her steadily but made no sound.

They left Celia after a while but had no sooner settled down themselves than the first pain began. She endured several to make sure it had really started, then she called out softly, "Mama." Her mother came to her, bearing a lamp, and Peter could be seen standing behind her in the flickering shadows. Emma did not want to talk about pains and child birthing with him there, and he sensed it.

"I'll go get the midwife," he said on his way out the door.

Everything seemed to be going well. The bishop and the ward teachers gave Celia a blessing. Peter got the midwife, huge Sister Willis, who had borne seven of her own and laughed with anticipation as she laid out her equipment. Here it was, two in the morning, with Celia gasping through a pain, and the little cabin was full of people. Emma clapped her hands sharply three times and jerked her head toward the door while fixing Quimby with a stern look. The men knew that look, and the cabin cleared except for Sister Willis.

First babies usually take a long time, and it was noon and hot in the cabin when Jed, Junior, arrived in the promised valley. No worse for the wait, he looked well, cried with strength and nursed immediately. Through the window, Celia heard Peter pacing about. Finally, he saddled his horse and rode off. She cried, saying the name of her dead husband over and over and shielding her child from the dirt that blew in the window.

Emma was tired for days after that night of commotion, but she took care of Celia and the baby while keeping up with the garden and the animals—chickens mostly. If that wasn't enough, she also worked at keeping that pesky Peter shooed away. *Let him mope someplace else,* she thought. *He is fretting Celia terribly, and the girl needs to relax and make milk.* Anyway, she did not have a confirmation of the spirit that Jed was dead, and she was feeling her own commotion about Quimby. He was a true saint and deserved to come home to a loving wife after all he did for his ward, not to mention farming his own land the live-long day. She remembered what Caleb had told her before he died and felt a quiet assurance of spirit that what she was feeling was right.

And so it was that Emma endeavored to wash her least faded dress when who should come down the street but Quimby Leighton, looking about with his cheerful, calm expression. He had a pair of rabbits swinging by their tails from his fist as he walked along. Emma's heart sank as she looked at the brightly colored dress in the wash tub and then at Quimby. She would have much rather been wearing what she was washing, but there was no use crying over spilt soap bubbles. Her

BROT

heart settled down, though, when she looked up and saw Quimby smiling at her. "Hello, Emma," he said so pleasantly that she just beamed. "Can I see you for a minute?"

"Come in, come in," she said, grinning and helping him through the gate.

As he held up the rabbits for her inspection he said, "The Brethren tell us to carry our guns to the fields because of the Indian raids, but it's hard to sling a musket across your back when you're irrigating all day. As long as I have to do it, though, I might as well get some benefit from it. I'll dress and skin these and you can make your wonderful rabbit stew."

"Which you will stay to eat," added Emma looking up into his face with sparkling eyes that locked with his own fond gaze.

"Thank you from the bottom of my stomach. My cooking is a violation of the Word of Wisdom." They laughed together. "How are Celia and Jed, Junior?"

"They are well and napping."

"When baby sleeps, mother sleeps, right?"

"Exactly."

"It is just as well, because I want to talk to you, if I may." Suddenly Quimby blushed and seemed to lose his courage.

Emma quickly strengthened him by saying, "I am pleased that you feel you can confide in me with what must surely be important information."

Quimby cleared his throat and opened his mouth to continue, but he was interrupted a second time. "How are Celia and the baby today?" came Peter's voice as he rounded the corner of the cabin.

"Be a good boy, Peter, and go dress these rabbits," Emma said dryly, without missing a beat or looking at Peter. She knew it would take him quite awhile, and that suited her just fine. Peter, in turn, looked at the game, looked at Emma, then at Bishop Leighton, and finally back to the rabbits. He took them from Emma and left without another word.

"Yes, Quimby," Emma repeated, pulling him down to sit beside her on their puncheon bench by the cabin door. "You were about to say . . . ?"

"Well, I . . . " He managed to take a breath and throw off his paralysis. ". . . I wanted to ask you . . . . Would you consider yourself . . . truly happy in valley?"

"We came in the belief that God would provide for us here," said Emma, thoughtfully. "Day by day that is proving to be true, and it is a testimony of God to me. Yes, I'd consider myself happy."

"And you don't regret coming here?" he asked in all seriousness, studying her carefully.

"How can you question that?"

"Well, as your bishop, I feared you might be lonely here. It's not easy to live by oneself. It's good to have the affection of loved ones . . . to have someone in whom you can confide . . . a comfort in work . . . a solace in adversity."

"I quite agree with you, Bishop."

"Sister Faraday . . . . "

"Yes . . . Bishop?"

This time it was Fennelly and his boys, in their blue-shirt hand-me-down spectrum, who interrupted Quimby. They came singing and capering down the street. As Quimby shot to his feet, almost knocking over the bench, Emma was thinking how she could hardly refuse to wash the Parsons' shirts, even though her work load had increased so since the baby. Then she noticed a solid, quite buxom woman beside Fennelly. Her hair was the color of straw, although straight bangs were all that could be seen under the bonnet which had failed to protect a sunburned nose. When the bonnet turned to face Fennelly (and Emma), she could see big, sky blue eyes, apple cheeks with freckles, and a creamy white double chin.

Fennelly was happily lecturing the woman and his boys. "Do not think when you gather in Zion that your troubles and trials are through. We must work hard if we are ever to have comfort and pleasure here. Isn't that right, my dear?"

"Ja!" agreed the woman earnestly.

"Each must do what he can and give something needful to the people. Then he will earn the support of the group to make his living."

"Ja, ja!" said the woman, with great support.

"But what can you do, Papa?" Amos interjected.

Emma waited for the explosion of self-righteousness, but it did not come. Instead, Fennelly looked down at his little boy with a perplexed gape and said, "I don't know, Amos, but I'm working on it."

Just then, Fennelly noticed Emma and the Bishop watching them. He led the woman over to the Faraday fence and the couple joined them at the gate. The boys gathered around. "Ah, Bishop, Sister Faraday, I'd like you to meet my wife, Kirsten. We were married at the time Celia had the baby. You were busy yourself then."

"How do you do, Sister Parsons?" said Emma with great relief, as Quimby mumbled the same. "I'm glad to see this family has a woman to take care of them."

"Ja, ja," agreed Kirsten.

"She doesn't speak English yet," Leonard informed them.

"Oh," said Emma and laughed at herself.

"But she makes good cookies!" piped up Amos.

"When we can get some sugar," added Leonard.

"Kan du tale Dansk?" Kirsten asked Emma earnestly, almost imploringly.

Emma put her hands on this new sister's shoulders and shook her head gravely. "No," she replied, "but we will all help you learn English."

"She's Danish. Came over from Dane-mark," said Fennelly.

"Does she like it here?" asked Quimby.

"She misses the fish," Fennelly said, putting his arm around his wife. "I took her fishing out to the Great Salt Lake, but they weren't biting too well."

"That's too bad," sympathized Quimby as he and Emma kept from looking at each other so they would not laugh.

Fennelly held up an empty sack, and they noticed each boy had an appropriately sized sack. "And we just went up the canyon looking for hazelnuts but some of our woodcutters told us they saw Indians, so we came back. I guess those Indians live around here someplace."

"I guess they do," agreed Quimby.

"We wanted to store away something for the coming winter besides that sagebrush we had on the trail," declared Fennelly, making a face.

"That wasn't sagebrush. It was sego lily," corrected Emma.

"I'll be hard pressed to forgive the Indians for teaching us how to eat that stuff," sighed Fennelly, looking up at the mountains. "I much preferred the peas we raised."

"Those weren't peas," muttered Leonard. "They were potatoes."

"Well, if we work hard, this year we'll have a better crop," the Bishop assured them soothingly.

Suddenly Fennelly's face turned positively bleak, and his chin actually dropped. "I don't seem to do so good with the land. I used to be a good piano tuner back in Pennsylvania, you know."

"Yes, we know," chorused Emma and Quimby.

"But they only got one piano to tune out here, and I already tuned it . . . ten times. President Young says I got to spend the rest of the time working the land. It ain't easy, I'll tell you that. Did I tell you I not only tuned pianos but I played them in church, the old church I belonged to before I became a Latter-day Saint, and later in our ward in Nauvoo? I composed, too. I got songs being played all along the Erie Canal. Did you ever hear of "My Gal Sal" or "Sparkin' on a Sunday Night"?

"Yes, I have!" exclaimed Emma; the surprise jerked the response out of her. To think that songs she had danced to when Caleb was courting her were written by Fennelly Parsons—it was remarkable, even outrageous.

"They were my biggest. I made some good money off my songs," mused Fennelly, looking afar off. "Of course, that was not honest labor like farming."

"I—I think I heard of the second one, the one about sparking with your girl friend," said the Bishop, trying to be helpful.

"I wrote a new one," said Fennelly conspiratorially. "Don't tell Brother Brigham. I couldn't help myself. It just came to me when I was trying to fix the plow I broke on that big rock. You remember, Bishop?" Fennelly turned to Leonard and made a little encouraging gesture. Leonard pulled out a harmonica and accompanied his father who sang his composition, "Golly, I'm Glad to Be Alive":

> I used to tune pianos and could always tell the pitch
> But it doesn't seem so helpful when I've got to dig a ditch.
> I used to know the scales and I'd make the music sweet
> But it doesn't seem to simplify the gathering of wheat.

The boys joined in on the second verse and Kirsten clapped her hands.

They have given me a farm and insist that I will thrive
But I can't raise enough to fill my plate.
Oh, golly out in Utah I am glad to be alive;
Oh, the life that we live here is great, very great!

Emma and Quimby found themselves swaying back and forth, tapping their toes, and grinning like fools.

It isn't very easy growing crops that you need
When you can't tell a weed from the sprout of a seed.
It isn't very simple when you try to rope a steer
And you don't know the front from the thing at the rear.

Oh, the life that we live here is rich:
But the thing you've got to know
Is where to use a hoe
And how to get water from a ditch.

Quimby led a little round of applause and then said, "Brother Parsons, I want to talk to you later about a ward choir."

Fennelly's face opened into an excited smile. "Oh yes, Bishop. Any time you want to talk to me . . . that would be wonderful."

The Parsons family strode on, waving gaily at Emma and Quimby.

"Well, uh . . . . " began Quimby, lamely.

"Come and sit down again," offered Emma firmly, putting her arm through Quimby's and taking him back to the bench. Once there, though, he refused to sit. Instead, he turned to face Emma and took both her hands in his. His voice was strong and decisive.

"Emma, we both married very well and for a long time couldn't think of ourselves marrying anybody else.

But marriage is the best part of life. Without it, there is no abiding happiness. I believe that your Caleb and my Alice want us to be happy and that we can all be happy together in the kingdom to come. I believe that, together, you and I can make a bit of heaven on earth here in this valley. Am I succeeding in communicating my feelings to you, Emma?"

"Completely, Quimby."

Bishop Leighton's feelings were also communicated to Celia, who had been watching through the cabin window after being awakened by Fennelly's song. It truly seemed to her a miracle, and she smiled hopefully as Quimby and Emma kissed a long overdue kiss.

Quimby and Emma sat together on the puncheon bench, Quimby's arm around Emma, her head on his shoulder. Peter could be seen making his way back to the cabin, rabbits in hand, all nicely dressed. At first glance, it appeared the rabbits had had the upper hand, Peter being covered in fluff and generally rumpled. As he reached the gate, he stopped and surveyed the serene picture before him. "Did I miss something?" he asked innocently.

It was just too much for everyone, and they erupted into laughter.

14

Troubled Homecoming

Jed, Jamie, and a band of twenty Battalion men entered Utah from the west. This laid an added burden on their faith in the Prophet. *How could Brother Brigham put the saints in a dirt bowl like this?* thought Jed. Unfortunately, they were at a disadvantage by traveling through the western desert instead of coming through the green mountains, as the pioneers had.

"I think if it were not for my Jerusha, I would turn right around and head back to California," Jamie declared, when he saw the valley. The sentiment was echoed by many of the men, including Jed.

"There is nothing that says we can't take our wives and families and do just that, Jamie," Jed assured him. "Unless there is something to this 'Salt Lake City' that we have yet to be informed of, California will be the land I call home."

His tired horse was no longer spirited and beautiful. Head down and shoulders lurching, the stallion also seemed to be homesick for California as he plodded along. Jed swayed and bobbed in the saddle. He was as loose and relaxed as he could be, trying to make good time for the last stretch of the journey.

It took them a whole day to eke their way over the huge desert valley that they were worried might be the "the place." However, they saw that it not only had no humans in it, but no other living thing of any kind. It was just dusty, dying sage and tumbleweed. If there were snakes, the horses must have avoided them by staying on open, uncluttered dirt. It was gorgeous at sunset, as they reached the crest of the valley's eastern ridge. They decided to camp there and enjoy it. The next pocket to the east was dark now and full of tangled ravines. Horses wouldn't go there even if men wanted to. It was good to be in a group. Nobody was confident enough of his skills or strength to face this country alone.

The next day, they clopped over a glistening white salt flat as bad as anything the Battalion had marched over. It was like riding a horse on an endless ballroom floor, which reflected the baking sun back up into a man's face, up under his hat. Soon they encountered the massive lake, heavy with salt.

The horses had worked their way around to the Great Salt Lake, turning the corner of a mountain range that ended on the lake shore. For the second time in his life, Jed was on a beach looking out over a vast body of briny water with a salty wind blowing up white topped waves. To come from a desert and arrive at an ocean in the middle of mountains was so strange that they all smiled at each other uneasily.

As the men pressed their mounts forward, they found themselves picking their way through stinking salt marshes. Each horse tried to find firm ground that trended usefully eastward while the men gauged their direction from the towering mountains ahead. The sharp peaks had jagged ruffs of snow extending down from their bald tops. Where the men were, the marsh reeds were so high that the huge lake was quickly lost to sight, even from horseback. The firm ground became easier to find, however, and they emerged from the reeds to finally catch sight the valley they were supposed to call home.

Perhaps the soft light of late afternoon helped the scene, but Jed was bound to admit it was a beautiful valley. The canyons coming down out of those east mountains ahead were all packed full of dark green forest. That meant streams running out of the mountains to water the east bench, which they could see running along the base of the towering rock massif. It was through those mountains their families must have come. What incredible mountains they were, at that! If nothing else proved pleasing to the eye, Jed saw plenty of beauty in the towering peaks ahead of him.

On the west side of the valley, as they looked south, there was a placid river running down the gentle trough cut deeply into the ground. It was lined by tall broadleaf trees, the cottonwoods they had seen and learned about in California.

Suddenly, Jamie yelled and pointed as he stood in his stirrups. All eyes followed his. They saw lights, lights in windows, clustered at the base of that east bench. The houses were formed in an angle made by two foothills. They wanted to sink spurs and gallop all the way, but they knew that was insane. They picked up the pace though, trotting eagerly, racing the lengthening shadows. The horses didn't mind. Their heads and tails were up. They smelled their own kind.

Fennelly Parsons was so excited his heart raced and his breath came in gulps, even though he was not moving an inch. He stood at the entrance to The Bowery and looked around to make sure everything was perfect.

The pine boughs laid on the lodgepole pine lattice overhead made a grand roof. The thick straight tree trunks with their furrowed bark made impressive posts to hold up the domed roof.

Looking out through those open sides, he could see the settlement all around, the huge streets marked out, the hasty fort they had built in the first weeks after arriving in the valley, the temple square Brother Brigham had tapped out with his cane and said, "Here . . . here will rise the House of the Lord." At this point, most of the people had moved out of their wagon box encampments into adobe or log houses that, although small and low-slung, were permanent.

To gaze at the settlement was to see order. The raw, dirty struggle to pull out huge tumbleweeds and sage was finished. Chopping irrigation ditches out of gravel, clay and sandstone was also complete. Indeed, enough stinking manure had been spread over chalky plowed fields to enrich the rocky soil and foster the growth of healthy crops. After months of eating sego lily roots and potatoes the size of radishes, the new crops meant new beginnings.

And now, at last, the people of the Fourteenth Ward were coming out of their houses in nice clean clothes and gathering at The Bowery for choir practice—Fennelly's choir practice. "Is that the last of the hymnals, Leonard?" asked Fennelly, still quivering as his sons finished laying out the battered books on the split log benches. The eight boys stood up from their work in various parts of the Bowery and stared quizzically at their father. "Thank you, boys," said Fennelly, quietly but intensely. "You can go play now . . . until bedtime. I'll join you for prayers."

"Go play now?" said little Amos. "Don't we have more work to . . . . "

"Come on," whispered Leonard hoarsely, grabbing Amos by the arm and pulling him toward the open side of the Bowery. Dazed, the boys first walked, then ran out.

"What's wrong with Papa?" wondered Amos as he ran. "Why don't we have to work?"

"Because he's happy now. We're safe, and he gets to do what he is suited to do," said Leonard calmly, slowing down and breathing deeply of the gentle evening air.

"Oh boys," called Fennelly after them, causing them to freeze in fear. "On your way to have fun, don't forget to sing 'The Choir Practice Song.' Let's get those people out!"

The boys sighed with relief. They loved to get the people out and they loved the song that did it from the moment Fennelly taught it to them. They formed up in single file, struck up an officious pose, and began marching around the Bowery as they belted out the song.

> Tonight is the night for choir practice.
> Our call is for quarter to eight.
> Come tenors and basses and all you sopranos.
> No one should ever be late.

Now men and women, well turned out in their cleaned and patched clothes, came out of their cabins arm in arm and joined the singing, led by the boys, as they walked toward the Bowery.

> The chorister's eager to lead in our singing.
> Our voices are ready now to rise.
> At quarter to eight in Great Salt Lake,
> Our hymns will be reaching to the skies.

First came Celia, carrying Jedediah, Jr. in her arms, her dress and bonnet clean and pressed. Her shining ringlets were arranged down the sides of her face, and her face was clean and smooth. Her smile was tight lipped, though, and she seemed distracted. Fennelly figured she was still troubled about the reports of Jed's death.

Then came Bishop Leighton with Emma Faraday on his arm. They made a beautiful couple and also anchored the bass and soprano sections of the choir. "Uh-oh, there is a tenor missing," noticed Fennelly. "Evening, Sister Rawson," he said, tipping his hat. "Where is your cousin Kimball?"

"He couldn't come." Her voice rose to a squeal of excitement and hope. "Our cow will surely drop a calf tonight."

"Wonderful," said Fennelly, with less enthusiasm, but several men laughed and cheered heartily.

"Evening, Bishop," rumbled Brother Willis, shaking Quimby's hand. He was as big as Sister Willis, the midwife. "What do you hear from Brother Stone?"

"He's still on his Denmark mission. The Lord has blessed him with the gift of tongues. He speaks like a native now." Quimby's face brightened still more. "He just sent over thirty more families." There was another cheer.

Fennelly cleared his throat officiously. "Let's have an opening prayer, shall we? Sister Tate?" All quieted and bowed their heads and folded their arms. Pert little Sister Tate intoned a sweet prayer as they stood among the benches.

With gratifying discipline, they came up after the "Amen," sat, and took up their hymnals. Fennelly grasped his rickety old music stand and lovingly smoothed out his stained and ragged hymnal. This was going to be a good choir, the best in the city. He just knew he could get all the moving parts and the close harmonies out of the talent he had here, and what a rich vocal production he would teach them.

"Brothers and Sisters," announced Fennelly, "For our choir number this Sunday, we will try that new song that Brother Penrose has been working on. Now, he's a little shy because he's not sure it's ready yet, but if it works like I think it will, the Brethren will have it in the Hymnal in no time. All right, get your sheet music. 'Oh Ye Mountains High.'"

As Fennelly conducted with two hands, his sure and knowledgeable movements called forth precise and energetic singing. People all around the bowery stopped what they were doing and listened to the beautiful music and the excellent words floating through the settlement.

> Oh ye mountains high, where the clear blue sky
> Arches over the vale of the free.
> Where the pure breezes blow and the clear streamlets flow,
> How I've longed to your bosom to flee.

Celia rocked slightly in time with the music and sang out the contents of her heart . . . her hope, her joy, her trouble.

> Oh, Zion, dear Zion, land of the free,
> Now my own mountain home, Unto thee I have come.
> All my fond hopes are centered in thee.

The baby loved it and stared up at her, reaching up with tiny outstretched hands. As they began the second verse, Jed was singing in her ear, "Oh the something ta dum and the wicked shall die . . . . "

She thought it was her dream again until he put his arm around her and she felt him and smelled him. Realizing that there were many new men's voices joining in, she turned and beheld a miracle. Fennelly had stopped conducting, his eyes and mouth wide open. Jerusha shrieked, "Jamie!" and Celia swooned, but Jed

Jerusha shrieked, "Jamie!" and Celia swooned, but Jed held her up.

Everyone turned to look at the battalion men who had crept into the bowery while the choir members were so entranced with their singing. The place erupted with laughter and whoops and cries. Everyone found somebody to embrace. Now the people around about who had been listening to the singing came out of their homes and rushed to The Bowery to join in and expand the hubbub.

Ecstatically, Fennelly sang out lustily. He waved his arms to start the song again and everyone joined in.

> Oh Zion, dear Zion, land of the free,
> Now my own mountain home, Unto thee I have come
> All my fond hopes are centered in thee.

To the surprise of absolutely no one, choir practice was over after one run-through of that appropriate song. Fennelly was a little crestfallen at the usurpation of his great moment, but what could he say with the battalion men arriving? Anyway, even in the glory of that moment, everyone was so appreciative of his conducting that he still felt secure in his calling. Even the battalion men, clinging to their wives, said they looked forward to next Sunday, as they pumped his hand. That gave him a grand feeling.

The sun was setting behind the Oquirrh Mountains. The Wasatch Mountains along the east side, at whose feet the settlement lay, were pink in the last sun rays. In between, the valley floor was purple. The corona along the crest of the western mountains was bright red. Jed looked at none of it. The beauty he craved was there beside him.

Jed and Celia walked along slowly, with her and the child still tightly enfolded in his arms. "Is this what you were trying to tell me about back in Winter Quarters?" Jed asked Celia, taking the baby from her.

"I tried to tell you, Jed, but your duty seemed more important."

"It may have seemed like that at the time, but there is nothing more important to me than my family." Jed cradled his son in one arm and his wife in the other.

"I named your son after you. It seemed like the proper thing to do."

"A beautiful wife, a strong, healthy son," Jed beamed with pride, " . . . how blessed I am. You endured the trek west alone, helping make a way for others to come join us here, safe and protected. Celia, my dearest, do you have any idea how much love and admiration I feel for you?"

"And I for you, good sir. You listened to your prophet and did your duty for the sake of everyone, thinking not of yourself. It is no wonder so many look to you for leadership, and your son will grow up just like you in a home filled with love."

Approaching the house, they did not speak. It was strange. Celia seemed to be tongue-tied. They got to a level plot of ground, maybe two acres, with no fence around it. There was Celia's wagon box and cabin home. They stopped and looked at it. Finally Celia spoke. "This doesn't have to be our final choice. I picked the best lot I could find. Others are already pulling out of the city and finding choice places up and down the bench and . . . . "

"This is our little home in the valley," said Jed, smiling. He kissed Celia. Then he peeked around the corner of the house. "You put in a garden?"

"A man helped me. He's still here."

"Oh, yes, I can hear him hoeing."

Her lip was trembling but Jed did not see because he was striding around the house to meet the man and inspect the garden. As the garden was revealed to Jed, he saw the tall man stand up from hoeing and turn to face him. It was Peter Van Cleef.

Peter dropped the hoe which clattered to the baked ground, raising a cloud of irritated locusts. He was agog, and torn with inner conflict. He smiled broadly and gasped. He even laughed as he called out, "Jed! You're alive!" Then his smile froze into a clenched teeth grin, and he looked in pain at Celia who was frozen into a tense picture of mortification. She looked only at the baby and rearranged his clothes so fretfully that he cried out.

Peter broke free of his shock enough to stride over to Jed and hold out his hand. Jed took it and shook it with a trance-like slowness. Like Peter, he also had a lop-sided smile stuck rigidly to his face. "Praise God, you are well and have returned safely," Peter continued to babble.

"Why? Did everyone think we were dead?" asked Jed almost dreamily.

Peter cleared his throat before being able to speak. "A . . . yes, yes they did, as a matter of fact."

"Matter of fact?" questioned Jed. "It's sure nonsense. Why would anybody think such drivel?"

"Because that was the news. We heard that the Mormon Battalion was wiped out, lost in the desert," Peter hastened to explain.

"Who brought that news here? You?"

"Well . . . yes . . . I did," said Peter, gulping. Then he spoke up louder with a sudden sense of outrage. "I risked my life to come here! I'm wanted for murder back in Saint Louis. I had to tell the Saints about the pursuit, about more persecution coming, and about the Battalion not coming back to help their families because the desert got you all, or the Comancheros did! We were given your sword by an army courier."

"We traded my sword to the Comancheros for an extra horse. We had a promise, and we are here." Jed felt rage well up inside him toward his old friend because of Peter's hasty actions. Although he felt like fighting instead of talking, he struggled to lighten the mood of the confrontation. Jed gazed into space for a moment and then thought of something that would interest Peter. "The war is over. California is part of the United States now, as is this place, I suppose. California is beautiful, and rich. I saw ranchos and towns that were very good. It has everything you've ever sought after, Peter."

Peter was glad to move the talk along to something safe as he replied, "Yes, and I am wondering if that is not the place for us to be."

But Jed returned to the moment they must deal with. "So, you have been living in Salt Lake? Taking care of my wife?"

"I'm living in Rockwell's cabin, taking care of my friend! Celia needed a man's help with this tough soil and bringing water here. You should see this new-fangled irrigation. When it works it's . . . . "

"Bishop Leighton and Emma weren't enough help? No ward teachers to . . . ?"

"Quimby and Emma got married and are working hard to survive on their own place. Ward teachers can't be here every day."

"But you can? Is that your job now? And what did you say about being wanted for murder?" Jed was trying to keep his voice low, but it kept going up into his tightened throat and gritted teeth.

"I had to," yelled Peter. "I had to take care of Celia!" Celia looked around to see if any neighbors were taking in this scene. So far, none were. "Just because you do whatever you're told by the Prophet doesn't relieve you of your personal responsibilities."

"The Prophet was right, and I earned the money to get her here!" retorted Jed with dignity that was also getting loud.

"Oh, and I can see you are well fixed! You could have been killed to no purpose!"

"But you see I'm not dead," retorted Jed icily with a thin-lipped smile.

"You left your wife," returned Peter, cut for cut. "If she were mine I would stay with her and protect her."

"But she's not yours!" The two men were unconsciously advancing on each other with one step per speech, shoulders back, chests bulging, eyes riveted on each other. Celia watched them with an agitation that became irritation.

They both were startled when Celia spoke up. "I'm not anybody's. I'm not a cow or a homestead that can be claimed."

It was her turn to be startled when they both turned their heads to look at her and bellowed together, "You stay out of this!"

That woke up the baby and made Celia cry. "All right, I will," she sobbed as she strode into the cabin.

Now Jed was furious as he turned back to Peter. "Don't talk to my wife like that!"

"Oh! But it is fine for you to order her about, eh?"

They had actually raised their fists but both noticed some wives doing chores, with little children hanging about them. They were all staring at the two bristling men. To make matters worse a flurry of huge, loathsome locusts unexpectedly buzzed into their faces, and they ended up swatting at themselves instead of each other.

Jed finally settled down a little and said, "Look, Peter, we have been like brothers. We are brothers in the kingdom and fellow elders. If only you had gone to the temple, as I did . . . . "

Choking with rage, hurt, and disappointment, Peter backed away. "You pompous . . . pious . . . farmer! You never made it through the temple, remember? There was a little matter of the mob! You're nothing but a

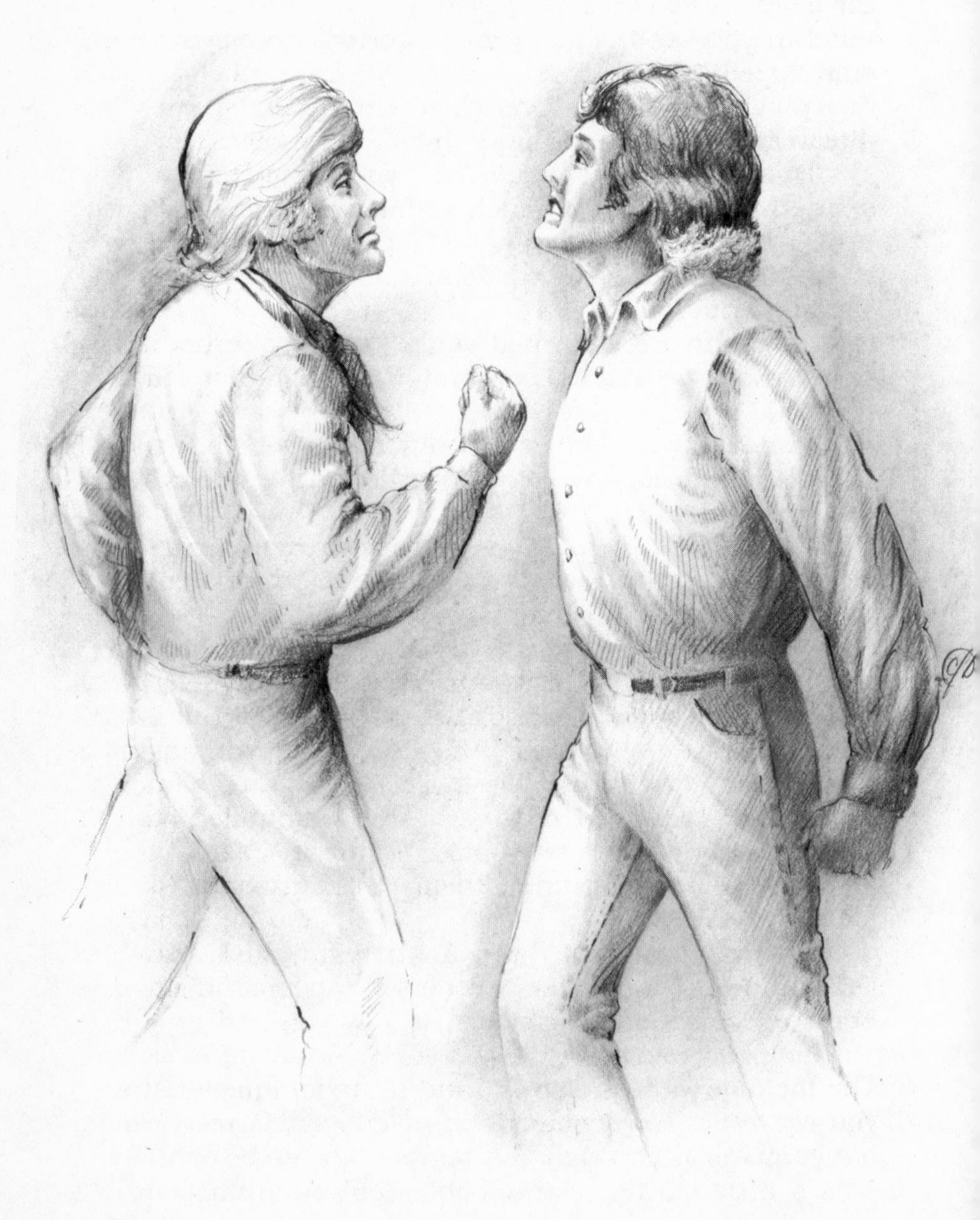

plowboy. I'm the man of affairs. I'm the creative one. I'm the one who could make a city out of a desert if I had a mind to—which I don't!" Peter turned and stormed off down the street. Locusts from the garden seemed to be everywhere and scattered from his path in all directions.

Jed stood alone in the garden for a moment. Then he stepped lightly to the window and called gently inside, "Celia, dear, what's for supper?" A small sack of very hard potatoes flew accurately out the window and slammed into his jaw. He flopped to the hard ground, raising a little dust cloud. As he sat there, with the heat of the baking afternoon sun reflecting off the clay and up into his face, he said to himself softly, "It's so good to be home."

Peter clumped into Porter's cabin and threw himself into a chair. It was hot in the cabin but hotter outside. Peter was deeply troubled and also extremely tired, so he moved to the bed in the corner of the cabin. Stewing in his own sweat and unhappiness, he closed his eyes.

"Seems like ever'time I come around, yer sleepin' in my bed!" boomed Rockwell, smiling as Peter lurched upright. Through the window could be seen the last crease of sunset glowing over the western mountains. Rockwell dropped his bedroll on the floor with a thump and crossed the room to Peter as the young man rose, yawning, on wobbly legs.

"Sorry, Port. I've been working hard fixing up Celia's place. I just came back to think a little and must have dozed off. It's good to see you. Did you have luck getting the mules?" Peter scratched his head and avoided Rockwell's staring eyes.

"Mules? . . . forget the mules, the Battalion is safe. The men are coming home! But then you knew that if you were over at Celia's . . . uh-oh. How long you been hanging about her place? What you been doing there?"

Peter pouted silently for a moment before he told Rockwell everything that happened over the summer since his departure. "Why am I always too late?" sighed Peter. "I should be married to Celia. I know how to take care of a woman, how to show her the good life. He'll always be leaving her. The Prophet will send him here. The Prophet will send him there. I about had her convinced to come away with me when Jed came back. He loves adventure more than he loves her." Peter chuckled ruefully. "I ought to kill him myself. Then he'd be dead for certain."

Rockwell's huge hands crashed against Peter's chest and the fingers clutched his shirt front. Peter felt himself heaved across the room like a rag. His back slammed into the wall. "Holy Moses, Porter! I was joking."

Rockwell advanced on Peter with hunched shoulders. Peter slid along the wall and then stood away from it, believing he would actually have to fight for his life. Rockwell abruptly halted his pursuit and spoke with an uncharacteristically low and broken voice. Staring at him in the now darkened room, Peter realized that Rockwell was weeping as he spoke. "I learned ya not ta jest about killin'. I almost killed the man who did ta me what you want ta do ta Jed. This is yer friend and the husband of this woman you say you care so much about . . . and he's the father of their child." Rockwell hesitated a moment as if it was painful to continue.

"Nobody's got too many friends, Peter. Even if you don't want ta be friends no more, he's still yer brother. Real men are rare. Everybody's against 'em, afraid of 'em, mad at 'em, particularly women that don't understand 'em. Us men have gotta do right by each other!"

Peter interrupted, "I don't understand either. Why did Jed go off to be a soldier in the army of the country that persecuted him, to fight in a wicked war of conquest? To get land for the same greedy slaveholders that drove us out of our homes? His wife, meanwhile, carrying his child, walks and drives oxen to drag all their possessions fifteen hundred miles into this God-forsaken valley full of dust and the nastiest looking bugs in anybody's nightmare? What kind of real man does that?"

"It ain't God-forsaken!" thundered Rockwell. "This is the place where we can make our headquarters. Then we can spread all over, cover the world if we like." He spread his hands out as if smoothing the paths of people going forth from the valley.

"So Brigham says. He has to think of the group. A real man has to think for himself and take care of his own."

"It was Joseph Smith who first saw this place in his mind's eye and told Brigham. Brigham didn't believe it at first either, but he came around. Jed did think for himself. He made up his own mind and then raised his arm ta the square . . . and he agreed. Celia knows that."

"I'm not so sure."

"Maybe not with yer stirring up mud from the bottom of the creek. Yer acting just like that maggot Alphaeus Higbee. He took my wife, my Luana. He took my children, even in the eternities." Rockwell sat on the stool and laid his head in his hands. Peter was shocked into stillness. Finally, Rockwell went on. "'Yer an adventurer,' she said. 'Ya ride off into the wilderness for causes, for excitement, to find out about life, and life is here, at home.' She was right. I'd be gone fer a year sometimes. I was exploring, trying ta learn, something crazy in me. Well, I learned all right. I learned that ya don't trifle with marriage. It's tough enough when everything is goin' right along. Family is the only pure and sacred thing in this wild world. By pleasing myself, I lost my family. Trying ta stay ahead of a sharp woman, that's the real adventure." Rockwell laughed as the tears fell down his cheeks.

"Don't forget you were out doing your duty by the Prophet Joseph Smith," Peter said comfortingly as he pulled up the other stool and sat next to Rockwell.

"That's right. I was the only one lookin' out fer him that understood sometimes a trigger has ta be pulled. If I'd been with him in that jail . . . . " His voice trailed off. "And, don't ya see, that's what Jed was doin'. He was out there because he knew it was his duty."

"I'm not so sure Celia understands that."

"Maybe, maybe not. But you ain't helpin' her none."

"And anyway, didn't Jed please himself, going off to be a big hero?"

"That ain't the way I see it. The Battalion men went off cuz it was their duty to *help* their families with that money and with that reputation they earned. They didn't want ta go. They knew their women was upset. They risked a lot more than just their lives."

Rockwell's words were arrowing deep into Peter's heart. He knew he should feel chagrin, but anger continued to burn, because his goal had been snatched away. He thought of something temporizing to say. "He insulted me when he said"—and here Peter mimicked Jed's pomposity—"'If only you had been to the temple, Peter, as I have.' I could have broken his jaw for that."

"Well, dang it, boy, you ain't thinkin' temple-like. How dare you think for a minute Celia would leave her man fer you and take his child with her? That's what my wife did, and are we sittin' here respecting her fer it?" Peter flushed at the comparison and pressed his lips together to stifle a groan at his anger and his loss. Rockwell saw and understood. He meant well with what he said. "And anyway, ya coulda had a true love in Mary Ellen. She was yers for the asking. It just goes to show ya, there's more than one quail in the covey."

Peter shot to his feet. This was too much. Rockwell knew everything and took everything away. Peter had just started to turn his thoughts back to Mary Ellen. He was remembering now what he hadn't paid attention to back then, realizing he could have had something wonderful with Mary Ellen. He stared wildly at Rockwell, who gazed back at him solemnly as he slowly shook his head.

A few miles away, Jed and Celia sat at the rough little table in their cabin, with Jed Junior asleep in a little rocking crib on the floor at their feet. They spoke in intense, hoarse whispers.

"I thought you were dead," moaned Celia.

"You hadn't thought I was dead for very long," said Jed with a tremble in his voice.

"I hadn't said anything to Peter. I hadn't given him anything. You know how he is. He rushes ahead. If I so much as meet his eye or tell him of my gratitude for the true service he did render, then he presumes all." Celia reached out and took Jed's hands in hers. Jed flinched away but then squeezed her fingers as he looked at her hands in his.

"Didn't you feel my spirit bringing you messages, while you crossed the plains?" asked Jed.

"Yes, I did," insisted Celia. "Especially at first, but they grew weaker. Finally, with all that Peter was saying, and his presence in your absence, there was nothing I could say, nothing I could do to make me believe you had not been killed."

"Peter's influence upon you was that strong?"

"Yes, it was." She bowed her head. "God help me."

"Then . . . . " Jed's voice cracked. "Did we do wrong to marry? Should you have waited for Peter?"

Now Celia's hands moved up to caress Jed's face. "No! No. I love you. You're the one I want to be with, forever. I was led away. I was weak. I should have had faith that you were still alive. I felt sorry for myself."

"Peter has good things to offer, doesn't he? He can give you the world. What else? What else does he have?" Jed was truly curious.

"Oh, never mind what he has," crooned Celia as she stood up, moved around the table, and sat in Jed's lap. "He doesn't have me."

But Jed stood up and held Celia in front of him, grasping her arms in his big, strong hands. "That is only because I got back here in time. I could have arrived to find that you had packed up and gone back to Saint Louis with him, isn't that right?"

She tried to twist out of his iron grip, "No! No, I would never go back there. I don't belong there."

"Do you belong here, in a frontier cabin with dirt blowing in the window and locusts hopping over your feet? He can put you in a mansion, with servants, and beautiful gowns." He stifled his voice as he glanced at the baby.

"Here I can build my own home with my own people. Don't talk like a fool!" She had torn away from him now and her eyes flared as she spoke, her clear voice starting to ring with her anger until she, too, brought herself under control for the sake of the sleeping child.

"A fool!" Jed thundered and the baby woke up. "Am I a fool, a country lout while he is a city gentleman? Is that it?" Jed Junior yelped and big Jed turned away in frustration. "Am I a fool to believe you now?"

Celia's shrillness turned to a cold, explanatory tone. "You are the greatest natural gentleman I ever knew, but you are foolish if you cannot see what he has done that you have not. You want to know what he has? It's a conviction that he knows best what he ought to do, and he follows his own road, a road he made for himself. And do you know what he wants the most? What is the goal at the end of his road? Me! My happiness! Me! He will do anything to be with me." Baby Jed punctuated her statement with a loud recital of his own needs.

"I'll have you know that I could take you to a beautiful valley in California that makes this place look like the Devil's leftovers. I have been offered shares in it. I could set you up in as rich a style as Peter Van Cleef. But should I have disobeyed the prophet? Refused the spirit? I thought you believed in obedience," Jed gasped in shock. "Celia, where are the testimonies we shared?"

She put her hands over her face and almost swooned as she spoke. "I know, I know. I do have a testimony. May God help me to understand this, but it is so . . . attractive, that strength of choosing and deciding. After all, why do we follow Brother Brigham? He thinks up what to do and he does it. He tells us and we can't think of a reason not to obey him."

"We do not obey him; we obey the Lord! Brigham is humble before the Lord."

". . . But not before us."

Jed drew himself up to his full height and looked down upon Celia with the utmost gravity. "You are an honest woman and a saint of the warm-blooded sort, not one of plaster as they say. But I did not leave you for the army to please Brigham Young. I went because I thought it right. Because of that army pay and army reputation, we can make a home wherever we choose, either here or in California, and we—you and I, together with our work and sacrifice—have helped our friends come away from the persecutors. Because of the Battalion, we can defend ourselves if the persecutors follow us here as Peter said they will."

Celia tried to calm the baby while Jed continued speaking at a disturbing volume. The cabin was small enough as it was. Loud voices only bounced off the log walls and sounded louder, but Jed continued all the same.

"I am no adventurer, Celia. I am a husband and a father. I am obedient, but only to the will of God, which is that you and I be united even if a certain duty parts us for a season. Every night in the desert, I begged God on my knees to bring me back to you. And I will build you a great mansion in a beautiful place. If that's what you desire, you will see. But this business with Peter has been a terrible thing. His willfulness has excited you. I cannot say I know what you prefer. It breaks my heart to say it, but I am not sure if I truly know your character."

Jed blanched as the last words left his mouth, because he knew an instant too late that he had gone too far. The arrows he sent forth had struck home. He had been well on his way to a contrite wife, which even he, in his innocence, knew was a rare thing. But now he had given her something to be devastated about. He had created a martyr.

Celia scooped up the baby and glared at Jed, chin aloft, as the tears rolled down her face. "My character is such that, when you left me pregnant at Winter Quarters, I brought *our* family to this new place in order to build the home you said you wanted."

She saw, though she dared not admit it, that she had stabbed him in the heart, unnecessarily. Jed was too shocked to do more than mutter, "That is what I want. Now enough of this. We can talk more tomorrow." Celia sat down to nurse the baby. Jed laid out his bedroll on the floor.

Meanwhile, in the other cabin of pain, Rockwell was snoring like a thousand sawmills in his own bed, reclaimed from Peter, while Peter fretted endlessly in *his* bedroll on the floor. He thought about the horror and agony of Rockwell's story, with its sundering of parents and children. He thought about sacrifice. Who had really sacrificed in this whole matter of Jed, Celia, Peter, and Mary Ellen, and who had indulged themselves? Celia wanted Jed, but he insisted on doing his duty far away. Would he always do that until it became clear that he was fascinated by the adventure of duty doing? Would Jed then end up like Rockwell?

Wasn't he, Peter, responding to an important duty by being what Celia wanted and fulfilling her needs regardless of some task assigned him in order to help someone else do *his* duty? But if he was to avoid the accusation of selfish indulgence of his own passionate needs, then what to do about Mary Ellen? Truly she had made genuine sacrifices. They could be called nothing else, because she had saved her beloved without hope of reward. Was there a way they could all be happy? Could there be some important lesson to be learned? Would Rockwell ever stop snoring?

Porter Rockwell, pistols and knives beside him in bed, was not a man to jog or roll over on to his side in the middle of the night. Peter rose and walked outside in just his shirt tails. Instantly, loathsome insects flew against his bare legs. He slapped at them in vain. The ground, even at midnight, radiated up the dry heat it had absorbed all day. Peter went back inside and sat on his bedroll with his back against a wall and gazed out the window at the moon.

15

Indians/Lamanites

Next morning, Jed stood up with a crick in his back. Sleeping on the ground was better than sleeping on a floor. Celia lay on the bed with the baby on her belly, both sleeping silently. Jed got his pants and boots on and finished dressing outside. In the gray, cool dawn, he looked around for water. There was a barrel about half full of good clear water, with a bucket beside it. Jed figured they must fill the barrel from the irrigation ditch which ran along the street in front of the house. He had to have a bath after his journey and disastrous first night home. He filled the bucket and drank it down. He filled it again and bathed. He filled it again and washed his clothes.

Changing to his only other outfit, which had stayed quite clean in his haversack, Jed refilled the barrel. He then tiptoed inside and got a double handful of biscuits left from yesterday.

Who should come plodding across the back of the lot with that unmistakable gait but his new father-in-law, Quimby Leighton? The good Bishop was leading one of the mules Rockwell had brought. The animal was in harness; the plow would be in the field, of course. Quimby also had a musket slung across his back with a rawhide sling, and he wore a powder bottle and shot bag at his waist.

"Good morning, Bishop!" Jed called out, hurrying across the yard, buttoning his buttons.

"Good morning, Jed!" returned the Bishop, equally hearty. Jed caught up, and they began walking toward the half-plowed field that Jed could now see.

"What are you putting in so late?" Jed asked, looking along the assorted fields around about, with their greenish-yellowish, ripening wheat and corn. The season was definitely well under way.

"Just more wheat," replied Quimby. "This will be our first harvest, and we want to have plenty for the winter. We haven't eaten well since we arrived in the valley."

"It looks like the heat and dryness are drawing crickets. Will they come every year, do you think?" Jed squashed one with his boot heel.

"Too early to tell. The Indians say some years they come and some they don't."

"Ugly critters, aren't they?" said Jed, curling his mouth in distaste as he batted some away from his face. "They've got eyes like goggles and legs like springs. By the way, why are you carrying your gun?"

"President Young has said that all men going to the fields should go armed. There have been more and more incidents with the Indians. They have been stealing. Our logging, up in the canyons, and the dams we built for irrigation have disturbed them."

"Have you seen any Indians this close in?" asked Jed, looking around.

"Sometimes. There is a hard-looking chief that boldly rides into the city and trades. Celia saw him. He frightened her badly, but Peter scared him away." This struck

Jed so hard that he stopped for a moment. Then he hurried on after Quimby.

In the field that curved along the bench, they hitched the plow to the harness and Jed watched Quimby struggle to make a straight furrow. "You were our best school teacher, I remember," said Jed gently as he took over the plow and got a straight, deep furrow going seemingly without effort.

"And you were one of my best students," replied Quimby, mopping his face with his kerchief.

"For a farm boy," chuckled Jed.

"That's what everybody said," chuckled Quimby in his turn. "But I have developed a greater appreciation for farmers lately."

"Do you like farming now?" Jed called over his shoulder.

"No more than before, but I do like eating," said Quimby with a wink and a smile. Suddenly, his face went sober as he peered at something in the brush along the stream bed that bordered the field. Jed turned around to see what it was. There, riding along in the brush, was the Indian chief.

"Is that the one that frightened Celia?"

"Yes."

"Should you go for your gun?"

"I don't think so. Look again," said Quimby, very quietly. Jed did look again and saw a war party of four braves, painted and feathered, following behind the chief. Using their rawhide lariats, they led two cows. Jed and Quimby stood very still while the Indians ignored them.

After the Indians had passed out of sight, Quimby began unhitching the mule from the plow. "We must report this," he said quickly.

As they walked up the street toward Brigham Young's house, Jamie Logan came dashing out to join them.

"Jed!" he cried. "Have you got a gun I could borrow? Like a fool I lent mine to Milo Jensen this morning. Now that I need it, it isn't here."

"Now don't get so excited, Jamie," replied Jed calmly, exchanging glances with Quimby. "What do you need a gun for?"

"Ma whole laundry was stolen off the line. I come home from the wars and then have the shirt taken off ma back. It's an outrage, Laddie, an outrage!"

"Who took them?"

"Who took them? Indians, of course!" Jamie was fairly jumping up and down.

"Now don't be foolish, Jamie," Jed cautioned, putting his hands on Jamie's shoulders. "You don't want to go shooting Indians."

"Oh, don't I?" yelled Jamie, breaking away from Jed. "Well, give me your gun and we'll soon see."

Men and women had gathered around and Jed tried to be soothing. "Now look, Indians have guns, too. We've had enough of war and dissension. If you want to go to the Indians, don't go as soldiers. Go as friends."

"It's easy enough for you to give advice. You're going to California," came a voice from the crowd. That stopped Jed cold, and he couldn't think of anything else to offer.

Zarabel burst into the group. "My cow's been stolen! I'm with ya, Jamie." Many men stepped forward with a growl.

Then the Bishop spoke. "Would you like to know what the Prophet of the Lord has to say?" The crowd fell silent. "Would you?" insisted Quimby.

Jed recovered enough to help. "Let's go see Brother Brigham." He turned and walked up the street toward the President's house.

Peter woke up because he heard his horse whinnying in the corral. At first he thought it was more of Rockwell's outrageous snoring, but as he struggled to push himself to his feet, he knew it was the horse. He staggered to the window and saw a young, small Indian in a breech clout, moccasins, and nothing else except for beads and paint, slipping a halter on the horse and vaulting onto its back. The young little brave reached over and pulled the poles out of the gate portion of the corral and tumbled them to the ground without ever losing his balanced, bare-back seat. He loped the horse past the cabin very quietly.

Peter vaulted right out the window and enclosed the Indian in a bear hug as the momentum drove them both right off the other side of the horse, and they fell to the ground. Peter saw that this was a teen-aged boy just as the kid put a stout kick right in Peter's chest, breaking Peter's grasp. The Indian was up and running in a flash and Peter decided to catch the horse rather than the Indian. As he led the horse back into the corral, he saw Rockwell looking at him out the window, scratching his beard.

"What are you lookin' at?" Peter said, dusting himself off.

"Yer right busy this mornin'." replied Rockwell. "Do me a favor, boy. The next time ya get a hankerin' to wrestle with some Injuns, try ta be a mite quieter, huh?" Rockwell flashed a sarcastic smile at Peter and left him to deal with returning the horse to the corral. With an exasperated grunt, Peter threw up his arms and kicked up some dust.

Rockwell wasn't the only one disturbed by noise. Brigham Young came out of his door to deal with the dusty hubbub that awaited him. He looked at the contorted faces and heard words above the babble like "laundry!" and "cows!" and "Indians!" He raised his hands above his head and called for quiet. He being short, the ones in front had to pass the word back into the crowd, and everybody settled down.

"Brethren, we understand what has happened. We are endeavoring to make contact with the chief of the Ute tribe in these parts. Try to understand that, for hunters like the Indians, this is a poor country, and we are scaring away such game as is here. The Indians are starving up in the mountains. We must find a way to ease their suffering so they are not tempted to . . . . "Brigham had the people in hand when suddenly Peter rode up and jumped off his horse, striding through the crowd.

"Indians are in the very town itself! I hope you know that, President!" announced Peter. Instant uproar followed.

Brigham glared at Peter and said through gritted teeth, "We are aware of that, Brother Van Cleef." Now the President had an idea that would get control again. He beckoned to Jed, praying that his trust in the blond farmer would be justified yet once more. "Brother Cutler, what condition are we in with regard to a militia?"

Everybody turned to Jed. "Well," he began. "With the return of many Battalion men, and other old veterans of the Legion, and weapons we brought here, we could show a good force. But why, after all our fighting and suffering, do we want to bring war and terror here?"

"It is the savages who bring the terror," came a voice.

"We must wash away terror, for the sake of the children. Blood begets blood. What have we learned from the Church of Jesus Christ?" replied Jed.

This broke the group up into several discussions and, once again, Brigham had a chance, but then Celia picked her way among the people to Jed's side and whispered to him. Unfortunately, a woman heard and loudly told her husband that Captain Cutler's mule—

one of the ones brought back from California—had just been stolen by Indians. Uproar reigned again.

After waiting a moment to let the energy run out, Brigham again called for attention. He had another idea. "Brother Van Cleef," he began in his humblest tone, struggling with the effort, "You have excited many of the members with your view of what ought to be done. What is your plan?"

Peter was taken aback for a moment, but he quickly straightened up, assumed a position where his audience could see and hear him, and began. "As Jed has said so well, we should avoid a war, if possible. As I have learned in my dealings with worldly businessmen not much less savage than these Indians"—all chuckled for a second or two—"it is best if you believe you could sign an agreement no matter which side of the table you sit on. But we must be strong. I suppose in negotiating with Indians, it is the same as in negotiating with any other powerful interest holder. You must quickly destroy his hopes for besting you. He must see immediately that your interests have him surrounded. He must feel lucky to get whatever you care to give him. He must know that if he does not negotiate in the right spirit, receiving honestly what you choose to give him in fairness, then he is in your grasp and will be destroyed. It is this approach that gained me everything I sought and kept safe everyone who relied on me. It is this approach that will get us security against the Indians now."

Both Peter and Brigham noticed how Celia looked intrigued and Jed looked appalled. There was a buzz of approval from Jamie and the war group.

"Thank you, good brother. Uh . . . who should go up into the Indian camp to negotiate in this manner?" asked Brigham innocently.

"Well, I suppose I should, since I have the experience with this kind of confrontation," said Peter blithely. This caused a silence to fall on his supporters, and Peter knew he had done something wrong. "Or . . . I could go with you, President, and advise you."

"Yes, advise me. I see." Brigham turned to Jed. "And you, Brother Cutler? There seems to be a body of the people that holds with you. What would be your plan?"

Celia looked up at Jed very intently and the big man was flustered, but he gulped for air and began. "Well, first of all, what I support is not *my* plan. We learned in the Book of Mormon that the Indians are a remnant of the people in that book. They came here as commanded by the Lord. So did we. They are the children of one tribe of Israel. We are the children of another tribe. We are cousins and neighbors.

"The Prophet Joseph Smith taught us to love them and bring them back to a remembrance of their fathers. You remember that Joseph went to the Indians of western Missouri and preached the Gospel to them. At least, he did that until the Missourians said he was a renegade stirring the Indians up to make war. It was totally the opposite. It was Brother Joseph bringing the Holy Spirit to those chiefs and bringing them back to a remembrance of their fathers that *kept* the peace on the frontier in those years. We should feed them, not fight them. We should be good neighbors. If we have driven away the game with our agriculture, then we should make up for that by teaching them agriculture. Nothing is more expensive than war. Peace is the best economy."

Quimby Leighton led a round of applause. Emma joined in and then so did Celia. Brigham stayed neutral, although he permitted himself an unnoticed smile. Then he said, "That is excellent, Brother Cutler. And who do you believe should go and deliver this message to the Utah Chiefs?"

"Well, you should, of course, President. You are our leader. This is only what you and Joseph have done many times in many places."

"It should be chief to chief then, eh?" laughed Brigham, and others joined in.

"Well, yes, so to speak," grinned Jed.

"Hmm." Brigham put his thumbs in his vest pockets and drummed his fingers on his belly. "What if I said you should do it, Brother Cutler? You should go and represent us."

"They'll kill him," came a voice from the back and Celia gasped, darting glances back and forth among the men. She watched Peter look hard at both of them and then drop his eyes.

"They'll never kill a man who rides in boldly and with honorable intent, isn't that right, Brother Rockwell?" asked Brigham, hailing to Porter over the heads of the crowd, which turned to see Porter sitting on a fence nearby.

"That's true enough, President. And, anyway, I'll be there to remind 'em of their beliefs," said Porter, pulling out his huge Bowie knife and whittling on the fence post. "Also, this man that's been comin' to town to see you and then boldly thievin' from the outskirts is a sub-chief. We better save our high mucky-muck for their high mucky-muck. We don't want to mess in their politics."

"Thank you, Porter," said Brigham, smiling sheepishly, genuinely humble this time. Then he turned to the group. "Can you sustain this, Brethren and Sisters?" he called out. A cheer answered him, and the people began to disperse.

Celia looked up at Jed, horrified. He squeezed her shoulders in his hands. "Celia, I have to go," he whispered fiercely, looking deep into her eyes, "but I will come back." After a moment of intense thought, her face broke into a serene smile and she kissed him and pressed herself against him. Then they headed off to home, arm in arm.

Peter stood alone in the street, twisting his hat in his hands, thwarted and hateful.

A well-organized and well-supplied group of four men left Salt Lake City, enroute to the Indian camp of the great Ute tribe. They traveled through the canyon passes to the east and deep into the mountain sanctuary of the Indian nation. Rockwell knew where the tribe was lodged and led the others on the shortest route through the twisting mountains. As they approached the village of the Utes, several braves rode out to meet them.

A little later, Rockwell, Jed, Quimby, and Jamie sat on blankets spread for them by young Ute women at the command of the chief they had seen stealing cattle in the city. "This feller is one of three brothers that run the Utah tribe," said Porter in Jed's ear. "His name's Wakara."

"Walker?" asked Quimby, trying to pronounce what he heard.

"No, Wakara," repeated Rockwell. "The other two are Arrapene and Kanosh. They live farther south. Kanosh is the eldest. He runs things. I'll bet Wakara here would like to settle this without Kanosh knowing what he's been doin'."

"That's fine with me," muttered Jed as a piece of meat on a stick was put into his hands by an Indian maiden. All the guests were similarly favored.

"Buffalo?" wondered Jamie.

"No," declared Rockwell, tasting, "Mormon cow."

"Our host has a lot of nerve," Quimby stated, eating carefully.

There was story-telling while they ate as various elders regaled the circle. Porter translated as best he could. They were stories about war, about Ute bravery in repelling invaders, about Ute cunning in robbing interlopers. All the while Wakara looked at his guests with a haughty disdain on his face.

"I believe this man has attended the Van Cleef School of Negotiation," whispered Quimby and everybody choked on their beef to keep from laughing, but Wakara saw it all.

When the food was gone, the braves danced with feathers and bells and beads. They were accompanied by keening singers who sat around the huge drum and pounded it in time with their music. Finally, they were ready to exchange gifts.

The Mormons gave flour, salt, and sourdough starter that made the Indians reel back with wrinkled noses, but they ate the samples of bread that demonstrated the finished product. The Mormons also gave potatoes and beans. All this they explained, asking Wakara to teach his people how to grow and use these things. He would not respond. It was not like trade goods from the mountain men. The Utes gave baskets of excellently woven lake reeds and riotously colorful blankets that Jed recognized from the camp of the Comancheros. They really were remarkable, and the Mormons made much of them. Wakara was pleased. Now they could talk.

Late that night in the Cutler cabin, Emma watched Celia struggle with the hungry baby, who beat his little balled fists on her breast. "Your milk isn't letting down because you're so worried," Emma said calmly. "Try to have faith. After all, they are on the Lord's errand."

"It is after ten, and they left at dawn. They only went some ten miles up the canyon," said Celia pettishly. Then she moaned and said, "I'm sorry. You're right. I'll try again."

Emma reached out her arms to Celia and said, "You hold your child, and I'll hold my child." Celia smiled and got up to go to her mother. Then she heard the clop of hooves and the jingling of a bridle outside. Instead of putting her head on her mother's shoulder, she gave Emma the baby and darted outside.

There, in the dark, stood Jed between his horse and his mule. "You got the mule back!" she crowed delightedly.

"I did," said Jed happily. "And here is a gift from the Chief that will go well on our bed," he continued as he handed her an Indian blanket. "He remembered you, and he complimented me on my taste in women."

Celia took the blanket from Jed and asked him what it meant to get such a gift. "All is well," he replied. "All is well."

16

Miracle of the Gulls

Jed's second night at home was far better than his first, and he arose at dawn as usual, with all others asleep, and crept out. This time, he and his clothes were clean . . . farmer clothes. The soldier's uniform and the rawhide accoutrements of the wanderer were put away. They would come out later for storytelling to little Jed. But Jed was a farmer with a decision to make—build a home in this valley and consecrate himself to the city of the saints, or partner up with Broderick and be an owner of Rancho del Capitan. In order to work this out in his head, he applied his hands and began the establishing of a farm in Utah, to see how it would go. After the harvest, he and Celia could talk about possibilities all winter long if they wanted to, and head for California in the spring if they were of a mind. He would show everyone he could go his own way, make his own decisions. "Come on, mule," Jed coaxed, after hitching his newly-returned prize to the plow. They made their way into the field, and Jed began his labor.

After weeks of sweat, combined with the efforts of Quimby and others, Jed was on his way to wonderful fields of wheat and other grains. It had meant long, hard days spent tending these crops in the hot sun, but Jed found it rewarding and fulfilling.

The heat of the season had not yet broken. Jed awoke one morning as usual, but there was a strange something in the air. The sun was barely over the east range of the Wasatch mountains, so the air was still cool and calm. No wind blew, and that meant the sun would bake the ground as it climbed higher. Jed wanted to get the tilling of this field out of the way first in order to prevent the mule from becoming exasperated with heat exhaustion as the day wore on. He carried a breakfast of biscuits and jerky into the field with him to avoid any distraction of his work later when Celia awoke and cooked for the family.

Jed was singing a song Fennelly Parsons had written for the return of the Mormon Battalion and didn't hear Peter approaching him from behind. "I thought you were my friend!" Peter roared. The suddenness of his proclamation startled Jed, and he whirled around to face his challenger.

"I am your friend, Peter, a better friend than you know. You came here as a fugitive from your world, and you ran around stirring up trouble in my world, and I never called you on it, for old times' sake. Don't you have anything productive you could be doing?" Jed's feelings were frustration and resentment, while Peter's feelings were those of rage and bitter hurt.

"This *is* the most productive thing I could possibly be doing, dear friend. I'm going to teach you a lesson in brotherly love."

Jed was confused by Peter's statement. He knew Peter felt cheated because of Celia. *But what does that have to do with brotherly love?* he wondered.

Peter didn't wait for Jed to ask. He pointed in the direction of town and said, "You put your brother, that's me, on the pillory of public ridicule. You're determined to destroy me, Jed, because you know Celia would have been better off married to me, and it came too close to happening to suit you!"

"Why deceive yourself, Peter? Celia knows your golden calf character. Your god is money and power. I didn't tell you what to say to President Young. That was your plan, no one else's. Aren't you man enough to accept the consequences of your actions?"

Jed's demeanor oozed insulting pomposity, and Peter wasn't about to take it. He clenched his fist and let fly with a punch that caught Jed's open mouth as he prepared another verbal attack, knocking him to the ground. Jed forgot all about his tilling and joined Peter's fight for brotherly love. Since both Jed and Peter were about the same size, neither one had much advantage over the other. Still, Jed's hands were hard and thick from farming. Peter relied on his cunning and speed. They took turns pummeling each other, but most of the fight consisted of a wrestling match. Jed was determined not to let Peter goad him into fulfilling Peter's own self-destructive desires.

The two men were too busy beating each other to notice Quimby standing not far from them. Quimby wasn't a coward, but he also wasn't stupid. Under normal circumstances, he wouldn't even think about trying to break up two, strong young men embroiled in combat. These were not normal circumstances!

"If you boys are so bent on fighting, maybe you should fight to save your people instead of to please yourselves," Quimby declared. Peter and Jed stopped their battle and looked up at Quimby. "Don't look at me, boys, look at that!" he continued, motioning behind him to a dark cloud slowly filling the morning sky.

Jed jumped to his feet and then helped Peter up. "What is it?" Peter asked, noticeably shaken.

"Crickets," Jed retorted. He felt his heart sink as he watched the cricket hordes swarm, unrelenting, from every direction.

"How dark it's getting," Quimby observed. "How black it seems." And black it was. The sky filled with clouds of crickets, turning the light to dark.

"What do we do?" Peter shouted over the monstrous, dissonant harmony of a billion humming insects. He looked at the other two men for some kind of explanation.

"We do what we've always done, Peter," came the reply from Bishop Leighton. "We put our trust in heaven, and then we fight like hell!" Jed was already making his way back to the house. Quimby and Peter soon followed.

Jed's first thoughts were the saftey of his wife and son. He would make sure they were secure and then do what he could against the blight that now threatened everyone. The other two men followed Jed instinctively, but stopped short of entering the house, in utter astonishment, to survey the enormous cloud of crickets overtaking them.

Within moments, Jed burst through the door of the cabin at a dead run. Peter and Quimby caught up with Jed as he headed out to the field. "Jed, no," Quimby said taking hold of his arm. "Never mind our field, it's already engulfed with crickets, and men are setting fire to it from all sides."

"It's not the field, Bishop. My mule is still out there. I've got to unhitch her from the plow!" Jed meant no disrespect, but he didn't wait for Quimby's response. He had to reach the mule before the fire did.

When he got to the field, he plunged through a gap in the perimeter of fire and ran to the terrified mule. She had strained herself into a lather trying to drag the plow, which only bit deeper into the earth. He grabbed the bridle and tried to calm the now demented animal. Running around to the plow, he managed to get it unhooked from the traces without getting hit by the mules flailing hooves. He leapt for the bridle again to lead the mule back through the gap in the encroaching fire. The mule, however, lunged forward, hitting Jed in the face with her shoulder and knocking him down. He still clung to the reins, though, and this maddened the mule even more. She kicked out, first with her front legs then with her hind ones. As she swung around in a circle with the force of her kicking, she caught Jed in the ribs just as he had gotten to his hands and knees. Jed was lofted a few feet and landed on his back, unconscious. The mule sensed the opening and ran out of the fire-surrounded field.

Back at the cabin, Peter was in the corral catching horses and putting blindfolds over their eyes to calm them as much as possible. He saw Jed's mule trot up to the corral and dip her nose in the water trough. Peter looked around for Jed, but saw no one. Standing on the top rail of the corral fence, he looked toward the burning field. It was clear where Jed was. It was clear what Peter must do.

Peter jumped off the fence and ran a few steps toward the flames and smoke. He could tell the fire was too dense to simply run through, so he ran back to the cabin and looked inside for a blanket. The gaudy Indian blanket Jed had brought back from Wakara was the first thing that caught his eye. Peter grabbed it and ran to the water trough, shoving the blanket under the water. With the streaming blanket under one arm, he set out again for the burning field.

When he got there, the gap in the flames was gone. There was a solid, roaring perimeter of fire, raging its way inward, but Peter was prepared. He looked for the thinnest part of the flame wall and put the blanket over himself. Strangely, he paused for just a moment and heard himself crying out, "Oh Lord, help me. Protect me that I may save thy more worthy servant." Then he sucked in as much air as he could, held his breath, and plunged headlong into the flames.

It is hard to run while holding your breath, Peter observed idiotically as he burst through the other side of the fiery wall and dashed toward the body lying in the middle of the field. When he got to Jed's side, he breathed again. Jed was completely covered with crickets and coughing from the smoke, even in his unconsciousness. Peter wiped the crickets off with his hands as fast as he could, because the flames were closing in on all sides. He tried to heave Jed up on his shoulders, but Jed screamed with the pain of his cracked rib. So Peter grabbed Jed's shirt front and pulled Jed to his feet. "Get up, farmer!" Peter yelled in Jed's ear. "Get up or you'll never see your wife and child again . . . at least in this life!"

Jed tried to muster his strength and raise his body to a standing position. Peter did all he could to help, but Jed had to do his share to avoid hurting his side. Twice he tried, and twice he failed. For a moment, it appeared to Peter that Jed had fallen back into unconsciousness, his body lying limp on a bed of crickets.

Peter grabbed Jed's shirt and lifted him until they were face to face. "You're not quittin' on me now, brother. You never gave up on anything in your life. Now move!" Jed opened his eyes slowly and looked at Peter holding him. He smiled and used all the strength he had left to stay on his feet. Peter wrapped the blanket around both of them and made for the edge of the flames.

"Where is my mule? Did the mule get out?" Jed asked weakly.

"Yes!" Peter yelled in Jed's ear. "Satisfied? Now shut up and keep moving." Wrapped in the blanket, they dashed with all their might back through the wall of

dashed with all their might back through the wall of fire.

As they stumbled toward the cabin with the scorched and singed blanket still around them, they saw Celia quickly approaching. They came together in a frantic embrace, and Jed winced but maintained his grip on his friend and his wife. The blanket slipped off and Peter caught it. They all looked at the smouldering remains. "That's a beautiful one-of-a-kind item . . . ruined," mourned Peter. He looked at the happy couple. "I don't suppose Wakara has another?" They all laughed, but then they faced the horror all around.

"The field is gone, then?" asked Celia.

"Yes," said Jed, with nothing to soften it.

Everywhere, the people of the valley fought the crickets—day and night. They fought until they lost track of the number of days of battle. And still the enemy advanced.

Brigham Young was busy organizing forces to combat the blight. Jamie and his group were sent to the fields that had already become covered with crickets. He was told to burn those fields, setting fire to all sides, from fire lines, so as to hem in the insects and give them no escape. Lorenzo and his group were sent to the less infested fields. They were to flood the land to drown the crickets and save the crop.

There were others, too—men and women who went forth with rugs and blankets, clubs and brooms. Anything they could find to beat the crickets with, they used. It was a terrible sight of pestilence and destruction. None were spared the horror of the advancing insects.

The smoke from the burning fields mingled with the incredible number of crickets flying above the settlement. It was hot, and it was miserable! The combined heat of the day and the fires made it very difficult to endure the onslaught of crickets. In the fields, both men and women fainted from heat exhaustion. Many more simply had to stop and take shelter.

"By the looks of things, the whole crop will be lost," Peter observed numbly. "Now can we all come away to California? We must pack up and get out of here while we can still carry a little food and make it over the mountains before cold weather." Jed and Celia clung to each other in an agony of indecision.

"Hallooo, you three!" They heard Quimby calling from behind them. They turned and saw him standing in the street with Emma, who held the baby. Emma and Quimby beckoned to them with waving arms. They ran over to the tall couple. "Come with us, President Young is touring the wards. He wants each ward in turn to join him in a prayer for deliverance."

They all moved as fast as they could to their little meetinghouse and went in. Every smoke-blackened, sweat-soaked man, woman, and child, was there with Brigham at the stand. As soon as the late arrivals were seated, President Young raised his arms, signaling all to be silent.

All heads bowed and Brigham began. "Dear Lord, deliver us, we pray, from these black Philistines. We beg you to reach down from on high and smite this filthy plague. If we are your chosen people, Father, and if this is, in truth, the promised valley, then you must help us, as you helped the Israelites of old. If we have offended thee with hard-heartedness or stiffneckedness, as was sometimes true of the children of Israel and, indeed, of the Nephites and Lamanites of this land, Oh Lord, we forsake such ways, and turn once again to thee, with all our heart, might, mind, and strength." Peter lifted his head and gazed into Brigham's face. He felt a rapturous smile spread all through him.

A little girl, sitting in her mother's lap, suddenly pointed out a window and said, "Angel!" as a pearly gray shape flitted past.

"Sssh," said her exhausted mother, trying to keep control. Another shape flitted past. It was a bird. Brigham asked Quimby for a song and the ward members sang "Come, Come Ye Saints," with Fennelly leading. Through their croaking, wheezing singing, the people heard a delicate screeching and cawing in the air outside. As soon as the last note was done, the people rose in a body and streamed through the door.

The ward meetinghouse sat on a little promontory that looked out over the valley. The ward members stopped still when they got outside and looked toward the Great Salt Lake. As on the terrible day when the cricket horde came, there was a huge artificial cloud blotting out the sun. "Birds!" everyone began to say. As the bug cloud had emitted a thunderous buzzing, so the bird cloud emitted a symphonic chirping. The bug cloud had come up from the south end of the valley, in from the desert. The bird cloud came in over the lake. The bug cloud was black. The bird cloud was a marvelously shifting array of blue and silver, gray and white as it spread over the fields.

"They are gulls, like sea gulls," said Emma. "Could they have come from the ocean?"

"That's too far, surely. How would they know to come?" answered Zarabel.

"It is a great salt lake, after all," mused Fennelly. "Maybe they are lake gulls."

"But they were never there before, in such numbers at least. How did they just materialize?" said Celia.

Milo was losing his hold upon his reason and cackled, "They've come to complete the destruction."

"No," said Quimby firmly. "Look!" He pointed to the bird cloud descending on the fields and breaking up into streams of gulls which fanned out over black patches of locusts. What had to be a million birds began to eat what had to be a billion locusts.

"Angels!" shouted the little girl who had seen the first gull. She jumped up and down, laughing and pointing.

"Yes, darling," said her mother, also ecstatic, "angels!"

A cry went through the little ward group standing on the hill, "The crop is saved. We are saved." Everyone dropped to their knees and bowed their heads, and a mumble of earnest prayer went up from them. Peter was on his knees, but his head was lifted and he studied the sky with wonder and awe.

The crickets the Mormons didn't burn and the gulls didn't eat fled to the streams and were drowned. Indians scooped them out of the water by the ton in their exquisite reed baskets. They sang their own thanksgiving songs as they dried and roasted the crickets for winter provender.

The Saints cleaned up and tried their hand at planting winter wheat to take the place of that which was lost. They were glad for the potatoes, carrots, and other tubers that were cricket-proof. And they harvested the grain that had survived. They sang, and they wept, and they ate. With renewed strength, they enlarged their cabins and adobes and thickened the roofs. They laid up firewood and dried foods of all kinds. Brother Brigham had grist mills built at all suitable locations, and the flour barrels were filled.

Peter, meanwhile, prepared to leave. He said goodbye to Porter Rockwell, who was himself preparing to explore the valley south and look for the terrain features described to him by an old mountain man named Etienne Provo. Peter then took his leave of Brigham Young, who agreed that, under the circumstances, it

was best that Peter go. Many good Saints, particularly those among the Battalion men who had seen the beautiful Upper California, had exercised the free agency Brigham had insisted he believed in, and had taken their families in new wagon trains west over the Sierra Nevada. "Go to California, then, and be damned to ya!" Brigham had said, hurt that the miracle of the gulls had not converted everybody to the promised valley. But to Peter he said comfortingly, "Go to California. Be a strength and a witness to the Saints who have chosen to live there."

Jed and Celia were bathing Jed, Junior when Peter came to say farewell. He looked good in his traveling outfit of wool and corduroy, with well-worn but well-oiled English riding boots. He was strong, straight, and clear-eyed. Celia could love him now as the friend and brother he had become. "I guess you have decided to stay," Peter said, splashing water on the baby, playfully.

"This is our home now, Peter," replied Celia, warmly. "President Young has guided us here by the Spirit, and we are determined to stay."

Jed reached out his big hand to Peter. "We'll miss you, though," Jed said. "I may even find myself feeling a little envious from time to time. Remember, I've seen this paradise you are bound for. You must find John Broderick and examine his rancho outside San Diego. I'm sure he will sell you the share he had reserved for me."

"No, with many thanks. I like to create my own deals . . . the Van Cleef School of Negotiation, remember." They both laughed with Peter, and the baby splashed to show his approval.

After a moment, Peter said slowly, "Do you remember, in Sunday School, when we studied the scriptures together? I loved the story of Father Lehi in the Book of Mormon with his Liahona, the compass that would always tell you in what direction you must travel. I am reminded that it only worked if you had the Spirit. Lehi had to have a compass inside and a compass outside. Thus, no matter what unexpected twists in the path of life require your bold decision, you can discover what is right for you. If you do that, you can always say of the spot where you stand, 'This is the place.'"

Celia and Jed were amazed and warmed by the sweet gravity of Peter's insight. Jed put his arm around Celia, and she laid her head on his shoulder as Peter continued.

"But do you also remember Lehi's dream of the Tree of Life, when he saw an iron rod bordering the stream of filthy water? Those who wished to reach the tree without falling in the filth had to hold to the rod. They dared not look left or right or back behind. If you walk the straight path with the rod of the Lord's anointed as your chastening guide, you will never find yourself lost and drowning.

"I am a Liahona and you are Iron Rodders. We both know what to do to enter the kingdom, but the Kingdom of God on this earth is invisible. Where is it? Where is the narrow gate? I will follow the Liahona and you will hold to the Iron Rod. We will both pound stakes of Zion deep into the earth, you here and I there, you in your way and I in mine. Together, we will all be a Zion people."

After embraces and handshakes, tears and laughter with Jed, Celia, Quimby, and Emma, Peter mounted his big-chested stallion and rode away. He rode through Salt Lake City, past road-grading projects, irrigation projects, and building projects, all designed and implemented to make a great city rise. Fennelly Parsons waved to him from his perch on a joist, supervising the building of a theatre which Brigham had commanded to be built. The Saints had always loved and encouraged the arts, so this was a natural addition to the growing city. *I guess good old Fennelly has finally found a way to put his talents to the best use,* thought Peter, waving back to the valley's consummate entertainer.

He did not head out of town west, toward the lake, because he would not go to California yet. Heading east, up Emigration Canyon, he would ride hard to beat the winter snow back to Saint Louis. He had left Mary Ellen there, defending him, hiding the truth for him, covering his troubles with her own sacrifice as she always had. Using all his money, all his power and wiles, he would try to resolve the whole matter of Bates and "The Mormon Plague." If he could win back Morgan Cain, he could win back the city and do a great service for the Church as well as himself.

This done, he would make Mary Ellen his wife, if she would still have him, and they would go forth together to conquer California.

At the top of the canyon, he stopped and looked back down on the valley and the city. Jed had said he might envy Peter. Peter knew he would envy Jed, but he also realized each would be content in his own world. Peter could imagine that, in years to come, the straight streets would extend like giant arrows for miles, and a temple, more massive and glorious than any other, would rise in the heart of the city. This would be the crossroads of the west, where millions would gather from all over the world. This is the place 'where none shall come to hurt or make afraid.' Peter had caught the vision of the Prophet Brigham Young, and he knew that, indeed, the valley would blossom as a rose.

A city that is set on a hill—or in the tops of the mountains—cannot be hid. It would be there as a beacon for him, wherever he voyaged. Peter said goodbye to the City of Joseph and the City of Brigham. He did not say goodbye to his friends, rather farewell, because he knew they would all remain linked irrevocably in that same unseen kingdom that knows no boundaries.

Turning his horse onto the trail he had chosen and with a kick of his heels, Peter Van Cleef was off to find his own promised valley.